Homecoming

Homecoming

Lacey Baker

St. Martin's Paperbacks

This is a work of fiction. All of the characters, organizations, and events portrayed in this novel are either products of the author's imagination or are used fictitiously.

HOMECOMING

Copyright © 2013 by Lacey Baker.
Excerpt from *Just Like Heaven* copyright © 2013 by Lacey Baker.

For information address St. Martin's Press, 175 Fifth Avenue, New York, NY 10010.

ISBN: 978-1-250-01922-6

Printed in the United States of America

St. Martin's Paperbacks edition / May 2013

St. Martin's Paperbacks are published by St. Martin's Press, 175 Fifth Avenue, New York, NY 10010.

10 9 8 7 6 5 4 3 2 1

To my Grandmothers

Doretha M. Wallace, Felicia R. Fleet, and Velma Moore

For always saying things you knew would come in handy later. You would be proud to know how much of your advice has stayed with me.

Chapter 1

There wasn't a damned thing funny, at least Nikki didn't think so. Hoover King and his band of jolly old men thought it was absolutely hilarious, despite the fact that this was the repast for one of the town's finest citizens. She had some choice words for them in that regard, too, but held her tongue. *Don't be rude to the guests.* That was one of the first rules to be learned in the hospitality business.

How about when said guest grabs your butt? Is it okay to be rude then?

Heading into the kitchen, she could do nothing but shake her head. Hoover King was a sixty-something-year-old man who'd lived in Sweetland forever. He was short, round, bald, and jovial, which was a complement to his wife, Inez, who was tall, rail-thin, and mean as a rattle-snake. She was most likely the reason Hoover stayed drunk more than he was ever sober, a fact that had most of the townsfolk feeling sorry for him instead of declaring him a public menace. With all that said, he probably didn't even know he'd grabbed her in an inappropriate spot.

No, that was bull, he knew exactly what he was doing and he'd enjoyed it. As for Nikki, she hadn't enjoyed anything since receiving the call about Mrs. Cantrell's passing.

Yet she'd agreed to come over and help out tonight. Actually, it had been a no-brainer. She worked here during the day as Ms. Janet's assistant manager, taking care of a lot of the day-to-day tasks and making sure the B&B ran as smoothly as it possibly could. Michelle took care of the restaurant, and they all coexisted in a peaceful harmony. She wondered how that harmony would hold up now that all the Cantrell siblings were back under one roof.

"Hey cutie-pie, you taking a mighty long time with that new pitcher of lemonade." Hoover's voice slurred, his portly body wobbling in through the swinging kitchen door.

"I'll be there in just a minute, Mr. King. Why don't you go back out and sit with your friends?" *Or go home and pass out next to your wife. That sounds like a better plan.*

"I came in here to help you," he said, stumbling toward her.

Nikki could hear his footsteps, but her back was facing him. She'd been just about to lift the tray with the two pitchers of lemonade on it when instinct warned her to put it down. The minute she did she felt him pressing against her back.

"I can carry it," he mumbled, then breathed over her shoulder. She thought she would collapse.

Even from behind she could smell the liquor on him. It was disgusting that he drank this way, especially since he also acted as the town's only cab service. The other thing that was basically nauseating was the way his round body was rubbing against her backside. She tried to turn, which really wasn't a good idea on so many levels. He breathed directly into her face then, hot and funky. And he pushed even closer to her, this time wrapping his arms around her like she'd asked for a hug.

She instantly pushed against him. "Mr. King, why don't we go back out and find your wife? She can take you home if you need to lie down." And he so needed to lie down and sleep off this latest drunken stupor.

"Nope, gonna stay right here with you, cutie-pie," is what he told her. He had the audacity to grind what should have been his pelvis but was actually even more of his protruding belly.

Nikki pushed at him, and he stumbled back away from her. He also had the wherewithal—even though she had no idea where it had come from—to grab her arms, pulling her forward with him.

"That's okay, I can stay right here," she argued, trying to keep from falling into the floor on top of him.

"Give me a kiss, cutie," he asked, poking his shriveled lips out from beneath a bushy mustache.

"Not in a million years," she whispered while turning her head. "I'll just go get your wife."

"Don't want her," was Hoover's slurred retort.

"Maybe that's the one you should want," a male voice said about a second before Hoover's heavy body was heaved away from hers.

Nikki took a step back and a deep breath, glad to be rid of Hoover's pawing and panting, not so glad to be caught in his grasp.

"Get your hands off me!" Hoover yelled but was cut short when a coughing fit hit him. He bowed over with the effort of standing, coughing, and talking.

"Time for you to head on home, sir. You need some rest," the man—no, the freakin' drop-dead-gorgeous specimen that had come out of nowhere—advised.

On second glance, Nikki decided Mr. Good Looking, still dressed in his church clothes and smelling ten times better than Hoover, was right where he belonged. His back was facing her but she'd know that back anywhere, would know those broad shoulders and that serious let's-get-right-down-to-business stance anywhere.

"You all right?" he asked when he'd turned to look at her.

I was before I saw you again.

"Fine," was her tight reply.

She never could get out more than one sentence around Quinton Cantrell. It was demeaning to realize that nineteen years after his departure, her vocabulary apparently hadn't improved.

"Don't need nobody telling me what to do," Hoover insisted.

"No, what you need is a hot cup of coffee and a bed. I believe there's someone in the other room looking for you," Quinn continued after looking away from Nikki. "She's right outside the door."

"You ain't got no business here, boy. Tis here is my town and she's . . . she's," Hoover stuttered and stumbled in Nikki's direction once more.

This time his feet tripped him up and he would have hit the floor face-first if Quinn hadn't reached out to catch him.

The muscles in Quinn's back bunched with the effort, and Nikki almost swooned. Yeah, swooned, like some high school girl.

Getting to his feet, Hoover mumbled something else, giving Quinn the stink-eye the entire time. Hoover looked so put out. He also stared Quinn up and down but probably figured he didn't have a chance in hell of taking the younger and clearly more physically built man down.

"I'll go," Hoover said, spittle flying out of his mouth, sweat prickling the top of his bald head. "But she's still my cutie-pie."

"Yeah, that's fine. She's cute all right. You go on home," Quinn told him.

It wasn't fine, and what did "she's cute all right" mean? And why, of all the men in this town, in this house as a matter of fact, did Quinn Cantrell have to be the one to come to her rescue?

"If you like being his cutie-pie I can get him back in here for you."

The deep voice snapped her out of what she would consider a deep state of embarrassment. Her heated cheeks would second that emotion.

"Hoover's harmless," she heard herself say.

"Looked like he was doing a good bit of harm fawning all over you," was Quinn's reply.

If it had been any other man, his tone might be construed as jealous and she might, just might have been flattered. As it was, it was Quinn and he sounded more along the scolding line, as he used to when they were younger. Nikki didn't like that. She'd never liked that, especially coming from Quinn.

Squaring her shoulders, she told him, "I can handle myself."

"Really?" he asked, his long arms folding over his chest.

And a beautiful chest it was, all broad and muscled. As he moved the material of his shirt had stretched much the way it had over his back a few minutes ago, so the outline of his upper physique was visible. And he was still too damned good looking. His honey complexion and smoldering dark brown eyes were the perfect complement to the strong jawline and aristocratic nose. Her mouth watered but she swallowed quickly, refusing the buds of arousal threatening to blossom. This was an old scene, one she'd vowed to resist. What she felt for Quinn Cantrell was over. Actually, it never truly began, at least not where Quinn was concerned.

"Really. And I have to get this lemonade out there before the rest of Hoover's crew decide to come in here and try their luck."

"Let me help you," he offered when she'd picked up the tray and taken a step in the direction of the door.

"No, thanks. You've been helpful enough already, as usual, Quinn."

Nikki slipped through that door before he could say another word, before he could look at her in that painfully platonic way a second longer. She'd known he was coming back to town, known he would be in this house, and should have known how her traitorous body would react to those facts.

Maybe it was time to admit she didn't really know as much as she thought she did.

This day couldn't possibly last any longer. Surely twenty-four hours had come and gone. Quinn certainly felt like it had. His grandmother's funeral had been at noon at the Redeemer's Baptist Church, the oldest church in Sweetland. It was now shortly after eight in the evening and the big yellow house at the end of Sycamore Lane that doubled as a bed-and-breakfast and one of the town's most popular restaurants, The Silver Spoon, was still full of people.

"Gramma would have loved the turnout," Raine said, coming to stand beside him.

Quinn had been trying to keep his distance from the people of Sweetland all day. Tonight it wasn't a possibility since the entire town seemed to have taken up residence here at his grandmother's house. And what a colorful bunch they were, he thought, remembering the encounter in the kitchen just a few minutes ago. Hence the reason he was now sitting comfortably in the farthest corner of the den he could find.

The den was decorated in hunter green and burgundy, the deep colors draping the walls and on the tablecloth. Heavy dark wood shelves filled with books were on two sides of the room, while a bay window took up more than half the other side. It was a spacious room that was now filled with about twenty people with heaping plates of food and lots of conversation.

"She did like a house full of people," he admitted, watching as his younger sister pulled an empty folding chair over to sit beside him.

And this house seemed to have met its capacity for

guests. Sure, there was the extension of the restaurant and the backyard was certainly big enough to hold at least fifty, but Quinn still felt crowded. Actually, he felt like the house would rip apart at the seams if another guest arrived. Townsfolk—that's what his grandmother would call them—were just like extended family. Right now they all seemed to extend his headache.

Despite how emotionally strained and physically exhausted he was feeling, Quinn had to smile at himself because it had been years since he'd seen Raine. At least five, he thought, remembering when he was in Atlanta for a medical convention and had spent the weekend visiting with her. She still looked the same with her slight build and soft-spoken demeanor.

"She loved the house and catering to all the people who stayed here," Raine continued after he'd slipped into comfortable silence once more.

Quinn nodded. "It was in her blood to take care of any and everyone around her." Talking about his grandmother, the woman who'd contributed to Sweetland's emergence into the tourist scene, the one and only Mary Janet Cantrell, in the past tense gave Quinn a melancholy feeling. The fact that she was really gone hadn't quite hit him yet.

"I'm going to miss her," Raine added, her voice cracking just a bit.

Because one of his biggest downfalls was a crying woman—a crying sister was a totally different level of torture—Quinn touched her hand. "We're all going to miss her. She was the glue that held us together."

Raine sighed, using the napkin she held daintily in her other hand to dab at tears that had formed in the corners of her eyes. It was an action that was so like Raine, so girlie and so classy at the same time. He looked at his sister's pretty face, the light coat of makeup that transformed her to a woman, and wondered where the little girl had gone.

"If you call what we are together," she scoffed.

Quinn shrugged. He didn't know how to respond considering what she'd said. However, she wasn't that far off the mark. He and his siblings hadn't seen one another in a while. He did talk to Preston via email a lot. Parker would call every now and then, whenever he wasn't knee-deep in some murder investigation—which wasn't very often. As for his sisters, Quinn knew it was bad but he usually only heard from them around the holidays. All of the Cantrells reached out during holiday time. Thanksgiving, Christmas—especially since Savannah's birthday was Christmas Eve—and New Year's were favorite times for the entire family no matter where they were in the world.

"We have our own lives," he said in defense. The words were familiar because he'd been telling himself this for years, using it as his excuse not to come back to Sweetland.

"But we're family," Raine insisted.

"That will never change," he countered. "No matter where we all live, we'll still be family."

"You don't know what'll change," a gruff voice interrupted.

Quinn and Raine looked up. Right in front of them was a wiry old man, hunched over slightly and clutching a cane to keep himself as upright as possible.

"Three days ago I sat right in this room with Janet having a glass of iced tea. Janet makes the best iced tea, with real lemons." He began to cough, and his thin legs shook.

Quinn immediately stood, going to help the man into a chair. "Get him some water," he told to Raine. "Just sit here, sir. We'll get you something to drink and you can catch your breath."

As Raine walked away, the man shook his head. "Don't need to catch my breath, just a little cough."

To Quinn's medical ear it sounded different, like

maybe a touch of emphysema or COPD. "Sounds like more than just a cough to me. How long have you had this cough?"

"You're the doc," the man said, looking up at Quinn with watery eyes.

Quinn nodded, sure he didn't remember this man and not very sure how the man knew Quinn was a doctor. "I am. And you are?"

"Sylvester Bynum," he stated, extending a hand to Quinn. "I live here. Have for going on three years now."

"You live at a bed-and-breakfast?" Quinn asked, more than a little confused.

His grandmother lived and had grown up in this very house with her parents, and so had their parents before them. About ten years ago she'd converted the huge yellow Queen Anne Victorian home with its sweeping towers and turrets and rounded porch that wrapped two-thirds of the way around the structure sitting at the end of Sycamore Lane like a light beckoning those lost in the dark—that's what his grandmother used to tell him—to a bed-and-breakfast. At that time Mary Janet had moved into the care-taker's suite located in the west tower. The six-bedroom, four-bathroom house was passed down through the seven generations of Cantrells that had lived in Sweetland. It had housed Quinn's ancestors, former mayors and founders of Sweetland, Maryland. To Quinn's knowledge his grandmother had run this B&B on her own since conception. Well, his sister Michelle helped out a lot, but Michelle had her own house a few blocks down. So the idea of someone actually living here and not just visiting, besides Mary Janet, was a little strange.

"I didn't have anyplace else to go," Sylvester continued as if he could tell exactly what Quinn was thinking. "No family. No nothing but my pension. Janet said I could stay here. I paid my way, so don't go thinking I'm some kind of mooch. But this is my home and I loved Janet for all she did for me."

The man looked adamant about what he was saying, his eyes watering even more as he spoke. Quinn didn't have the heart to continue questioning him. "Okay, well I'm glad she was here for you," Quinn said. "Now about that cough?"

Across the room loud laughter sounded, grabbing Quinn's attention. He looked up through the crowd of people and zeroed in on her.

It was the same woman from the kitchen, and it appeared men couldn't keep their hands off her. She'd just hugged someone, a tall, lanky guy in a police uniform. The embrace hadn't lasted long, which Quinn shouldn't have noticed at all. But as she pulled away her eyes were alight with the huge smile that covered her face. *A cute face,* he thought. *No, a really pretty face,* was the realization when that thought translated to a quick pang in his chest. Her hair was a riot of curls, which only added to the perpetually cheerful look she possessed, the look that shouldn't be sexy but actually was.

"Can't spend all your time alone," Sylvester said.

"What?" Quinn asked, returning his attention to the old man.

"The people." Sylvester nodded toward the crowd. "You don't like them here. Do you?"

"I don't see the point. We've already had the funeral. She's gone and she's not coming back," he said, sinking back down in his own chair. That enormous burden was weighing on Quinn. From the moment he'd received Michelle's call saying their grandmother had passed away in her sleep, he'd felt like yelling or screaming or punching something. Of course, he hadn't done any of those things, but the tension was continuously building inside him. Verbalizing that his grandmother was gone almost broke him.

"She'll always be here," Sylvester said, clapping his

shaking fingers over his heart. "You need to remember that."

Before Quinn could say anything else Raine had returned with the glass of water. Sylvester politely took a sip then waved both of them away as he struggled to stand. Raine stood closest to him now, and the old man touched a hand to her cheek. "You've got lots of love in you. Janet knew it and I can see it in your eyes. Don't wait forever to share it."

He limped away, leaving Quinn and Raine to stare after him. "Who was that?" Raine asked in a conspiratorial whisper.

"A friend of Gramma's," he answered simply even though he was thinking the man may have been more than a friend to their grandmother. She had definitely provided him with some sort of companionship, and he'd most likely reciprocated. That was something neither Quinn nor his siblings had done since leaving town years ago. Now he could add guilt to the storm of emotions reeling through him. He would give anything to turn back the clock to when he was in Seattle, sitting in his office reading the latest in stem cell research. He was in his element there, safe from all the bad memories that wanted to haunt him, safe from the pretty little Bay town of Sweetland.

And definitely safe from the picture of the pretty woman with the curly hair that kept entering his mind.

Chapter 2

Just put one foot in front of the other. That's what Nikki Brockington whispered to herself as she walked out of the house and to her car this morning. The sun was shining way too brightly considering they'd just buried one of the best people she'd ever known.

Mrs. Cantrell had been Nikki's mentor, her surrogate grandmother, and just an all-around nice person. She'd given Nikki guidance when she hadn't wanted it, a swat on the butt when she needed it, and a shoulder to cry on when Nikki didn't know it was a good cry that she needed. She'd been a huge part of Nikki's life and now she was gone.

When she'd awakened this morning, she'd rolled over onto her stomach, burying her face in her pillow and seriously considering staying right there. But as she thought about how she could possibly make it into The Silver Spoon where she worked as assistant manager, she heard Mrs. Cantrell's voice just as clearly as if the woman had been standing at the foot of her bed.

You're gonna get up and put one foot in front of the other.

Nikki shook her head. It couldn't possibly be that easy.

Especially not after last night. After what might just be one of the most embarrassing moments of her life.

Maybe he'd be gone. None of the Cantrell siblings lived in Sweetland so there was a good chance they'd all packed up and headed out early this morning. No, the will was being read today so they'd still be there. *Dammit!*

She would just ignore him, that's what she'd do. She hadn't seen him in years, hadn't heard a word from him, not that she'd expected to. To Quinn she'd been his sister's friend. To her, he'd been everything. A foolish girl's dream. But Nikki wasn't a foolish girl anymore.

Of course some would say differently considering her track record, but she didn't care. They could all think what they wanted; she knew who she was and what she wanted out of life. At least she did now, and that was thanks to Mrs. Cantrell. So she wasn't about to let Quinn waltz into town and throw her off track.

This morning would be the first Sunday she'd walk into The Silver Spoon and not hear Mrs. Cantrell singing hymns as she moved about the dining room preparing for breakfast. This morning could quite possibly be the last Sunday Nikki walked into The Silver Spoon, but that was a whole other can of worms she didn't want to open right now.

It was better to keep focused on the here and now, the things she could control. As the restaurant was an integral part of the B&B, all the guests were offered a continental breakfast, Monday through Friday, which was included in their room rental, and a generous buffet breakfast on Sundays. Nikki usually arrived just as the setup was complete. Michelle supervised the kitchen and made sure everything was brought out, remained hot, and tasted marvelous. Nikki's job was to make sure everything ran smoothly, and no matter what she swore to do just that today.

That was the thought on her mind as she pulled into the B&B's side driveway.

They had two couples in residence this weekend. Both would be checking out later today. She'd wanted to cancel them when Mrs. Cantrell had been found dead, but she'd spoken to Michelle and they were both convinced she wouldn't have wanted to turn customers away. So upon their arrival she'd been sure to greet them herself. Natalie, the part-time clerk, usually checked in their guests, but she'd already been summoned to help her mother with the cooking. Whenever somebody died in Sweetland, all the ladies of the town began cooking. Cakes, pies, casseroles, biscuits, fried fish—you name it, they cooked it. Then brought it all to the house of the dearly departed, for their family to either feast or faint.

Nikki told the guests of their loss and they were all very consoling, just before they headed out to enjoy their cruise on the Miles River. For the most part their weekend had been full of excursions, which had worked out well for Nikki and the Cantrells, because citizens of the town piled into the big yellow house immediately after yesterday's burial. Now, today should be quiet. No more food would be brought; the family had one big meeting this morning then they'd most likely be heading out of town themselves. None of them liked Sweetland much, or at least that's what Nikki figured since they'd all left the second they were old enough to do so.

"Breakfast is right on schedule," Michelle said to Nikki the moment she walked through the back door.

It led directly into the kitchen of the beautiful old house and right into Michelle's domain. Just last year it had been remodeled to further suit Michelle's needs. The floors were a retro black-and-white check with gleaming black countertops and pristine white cabinets. All of the appliances were stainless steel, including the huge industrial stove and ovens that had been shipped from Annapolis. The color came with a quick flash, just like Michelle's smiles usually did. Bright yellow eyelet curtains hung at the long stretch of windows just over the sink and at the back door. All the dish towels and cloths were yellow, and there was a huge yellow sunshine magnet on the side of the stainless-steel refrigerator, courtesy of Godfrey's Market and the special they'd run last summer on Morningside Orange Juice.

"The meeting with Mr. Creed is in another half hour. You should be heading into the parlor with the others," Nikki said while dropping her keys into her purse.

After she'd closed the door behind her—because hopefully the air-conditioning was running, since outside the humidity was already rising—Nikki hung her battered old leather bag on one of the huge white pegs near the basement door.

"I've got time. My siblings are not morning people," Michelle said, pouring apple juice into a shiny white carafe.

They always used the Haviland china for breakfast. Its cute and colorful peony design had been Mrs. Cantrell's favorite.

"Tanya's helping out this morning. She's already in the dining room setting the buffet. And the Smiths have already come down." Michelle continued clamping the top on the carafe and putting it on a tray with a pile of saucers and linen napkins.

"Then I'll go in to greet them. Henry's already out doing the omelets, I presume," Nikki stated, moving to the counter to take the tray before Michelle could lift it herself.

With a slight frown Michelle nodded. "Yes, he's already in there. I should go in just to make sure he's offering the crepes with all the toppings."

Nikki shook her head. "I'm sure he's offering everything on our usual menu. Now, you take off that apron and head on into the parlor with your family."

Again Michelle frowned. "They're probably all packed and ready to catch the first thing smoking out of town."

Nikki couldn't help but take a moment. She stopped her procession to the dining room and looked at Michelle Cantrell, who had been born Mary Michelle Cantrell: It was customary for all firstborn females in Sweetland to carry the name Mary in honor of the wife of the town's founder, Buford Fitzgerald. She was six years older than Nikki, but Nikki had known her forever. Nikki had been working closely with Michelle these past eleven years so the two of them kind of leaned on each other here and there. Right now was definitely a here-and-there moment.

"You don't know that. From what I've seen of them these past few days, they're all shell-shocked right now. They don't look like they know what to do or where to go for that matter."

Michelle shook her head. "You don't know my siblings. They're all too intelligent and too headstrong for their own good. They always know what they want and how to go about getting it. That's why they never stayed in Sweetland."

"But they're all back now. That's something, isn't it?" Nikki tried to sound optimistic for Michelle's sake. She wasn't sure how being back in Sweetland was going to help them keep the B&B.

"Only because Gramma died," Michelle continued. "Believe me, I've tried and tried to get them to come back before. They just hate it here."

"Did you tell them what's going on?" Nikki asked.

From the look Michelle gave her, she'd say the answer to that question was a resounding no.

"They won't care," Michelle said with a huff. "It's not their responsibility."

Nikki strongly disagreed, but wisely kept her two cents to herself.

"Go on." Michelle waved her away. "Take that out there before Tanya comes back here screaming that we've run out. I swear that girl's as nervous as a baby chick."

Nikki laughed as she pushed through the swinging kitchen door that led directly into the dining room. "That's why you're the one in charge of training her. You're the best mother hen around these parts."

The last had at least made Michelle smile. Nikki and some of the other staff at The Silver Spoon often joked with Michelle about being a mother hen to anyone who walked into this place. She'd gotten that honestly from Mrs. Cantrell. Two more caring and compassionate people, Nikki had never met.

Immediately upon entering the dining room, she was assailed by the smell of breakfast food. It reminded her that she hadn't eaten anything before leaving the house this morning—too busy convincing herself she needed to come to work, most likely. Two long buffet hutches sat permanently along one side wall. An eight-foot-long cherrywood table was in the center of the room with ornately designed chairs to match and the fifty-year-old Victorian lace tablecloth Mary Janet had received as a wedding present on top. Glasses, plates, silverware, and napkins were on a smaller hutch on the opposite wall. Straight to the back of the room was a set of bay windows with potted plants soaking up the morning sun.

Nikki headed right to the buffet to replace the just-about-empty carafe of juice with the now-full one. They offered a choice of Grand Marnier blueberry cheese blintzes, caramel French toast, made-to-order omelets and crepes with all the freshest toppings, eggs Benedict, cheese grits, Belgian waffles, and the area's fluffiest pancakes. There was more by way of breakfast meats, bagels, and of course Michelle's famous cheddar cheese biscuits. Nikki almost swooned she was so hungry.

Mr. Sylvester walked in with his usual morning banter.

"Good morning to all who were blessed to see another day," he said in his crackly voice.

Mr. Sylvester had been here for a few years now. He'd simply showed up one day, no reservation, and hadn't left. Nikki got the impression, sometimes, that he was sweet on Mrs. Cantrell. She'd often wondered if Mrs. Cantrell had any idea.

The Smiths—Robert and Laurie—both smiled over cups of coffee. Sylvester walked past them with a nod. He normally used a cane to get around, but didn't lean on it much; sometimes Nikki thought he could actually go without it. This morning, however, without the cane, he would have surely fallen over. His eyes looked red-rimmed, like he'd already been crying. Instinctively Nikki reached out a hand to touch his shoulder.

"How are you this morning, Mr. Sylvester?" she asked, knowing he wasn't doing nearly as well as he planned to tell her.

"I'm just fine, pretty lady. Just fine," he said with another nod.

He reached for a glass, and Nikki helped by pouring him some orange juice. He always had orange juice before his morning coffee.

"That lawyer fella's coming this morning," he told her after two short sips.

"I know." She nodded, taking the napkins from the tray and placing them on the table. She offered the Smiths a smile as they continued eating. "Let me know if you need anything else," she told them.

"Gonna be something for those kids to hear, you know."

He was moving right behind her now, haltingly but still there. Nikki slowed her steps as she checked the dishes on the other side of the room and then moved to the windows to make sure the plants didn't need any watering.

"Well, we don't know what's in the will. And they're

adults. I think it'll be okay," she said even though she wasn't totally sure. There was bound to be something in the will about the taxes that were owed on this property and the town council's threat to foreclose if the bill wasn't paid soon.

Behind her she heard him clucking his teeth, something he did when he was about to go into a rant about the good old days, which Nikki did not have time for. She had some receipts to look over today, and then she'd have to help Tanya with the rooms as soon as both guests had checked out. The Cantrell siblings were staying in the remaining four rooms at the B&B. The twins, she thought, were sharing the biggest room, while the others had their own space and of course Michelle lived just down the street. Mr. Sylvester had the only first-floor room, which was toward the back of the house. It had once been a pantry, but Mrs. Cantrell had the contractors knock out the back wall of the house to extend it enough so that now it looked more like a one-bedroom apartment. She'd said it was meant for long-term guests—which turned out to be exactly what Mr. Sylvester was.

"I think they're all in for a surprise," Sylvester told her.

He was trying to keep his voice low, but it wasn't working too well. The best Nikki could do was steer them away from the table and the ears of their guests.

She turned around and almost knocked him over. "Whoops, excuse me," she said and backed up because it didn't seem like he was going to move. "Do you know what's in the will?" she asked even though she stood firm that it was none of their business.

Just because they'd loved Mrs. Cantrell as much as her blood relatives didn't mean they had a right to know her personal business. Nikki's mother, Odell, had always been firm about minding their own business and leaving other folks' alone. Even when you lived in a town the size of Sweetland. Or especially so.

Sylvester shook his head. "Don't know. But I did know Janet and there was nothing more important to her than getting these kids together and keeping them here in Sweetland."

Nikki nodded because that sounded right. "Yeah, but they're adults. You can't make people do what they don't want to do," she said, using her shoulder to push through the kitchen door.

"You never know." Sylvester kept right on talking, mostly to himself now. "You just never know."

Morning came as they tend to do in the grand scheme of things. *Joy will come in the morning*—Gramma used to say that a lot, Quinn remembered. Heading to the shower, he thought about his grandmother and things she'd tried to teach them while they were growing up. It was a welcome change from the lustful thoughts he'd had all night.

It was the girl from the kitchen, the one with the smile and the obvious curves. Late into the night he'd thought about those curves and his hands having their own meet-and-greet with each and every one. He'd moaned with his eyes closed because his body had reacted to the thought of the curves and his hands and the ultimate outcome of said interaction. Then he'd decided to open his eyes, to stand at the window and look out into the quiet of the night in the sleepy Bay town.

That hadn't worked, either.

He could hear her laughing, saw her as she was last night in the arms of that cop, and wanted to tell the guy to get his grubby hands off her. Crazy, yeah, he knew that. And nobody had ever called Dr. Quinton Cantrell crazy. Sleep had finally come amid thoughts of the curly-headed vixen and the mountain of work he'd left back at his office.

Now morning was here and a new wave of concerns had hit him. They all circled around his family.

For all intents and purposes Mary Janet had been more

of a mother to Quinn and his siblings than Patricia ever had, though that was no fault of Patricia's. Quinn did not blame his mother for her shortcomings. She was not cut out to be a mother, but his father loved her and she apparently loved him—that's why she'd left her big-city home of Chicago to come here. But this town wasn't for everyone. Quinn had learned that the hard way.

Sweetland was located in the heart of Maryland's Eastern Shore, nestled quaintly along the Miles River. If ever there was a town removed from the big-city life, this was it. With only about a thousand residents, the feeling that whatever you said or did was known to every one of them could get kind of claustrophobic after a while. When his father died, twenty-two years after Patricia had come here, she'd left. Quinn always thought that decision had been made long before his father's death. Still, her leaving hadn't mattered that much to Quinn because he'd already been away at college. On the other hand, losing his dad before he graduated had been devastating. The fact that the loss came four years after Sharane's death had only pushed him deeper into his own depression— too much loss, too young to know how to handle it, too long ago to think about it right now.

This morning Quinn would face one more family hurdle before he could finally leave this town and all it held for him behind. Gramma's will was being read in the parlor promptly at nine thirty. That's what the lawyer, Edison Creed, had told them last night. So Quinn showered, dressed, and headed down the stairs toward the parlor. He wanted to be on time and he wanted this to be over as soon as possible.

Gramma loved colors as much as she loved life, and it showed in the decor of the house. The parlor had wallpapered walls with a cream background and pale pink rosettes. The plush carpet was a deep crimson, while the curtains were pink with a matching crimson brocade drape over the top. The furniture was mostly antiques. A huge coffee table sat in the center of the room with a couch on each side. Four high-backed Victorian chairs were positioned between the couches. But the focal point of the room had to be Gramma's collection of antique lamps. Along one wall a set of four matching 1900s wall sconces hung. On a small table beside the entryway was a pair of green Bohemian lamps with crystals. She also had crystal lamps with prisms and a pair of cranberry Victorian lamps with gold prisms.

Quinn was an antiques fanatic, one of the things he supposed he'd inherited from his grandmother. Although he didn't have time to collect a lot of antiques himself, he knew them when he saw them and was in awe of what he figured was a small showing of his grandmother's collection.

"How long is this going to take?" Savannah came in first, heading directly to the sideboard that always held a pitcher of iced tea and a pitcher of iced water. She picked up a glass and poured herself some tea.

If he didn't know for a fact that she'd been born right here in Maryland, Quinn would swear his sister was a twenty-first-century southern belle in complete harmony with her name. This morning Savannah wore a sundress— it was May, the prelude to summer in Maryland, which meant that eighty-plus-degree days with matching humidity were not unusual. But Savannah's entire back was bare, down to her waist. The dress tied around her neck and hugged her bodice. Her shoes were sky-high heels that made her look even more alluring, if that were possible. Quinn's temples immediately began to ache at the sight of his baby sister dressed this way. He'd kept a close eye on her career and was the first person she called if she needed anything, which wasn't often since she probably made more money than he did. But he'd never get used to the idea of her as a grown woman.

"Mr. Creed said not more than an hour." Raine had

already been in the room and seated in one of the high-backed chairs, which actually looked like it would engulf her slim fame.

Quinn made his way to one of the couches and took a seat looking from one of his sisters to the other. If ever there were two people who were more different . . . and yet their resemblance was clear. They shared the same wide pretty smile and brown eyes, even though Raine's were lighter than Savannah's. Savannah's butter-toned complexion was in contrast with Raine's cinnamon brown. They had the high cheekbones that were part of the Cantrells' half–Native American heritage, and both were built tall and slim like their mother.

"Surely you can stay in town another hour," Michelle stated as she entered the room.

Now, here was where the differences really came into play. Michelle was two years younger than Quinn, and he knew her probably as well as any of the others. Michelle had always taken responsibility for her siblings, which in her eyes made her the boss. And truth be told, next to Gramma, Michelle did most of the motherly things for them, including making sure she called each of the siblings when they went too long without calling her.

Michelle also looked most like their grandmother with her chocolate-brown complexion, thick arched eyebrows, and infectious laugh. She wore a sensible business suit in a pale shade of yellow and high heels that confirmed all of his sisters had grown up while Quinn hadn't been looking.

"I didn't say I couldn't," Savannah quipped. "But I do have things to do."

"Things that are more important than hearing Gramma's wishes." Michelle shook her head. "You haven't changed one bit. Still spoiled and selfish."

"And you're still bossy and evil," Savannah replied.

Raine rubbed her temples. "Please, you two. It's too early for this."

"She's right, it is early," Preston said, walking into the room in khaki shorts and a white polo shirt. His sunglasses were pushed up onto his head, and he rubbed his eyes as if he were still half asleep.

"What time did you get to bed last night?" Michelle asked him.

Preston groaned. "I don't even know. That O'Hurley girl can talk."

"I know you weren't hanging out with Casey O'Hurley, the youngest of the O'Hurley girls?" Michelle asked. "And when I say youngest, that's exactly what I mean. She's barely twenty-one."

"And I'm only thirty-three. Come on, she's an adult and so am I. Help me out here, Quinn; she's legal, right?" Preston looked to him.

Quinn, who had been quiet, simply sitting back watching the familiar exchange between his siblings, frowned to bite back a grin. Preston loved women. He and his twin, Parker, had broken so many hearts during their teenage years in Sweetland, they were legendary. As adults they hadn't changed much in the women arena. Quinn couldn't help but feel a hint of pride at the men his brothers had grown into; after all, he was the oldest and had been the only male figure in their life after their father's death. However, at this moment he wasn't so sure that was a good thing.

"She's a bit on the young side," he told Preston honestly because really, they weren't teenagers anymore.

Savannah chuckled. "You're the star attorney. You should know better than the rest of us how wrong that is."

"What? She's legal," Preston insisted amid continued laughter from Savannah and even Michelle.

For a minute it felt like old times, and Quinn enjoyed it. He actually liked being back in his grandmother's parlor with his siblings. It had a really comfortable feeling, almost like they all belonged right here at this very moment. Then Mr. Creed came in and the atmosphere shifted.

"Good morning. Is everyone here?" he asked, all business in his three-piece mud-brown suit and mustard-yellow shirt. He was a short man with a gaunt look and quick steps. His balding head glistened with whatever product he smoothed on to keep the remaining strands down, and his wire-framed glasses slid to the end of his nose as he tilted his head and looked over them.

There was a small desk in one corner of the room where Gramma used to write her correspondence, as she would say. Creed plopped his worn leather briefcase on top and began pulling out papers.

"I'm here," Parker said, coming in last and taking a seat on the couch next to Quinn.

"Good. We can get started," Creed stated, licking his finger then sifting through papers.

Preston frowned. Raine shrugged and Savannah crossed her legs, letting the top one dangle with her impatience.

"I'll skip the formalities and get right to it," Creed began, folding a set of papers back at the stapled edge. "I, Mary Janet Cantrell, leave and bequeath all my monetary holdings to my six grandchildren: Quinton Clifford Cantrell, Mary Michelle Cantrell, Preston Reece Cantrell, Parker Roland Cantrell, Raine Marie Cantrell, and Savannah Lynn Cantrell. It is also my wish that The Silver Spoon be given with joint ownership to my grandchildren."

Quinn let out the deep breath he'd been holding. It was as he'd suspected. Besides them, Gramma had no other family and he knew she'd never leave any one of them out of her will, even though she probably had good cause to. So it was done, he thought with relief. Now he could go back to Seattle.

"Okay, so we need to figure out what to do with the B and B," Savannah was first to say.

"We're not selling it if that's what you mean by 'figure out,' " Michelle stated adamantly.

"That's not what I meant," Savannah huffed.

Creed cleared his throat. "I'm not finished."

The siblings looked at one another with questioning shrugs, but all clapped their mouths shut to listen to the attorney once more.

When Creed lifted a small brass bell, shaking it so that it rang with a loud clanging sound, they all looked even more confused. Sylvester came into the parlor, a smile on his face that showed his white teeth against his leathery cocoa-brown complexion. On a leash was a dog. A female—no, the female from last night—came in behind Sylvester with a kennel holding a bunch of yapping puppies. She looked fresh as a new day, yet just like Quinn remembered her from last night—her hair unruly but sexy, her body petite and curvy enough to garner a second look. And then a third. And finally, Quinn paused to take a quick breath. She wasn't the focus here; he presumed the dogs were.

"I also bequeath to my grandchildren as follows," Creed began reading from the will again. "To Mary Michelle, Ms. Cleo and Lily."

Sylvester walked the larger dog over to Michelle and handed her the leash. The female reached into the kennel and after a few moments of searching pulled out a puppy that was identical to the larger dog. She walked over and sat the puppy in Michelle's lap.

Creed read on, "To Raine, Loki. To Savannah, Micah. To Preston, Coco. To Parker, Rufus."

As he read, Quinn had been holding his breath hoping against everything he knew that the kennel would be empty by the time his name was called. He should have hoped something else.

"And to Quinn, my Sweet Dixi."

The puppy who was dropped in his lap instantly hopped

down as if she were afraid for her life. She landed at his feet, where she danced around for a few seconds then fell back onto her bottom like she had run out of options.

"It is my last wish and desire that each of you cares for my precious Labs. They meant the world to me, the family in place of my real family. In the event that you feel you cannot handle this task, be not worried, Gramma understands. I ask, however, that you take time and good care to find loving homes for them."

The room was silent except for the puppies, who seemed to be having a conversation of their own.

"Now I am finished," Creed concluded with a nod of his head and dutifully began putting all his paperwork back into his ragged briefcase.

"He's kidding, right?" Savannah asked with a squeal as she swatted at the puppy licking her shoes because she hadn't hesitated to remove it from her lap.

Michelle sighed, rubbing a hand over what Quinn assumed was the mother dog's, Ms. Cleo's, brown head. "I don't think so."

"What am I supposed to do with a puppy?" Preston inquired with a frown.

"We're supposed to do as she said," Quinn added. "Take care of them." He looked down to the floor and held in a curse of his own as the puppy he'd been assigned, Sweet Dixi, unceremoniously peed on his shoes.

Chapter 3

"We can either keep them and take care of them or find a good and loving home for them," Michelle stated, rubbing a hand over Ms. Cleo's head.

She was a show-quality Lab but Gramma hadn't wanted to put that kind of stress on her, especially after the previous owner had barely fed her and trained her until she was sick. Gramma had found Ms. Cleo at a rescue shelter on a trip to Easton about two years ago. Since coming to Sweetland, Ms. Cleo was just as happy running around the couple of acres of land that surrounded The Silver Spoon. She'd entertained guests and their children since that first day, and when Judson Heathrow suggested Gramma let her try breeding, Gramma had gone along with the idea, figuring Ms. Cleo would love to be a mother. Besides, the previous owners hadn't bothered to have her spayed. Unfortunately the male who'd been used in the breeding had been hit by a truck when he'd gotten out of his kennel and wandered all the way up to Interstate 33. Mr. Heathrow let Gramma keep all the puppies, and she hadn't entertained any plans to sell the purebred pups.

"Good," Savannah said quickly. "Where's the dog pound

so I can drop her off?" She was again swatting at the puppy, who was sniffing around her shoes. But her moving arm only caught the dog's attention, resulting in quick laps with the puppy's tongue over Savannah's exposed arm. "Yuck!" she squealed, pulling her arm back.

"It's a dog, Savannah, not a disease," Raine told her younger sister.

"And she's a he," Michelle informed her. "His name is Micah."

"Whatever it is, it's not mine and I'm not keeping it," Savannah said, sounding contrite. It was her usual where her siblings were concerned, so none of them looked shocked at all.

"Then you'll have to find a good home for it," Preston said, holding his puppy in his lap, letting her lick all she wanted up and down his arm. When she noticed his shiny belt buckle she immediately diverted all her attention there.

"I don't have time for this," was Savannah's next reply. "What am I going to do with a puppy?"

"I think Gramma's trying to teach us something," Quinn said. Michelle was grateful.

Quinn was older than her with a very reserved manner about him. He took everything in stride, with the same monotone demeanor. Nothing upset him; nothing ruffled his always-smooth feathers, ever. Even now, after the puppy he'd been assigned, Dixi, had already peed on his shoes—the leather tie-up ones that he'd untied and taken off, pushing them to the side as he used tissues to wipe up the wetness from the floor—Quinn's voice sounded as level as it had twenty minutes ago.

"You're probably right," Michelle added. "She was always teaching us lessons." And Michelle prayed her siblings were open enough to learn from this one because it was going to take everything they had to make sure that all their grandmother had worked so hard for continued to thrive.

Preston nodded. "Life lessons, that's what she called them. Said they'd teach us to lead a better life."

"Not giving me money to buy a new dress for the ring dance was not a life lesson. I had to wear one of Raine's old dresses instead. It was embarrassing."

Of course this was Savannah. The one who was blessed too heavily in the looks department and not enough in the brains department, as Michelle always said. Gramma would scold her for that. She swore Savannah was smart in her own way. Michelle figured somewhere under all the makeup and hair spray Savannah might have a brain; she just wished the girl would learn to use it instead of her looks to get ahead.

"I think it might be something a little more poignant than a dress, Savannah," Preston told her.

"It doesn't matter because I have a life. I do not have time to find a home for this thing." Micah had pushed himself close to Savannah's legs, his chin and ears flopping down to cover the buckles of her shoes. Savannah had been trying to move out of the way, but short of getting up and walking out of the room there really wasn't much she could do to escape the friendly dog.

And speaking of friendly, Michelle noted that Quinn's pup was not. Dixi, who was normally very happy and very sociable, had moved about a foot away from Quinn and sat with her back to him. Quinn didn't look like he minded the distance because he definitely did not like that his shoes were wet. Another thing Michelle remembered about her brother was that he'd always been a neat freak. Everything had its place, and if something wasn't where it belonged, Quinn wasn't happy. She almost smiled to herself as she wondered how he was going to deal with the pampered and spoiled Dixi, who didn't care where anything belonged, only worried about what she wanted and how fast she could get it.

"We're abiding by Gramma's rules," Quinn said with a solemn type of authority.

"That's easy for you to say." Savannah was the first to argue.

Not that anyone was surprised by that fact.

"I don't have a nice house in the coveted Maple Leaf neighborhood in Seattle. I have an apartment in New York that I'm not even sure allows dogs. Not to mention the fact that I'm hardly ever there, or in any one place for that long, which means I cannot take care of a dog," Savannah continued.

"Do these types of dogs require a lot of attention?" Parker asked. His puppy had long since wandered off in search of something much more exciting than Parker.

Michelle had noticed him watching where the puppy went in the room but he hadn't gotten up to retrieve him, which told her he was still trying to figure out just how close he planned to get. *Cautious* was not a word she'd normally use to describe this brother. That was usually reserved for Quinn.

"Yes, they do," she said. "There's a book in the living room that tells all about what they need. Gramma bought it at Nan Giles's bookstore when she brought Ms. Cleo home with her."

"So I take it she really loved these dogs?" Quinn asked.

"Yes, she did," Michelle answered. "Just like she loved all of us. I agree with you, I think we should follow the mandate of her will."

"I think that's a given," Preston said. "But there are obvious problems with that idea. For one, if we all own a part of this bed-and-breakfast, which one of us is going to run it? None of us lives here."

Michelle frowned. "One of us does."

"I apologize," Preston added. "What I meant was that only you live here and it's not fair to ask you to take on the brunt of running this place by yourself."

"I've been here since the place opened. But I'd have to admit that I know more about the menus and the grocery expenses for the restaurant than I do about renting out the rooms. Gramma and Nikki did all that kind of work."

Parker sat up in his chair, peering around the back of the couch, finally in search of his puppy. "Was that little Nikki that you used to hang out with, Savannah? The one who brought the dogs in?"

Savannah nodded. "Yes, that was her. I haven't seen her in ages. But she looks exactly the same."

From the totally uninterested tone of her voice Quinn couldn't tell if that was good or bad. And truth be told he was more interested in the fact that little Nikki Brockington had grown into such an attractive woman—a woman he'd almost had a wet dream about.

"You two were pretty close. It's a pity you haven't kept in touch," Raine told her.

"Yeah, it's a pity I've been working," Savannah said with a smile. "What? Don't look at me like that. I did miss her a little but I just didn't have time to call every five minutes."

"Didn't have time or just didn't want to?" Michelle asked.

"Okay, that's enough," Quinn said, his voice rising above the high pitch of the females. They were giving him a headache, or maybe he'd had one when he'd gotten up this morning, or maybe it had come on when he learned he'd been lusting after a female as young as his youngest sister. Whatever the cause, he had to get a handle on it and quick. There was more than enough stress in his life for any number of chronic ailments. He was lucky the headache was the only one to appear.

Besides, in another second Savannah would jump up

from the chair in full argument mode, which included yelling and screaming if she thought that would get her point across. Michelle was much more somber in her attacks and would remain calm but would not back down against their little sister. Raine would roll her eyes and become frustrated with both of them. Parker would ignore the chaos, being so used to producing enough of that on his own, and Preston—well, Preston was just too laid-back or preoccupied with whatever went on in his legal-beagle head to ever get involved in sisterly affairs.

"None of us is innocent of leaving Sweetland and not looking back," he continued.

"Michelle is because she's Miss Perfect," Savannah quipped.

Raine frowned but didn't argue against Savannah's words, which said she kind of supported the younger sister's comment.

"I did what I had to do," Michelle told them.

"And so did we," Quinn announced. "Besides, now is not the time to rehash old grudges. We're all adults now. We're going to handle this will and Gramma's wishes like adults." The look he gave them all solicited no argument. "Now, as soon as I clean my shoes and change my socks, we can talk about hiring a manager for the B and B. Let's all try to recognize that this has to be done relatively quickly since we all have lives and careers to return to."

He'd seen Michelle shake her head, which meant she didn't totally agree with what he'd said. But then she cleared her throat. "We should hire Nikki Brockington. She just got her degree in hospitality and hotel management and she was Gramma's assistant manager. She knows this place inside and out. You're not going to find a better candidate," she told them.

"And you sound like you're not going to vote for another candidate if we do find one," Parker added with a chuckle.

And because it was Parker, the most fun loving of the Cantrell siblings, Michelle laughed along with him before saying, "You're absolutely right."

"Then as soon as I come back we'll go talk to Miss Brockington," Quinn said, picking up his shoes and heading out of the room. He didn't know if Sweet Dixi followed him or not, and at the moment he didn't really care.

As Quinn took the stairs he couldn't help inhaling the scent of lemon and the warm breeze coming through open windows. At the top of the landing there was a white iron table with an antique lamp, a box of tissues, and a bowl of what looked like potpourri. But that wasn't what gave off the citrus smell. That was coming from the left.

His room was down that way, all the way at the end of the hall. With still-damp socks he walked along the shined wood floors and was stopped by humming and a burst of sunlight. When he paused at the open door to the room right next to his, he expected to see a housekeeper or possibly one of the guests who'd been booked here over the weekend. Either way, Quinn didn't expect them to have the most delectable backside he'd ever had the pleasure of seeing in an upright position.

She was on her hands and knees, in the center of a king-sized bed, pushing pillows to one end, crawling backward to smooth the sheets and situate another set of plump pillows. He almost groaned at the word *plump,* especially since he wasn't really looking at the pillows when he thought it. Quinn knew at that moment he should keep right on walking, but of course he didn't.

Instead he stood in the doorway of the sunny yellow-painted room and watched as the female whom he was almost positive was Nikki Brockington made up the king-sized bed. The comforter was a pale sage design, which complemented the room's decor perfectly. To the left the wall was exposed brick, just like the right side wall in his room. A lot of care and attention to detail had been put into decorating these rooms, he thought with a great deal of pride, because he'd known his grandmother had worked hard to make this place something. From what he could see she'd done a damned good job.

Something could be said about such a perfect rear end as well. Something along the lines of *Damn, that looks good!* He certainly wasn't going to say that, but the thought was plastered in his mind so that he didn't think he'd ever be able to look at her again without thinking it. And she was on her knees. Somebody really needed to just shoot him right now.

Okay, that wasn't going to happen so he'd have to be the bigger person and walk away. Quinn was just about to leave, to stop gawking like a horny teenager and return to his room like he was supposed to. The moment he turned he heard it.

Barking.

It grew louder and more frenzied until he saw the fuzzy chocolate ball take the top step then lunge down the hallway. He knelt, reaching out an arm to stop the procession, but the rascal slipped right through his hands and bolted into the room. When he turned to check where the puppy had ended up he was startled to see that the gorgeous backside had not only turned around but was no longer on the bed. Now she was kneeling on the floor much like him, catching the puppy in her outstretched arms.

"Hello, little lady. How are you?" she was saying as the dog happily licked every part of her face. "You're happy to see me, huh? Well, I'm happy to see you too, Sweet Dixi."

So this was his ward, Quinn thought, the puppy who had been assigned to him. Had she followed him up the stairs? Not likely; the two of them hadn't gotten off to such a great start.

"Oh, hello," Nikki said, and Quinn realized she was now talking to him.

"Hello," he replied, slipping the hand that didn't hold his shoes into his front pocket. "I'm sorry about her."

"No. No, don't apologize. Sweet Dixi and I are great friends. I was there when she was born." She scooped the puppy into her arms and stood.

Quinn now looked into a small round face with hair that was way too big and unruly, but somehow just right.

"Nikki Brockington?" he asked, only because now that he knew who she was, he remembered her from when they were younger. Or rather when she was younger and had hung out with Savannah.

"That's right," she said and gave him what Quinn thought was an exasperated look. "I'm Nikki and you're the Mighty Quinn," she added drily.

"Excuse me?"

She looked down at the puppy, snuggling it closer to her face, offering her cheek for an exuberant lick. Quinn swallowed hard and mentally kicked himself for wishing he were a dog, that dog in particular, to have that privilege.

"When Savannah and I were young we used to call you that. Of course you were never around when we said it—we were too afraid of what might happen if you found out. Well, I was afraid of you; Savannah, as you know, thought she could beat the world. And whoever she couldn't beat she could certainly woo with her pretty smile."

Memories of hot summer days, cherry-flavored snowballs, and swimming down at the lake came to mind as she talked. Her voice was light, like any minute now she'd laugh. And Quinn waited, hoping, as if he'd never heard what he knew would be a lovely sound before.

Then she smiled. Her pert lips spread to show brilliantly white teeth, and her dark eyes lit up with excitement as Dixi licked her face once more. She seemingly liked this dog a lot, and the dog obviously returned the feeling. He couldn't help but look at her hair again, a mass of springy black curls that he'd bet all the money in his wallet were as soft as the sheets on that bed.

The thought came quick, slapping against his brain like a whip, and Quinn sucked in a breath. He wasn't a stranger to women or to physical attraction. But to put it simply, this was not what he'd expected. Not now and certainly not here. He'd blame it on the coffee he had before coming downstairs or the fragrant Chesapeake Bay air, or whatever would get it out of his mind. But the reason might be simply that she was a very attractive woman.

"We were just talking about you," he said, pulling himself back to business. The safest place Quinn knew.

"Really?" she questioned, taking a step closer to him. "Is something wrong with your rooms? Or did you need me to get anything for you?"

The scent was hers. As she grew closer, his lungs filled with lemons. No, it was more like a tall glass of homemade lemonade with plenty of sugar and ice cubes, which would melt over her skin like . . .

"We," he began and then had to clear his throat. "My siblings and I just want to talk to you about the B and B. If you're finished in here we could go down. They're waiting in the parlor," he told her.

She nodded. "Just give me another second to put things in order here."

In her arms Dixi had been scrambling as if the dog couldn't keep still to save her life.

"She's a handful. I can take her," he offered and reached out. He dropped both his shoes and cursed because he'd forgotten they were in his hands.

They both bent to pick up the shoes.

Dixi jumped out of her arms and found one shoe before either of them could grab it. She was inside licking before she could be stopped. Which neither of them attempted to do because their hands touched, his left against her right as they reached for the shoe that had been quickly taken from them. Heat sizzled up his arm; he thought maybe it crackled in the air, too, because Nikki looked taken aback as well.

"I'm sorry," he offered quickly.

"No," she said, pulling her arm back as if it had touched the same flame he felt ripping through his body. "It's okay."

He had to look away from her, had to move away from her actually because he might do something he'd never done before. He might kiss this woman whom he hadn't seen in years and who could be his little sister.

"Give me that," Quinn directed at Dixi, pulling the shoe away from her. "You've had your time with my shoes."

Standing, Nikki gave a nervous chuckle. "I see you two are getting along nicely."

"I wouldn't say that exactly," he replied, coming to a standing position, shoes once again in tow. "I don't think urinating in your new owner's shoes is a good way to start a relationship."

Now her laugh came in swift guffaws that sounded oddly feminine, yet more than a little contagious.

Quinn found himself smiling. "I didn't think it was funny at the time."

"I'm sorry. It's just that Dixi is the nicest of the bunch. She's always friendly and playful. I can't imagine her doing such a thing."

"Well, she did." Quinn held up a shoe. "I've got proof."

Nikki nodded. "And it looks like she's not quite finished with your shoes yet."

Dixi was yipping and dancing around Quinn's feet as if she expected him to maybe lift one of those up for her to urinate on next.

"Sit!" he ordered but it was as if he'd said it in German because Dixi didn't so much as take a pause.

"Poor Sweet Dixi. I'll just take her down with me,"

Nikki said, shaking her head. "You go and get, ah . . . another pair of shoes."

The way she looked at him said she was about to laugh again, but she bent down, taking Dixi into her arms once more. Lifting one of her paws, she made like the dog was waving at him. "We'll see you downstairs in a bit."

Quinn was not amused and walked away thinking it was going to be a horrendous task keeping that dog.

But once he was back in his room he went to the window; his suitcase was propped against the wall just beneath. He dropped his shoes beside it and was just about to bend over and open the case to find another pair when the outside caught his attention. The room he was staying in faced the back of the house, which in turn faced a line of maple and oak trees as big and full as if they were perfectly drawn in a picture book. The grass was emerald green, almost too green to be believable. The sun sprinkled its golden rays down in abundance, until it looked like another place and time entirely. Surely this could not be the town he'd left more than nineteen years ago. He never remembered it being this beautiful on a Sunday morning.

Then again, Quinn and his siblings usually spent their Sunday mornings sitting on a pew at the Redeemer's Baptist Church. They'd all sat there yesterday, in the same old church that Gramma had dressed them up for and dragged them to every week. But yesterday they'd said good-bye. He'd looked down into that pale rose casket to the body of one of the only women he'd ever loved. Even in death she looked happy and healthy and ready to take on the world. Gramma hadn't been afraid of anything. She'd said that only fear itself was scary; that's why she didn't allow it into her heart. She always looked forward, always kept her head up. On a long sigh Quinn was determined to do the same.

He'd known that coming back here was going to be

hard. But it had to be done. And now it was almost over. He'd just about made it without any issues.

Then he saw the old man from last night. Sylvester Bynum. He walked with a significant limp this morning, his cane's bottom disappearing in the lush grass as it assisted him out to the line of trees. He walked down farther, past the old gazebo, to where Quinn could see a lone bench and a couple of colorful bushes—azaleas in all shades from white to fuchsia. Sylvester sat down with a tired plop, using both his hands to hold the cane in front of him. Then he simply stared. At what, Quinn wasn't quite sure. But he recognized the stance, almost read the thoughts in the man's head. He was grieving.

Quinn didn't do grief well. No, he didn't do it at all. He loved hard, worked even harder, but let the dead bury the dead. That was all, and he'd never really had any other choice. It was what worked for him.

Tearing his gaze away from the window, he reached into the suitcase and grabbed another pair of shoes and socks. When he'd slipped on the leather loafers he went into the bathroom and washed his hands. Leaving the room, he was more determined than ever to hire a manager for the B&B and get the hell out of this godforsaken town, once and for all.

Chapter 4

Quinn Cantrell still did something to her, Nikki was the first to admit when she'd finished that room and walked down the steps with Dixi in her arms. She'd moved a lot faster than she'd planned, partly because she didn't want to be stuck going down the steps with Quinn. Not that *stuck* was the best word.

She'd always avoided him. *Like the plague,* she thought seriously. Savannah said he was mean and liked to yell at her all the time. But Nikki had never believed that, not entirely. Savannah was spoiled and could be a bit of a brat. She hadn't spoken to her much in the years she'd been away from Sweetland, so Nikki wasn't sure if she'd grown up any—she wasn't really betting on it. And they hadn't had a moment to talk during this trip. Savannah had arrived yesterday morning just in time to climb into the limo and head to the church.

But Nikki's best recollection of Quinn was his sad brown eyes, the same ones that had stared at her when she'd played with Dixi. A part of her had wanted to invite him to come down and play with the dog with her, but she hadn't. Quinn Cantrell did not play with puppies. Hell, she'd thought he didn't smile, but she'd seen one today and figured it was almost as perfect as the picturesque scenery outside. And as if the smile weren't enough, they'd touched, like skin on skin—which was a thought that made her burn within, but that was another story. And just like last night when he'd looked at her as if she were just another citizen of this lovely town, he'd given her his signature scowl and she'd felt like crap. He even looked at Sweet Dixi like she'd just come in on a bus from hell.

"He just doesn't understand us does he, Sweet Dixi?"

Her answer came in another boisterous licking of the face and a wagging of Sweet Dixi's otterlike tail. Nikki doubted Quinn understood anything but his high-class job at that fancy hospital in Seattle. At the funeral Ms. Marabelle and Ms. Louisa had been talking about the Cantrell siblings as if they were all on the cover of some tabloid magazine. Then again, Marabelle and Louisa could be called Sweetland's live version of the *National Enquirer,* only they didn't bother to write down their glamorous and often over-the-top stories, they just sat in the front pew of Redeemer's Baptist and let it all out. When they weren't sitting in church gossiping, they were at Jana's Java Shop sitting right in front of the window so they could get a good look at everyone walking down Main Street, all of them fair game for their commentary.

Anyway, they'd been saying that he'd gone to the top schools and graduated at the head of his class—Quinn, that is. Then he'd worked at the famous Johns Hopkins for a while but thought he was better than those fine folks there, including Dr. Ben Carson himself, and picked up and moved all the way to Seattle where he ran some part of the hospital all on his own. Quinn looked like he was used to being in charge—after all, he was the oldest sibling. He also looked like he needed to loosen up a bit, if Nikki were really looking at him, which as she got to the bottom of the steps she decided she definitely was not—or at least she didn't plan to anymore.

When she entered the parlor she heard Raine—the quiet and pretty Cantrell sister—remembering a particularly memorable fiasco the "Double Trouble" Cantrells had gotten themselves into. Preston and Parker were well known around town for their practical jokes as well as the long line of broken hearts they routinely left in their wake. Looking at them now, Nikki figured they hadn't changed a bit.

"Hello," she said upon entering and moved to stand closer to Michelle, since she knew this sister better than the others at this moment. "Quinn said you wanted to talk to me."

"Oh yes," Michelle said, standing and grabbing Nikki by the arm. "You all remember Nikki, right? Her father's the fire chief."

Dixi took that as her cue to jump down and join her own siblings as they played in the middle of the floor. For some reason they loved the old Aubusson rug in this room and routinely spent hours here just entertaining themselves.

"Hi, Nikki." Raine was first to speak. "You've done a great job here. I love the feel of the B and B as soon as you hit the front porch. And I hear the place is quite popular."

Nikki smiled, her cheeks heating only minutely. "It was your grandmother's vision, I just came by to learn from her and ended up staying."

"She's done a great job. Her personality is what helps keep word of mouth traveling. Nikki wrote the verbiage for our brochure and she does all the advertising. Everyone in town knows her and her family, so that's another hometown connection to The Silver Spoon as well," Michelle told them.

"But it's Michelle's cooking that really keeps them talking," Nikki added. "We've had some pretty important people stay here just to get a taste of her food."

"But they could just come into the restaurant without staying, right?" Savannah asked.

"Yes," Nikki replied. "But I try to develop attractive packages that will keep them here. For example, earlier this year we had Drake Sheridan and his crew come out and convert the sunroom to a small gift shop. Now we have everything here that a tourist could want."

"Except a pool," Preston was quick to point out. "And a gym. I like to keep up with my workout regimen while I'm on vacation."

"But that's not what The Silver Spoon is about," Michelle told him. "We're about creating that home-away-from-home feel. Not the impersonal touch of a hotel."

Parker nodded. "I can see the appeal." Then, leaning forward with his elbows on his knees, he continued onto a totally unrelated subject. "I heard your sister got married a few years ago."

He wore jeans that looked old and worn, but great nonetheless because they were on him. His good looks were so stark and in-your-face they'd always intimidated Nikki. Not like Quinn's, which just kind of snuck up on you and settled right in the center of your chest. She coughed at the thought.

"Yes, she did. Barry's doing his second tour in Iraq. He and Cordy have three kids now, one boy and two wicked pretty little girls," she told him.

"Is that so? Wow, I can't imagine Cordy with kids. Can you, Preston?"

The brothers shared a secretive smile. Nikki just shook her head. She did not want to know what that meant. Cordy had been in love with Parker Cantrell most of her teenage years, until he'd graduated and left to join the police academy in Baltimore. That next summer Barry and a busload of soldiers had come to Sweetland on one of those crab-feast-slash-shopping day trips that were very popular in Bay towns and swept Parker right out of Cordy's mind.

"So does this place make a lot of money?" Savannah asked, to Michelle's instant chagrin.

Nikki wasn't bothered by Savannah's candor; she'd already figured her onetime good friend hadn't changed much. It was almost funny to realize how right she'd been.

"About a year before Mrs. Cantrell opened this place some developers came down and spent a week in town measuring and checking out everything. Mayor Yardley took them all around, giving them the history and showing them our best sights. At the end of the week they made an offer to wipe the entire town out and build a resort and golf course instead, said it would be a huge vacation destination. The town council vetoed that idea, and the next year Yardley was voted out of office.

"Now Liza Fitzgerald is mayor, and one of the first things she did was begin the revitalization of Sweetland. She even named new members to head up the chamber of commerce. Mrs. Cantrell supported that revitalization wholeheartedly and decided to convert the house into a B and B and specialty restaurant to make Sweetland more appealing to tourists. The construction on the extension to the house for the restaurant took about three months. She called it The Silver Spoon because she said when she was young kids always teased her about being born with a silver spoon in her mouth, when really her family had to scrimp and struggle just like the rest of the citizens in Sweetland. Right after that other shops began to open on Main Street. A few newcomers hit town with their ideas, and since then we've seen both an eighty percent growth in full-time citizens and a booming tourist season that kicks off at Memorial Day and holds steady right up to the Labor Day weekend."

Nikki paused for a moment, hoping one of them would say something or at least ask her another question. But they all remained quiet, staring at her expectantly.

"Like most of the other businesses in town, the summer's our peak time," she continued, acting as if she were pitching the B&B to a bunch of tourists. Which was kind of what the Cantrells felt like after all this time.

"As a matter of fact, we're completely booked starting this coming weekend and through the second week in June. Each month of the summer we have at least three reservations already. And the restaurant does well steadily because the citizens as well as visitors have come to love Michelle's cooking."

She stopped talking then and was determined not to say another word. For one thing, she was sort of out of breath from that recitation, and for another . . . well, the first reason was good enough.

"Sounds like you have a handle on things around here," Quinn replied.

Nikki turned to his voice because she hadn't realized he'd reentered the room. He was so tall, his appearance so dominating that she had to take a quick breath. It felt like he'd sucked all the oxygen out of the room with his arrival.

"I know this place like the back of my hand. And I know what Mrs. Cantrell wanted for its future. I can write up a report so all of you will have an idea as well," she offered.

"I told you she's the best person for the job," Michelle added. "If we want to keep this place going without any hiccups because of Gramma's passing, making Nikki manager is our best option."

Nikki's head snapped around to face Michelle. "What? Me, manager?"

So many thoughts had filtered through her mind since Mrs. Cantrell's death, but this was not one of them. Of course, Cordy had asked her what she thought would happen to the B&B, but Nikki had kept that to herself. She hadn't voiced to anybody that she didn't think the B&B would continue to be run by Cantrells. And now, as she looked at Michelle, she got the sinking feeling that none of the siblings here considered that to be a possibility, either.

"You have a degree in hospitality management?" Preston asked.

"Ah, yes," she answered, still a little stunned that this conversation was actually taking place. "Hospitality and hotel management. I minored in accounting."

"Smart girl," Parker added. "I vote yes." His smile was slow forming—a practiced move she'd bet her biweekly paycheck on. Once it was complete it was dazzling, his dark eyes so expressive, so charming. He was still a heart-breaker, she thought, almost shaking her head. A damned good heartbreaker, she suspected.

"Are you married?"

Nikki turned quickly again. She was going to have one sore neck by the time she went home tonight. "What?"

Quinn moved from where he'd been standing in the doorway and stopped when he was only a couple of feet away from her. "Married? Kids? Other responsibilities that might hinder you from performing your job duties here one hundred percent," he continued.

He was serious, his brow furrowing just a bit, his jaw set in that intense line that almost looked painful. The puppies still played and barked as if none of the humans were standing there. Nikki let their sounds calm her racing heart. Quinn Cantrell was giving her that intense look that sent trickles down the base of her spine, and he'd just asked her if she had a man, a family. She felt like a colossal idiot for the answer she had no choice but to give.

"No," she stated quietly. Then she cleared her throat and spoke with more conviction. "I'm not married and I don't have any children. I live in the apartment over my parents' garage. I go to church on Sundays and I shop at Godfrey's Market just like everyone else in town."

"And you plan to live here for how long? Forever?" he asked with that clear look of his.

Maybe she didn't like Quinn Cantrell as much as she used to.

"I was born in Sweetland and don't see any reason why I should leave. It's my town, my home. Can you understand that, Quinn?" She asked him that but really had no idea why. In fact, once the question was out she wished she could yank the words back. But that was futile. If there was one thing Nikki knew with startling clarity, it was that the past just could not be undone.

"So you could move into the caretaker's suite as soon as possible?" he continued.

Nikki lifted her chin just a bit because it was clear to her that Quinn Cantrell was used to calling all the shots. She'd bet he walked around that big fancy hospital with his shiny tie-up shoes—pre-Dixi-urination—and crisp pressed pants and dress shirt. His tie would be perfectly straight just like his posture. He'd give his staff that look with the furrowed eyebrows and deep dark eyes and order them around just as he was attempting to do with her. Well, this wasn't Seattle, and until she accepted the position, Quinn Cantrell was not her boss.

"I don't know that it's necessary for the manager to live on premises. Mrs. Cantrell did because she grew up in this house. It was her home. I already have a place that I grew up in. And when I decide to move I'd like to select my own residence."

"And that's just fine," Michelle intervened. "I live down the street and we could always hire an evening assistant manager to take care of anything that could happen in the off hours."

"That sounds like a good idea," Raine added. "That way Nikki could still have a personal life. She's too young to be tied to this place twenty-four seven."

Quinn didn't waver at his sister's words. "It's a twenty-four seven job."

"How would you know?" Savannah asked him. She'd been quiet for most of this exchange so Nikki was a little stunned to hear her speak. But when she did it was with that same Savannah-esque attitude, complete with the pouting lips. "You've never run a B and B. I'm sure this isn't the machine your clinic is. And besides, she's been here since the beginning. She's the best person for the job whether she lives here or in a box by the river. Not that I would suggest that, mind you," Savannah finished with a weary look at Nikki.

Nikki remembered that look and smiled, shaking her head. "That's not an option I was considering."

"Good. That's settled, Nikki gets my vote," Savannah announced with a smile then stood frowning down at the puppy who instantly ran toward her with an obvious don't-forget-me look on his precious face. "I'm sick of sitting in this house. I'm going out for some air."

Savannah was more than a little chagrined to find she wasn't doing that alone. Micah, her brown pup, was right behind her. "Be quiet if you insist on tagging along," she scolded impatiently as she walked out of the parlor through the living room.

A few seconds later they heard the door slam.

"She's going to drive that dog crazy," Raine said as she stood and shook her head. "Nikki has my vote as well."

"Mine, too," Parker chimed in. "Now I'm going for a swim."

"I'll join you," Raine said. "You coming, Preston?"

Preston, who had been watching Nikki with amused interest, shrugged. "I think you're the best person for the job, Nikki. We really appreciate your devotion and look forward to working with you," he told her as he stood and came to shake her hand.

Professional, debonair, intimidating: Those were the words she'd use to describe Preston Cantrell. He and Parker weren't identical but you could definitely see they were twins, so saying he was handsome would be more than repetitive on her part.

"Thank you, Preston. And thank all of you for your faith in me. I'll try to do everything Mrs. Cantrell would have wanted," she told them. Even though she still wasn't sure why she was taking the job, all things considered. No, she was sure, it was because Quinn didn't think she could do it, or he did but had reservations. Either way, she was determined to prove him wrong.

Preston shook his head. "We'll be happy if you just do the job the way you see fit. I'm sure my grandmother respected your vision and your skills or she wouldn't have had you here."

She could only nod. Was she really going to manage The Silver Spoon B&B all by herself? Talk about coming a long way, she thought with an inner pride that left a lump in her throat.

Michelle came over to hug her. "You'll do just fine. Now I've gotta go work on this week's menus. I'll be in my office if you need me."

Nikki held on to her when Michelle would have pulled away. "You didn't tell them?" She whispered the question in her ear.

"Later," Michelle replied. "We'll talk about it later."

Nikki wasn't in agreement with putting off the inevitable, especially not when "later" could very well mean after all the siblings had returned to their homes. As the primary bookkeeper in the last years, she knew how much was owed and had been told by Mrs. Cantrell that she'd taken care of it. Nikki partially blamed herself for not knowing that something was wrong sooner, but she'd trusted Mrs. Cantrell. This place meant the world to her; she would never intentionally do anything to lose it. At least Nikki didn't think she would.

Clearing her throat after Michelle had pulled away, Nikki tried to sound as if nothing were wrong. "Both our guests have checked out. We're clear until Friday. But my mom wanted me to remind you that the women's auxiliary is having a class down at the municipal building on Tuesday morning. Afterward they're all heading down here, so that's about fifty for lunch or early dinner."

It was Michelle's turn to nod. "I'll give her a call to see if she wants something special served. Talk to you later," she said with a wave. Then she stopped and gave her older brother a look. "Behave," Nikki heard her whisper.

When they were alone, she and Quinn, Nikki couldn't think of any reason to stay. She began walking to the door but knew instinctively her getaway wouldn't be that easy.

"Where can I get supplies for this dog? And is there a shelter here in Sweetland or should I contact the one in Easton?" he asked.

Again, Nikki was turning with a start. "You aren't going to keep Sweet Dixi?"

Quinn slipped his hands into his pockets as he stood there watching her. "I work long hours at a cancer clinic. While I have a big enough house, I also have a maid service that comes in once a week. There's no way I can provide twenty-four-hour care for her. Besides, my siblings aren't animal people, either. Case in point," he added, pointing to the four pups who still played in the middle of the floor.

Dixi, Rufus, Coco, and Loki seemed oblivious to the fact that they'd been left. Michelle had already had Ms. Cleo and Lily kenneled up when Nikki had come back into the room. Then again, Michelle was the only one, besides her, who was used to this rambunctious litter of Labs. The others came from the big city and their own lives, their own responsibilities. The dogs were just an inheritance, one they didn't seem proud of accepting.

"Kraig Bellini is the town vet. He's over on Trailway and usually stays open to around seven in the evenings. He does house calls when necessary. You could go over there and talk to him about your plans. I'm sure he has some connections."

"Thank you," he said blandly.

"You're welcome," she said and continued to walk away because he hadn't changed. And probably never would. Quinn Cantrell was certainly welcome to be the rigid jerk she remembered, and he was more than welcome to take his big-city ways back to the big city that he came from. Sweetland had been doing just fine without him. And so had she.

Chapter 5

The Silver Spoon was crowded, and that was unusual for a Sunday evening. Generally, when it wasn't tourist season, the citizens of Sweetland attended the church of their choice on Sunday mornings, or hit the water for some fishing, or just piddled around their homes doing things they hadn't grabbed enough time during the week to do. This gave them all day long to prepare what they liked to call "good Sunday meals."

When Michelle took over the kitchen at The Silver Spoon—about ten minutes after Janet decided to open a restaurant and a bed-and-breakfast—she'd planned to offer a light "good Sunday meal." Over the years she'd changed some items and added new ones, and today Sundays at The Silver Spoon was a good place to be if home was not an option.

Tonight she'd planned an extra-special dinner, adding a few items to the menu that would not likely be offered again. That was because tonight was special. All of her family was home, where, in her opinion, they belonged. For years she'd wanted her siblings to come back to Sweetland. They'd been born here, had roots in this town that sprouted with their grandmother and continued with the legacy she'd left them. The Silver Spoon wasn't only a place to eat and sleep, it was the dream of a woman who'd dreamed all her life. Who had loved home and family above all else. And who in the end hadn't been able to keep either one on her own.

Unfortunately, tonight Michelle would have to tell them the truth. She would have to let them know the real situation of The Silver Spoon, the situation she'd been praying about for the last eight weeks.

"Business is doing just fine tonight." Sylvester came into the living room talking as if he were in the middle of a conversation as opposed to just starting one.

He wore his Sunday suit, the summer one, Michelle noted—a pale blue seersucker suit complete with navy-blue suspenders and red-and-white bow tie perfectly tied.

"I heard. The beef stew is going fast, too. Good thing I added a couple of selections to the menu," Michelle said, moving to one of the counters to pick up another order off the wheel overhead.

Tonight she had five waitresses working the dining room with its twenty-seven tables. Two students she'd hired as interns from the culinary college she'd attended in Baltimore worked on preparation, and Tanya and Lisa Kramer were also working in the kitchen as they were home from college and ready to start their summer positions. She needed a sous chef badly and had been hoping to hire one this summer, but with the current situation she wouldn't be able to afford one. Hopefully all the extra catering jobs she'd been picking up would help.

For tonight, Michelle had cooked most of the food, or at least started it when she'd come in around five this morning. She'd made the dough for her dinner rolls late last night when she couldn't sleep and brought it in with her. Now, at only twenty minutes after seven, she was hustling back and forth trying to make sure everything was perfect for her own dinner celebration.

"I saw that," Sylvester said. "Also saw you have that big table in the back set up. Got a party coming in tonight?"

"The Cantrell party," she announced with a nervous smile. "I figured since we were all here it would be good to sit down for at least one meal together. Before they all leave," she added a little more quietly.

"Good move," Sylvester said with a sly grin.

Michelle really liked Sylvester. She figured this was exactly what her grandfather would have been like had he lived to see any of them. And her grandmother had liked him a lot, too, which was probably the real reason Sylvester had hung around Sweetland as long as he did. He was a drifter, as he'd told Michelle before. He hadn't lived in any one place longer than it took him to get a few pieces of mail or impregnate some woman. The latter he'd done on three occasions. It was his youngest daughter whom he'd lived with after his stroke five years ago. The hospital had notified her and she'd come, much to Sylvester's surprise. Then she'd taken him back to her house to live. It wasn't for another four months that Sylvester figured out why she wanted him there. His Social Security check was proving to be extra income for her. He said he hadn't squawked but gave her what money she asked for, figuring it was the least he could do for her since he hadn't really played an active part in her life. But when her boyfriend moved in with them, everything changed, fast. In the end they moved to Atlanta and Sylvester wasn't invited to go along. With his health almost 85 percent intact he set out on his own travels once more and ended up right here on the steps of The Silver Spoon. That was three years ago. He'd been here ever since.

"You're invited to join us, Mr. Sylvester. You're just like family, and Gramma would have wanted us to all continue to treat you that way."

Sylvester was quiet for a moment, then simply nodded. "I'll go and take my seat."

She watched him walk out of the kitchen and smiled. Hopefully, her siblings would be so easy to deal with.

"Charlie still has his spot down by the pier," Parker was saying to Preston, who sat to his right.

Quinn had just arrived and was pulling out his chair to sit on Parker's left. They were the first three to arrive at Michelle's special dinner. "And let me guess, you're thinking of going down there to get drunk . . . legally, this time," he said to Parker.

Parker was already grinning, rubbing his hands together. "You've got that right. You know when the last time was I've been able to unwind with a drink? Hell, man, I can't even remember."

"I hear you," Preston added. "Business has been good, I'm not complaining. But I haven't had much time to myself lately."

"And by 'business has been good' he means that there's been an increase in murders in Baltimore City so we've both been pretty busy. I swear if I have to knock on the door and tell another mother that her fifteen-year-old son has been shot and killed I'm going to lose it," Parker said with a groan.

Tanya appeared then with her quietly pretty face and ready smile. She looked like she was in her early twenties, fresh and ambitious. Michelle had told Quinn earlier this afternoon—they'd been sitting on the front porch drinking lemonade and looking up and down the street instead of talking about what was really on her mind— that Tanya and her sister Lisa had been working here during their summer breaks for the last three years. Seeing her now made him wonder how many more summers she would walk around this old house, taking dinner orders, scrubbing floors, and making beds. How long before the eleven hundred occupants of this small patch of land started to suffocate her?

"Can I get you guys something to drink?" she asked.

"Rum and Coke," Parker requested immediately.

"I'll have whatever is on tap," was Preston's reply.

"I'll have the same," Quinn said. It appeared Parker was very serious about relaxing tonight.

When Tanya had left them, Preston related to what his twin had said. "And I'm defending the other fifteen-year-old who pulled the trigger. It's getting so now I hate to watch the news at night because I know my phone's going to ring first thing the next morning and it's going to be some distraught mother begging me to get her son out of jail."

"So switch to civil law," Quinn suggested, toying with the napkin on his table.

Preston had gone to the University of Maryland and the University of Baltimore School of Law. He'd practiced as a prosecutor for five years and for the last two years had run a very successful defense firm with his former classmate and now partner, Joseph Baskerville. Preston had been talking about becoming a lawyer since he and Parker were sixteen and were pulled over on their way home from Ocean City. He'd argued for weeks that they shouldn't pay the ticket; they should go to court instead, especially since the officer had reeked of alcohol. In the end, Gramma had sent a check to the court for the ticket and Preston had vowed to fight the good fight for the wrongly accused. Now, Quinn thought with a frown, his younger brother seemed to be growing tired of that fight.

Preston shrugged. "I just might do that," he said.

Their drinks arrived and Parker finished almost half his glass before saying, "So what's your advice for me, big brother? Should I quit the police force?"

Younger by five minutes, Parker had always been the true wild child of the Cantrell family. *Headstrong* and *reckless* were words people in the town had used to describe him. Quinn saw something different. He'd always seen a young man trying to find his way, to make his mark on the world. And truthfully, Quinn had been a little envious of Parker growing up because even though he was younger Parker always knew what he wanted and how to get it. He also knew how to live life to its fullest without worrying about recriminations or repercussions. Quinn had always worried about how what he did would affect others, almost to the point of distraction. That hadn't changed over the years, and he was beginning to feel the strain from it all.

"You don't want to be a cop anymore?" Quinn asked in an attempt to remain focused on his brother's life and not his own.

"I want to stop spending every waking moment staring at death. It's depressing."

Quinn could certainly relate to what Parker was saying. Still, he couldn't help but ask, "What else would you do? I mean, the force fits everything about you. They allow you to carry a gun and get into people's faces legally."

There was a joined chuckle as the brothers continued to wait for their sisters. Each of them looked around the dining room, watching as people came in, took seats, ordered food, and were served. Quinn couldn't speak for them but what he saw was a pretty smooth and profitable business.

"What about you?" Preston asked. "Everything going okay with you at the cancer center?"

Of course the conversation would eventually shift to him; the Cantrells liked to know what was going on with one another. That was a family thing, he knew, and he really shouldn't have been put off by it. Truth was, Quinn simply wondered how to answer the question when he wasn't totally sure himself. He'd been working at the

Mark Vincent Cancer Center for five years as their chief medical oncologist. He watched his patients come in for treatment after receiving the worst news of their lives; some would die, and some would go into remission. Quinn refused to have a feeling at either outcome. He simply did his job. Day after day.

"Everything is okay," he answered but not with total honesty. He didn't think either of his brothers would pick up on that.

And as if he'd personally summoned something to change the subject from him and/or his career, Raine and Savannah arrived. Savannah wore a long yellow dress with earrings as bright and as big as the heels on her shoes and Raine, very understated white linen pants and a lavender blouse. Quinn could tell a lot about a woman by the way she dressed. He'd had ample practice watching his three sisters argue over clothes and giving their endless opinions about what the others were wearing. It had provided him wonderful insight for his future. Unfortunately, he rarely used any of the knowledge he had about women. Not since Sharane.

"So have we ordered? I'm starving," Savannah said, reaching for a menu.

"I think your sister has a special menu planned for you tonight," Sylvester told her as he took a seat at the end of the table. "And she's a fine cook so I'm sure you won't be disappointed."

"I want seafood," Savannah insisted, Sylvester's comment notwithstanding.

"That beef stew is smelling mighty good," Preston offered.

Raine shrugged. "Whatever Michelle cooks will be fine. I really like what they've done to this place."

"It's a good establishment," Quinn said, grateful for the change of subject both verbally and mentally. "Michelle gave me the rundown this afternoon on how things have been working over on the restaurant side. And from the look of the last financial statements, they've been operating in the black for quite a while."

"That's good. Daddy would have been proud," Raine said.

"Your grandmother certainly was." Sylvester lifted his glass of water to his lips and drank. "She loved this house and this town. But mostly she wanted to leave you kids something. A piece of your heritage."

"She could have left out those danged dogs," Savannah said with a groan.

"Speaking of which," Preston offered immediately, "I've listed my puppy on one of those websites. My secretary is an animal lover so she knows about all this stuff. When I emailed her about the will she suggested I give this place a try since there's no way I can take care of a Lab puppy working the hours I do."

"That's a great idea," Savannah said with a smile. "What's the web address so I can get my little hellion listed on there, too?"

"So nobody's interested in keeping their dog?" Raine asked with a frown.

"I'm on the streets for twelve, sometimes twenty-four hours straight. I barely remember to go to the grocery store to buy my own food, let alone remember to feed a dog." Parker had signaled to Tanya for another drink.

Quinn watched the girl's hesitant look and figured she'd probably serve him a much more watered-down version this time.

"I just thought since Gramma wanted us to have them," Raine began. "I mean there has to be a reason she'd call us all back here and give us these dogs to take care of."

"It's a simple reason," Michelle said, finally joining the rest of them and taking her seat at the head of the table. "Gramma wanted you all to come back to Sweetland to live. I need you all to come back to Sweetland to help save The Silver Spoon."

Before the grumbling could start Michelle raised a hand that silenced everyone . . . at least for the time being.

"Let me just say this all at one time then we'll open the floor for questions and comments." She took a deep breath. "About two months ago Nikki came to me with a tax bill for more than fifty thousand dollars. Gramma hadn't paid the taxes in a couple of years, and with all the penalties and interest the amount continues to grow. The town council is now threatening to foreclose on the property."

"What? Why didn't Nikki pay the bill? I thought she was doing the managing thing?" Savannah asked right after she'd slapped a hand down on the table.

"Nikki went over the books but Gramma continued to write the checks up until the day she died," Michelle answered quietly.

"So we have to come up with fifty thousand or this place goes to the town," Quinn stated slowly, shock still resonating through his mind.

This was almost as much of a shock as his grandmother dying.

"Who has that type of money?" Raine asked almost in a whisper. "If we lose this place it'll be a disgrace. All Gramma worked for will be gone."

"That town council must be a bunch of asses!" Parker raged. "Gramma helped build this town. Our great-grandfather was even the mayor at one time," he went on, as if they all hadn't already heard the history about the Cantrells in Sweetland.

"It was almost a hundred years ago that Cyrus Cantrell was mayor. And since then the Fitzgeralds have been firmly in that seat at city hall," Preston argued.

Michelle shook her head. "And before Liza they'd all been hell-bent on stopping progress and keeping down anyone who disagreed."

"Sweetland is a democracy, Michelle. The Fitzgeralds may think they own this town because good ol' Buford was the founder. I would think the town council and the voters would be interested in preserving its history," Quinn stated.

"And didn't Nikki say that the current Fitzgerald mayor is working for the growth of the town?" Raine asked.

"First, Liza married into the family so she's not crazy. Yet. Also, Hoover and Inez King are still sitting council members. With only dollar signs in their eyes, they're still rallying support to sell chunks of Sweetland property to some big-shot developer. On the days that Hoover's sober enough to negotiate," she added.

Hoover King had been the man Quinn pulled off Nikki last night. Now that Michelle had said the name and mentioned the liquor, he remembered the man and his intoxicated antics clearly.

"So what? Now progress means we're going to lose this house? And if they sell it to a developer, it will undoubtedly become something like a huge resort or maybe a casino. Both of which will bring considerable money to the town," Preston said.

Michelle was already shaking her head. And Quinn immediately felt bad for her. She had been burdened with the task that their grandmother could not complete. But he also understood where the rest of them stood. Gramma had always told them to live life to its fullest and to be the very best people they could be. Well, unfortunately for them, that life wasn't centered on Sweetland.

"Giving us a puppy wasn't going to be enough to make us stay here. Gramma had to know that," Quinn said, his tone low and consoling so as not to upset Michelle further.

"What are you saying?" Michelle asked.

He didn't want to say, didn't quite like the sound of it

even in his head, but he didn't hold back. "I'm wondering if this isn't another one of her life lessons. Puppies wouldn't keep us here, but the threat of losing this house just might. At the very least it would bring us all together to figure out what to do next."

"She wouldn't do that," Michelle interjected, but she didn't sound like she was even convinced of that fact.

"What I've been wondering since Michelle called me about Gramma is how she really died," Preston added, resting his elbows on the table, fingers steeped to rub along his chin. "I mean, how did it happen? Who found her? Had she been sick?"

Quinn could see just where his brother's lawyerly mind was going. He didn't like it. Hell, he was beginning to hate this entire situation, but he could see Preston's line of thinking as plain as day.

"I went looking for her when she wasn't up getting ready for the day like she normally is. We used to have our first cup of coffee together right on the back porch," Sylvester said grimly. "I went to her rooms and knocked and knocked. Finally, I just opened the door and there she was, lying in her bed like she was still sleeping. Only I knew she wasn't waking up."

Michelle cleared her throat. "Sylvester called me and I came down immediately. We called the coroner right after that."

"But how had she been feeling?" Preston pushed on. "Was she okay the day before? Did you talk to her about the taxes before she died?"

Michelle shook her head. "I didn't and I don't know why," she told them. "You know how Gramma was, Pres. She never complained, never wasted time on things she couldn't change. Said God had a plan for her and for all of us."

Preston sighed. "So you thought this was somehow a

part of God's grand plan? For her to lose this house and then to die without any of us knowing why?"

Quinn didn't know what to believe at the moment. What he did know was that getting into a heated debate and turning on one another wasn't going to help.

"I agree with Preston, we need to know if there was a medical reason for Gramma's death. As for the taxes, we're going to have to come up with something. I don't know what right now and I don't know if that means we'll all have to stay here. What I do know is that Gramma loved us beyond all our faults, and she believed in us until the very end. We owe it to her to at least try to find a solution."

"Michelle, who was Gramma's doctor? I'll give him a call to see if there was anything going on we should know about."

"Why?" Michelle asked. "Can't we just let her rest in peace?"

"There are too many questions, that's why," Preston argued.

Parker shook his head. "I have to agree with Pres and Quinn. How did Gramma know to write in her will for all of us to take a puppy? From what Nikki told me earlier, those pups are only eight weeks old. Did she rewrite her will within the last eight weeks? And why was there no mention of the taxes owed on the property in the will? I guess we could ask Mr. Creed that question. Either way, I think it's worth us looking into, just so we can have some closure."

"I agree," Quinn said, even though he wasn't a huge advocate of that "closure" philosophy. It had never worked for him. "I'll find out who her doctor was and talk to him. Preston, you can talk to Mr. Creed. Raine and Parker, maybe you two can look around in her rooms to see if there are any clues there."

"I think I should be the one to clean out her rooms," Michelle insisted.

Quinn nodded. "Maybe all of the ladies can go through them."

Preston took another drink and put his now-empty glass down in front of him. "I'll ask a few questions around town. You know secrets don't last long here in Sweetland. And I'll check into the back taxes to see what we can possibly do about some of the interest and penalties."

"I'm keeping my puppy," Raine said abruptly and sternly. "Gramma wanted me to have her and I'm keeping her. And I have some money saved up. I'll give every dime I have to save this house."

"Always the Goody Two-shoes," Savannah huffed. "I swear you and Michelle run a race to see who can kiss up the fastest."

Quinn rubbed his temples because this was just how their old Sunday dinners used to progress. They all bickered over one thing or another. In fact, it reminded him of the last board meeting he'd attended. All of which was collectively working on his last nerve.

"We're all adults," he started, his voice raised slightly. "We will make the decision that is best for us. That's all anyone can be expected to do. Right, Michelle?"

It was so obvious she didn't agree. Her brows had furrowed, her lips clasping tight, but she took a deep breath and released it. The smile she gave was shaky, and it skipped Savannah entirely. But when she spoke, her voice was calm and clear.

"You're absolutely right, Quinn. As Gramma used to say, we all make our own beds and at some point we'll have to lie in them . . . no matter what. So why don't we say grace and have some dinner."

The agreement was silent as everybody at the table could most likely recall Gramma saying just that. Mary Janet Cantrell was full of sayings, some she made up as she went and others handed down to her by her mother or father. Still, Quinn thought after the grace when the buttered biscuits, steaming cream of crab soup, and Michelle's crispy fried chicken were placed on the table, there were always one or two that would hit their mark.

Quinn was afraid that along with her delicious food, Michelle had just served up the winning one.

Chapter 6

The next day Quinn was awake a lot earlier than was his norm. His residency hours at the hospital had been grueling: thirty-six-hour shifts, days without seeing sunlight or anyone other than patients and other humans in white coats or uniforms. When he'd moved to Seattle, the hours had gotten a lot better. As the chief medical oncologist he was in his office five days a week, seeing patients until two, then handling administrative duties until five or six in the evening. A couple of days out of the week he worked on his research, applying for grants and tracking the success of their innovative treatments. None of which required him to be up and out of bed before four in the morning.

Sweet Dixi apparently had other ideas.

She'd been barking persistently for about fifteen minutes now. Trying his level best to do right by Gramma's will—at least for the time being—Quinn had retrieved a small carrying box from the basement and set it up in his room. The idea was to assume full responsibility for a puppy who couldn't stand him. This was before he knew that full responsibility consisted of early-morning hours.

Pushing the covers back, Quinn stepped out of the bed and headed over to the kennel.

"What's the problem, little lady?" he asked, switching on the lamp so he could see inside.

Her moist nose was right at the bars and she stared at him with almond-shaped brown eyes. Everything about this dog was brown, from the rims of her eyes to the tips of her paws. She danced around the kennel in response.

"Bathroom?" he asked, going on instinct. When there was no definitive answer—meaning one spoken in English, for which he was grateful—Quinn took the continued barking to mean he was correct.

He found his slippers then unlatched the kennel. Dixi bolted out, her little feet carrying the rest of her weight to the door in a clumsy shuffle.

"Wait a minute," he said, following behind her then leaning down to pick her up. "You can't wake up everyone in the house because you have to pee."

For a second she was still in his arms, her stomach heaving with all her barking exertions. Then she looked right at him and barked again.

"Simple dog," he mumbled and left the room.

Early mornings in Sweetland were like a page out of a storybook. At least that's how Quinn began feeling once he was outside. He groaned at the realization that even the sun was still basking in the night hours. The sky was a dusky shade of black, as if it weren't entirely sure it wanted to be totally dark, but didn't have much choice. He went out the front door because the stairs led to the foyer that pointed in that direction. Of course he could have circled back and gone through the parlor to the kitchen and out the back, but hell, he was too tired to think of that.

The screened door closed behind him—yes, Gramma still had a screened door so that she could keep the front door open in the summer months. Quinn figured they didn't do that often since summers in Sweetland were very hot, like hundred-degree-plus weather with humid-

HOMECOMING 69

ity that could choke a cow. Dixi squirmed in his arms, desperate to get down. He was reluctant even though he knew the purpose in bringing her out here was to do something he definitely did not want done in his arms or on any other part of his body, again. He took the steps two at a time, loving the sound of his shoes on the old-fashioned wood, when others who had done any sort of remodeling would have definitely used cement.

That was just one element of the charm of The Silver Spoon. The expertly landscaped yard with pristinely kept shrubs that wrapped completely around the house was another. The portion of the property that faced the street was surrounded by a three-foot-high black iron gate with spiking posts. In the front yard there was a huge maple tree that looked like a silhouette in the night. Speaking of which, Quinn cursed. He hurried back into the house, heading to the kitchen to search for . . . what? He found it in what he hoped was good timing. In seconds he was back outside with a bag in hand, for Dixi's bathroom purposes.

Of course by now he couldn't see the puppy and was forced to call her name at a whisper he hoped she at least could hear. He was out of the front yard and heading down the sidewalk when he saw Dixi next to a lamppost. Grumbling and deciding the first thing he would do in the light of day would be to go and buy her a leash, Quinn headed toward her. It was then that he saw another shadow, a human one.

The Silver Spoon sat on a chunk of land at the end of a dead-end street. There was a turnaround that would take unknowing cars into a swift circle and bring them back onto the street to get out. In the center of the turnaround was a flower garden that boasted some of the brightest and prettiest flowers Quinn had ever seen. Houses lined both sides of the street all the way down. Sycamore stretched the length of Sweetland, dropping off at Old Towne Square and picking up again on the other side of the pier. Michelle lived in a house almost two blocks down on the right-hand side.

The shadowy figure was skulking around the house two doors down from The Silver Spoon, on the left-hand side. Quinn kept his eyes on the guy—he figured it was a guy based on his tall stature and squared shoulders. Another one of Gramma's sayings was that if you were out past two AM, which was the time all good and decent bars closed, you were up to no good. Now, Quinn had an excuse: His dog apparently had an overactive bladder. But this other guy, he wasn't so sure.

When Dixi seemed to be finished, Quinn picked her up again. Of course she made noise; he should have known she would. Those were the two things this dog seemed to do very well—pee and bark. The shadow didn't make a move to run or act as if he'd even heard her, which was so not a good sign. Quinn walked across the street, not bothering to look both ways because nobody in Sweetland would be driving around at this time.

Now the guy had come all the way to the front of the house. He stood there looking up at the window. Quinn was able to walk right up behind him without the guy even hearing him or turning around.

"Excuse me, sir," Quinn said, tapping him on the back.

Now the man did turn, and when he did it was with clenched fists raised and ready to swing. Quinn lifted his hands as if to show he was not a threat. "It's okay, buddy. I'm just trying to help. Are you lost?" he asked.

The man was wearing pajama pants and a T-shirt. On his feet were worn leather slippers; his hair was ruffled like he'd just rolled out of bed.

"I'm going home. Going back to bed. I just got turned around," he said, lowering his fists. He kept one hand raised and used it to scratch his head. "Went to pee and now my bedroom's gone."

With a yipping Dixi tucked under one arm, Quinn

reached for the guy's elbow. "Okay, well, why don't we just go inside my house for a minute and see what's going on."

He was immediately thinking Alzheimer's, a disease that chewed away at the brain and a person's memory with ferocity. While working his residency at the Johns Hopkins Hospital in Baltimore, Quinn had seen his share of Alzheimer's patients during his geriatric rotation. It wasn't pleasant. Then again there wasn't a whole lot of the medical practice that was, a fact that had been gnawing at him for some time now.

"I don't live at your house," the man told him.

"I know," Quinn said, still leading the man toward the end of the block where The Silver Spoon stood majestically, arms open wide for all who were willing to come in.

This morning it was going to a guest without reservations, but one who needed refuge as badly as anyone else. Probably more so.

"Your dog's pretty worked up," the man said as they made it across the street and stepped up onto the sidewalk.

"Yeah, she's a little hyper."

The man surprised Quinn by laughing. It was a hearty laugh, one that sounded like it was released often and enjoyed by many. One that made Quinn think of his father.

"Those kinds are like that all the time. Had a sister with one of those . . . ah . . . they're called . . . um, I know the name."

Quinn nodded as they headed up the walkway. "Yeah, that's what I've heard about Labs, especially when they're still puppies."

The man wouldn't like Quinn blatantly correcting him, or giving him the answer he already figured he knew. Alzheimer's patients tended to be a little on the moody side as well. Anyone dealing with them had to possess a phenomenal amount of patience and compassion. Quinn prided himself on both, especially after working with patients who had been given the ultimate death sentence. He'd had no other choice.

"Yeah, my cousin had one of those. Pretty little pup, then they grow up and they're knocking over everything you own."

He kept on chuckling and walking as if he were now 100 percent sure of where Quinn was taking him. They took the steps and headed inside to a house still quiet with sleep. Quinn helped the man take a seat on the couch and turned on one of the standing lamps in the corner.

"Would you like some tea or coffee?" he asked. The man looked to be contemplating his answer.

"I think I like tea," he replied finally.

Quinn left Dixi in the living room. It seemed like the right thing to do, and surprisingly as soon as he put the dog down she plopped right onto her butt in front of the man, looking up at him expectantly. He leaned forward to pat her head, and she barked happily. Silly dog, loved attention.

If she had to choose a favorite time of day Nikki would say dawn every time. It wasn't the gorgeous sunrises that lit up the Bay like a beacon, because some days were cloudy. And it wasn't the sound of chirping birds already up and about for the day, because birds flew south for the winter. No, it would have to be the delicious scent of the seashore, the tinge of saltwater and fresh dew that crept through her window on summer mornings and whooshed into her door the minute she opened it in the winter. It was the quiet scenic town that she'd loved forever and the crisp air that blew in only from the Bay. It was her home.

Maybe she'd like dawn in other states, with other scenery and other scents, but she doubted it would be the same. And one of her favorite things to do at dawn was swim. Crazy yes, because she didn't swim in a pool. Still invigorating and one of the best forms of exercise she could think of living in Sweetland where there was no such thing as a fully equipped state-of-the-art gym like the ones she'd seen on television.

Fitzgerald Park was the best place to swim in Sweetland, there was no question. But she didn't have time to stop there and still make it to the B&B before the Cantrells awoke. She wanted to be there early, to start her new job as the manager on a good foot.

As she climbed out of her car, parked in its usual spot in the back driveway of the B&B, she bypassed the back kitchen door where she normally entered and trotted right down to the river. Her flip-flops flipped and flopped as she moved over the damp grass, dew tickling her hot-pink-painted toes. Energy buzzed through her system like a chain saw, and she picked up her pace. At the border of the grass she flipped the flops off and dropped her huge bag, which carried everything she needed for the duration of the day. An almost cool breeze blew when she took her shirt off. As she moved down the small hill of rocks where medium waves of water reached up to greet her, the shorts came down.

She was under the water in seconds, absolutely loving the freedom of swimming right alongside crabs, fish, and whatever else was traveling about the Miles River. Coming up for air, she pushed her hair back out of her face and rubbed her hands over her eyes. She should have worn goggles but hated how dorky they made her look. Who cared if her eyes would be bloodshot for the rest of the day? Nobody would think she'd had a long night of drinking as Ms. Marabelle had once accused her. Nobody who mattered would think that anyway.

It was still pretty quiet, though a few birds had come out to play as the sun began its blush-pink arrival.

Until she screamed.

Loud and long.

Then he smiled and her mouth closed like a trap.

"Sorry to disturb you," Quinn said, one hand in his pant pocket, the other rubbing along the line of his jaw.

"Dammit!" she cursed because she didn't know what else to do or say, for that matter.

"Water cold?" he asked, still smiling, the idiot!

"Spying is not attractive," were the words she finally came up with.

"I'm not spying. Or at least I wasn't," he had the decency to admit.

She was already walking toward the bank as he continued to talk.

"I was in the kitchen when you pulled up. When you didn't come in right away I was concerned and I came outside to make sure everything was all right."

"Everything is fine," she snapped and reached for her shorts.

"From the looks of things I'd have to agree."

That's when she remembered what she'd been swimming in. A bikini top that was two years too small and barely covered her nipples and a thong bottom that wasn't originally a thong—but after she'd mistakenly washed it with her white clothes in steaming hot water and bleach, it had taken on its own new size. She had other bathing suits, pretty ones, sexy ones. Why the hell had she put this one on this morning?

"Yes," she said through clenched teeth, hating the fact that her legs were so wet, her shorts were taking their own sweet time riding up her legs. She was shimmying into them as she continued to talk, feeling miles and miles of embarrassment mounting around her.

"I. Am. Fine. You can go back into the house," she told him, and dammit her teeth were chattering.

As if this predicament weren't already the worst she could possibly imagine, as she stepped up the hill of rocks—

an act she'd done so many times she had probably memorized every stone here—she slipped.

Quinn was right there to the rescue, wrapping one strong arm around her waist and lifting her off her feet. The arrogant bastard!

"I'm fine," she quipped when they were safely away from the rocks.

"I already agreed to that," he said his breath a warm whisper over her face.

She wanted out of his grasp so she pushed against him. But that backfired. Of course it backfired, what else did she expect? What the action did was plaster her body closer to his because he held on to her so tightly. They were face-to-face, his arms wrapped around her, and he was so hard and so hot even first thing in the morning. She wanted to squirm, needed to so the tension building between her legs would somehow be released. No such luck.

"Put me down," she said slowly, refusing to move another inch. Because if she did, dear God she might actually combust.

"Anything you want," he told her in that slow, deep, alluring voice of his. She'd heard it before, but not speaking to her. It was different now to see what might be a hungry look in his eyes. To feel . . . what the hell? Was Quinn Cantrell aroused?

Yeah, he picked that moment to let her go and to step away from her. She could no longer feel the rigid length of him against her leg. But she could look. And she did. And he was.

"I'm making tea," he told her, his brow furrowed.

Then he was gone. Just like that he'd turned and walked away from her as if he hadn't just seen her half naked—well, just about naked—and she hadn't just been in his arms and he hadn't just been hard as . . .

Shaking her head and cursing quietly, Nikki pulled on

her shirt and grabbed her bag. Her feet slipped all over her flip-flops until she finally just picked them up and tossed them in her bag.

So much for making a good impression on her new boss.

In the kitchen once again Quinn switched on a light. He planted his palms firmly on the counter and lowered his head, concentrating . . . on breathing. From the moment he'd seen the bag, the shorts, the shirt lying on the rocks his body had been rock-hard, no pun intended. Everything about him had stiffened and hungered and he knew who would be in that water before her head had even surfaced. It also appeared that she would be naked, or at least if there was any help for men in this divine universe, she would be naked.

Well, she hadn't been . . . naked that is. But she had been the sexiest female he'd seen in a very, very long time, dripping wet and filling out a very, very small bikini. He'd salivated, something Quinn didn't think he'd ever done before. And he'd wanted to touch her, something he told himself he wouldn't do. Yet he did, and he liked it. Liked it way too much.

He grit his teeth because there was a much more serious matter at hand that he should be dealing with, not trying to rid himself of a mega erection that had no doubt shown itself to the young and probably impressionable new manager of this B&B.

When he thought he finally had himself together, when thoughts of baseball had nicely replaced thoughts of breasts and buttocks, and he was just about to head toward the cabinets in an attempt to figure out where tea bags were kept, the back door opened.

"Mornin'," she said brightly and as if they hadn't just met under . . . different circumstances.

She closed the door behind her and continued to speak

to him like this was their first meeting of the day. "You're up mighty early."

Lust punched at him like a washed-out boxer hitting and missing. Only the hits landed in all the wrong spots and Quinn wanted to curse. He was more together than this, more mature than to be losing his mind over some shapely young woman. With his new train of thought the hair that she'd pulled back into a tight, still-wet ponytail was fresh and pretty and shouldn't have agitated Quinn, but it did.

"Yeah, not by choice. Do you know where the tea bags are?"

"Oh, you couldn't sleep, huh? My dad says warm milk is better for falling asleep. But I don't like milk so I usually go for hot chocolate in those little packets."

She talked as she moved around the kitchen, pulling down a mug then grabbing the silver-toned teakettle from the stove and sitting it inside the sink. When she switched on the water to fill it, Quinn got a look at her backside one more time. It was as if his gaze was automatically drawn there whenever she was around. The real kicker was, Quinn did not consider himself what Parker would call a "booty" man. Normally he tended to lean more toward breasts. Nikki had nice breasts, too. And he'd been lucky enough to see a lot more of both body parts mere minutes ago.

Inwardly, he groaned and wanted to kick himself. He couldn't think about her in this way and told himself he wouldn't any longer because it felt too much like a betrayal—like he was cheating on the one he knew damned well was no longer here. It was crazy, yes, but Quinn had thought that lately he'd been going a little crazy anyway. He had a past in Sweetland, one he wanted to leave in the past. And yet he'd been drawn back here for a present situation that he wasn't quite sure he knew how to deal with. None of which made for a positive outlook on the future.

"I wasn't having trouble sleeping," he replied tightly, his throat more than a little dry.

"Really? So why are you up before dawn wandering around outside—" She stopped, pressed her lips tightly together, then began again. "Why are you standing in the kitchen looking for tea bags? Bad dream?" This was asked with what she tried to pass off as a smile but looked a little strained as color stained her cheeks.

Why that, too, was sexy and damned irresistible, Quinn had no idea. The quick conclusion would be he was in dire need of some female attention. Work had been keeping him extremely busy. He probably should have listened to his PA—physician's assistant—Elena Matthews when she suggested he go to happy hour with them one Friday. All work and no play was obviously making Quinn a horny nutcase.

After clearing his throat and hopefully his sordid thoughts, Quinn replied, "I'm fixing a cup of tea for the man I found wandering around outside. He says he got up to pee and now he's lost his bedroom."

"Oh," she said, closing her mouth with a snap. Then she flipped the nozzle down on the teakettle and moved it to a front burner on the stove. "Who is he? Does he live around here?"

"I don't know his name, but I would presume he lives around here. Unless he's been walking for days instead of just a few minutes."

"Where'd you leave him? I hope not outside." She sounded alarmed.

Quinn shook his head, a smile touching his lips at the absurdity of her question. He'd taken an oath to care for patients—people—so why would he leave one who was apparently not well outside?

"He's in the living room being entertained by Dixi."

"Oh, Sweet Dixi, she's such a caring little thing."

"Is she really?" Quinn asked before reaching across a counter to retrieve the sugar canister. He'd seen that while he'd been looking around trying to decide where the tea bags would be.

She pushed the mug toward him as she replied, "She's a very loving dog. I was there when they were born and when Sweet Dixi finally came out, it was with her eyes open, like she was ready to take on the world."

Quinn shook his head while he scooped sugar into the man's cup, hoping he liked sweet tea. "She's certainly more than ready to take me on."

"And you're not used to that, are you, Quinn? You're used to everyone doing what you say, when you say. If they question you, or dare to go against you, they face your wrath."

"Whoa," he said, looking up to her. "Where did all that come from?"

Nikki shrugged. Her skin had a smooth appearance, like a very heavily creamed cup of coffee. It was in direct contrast with the black riot of curls on her head, yet this morning he could see that the subtle and the extreme worked together perfectly.

"Sorry," she said, turning her back to him and going to stand near the stove. "Just an observation. I tend to make them and before I know it they come spilling out of my mouth. My dad says I have a hole in my lip."

That's not exactly what Quinn would say about her lips, but he was supremely thankful—and at the same time a little regretful—that she'd turned away from him. He'd begun staring as she talked, watching as her pert nose wrinkled when she was perplexed or her small lips moved quickly as she prepared to smile. For lack of something better to do with them, Quinn put his arms behind his back and clasped his hands. He hadn't been this in tune to a female in a very long time.

"Well, that wasn't an accurate observation of me, but we'll have to discuss that another time," he told her a few seconds after a loud crash came from the living room.

Thankful she'd dodged said discussion with him, Nikki breathed a sigh of relief. He'd already left the kitchen without the tea when she said, more to herself than to the empty kitchen, "No way, no how am I making a fool of myself for you again, Mr. Cantrell."

"Why, Mr. Riley, what are you doing all the way on this side of town?" Nikki asked the moment she entered the living room with the cup of tea Quinn had left behind in his hurry to see what was going on.

The man she'd called Mr. Riley was dressed in pajama pants and slippers. When Quinn had come in he'd been on his knees trying to pick up the lamp either he or Dixi had knocked over. Neither of them made a confession as Quinn returned the lamp to the end table where it belonged. Now he sat on the couch with Sweet Dixi in his lap, one hand rubbing behind her ears. He looked a little weathered, his skin thin with prevalent liver spots.

Nikki put the cup of tea down on the same table as the lamp and stood back to look at him. Undoubtedly she was watching the dog as well; they seemed to have a special bond.

"I should have figured you'd know him," Quinn whispered to her conspiratorially since they were only a couple of feet apart.

"His wife is Margaret Riley. They have two children, Bill Junior and Katherine; neither one of them lives in Sweetland anymore. He lives over on Trailway, right around the corner from my parents," she replied in her own James-Bond-ish whisper that almost made Quinn laugh.

"And he walked all the way over here?" he questioned instead. While Sweetland wasn't a huge town, it had more than enough space for its one thousand or so inhabitants. *Across town* usually sounded a lot farther than it really was. But the walk from Sycamore to Trailway could easily take half an hour to forty-five minutes for a completely healthy eighteen- to possibly thirty-year-old. This man was certainly out of that age bracket, and Quinn wondered if he'd really been out that long.

"Been walking around Sweetland all my life," Mr. Riley said quietly, looking down at Dixi.

"But you had no idea where you were walking to?" Quinn asked, moving closer to the man.

"I was looking for my bedroom," he replied sullenly.

"Do you mind if I just check a few things out? I'm a doctor," Quinn told him by way of explanation.

What he received in response was a clear glare from Mr. Riley. Dixi, of course, looked up at him with her own sort of frown, which made Quinn feel like a colossal jerk for extending the offer.

"Doctors don't have nothing but bad news for me," he told Quinn.

It was Nikki's turn to lean over, but because Quinn was so much taller than her she had to put a hand on his shoulder, pulling him down to her level. He readily obliged and was rewarded with the warmth of her touch, the softness of her voice, and her sweet fragrance seeping upward into his nostrils so fast he was almost dizzy.

"He was diagnosed with brain cancer about a year ago. I hear he and Mrs. Riley just came back from another doctor in Annapolis who told them there's nothing that can be done."

With a sad sigh Quinn now understood exactly what was going on. He nodded to Nikki and stood upright, taking another step toward Mr. Riley. "Are you taking any medications, sir?"

"All they give me now is pills. I don't know what they're for. Peggy just tells me to put them in my mouth. I do what she says."

Quinn nodded. "Did they talk to you about side effects?" he asked.

Mr. Riley shrugged.

"But you had chemo treatments, correct?"

Again the older man shrugged, this time with a wave of his hand to punctuate the fact that he didn't want to talk about this. Quinn wasn't offended by the actions; he knew they weren't personal. A lot of his patients became surly and resentful toward the end. It was an unfortunate situation, but one he was more than used to dealing with.

"Can you call his wife?" he asked Nikki.

"Sure," she said with a quick nod.

"Mr. Riley, you can sit right here and play with Dixi as long as you like. But I don't want you to go anywhere. We'll find your bedroom together. Right now, I'm going to run upstairs and get dressed. I'll be right back. Is that okay?"

Dixi had come up on two legs; the other two were planted on Mr. Riley's chest so she could lick his face.

"This is one happy dog you got. Pretty eyes just like my cousin's dog. Can't remember the type of dog it is, but I swear they're the happiest things on four legs."

"That certainly seems true," Quinn said, watching the dog with the man.

Mr. Riley didn't want to hear a word Quinn had to say, but he'd be just as content to sit there with his cup of tea and that puppy licking all over him for the rest of the day. At least he'd made a connection, had some sort of comfort at this time. It couldn't be easy admitting to yourself you were dying and losing all your thoughts and general sensibilities in the interim. It was a cycle Quinn was all too familiar with. And as he walked up the steps to his room, he thought with fretful clarity, the familiarity of his personal connection to the disease wasn't something that happy little pup down there could make go away.

Chapter 7

He was too damned handsome. And way too bossy for her to even consider liking. But she did—like him, that is, Nikki thought with a deep sigh. She'd just hung up the phone in the parlor after talking to Margaret Riley, who had been about to call the police to report William missing. The woman had sounded frazzled and tired. They'd been dealing with Mr. Riley's cancer diagnosis for more than a year now.

She stood for a few seconds, wondering how it would feel to have someone you'd been married to for more than thirty years take sick and be told he was going to die. Of course, everyone was going to die at some point, but knowing that point was in a reachable distance was heartbreaking. Watching Mr. Riley sit in that living room without a clue as to where he was had been just as heartbreaking for her.

After the call, she went into her office to change into her work clothes. Of course her traitorous mind would pick now to think about him yet again.

She'd first noticed Quinn, *really* noticed him, when she was about nine. That would have made him seventeen and just about to graduate from high school. She remembered peering around the wall that now served as the entrance into the foyer from the living room and watching him stand in the doorway. He'd worn shorts then with dock shoes and a sleeveless T-shirt that showed off his muscled biceps. She'd been waiting for Savannah to come down-stairs because they were going to a swim party at Meg Fitzgerald's house.

Quinn stood in that doorway for the longest time just staring out to the afternoon like he was maybe waiting for someone, too. He hadn't known she was looking but Nikki remembered thinking that this was exactly the kind of man she wanted to marry—tall, handsome, strong. In her little girl's prepubescent mind he was everything.

And then he was gone and Nikki had to grow up and find another Prince Charming. Of course the next sup-posed love of her life had showed up driving a sleek silver Jaguar and had sugary-smooth lines that melted her heart and had her giving him everything he asked for, including her virginity. Needless to say that little soiree into the adult world had opened her eyes and hardened her heart.

This older Quinn was much more reserved and just a tad colder, she'd venture to say, as if his years in Seattle hadn't been kind to him. Then, strangely enough, this morning—after the swim, the embarrassment, and the now-infamous arousal—she'd seen a more compassionate side of him. The way he'd talked to Mr. Riley said he un-derstood what the man was going through and genuinely wanted to help.

"Get over it, Brockington," she told herself as she rested her forehead against the glass of the front window. "He's still so far out of your league he wouldn't hear you if you yelled through a bullhorn."

Quinn lived in a big city where there were undoubt-edly gorgeous, sophisticated women throwing themselves at him left and right.

"To hell with him, he can just run right back to the big

city with them," she stated with more force and a little more volume.

Turning, she made sure she was still alone. The sun had completed its daily arrival and now sat cheerfully in the pale blue sky. Birds chirped their morning salute loudly as the rest of the town slowly awakened. There was a knock at the door, and Nikki cleared her throat and began walking to answer it. On her way she reaffirmed that she was a good and successful woman who had worked hard for what she wanted and received it. She didn't need a man to validate or please her. She didn't need Quinn Cantrell.

When she put her hand on the knob to pull the door open and head back into the living room, she was almost sure of everything she'd just told herself. Almost.

"So you think he's losing his memory because of the chemo?" Margaret Riley asked, sitting in the living room of The Silver Spoon.

It was just after seven in the morning now and Michelle had arrived to start preparing for the breakfast crowd. When she'd seen she wasn't this morning's only early riser, she joined them in the living room.

"I do," Quinn said. He was standing near the sofa where Mr. and Mrs. Riley were sitting.

His arms were folded, one hand rubbing along the line of his jaw. The strong, imperceptible line of his jaw that held Nikki's gaze longer than it should have.

"Wow, they didn't tell us something like this could happen," Mrs. Riley said, sitting back in the chair. "They give you so much information and then it all boils down to nothing." Her voice cracked at the end, and Michelle was at her side instantly.

She rubbed her shoulders. "It's okay, Mrs. Riley. Quinn's a very good oncologist. If they told you something wrong I'm sure he can correct it."

Quinn didn't look like that was his plan. Then again,

Nikki noted how concentrated his expression looked. He'd changed into jeans and a button-up white shirt and leather loafers that looked really expensive. She hoped Dixi behaved herself this time around. Even though his attire was relaxed, Quinn's demeanor was as intense as ever.

"With a diagnosis of brain cancer there's some memory loss or cognitive dysfunction to be expected. Without his records I can't tell you specifically if it's the chemo medication or just another stage in the cancer. Who's your doctor?"

"Howard MacNamara at General Hospital in Annapolis. He's been seeing Bill since they found the tumor."

"Did he operate?" Quinn asked.

Margaret shook her head vehemently. "No. He said it was too big and in a bad spot. And because of Bill's age, high blood pressure, and heart disease, he'd never survive going under."

Quinn nodded.

"With your permission I'd like to give him a call, just to ask a couple of questions."

"Sure," Margaret said. "Go right ahead. You know your grandmother talked so much about you, about how you were healing people and all that. She said that since your girlfriend had died of cancer and then your father, too, you were determined to find some kind of cure. Well, I say God bless you, Quinn Cantrell. I don't know what would have happened had Bill kept walking around."

The moment she'd mentioned the girlfriend Nikki had a spurt of memory. Her name had been Sharane Houston; her father, Brett, owned The Cigar Shop on Birch Street. Sharane died the year Quinn graduated from high school. But for about two years before then he and Sharane had been just about glued to each other.

"Thank you, ma'am," was all Quinn said before leaving the room.

The rest of the day for Nikki proceeded without any

further incidents. After seeing the Rileys out she went into her office to work on the books. They appeared to be in the black, just as they had in all the years she'd been working here. Why the taxes hadn't been paid was still a mystery to her. And the bad part of that mystery was that there wasn't enough cash on hand to simply pay the taxes and be done with it, not without sacrificing their credit standing or leaving most of their employees unpaid. Neither of those was an option Nikki wanted to explore. So instead she tried to be as optimistic as possible. Their summer promotions quickly came to mind. They would certainly hit all the normal promotions that ran throughout the town: romantic getaways, family reunions, and crab feasts. There was a developer looking at acres of land on the other side of Yates Passage. Nikki had heard he planned to build a new resort complete with a golf course, which would definitely be competition.

For right now, however, the romantic getaways and crab feasts worked best for The Silver Spoon. Michelle had a standing agreement with Walt Newsome, a third-generation crabber who ran The Crab Pot restaurant down at the pier. For any crab feast they booked, Walt would send up his best Chesapeake blues already steamed and seasoned with his famous mix that started with good old-fashioned Old Bay Seasoning. Michelle would provide the other crab feast staples: corn on the cob, pulled barbecue pork, barbecue ribs, potato salad, coleslaw, and hot dinner rolls.

To that end, crab feasts were instant moneymakers for them. Nikki scribbled notes on her pad describing a little of what they could offer, from the scenic Chesapeake Bay views to the luxurious and quaint rooms, and ending with the renowned Chesapeake Bay–style cooking of Chef Michelle Cantrell. She worked on the brochure a little longer then pulled up the accounting software on her computer and paid some of the B&B's bills. The last thing on her to-do list was to make the supply orders Michelle had given her.

She had just finished writing a check when the phone on her desk rang.

"You busy? Please say no," Cordy began. "I really need to get out of here. My roots are screaming for help, cuticles are getting so big they're threatening to take over my entire hand."

"Hello, Cordy. I'm fine and how are you?" Nikki asked, sitting back in her chair and cradling the phone to her ear.

"I'm not fine, didn't I just say that? But it figures you are since you're closed in that big old house with those gorgeous Cantrell men."

"They're not all here right now, I think," she replied. She'd been in here for hours so she had no idea where anyone was. But Savannah was leaving in about fifteen minutes so Nikki suspected her siblings would be at the door preparing to see her off. Which, by the way, Nikki figured she should be doing as well.

"What time do you need me to babysit?" she asked. Sometimes it was easier to just cut to the chase with Cordy. The woman could go on and on and on. Nikki attributed that to the fact that she was closed up in the house with three kids for hours on end. The minute she had the ear of an adult she didn't know when to stop.

"Simone says she can fit me in at five. Can you be here by then? Please say yes," Cordy pleaded.

"Sure," she said absently, fingering her own springy curls. "Hey, while you're at the salon, can you ask Simone if I can come in early tomorrow morning?"

Nikki was not like Cordy, meaning she wasn't a girlie-girl. Her nails featured permanent cuticle overgrowth; the last time she'd had a manicure was for her senior prom. She rarely did anything with her hair beyond washing it and letting it air-dry, which was why it always had that crazy-frizz-curl look that she figured was like her signature by now. And since she was a little on the skinny and short side, her hair was normally the biggest thing on her. Or at least that's what her brothers joked.

"You want to get your hair done? Hallelujah! I'll tell her you can be there first thing in the morning."

"Ha. Ha. Very funny. Not first thing. I have to come into work first. Maybe around ten thirty so I can be back in time to help Michelle with that luncheon Mom's having."

"That luncheon that she's making me come to even though I told her I didn't have a babysitter," Cordy said sarcastically.

"So who's watching Mimi and Zyra?"

Cordy had three kids: Josiah, who was six years old and happily being bused to the elementary school in Easton; Mimi, a four-year-old girl who loved to primp and prance around as much as her mother did; and Zyra, who was only two and too young to know the difference between professionally teased hair and naturally curly—in other words, Aunt Nikki.

"Caleb's on the night shift for the rest of the week so Mom had Dad threatened him with another two weeks of it if he didn't keep them."

Nikki laughed. Of her two brothers, Caleb was the one who swore he was allergic to children. Brad wasn't allergic to them, just the women they came from—hence the reason he never stayed in a relationship long enough to produce any.

"That should be fun. Okay, I've gotta go, Savannah's leaving today and I want to say good-bye."

"Again? I knew she wouldn't stay here long. That girl has always had her head in the clouds."

"That's what they used to say about me. Savannah's head was always in beauty magazines—and rightfully so, she's made a huge name for herself."

"Yeah, but what kind of life does she have? Running from town to town, taking pictures with clothes on and clothes off, having people staring at her all the time, whispering stuff about her. It's not a happy life if you ask me."

"She's super-rich, though," Nikki said, now slouching in her chair as if that was going to make the sudden feeling of inadequacy disappear.

"Money does not buy everything, Nikki. That girl is miserable. I can see it in her eyes in every one of those pictures she takes. Problem is, she doesn't know what to look for that'll make her happy."

"I think a lot of people have that problem," Nikki replied thoughtfully.

"Really? You looking for something, little sister?"

This was not a line of questioning Nikki wanted to get started on with Cordy. "No. I was just saying. It seems to me that all the Cantrell siblings are looking for something."

Cordy agreed. "Probably the home they left so fast. Michelle's the only one with a good head on her shoulders."

"And yet she's not married with kids, either. It makes you wonder what happiness means to most people."

"Well, if you live in Sweetland it means graduating from high school, finding a good husband and a good job, and having some halfway decent kids. We're very simplistic around here."

Nikki nodded even though she knew Cordy couldn't see that motion. "Well, maybe we're too simplistic for some folks."

"Not for an entire family of folks, Nik. Their mother left right after the father died. Then one by one each child left as soon as they graduated. It was like they were all being held hostage until their eighteenth birthday."

"But they went away and became very successful individuals." Why she was defending them, Nikki had no idea. But having grown up elbow-to-elbow with Savannah, worked with Mary Janet, and grown to know Michelle, she kind of felt like they were relatives. And if Sweetland was a simplistic town, there was something else that went right along with that simplicity—loyalty.

"Success isn't always in the amount of money in your bank account. All those degrees and titles they have and they all sat right at that funeral and cried for Mary Janet the same way we did. You ask me, they should all be staying here and helping to run that B and B. She left it to them, didn't she?"

"Yeah, she did. But they asked me to be manager." Cordy lived a few blocks away from Nikki and their parents. She usually saw her a couple of times a week but last night she'd wanted to go home and get in bed. Quinn Cantrell had stirred something in her she wasn't about to share with anyone.

"What? You're managing the entire place now?" Cordy bellowed.

Another difference between Nikki and her older sister was that Cordy had a very loud and boisterous personality, which was probably why she'd been captain of the cheerleading team during her high school years. Nikki had been on the team but she'd always been on the bottom tier of the pyramid, even though she was the smallest girl on the squad.

"Michelle's managing the restaurant. I handle the B and B."

"Nik, that's still huge! Did you tell Mom and Dad? You know Mom would want to do a dinner or something."

She was already shaking her head. "That's exactly why I haven't told them yet. I don't need a celebration. It's a promotion and it was nice. That's all."

Cordy was quiet.

"That's not all. Something's going on, I can hear it in your voice. Why don't you want a celebration when you know that means Dad will put out the grill and slap barbecue on every kind of meat he can find at Godfrey's. It's your favorite, so why would you intentionally try to avoid it?"

Cordy was also very intuitive. Nosy, pushy, and intuitive.

"Just in a mood since Mrs. Cantrell passed, that's all." *And her oldest grandson saw me just about naked.* She wisely left that part out.

"Okay, I guess so. But we're going to celebrate. I'll call Mom and we'll schedule it for sometime later in the week when things get back to normal."

"Right. Normal. Look, I've gotta go. I'll be there at four."

"Great. Thanks. And Nik—" Cordy always called her Nik, which always reminded Nikki that she was the little sister. "—congratulations. You're a great success."

"Thanks, Cordy," Nikki told her before hanging up. Leave it to Cordy to end up making her feel better.

But her sister's words left her wondering if success was the only thing she'd get out of her life.

"This is not acceptable! What kind of place is this that there are no taxis or car services or anything civilized?" Savannah screamed.

"Calm down, Savannah," Quinn said, moving one of Savannah's many bags out of the way so she wouldn't trip on them. "The only taxi here is Hoover King's and I know you don't want to ride with him."

The puppy who'd been designated to Savannah followed her every step with paws that seemed too big for his small frame and ears that followed suit.

"You calm down, Quinn! I'm stuck here and I'm going to miss my plane," she said.

"Savannah, it is not the end of the world. So the service got your reservation mixed up. When did they say they would be here?"

"They have the reservation for Thursday, not Monday," she complained.

Quinn had come downstairs to see his sister off and to

make his way to the veterinarian's office. He had some questions about Dixi and wanted to know what he should be looking for in a new owner. Preston had told him again that he'd posted a listing on a website to get rid of his dog. Parker hadn't said much about his, but seemed to be bonding with the dog. Parker also seemed to be more than content to hang around Sweetland for an indefinite amount of time, despite his job in the city and the fact that his motorcycle was most likely driving the people of this quiet town insane.

Raine had already made it known that she was keeping her dog, and she didn't seem to be ready to leave Sweetland, either. She'd also been the only one to commit any money to help save the B&B.

Quinn would be the first to admit he hadn't been with his siblings like this in a very long time, but he prided himself on knowing them at least generally. Raine's and Parker's behavior seemed a little off to him.

As for Savannah, this was her norm. So much so that Michelle had already left them standing in the foyer. For all that Michelle seemed to share their grandmother's personality, she had no tolerance for Savannah at all.

"Did they have any vehicles that could pick you up today?" he asked, still trying to console her. Quinn didn't really know if he blamed her or not.

"No. Everything is booked."

"Then why don't you see about moving your flight to Thursday? Do you have any shoots scheduled this week?" he asked because he was curious about how her job was going. Savannah wasn't much for opening up and sharing her feelings, but just like with Raine and Parker, Quinn sensed something wasn't totally right with his youngest sister.

"No, I don't. But Quinn, you don't understand," she whined. He almost winced. This was exactly the way she'd acted when she was younger. The years had obviously done nothing toward maturing her.

"I do understand, Savannah," he said, nodding. "You're acting like a child over something that's fixable. Either you try to call another car service or you move your flight. It's not that hard."

"I don't want to stay here another day," she told him.

"Why?" he asked. Savannah was normally spoiled and self-centered, but there was something else behind her urgency to leave town. Quinn didn't know how he knew that for sure, but he did.

Savannah turned away to stare out the door. They both knew there wasn't any car coming to pick her up, so this action was futile. But Quinn waited because something else he knew was that Savannah—even though she could be very self-centered—could also be very vulnerable.

Her arms were folded over the buttoned-up top to the white dress she wore. On her feet were natural-colored sandals that matched the bangles on her arms and earrings in her ears.

"Nobody likes me here," she said softly.

So softly Quinn almost didn't hear her. Eventually he stepped closer to her so he wouldn't miss another word.

"You're crazy, you know that? What do you mean nobody likes you? They don't even know you. You've been gone for ten years," he told her.

"It doesn't matter. They don't forget. None of them does. Did you see how Marabelle and Louisa looked at me at the funeral? Like they remember every wrong step I've ever taken."

"Marabelle and Louisa have likely taken some wrong steps themselves. And since when do you give a crap about what somebody's saying about you? Those two ladies have been talking about every citizen of Sweetland probably since the day they were born," he told her. Then Quinn touched her shoulder, turning her so that she faced him. "Now come on, tell me what's really bothering you."

She kept her arms folded, her bottom lip pouting, and

Quinn almost smiled. As much as she wanted to be an adult, had the body of one, and actually should be one right about now, Savannah was still just his baby sister.

And that's precisely what he should have been thinking about and not the female who chose this moment to walk into the foyer.

"Oh, sorry if I'm interrupting," Nikki said, tucking her hands into her back pockets. "I was just coming to see you off, Savannah. I was hoping I hadn't missed you."

Savannah shook her head and sighed. "No. I'm not gone yet because the idiot car service got the dates wrong and now I have to find another service to take me up to Baltimore to catch a flight."

"Really? Wow. I think Emory Newsome goes up to Baltimore once a week to deliver his fresh-picked crabmeat to the markets. I don't recall which day but you can check with him to see if he can give you a lift," Nikki offered.

"He only goes once a week?" Savannah asked, almost appalled by the thought. "How is that considered fresh?"

"Emory's getting older. Remember he used to be out in that old raggedy boat of his at the crack of dawn each morning. We could see him as we walked past the pier to the bus stop, waving as if we were going away forever."

Quinn could be wrong but he thought Savannah had actually smiled at that memory. Nikki sure did and Quinn caught himself looking at her, captured by that small smile that emanated so much.

"Now with other bigger picking houses taking over most of his old accounts, he doesn't have to go into the city so frequently. Just a few old private-owned stores that keep him in business," Nikki told her.

"Oh, that's a shame," Savannah said thoughtfully. "I guess I could give him a call. You'd think I'd be able to rent a car someplace."

"You can if you get to Easton or Annapolis," Nikki replied.

"If I could get there I could get to Baltimore," Savannah added with a sigh.

"Or you could just make the best of a bad situation," Quinn offered. "You're not in a strange place, Savannah, you grew up here. Just get on the phone and reschedule your flight and car. Then go for a walk or something to take your mind off whatever is really bothering you."

At that she shot Quinn one of her seething looks. The look had improved over the years but Quinn wasn't impressed. "You don't have all the answers, Quinn," she told him. "Just because you're older doesn't mean you're smarter. You have no idea what I've been through or how hard it was to come back here."

"But I do have an idea of what it feels like to suck it up and move on. Maybe you should give that a try," he snapped.

Quinn thought she was going to stomp her foot or punch him—hell, she was probably considering some combination of both. To her credit she didn't do either, but her fists did clench and unclench at her sides, which told Quinn he'd really hit a nerve. The thing about Savannah that a lot of people didn't understand was that the way she acted was sort of justified. She was only thirteen when their father died and their mother left town. In most cases the death of a parent is traumatic enough, but to lose both parents at one time was devastating, especially for an impressionable thirteen-year-old who had loved her father dearly and just about worshipped her mother. Savannah's petulant and surly behavior had started almost instantly upon their departure so that Gramma had a time raising her through the rest of her teenage years.

Of course she was an adult now, and you'd think she would have grown out of all her hostility and immature reactions. Still, Quinn had to give her credit: For the most part she had. Through the years when Quinn had seen her or called to check up on her Savannah appeared to indeed be a grown-up. She had a budding career and a good head on her shoulders. She'd invested a lot of her money and made sound purchases with the rest, there were no stories of her in this man's bed or another, and she was very professional. Coming back to Sweetland had definitely done something to her.

As if on cue the puppy who had been graciously licking Savannah's sandals sat back and looked up expectantly. He caught her attention and she looked down. "And you, little mongrel, are going to buy me another pair of shoes?"

When Savannah stormed out of the room Micah happily ran after her, leaving both Quinn and Nikki a little amused.

"She's going to hurt that poor dog," Nikki said, coming to stand fully in the foyer.

She moved to one of the tables that ran along the wall behind the door, straightening the huge flower arrangements that sat there. It seemed like a natural enough move, but Quinn suspected it was more of a distraction.

"Now that, I can relate to," he said with a sigh. "Sweet Dixi and I don't seem to get along at all. Makes me wonder what Gramma was thinking giving us all those dogs."

"Really? You're questioning Mrs. Cantrell's will?"

There was a hint of alarm in her voice. "Not like that," was his quick reply. He'd already pissed Savannah off. Going for another woman's irritated looks and remarks was not on Quinn's agenda. "We were all talking last night wondering why she thought it was a good idea to leave us the dogs as well as the house."

Nikki turned, resting that delectable backside against the table, and looked up at him. "I think she was trying to share a part of herself with the people she loved. All of you were so busy with your lives in other places, you rarely had time for her. Maybe she thought this way you'd have a piece of her forever."

She seemed serious about what she'd just said, as if Gramma had told her this for herself. Quinn wasn't entirely sure of that, and he found himself focusing a little more on the physical reaction his body was having to her proximity.

"Why didn't you mention the taxes that were due on the house?" he asked by way of distraction and because he wanted to know.

She looked only slightly startled that he'd asked. Then she looked professional and oddly serious.

"It wasn't my place. Michelle said she would handle it."

"But you're the manager now," he continued, not sure what reaction he was reaching for, but wanting one just the same.

"I can't afford to pay the back taxes. If I could, I would, because I know how much this place meant to Mrs. Cantrell. And the business is doing well—we don't owe anybody except for the taxes. I can't say for sure why they were never paid, but I think she was hoping you and your siblings would all pull together and save the B and B."

Quinn had thought that as well. In fact, he was almost positive that's what his grandmother had been thinking. Nikki had just confirmed his thought that the place was doing good business so there shouldn't have a been a reason Gramma didn't pay the taxes. And yet they were presumably delinquent. Quite convenient when he considered the timing of his grandmother's death along with what had to have been a quick change in her will.

"Well," he replied finally. "I don't know how well that's going to work out."

"Is it that you don't want Dixi or you don't want to save the B and B?" she asked.

The question was posed more like an accusation, and Quinn figured that reaction he was looking for was just about ready to erupt. "I didn't say that."

She shrugged. "You didn't say you did, either."

"Were you always this contrary?" he asked out of the blue. "I don't really remember you being this way. But ever since I've been here we've been at odds about one thing or another."

"I wouldn't say that exactly. Maybe you're just not used to anybody questioning you."

Maybe he wasn't used to women who looked like she did turning him on the way she was. Or maybe he was just annoyed at how much she turned him on and how guilty that ultimately made him feel. Quinn considered himself a smart man . . . apparently not smart enough to stop his feet from moving him closer to her, but still pretty damned intelligent. On a good day he knew right from wrong, up from down, and basically how to make his way in this big old cruel world. Today, right at this moment, he wasn't quite sure. There were other forces at work here, forces he didn't know if he had the strength to fight.

"Maybe there's something else going on between us that's making us edgy," he said lowering his voice. He was edgy all right, and horny as hell. Both of which were not the norm for him.

She had to crane her head upward to see him, her eyes blinking fast. Pretty brown eyes, he noticed.

It was as if she refused to look away. Her shoulders had squared and she almost seemed to rise up a little taller. "You never paid enough attention to me to know if I was contrary or not as a child."

"I'm paying attention now," he told her because it was the God's honest truth. Whatever else he'd convinced himself was true about her, the fact that he was obviously attracted to her was a given. And Quinn didn't make it a habit of walking away from a physical attraction.

She looked as if she were carefully contemplating his words, like he'd made her a business offer she had to consider. There was an unmistakable flash of heat in her eyes, then a purposeful retreat in her tone. "You should walk your dog. She's dancing around at the door like she's about to pee on the rug. And that's a three-hundred-dollar rug. As the owner of this B and B you'd want to take very good care of your property."

Her words were said with a cool seriousness that was belied only by the heated look in her eyes and the slight blush along her cheeks. And even though she walked away quickly after she'd spoken them, Quinn knew he wasn't alone in this attraction thing. The thought made his attitude toward Dixi a lot lighter—until he took two steps toward the dog and knew instinctively what she was about to do.

His curse was long and low as he made a mental note to go online and look for a replacement rug this evening.

Chapter 8

Cordy's house sat on the corner of Birch Street and was surrounded by grass and miniature bushes that she trimmed herself twice a month. "Autumn Frost" hostas lined both sides of the walkway, draping over onto the sidewalk since Cordy's house received every bit of the sunlight Sweetland enjoyed. In the spring and summer, Nikki always felt like she was making a grand entrance when she walked to her sister's front door. The gorgeous green leafy border plants served as their version of a red carpet and she hummed as she moved along the path.

"Endless Summer" hydrangea bushes in plump lavender and creamy pale green colors hugged the width of the white shingled house. And on each side of the three steps leading to the door were azalea bushes in vibrant pink. It was a riot of color that never failed to put Nikki in a happy mood.

She'd actually been able to leave half an hour before her original plan as nobody had walked in for a room and Michelle indicated she was fine preparing for the dinner rush at the restaurant on her own. Nikki had driven her car over but wondered if she should have walked instead. Walking always helped clear her mind, and right now there were a few big issues battling for her attention. As she turned the knob and entered Cordy's house, she heard the low hum of her cell phone vibrating in her purse. Snatching the purse off her shoulder Nikki tossed it on the couch as she continued walking through the living room. She knew who was calling and would rather not talk to him again today.

"I want it!"

"Mine!"

"I had it first!"

"No!"

"Did too!"

It was an argument Nikki had heard before, in the high-pitched voices of two toddlers who were not very happy with each other. Since Zyra had just turned two in January, her vocabulary was a little limited; the one-word replies belonged to her. She'd mastered *no* fairly early in her talking life. Mimi didn't care how old her sister was, though: When she wanted something that was all that mattered.

Before Nikki could make her way back to the second of the three bedrooms in the split-level house she heard adult footsteps and almost groaned. Cordy had heard the argument.

"Mariah Charise Brockington-Simmons, I know you are not bullying your sister," Cordy yelled before she entered the room.

Nikki bumped into her sister as their paths crossed in the hallway.

"Oh hey," Cordy said. "I'm about to go in here and strangle one of them."

Nikki laughed. "You lie. You could no more hurt those children than you could yourself. Barry's the disciplinarian in this house, that's why they're carrying on the way they are now."

"Who asked you? Your expertise is in the hotel business, not the child-raising business," was Cordy's quick retort.

"Well, I'm the babysitter and I'm here now. So I'll handle it," Nikki told her, inching her way by to slip into the bedroom ahead of Cordy.

"Sneaky little brat," Cordy mumbled, leaning against the doorjamb to watch how Nikki planned to handle the situation.

For Nikki, dealing with children wasn't so hard, another feather in her personality cap. However, dealing with Mimi and Zyra was totally different. They weren't your ordinary girls and could easily serve as an effective form of birth control.

"Hey girls, what's going on?" Nikki asked, lowering her voice and instantly going to sit on the edge of Mimi's bed.

The girls shared a bedroom—a princess-themed, pink, yellow, and white, froufrou room with more lace and fluff than Nikki had ever seen. They had a huge window on the wall opposite their beds—Mimi's a pink-and-white canopy and Zyra's a white framed toddler bed in the shape of a princess crown. Yellow lace curtains hung from the window, letting in spears of sunshine since their room faced the front of the house. The walls were painted the palest shade of yellow with each of the girls' names painted in glitter pink cursive letters. There was a three-foot-high dollhouse that Nikki remembered playing with when she was a little girl. Their maternal grandfather had built the dollhouse and all its furniture while their grandmother had made all the curtains and linens to match. In one corner was a dark yellow beanbag chair; in another, a white trunk full of dolls and jump ropes and any other toy imaginable for a young girl. Barry hated the time he was required to spend away from his family, and he often repaid them with material possessions that none of them complained about.

"I want that dolly," Mimi said with a pout, her little arms instantly going over her chest.

Mimi was just about three feet high with an adorably chubby frame that started with plump toes, nails painted neon orange, and ended at the most pinchable cheeks ever made. She preferred her sandy brown hair be left out to curl adoringly around her face—similar to Aunty Nikki's—but Cordy insisted on pigtails with coordinating hair accessories.

"Mine!" Zyra screamed in her tiny voice as she gripped the doll in question even tighter.

Zyra had an angelic look, her tiny body complete with a round face and heart-shaped lips. Her hair, having just started to grow, was usually highlighted by coordinating headbands, because Cordy just wouldn't have it any other way. To Nikki they were the most adorable girls in the world and she loved them more than anything. They filled a void in her she'd long since figured would never heal.

"Who does this pretty little dolly belong to?" Nikki asked, pulling Mimi closer so that her chubby little thighs were alongside Nikki's jean-clad leg.

"It's hers but Mommy says we gotta share," Mimi answered.

Zyra shook her head. "Mine!"

And she was definitely not in the mood to give up her dolly—which by the way was missing her pants and only had on one sock to match her white shirt.

"Well, if she wants to play with her dolly right now, Mimi, why don't you play with something else? I see lots of dollies in your toy box."

"I don't want those," Mimi crooned.

Of course she didn't want those; that would be too much like right.

"But you have some really nice ones over here." Nikki got off the bed and headed over to the toy box. Going to her knees, she began picking through the toys.

"Look, this one is yours. I know because I gave her to

you for your birthday. She looks like she'd like to play," Nikki said, waiting for Mimi to come and join her.

She was a stubborn child so trying to convince her of anything was a struggle. "She's missing a shoe. Maybe you can help me find it."

"I don't know where it is," Mimi said. She was still pouting, Nikki could tell by the sound of her voice even though she hadn't turned back to look at her.

She just kept moving stuff around in the toy box. "She needs her shoes if she wants to go out back and ride the swings. And she might need a sweater if it gets cool outside."

"It's hot 'cause it's almost summer," was Mimi's reply.

"Then maybe she'll need a bonnet to protect her from the sun. Oh, here's her shoe!" Nikki put the shoe on the dolly, still not looking back at Mimi.

A few seconds later she heard a rustling then felt the whisper of Mimi's breath as she leaned over her shoulder and said, "She has a green bonnet with little flowers on it. It matches her shorts and Mommy says it's good to match."

Nikki nodded. "It is and you're getting so good at it. Can you find the bonnet for me while I make sure Zyra's dolly has another sock to wear outside?"

"She's too small to ride swings." Mimi pouted, pushing past Nikki to bend her small frame into the toy box moving stuff aside as she looked for the bonnet.

"But the sliding board is just right for her. It's short so she doesn't have far to go, and when she lands she'll go right in the sandbox."

"And get sand in her Pamper. Mommy says that's gross," Mimi declared, sounding much older than her four years. "But Zyra likes it. She says it tickles."

Nikki had moved to the other bed and extended her hands to Zyra. The baby happily gave over her dolly, which led Nikki to believe that it was only Mimi whom

Zyra didn't want to have her doll. She almost smiled, re-membering treating Cordy the same way when they were young. Then Zyra crawled to the top of her bed and reached under the pillow. She smiled as she offered Nikki the dolly's other sock.

"As soon as Mimi finds her dolly's bonnet we'll be all set to go outside."

"Got it!" Mimi said, holding up a green-flowered doll bonnet.

"Great, then let's go." Nikki handed Zyra her doll and helped the baby off the bed. As she walked she extended her other hand, and as expected Mimi took it.

When they arrived at the doorway it was to confront a smugly smiling Cordy. "You're too good at that to remain childless."

"Please, babysitting yours suits me just fine," Nikki said, moving past her sister and heading toward the back door.

"That's what you think," Cordy whispered as she watched her sister walking away with her daughters.

Nikki had so much love inside her, so much compas-sion and so many smiles to give to children, to a man she loved, to a family she could come home to every night. Cordy hated to see her walking down the old-maid path. Before long she'd be sitting inside the coffee shop right beside Marabelle and Louisa talking about everybody who walked up and down Main Street. Cordy groaned at the thought.

Maybe because she'd fallen in love and had a gorgeous family, she wanted that same type of happiness for her little sister. Or maybe it was because she knew Nikki better than anyone else. She knew that Randy Davis had broken Nikki's heart a few years ago and caused her to give up on men entirely. And she knew without a doubt that Nik-ki's no-men declaration would lead her to a very solitary and unhappy life.

That's why she prayed for her little sister every night.

Prayer worked, Cordy knew this without a doubt. It was the only thing that got her over Parker Cantrell and his smooth talk and rude departure. It was what kept Barry safe while he was away fighting a war she didn't really understand. It was what brought her lovely babies safely into this world. And it was, she thought with a small smile as she stared out the back window to see Nikki, Mimi, and Zyra playing happily in the backyard, what would save her sister's life.

Quinn strolled down Main Street on his way to the vet's office. The decision to walk was kind of made for him since he hadn't rented a car to come to Sweetland from the airport, either. He'd simply reserved a sedan service to bring him into town and really hadn't thought he'd need to get around, or be available to take his sister to the airport, for that matter. He'd come here to attend a funeral. A limousine provided by the Brinks Funeral Home in Easton had taken the family from the house to the church and back again. His plan to get back to the airport was to hire that same sedan service to pick him up. As for when he was leaving Sweetland, well, Quinn had had enough forethought to give himself the whole week here. He hadn't known what Gramma's will would say or how long it would take to make sure all her affairs were in order.

Now he was walking the same streets he had as a child with his father and then again as a teenager when it wasn't so cool to walk with one's father. He'd stopped at the municipal building, had even gone into the only completely marble building in Sweetland and walked around for a few minutes. The portraits inside—the one of Hubert Fitzgerald, the first mayor from 1900 to 1904, and the one of the very familiar-looking Liza Fitzgerald, the current mayor—were on prominent display in the hall that greeted visitors as soon as they walked through the brass entry doors. All other mayoral portraits—including the one of

Quinn's great-grandfather and Gramma's father, Jerry
Davidson, who served two terms from 1920 to 1928—
were located down an adjacent hallway.

It wasn't quite the season for tourists yet so they weren't
out in full force, asking questions and pointing fingers,
staring in awe at the people they most likely considered
country for living in this small town. In another two
weeks, the weekend of Memorial Day, the town would be
brimming with them, all looking for Sweetland's reputed
serenity and delicious cuisine. The last time he'd been
home had been at the peak of the season, the week of the
Fourth of July and Sweetland's annual Bay Day celebration. The atmosphere had been practically giddy, the pull
to stay and enjoy the festivities as alluring as that of any
controlled substance. Yet he'd still returned to Seattle. To
his pristine, expensive, coveted, empty-as-sin town house
and the job that was beginning not to need him as much
as he needed it.

Coming out of the municipal building he sat on the
benches across the street at Old Towne Square, watched
as others walked their dogs and listened as Dixi barked.
He'd thought about letting her out of the carrying case but
decided against it. Chasing her around town wasn't his
idea of a nice leisurely walk through the streets where
he'd been born. No, he wanted some quiet time to absorb
everything that he'd left behind, to see whether—if he
opened his hands wide enough—he could grasp what it
was that kept Michelle here and made Gramma such an
advocate for this small town.

Half an hour later he was walking again, taking in all
the new shops that had popped up since the last time he
was here. There was Boudoir, a shop that sold women's
clothes, soft and frilly things like negligees and other
night apparel. The front window was garbed in pink-and-
white silk, lots of lace, and other things that put men in
mind to go in and spend a bundle. Just across the street

was Wicks & Wonders, which looked like a candle shop, but with all the stars and moons dangling in its front window Quinn figured it might be geared toward a more mystical clientele. Then again, a candle shop could be the next stop after the nightie store. That would be a great marketing strategy and he wondered if the owners had teamed up on the plan.

At the top of the street was Jana's Java, which Quinn knew he'd visit at least once before he left. At home it was Starbucks that kept him coming back for more and more, until Tiffany, the morning clerk, knew his order by heart—venti caramel macchiato, extra hot, extra caramel. This shop looked strikingly different, however, with a beige awning that stretched almost to the curb providing a sort of patio for its customers, who sat in high-backed wrought-iron chairs at round high-boy tables sipping brews. Here, the marketing ploy was undoubtedly to have whatever the outside seated customers were drinking omit a scent that would eventually engulf the entire block until, Quinn decided, they just had to have a cup. He rationalized his decision to go inside was that it was on his way—the vet was just across the street on the corner of Trailway—and not that the marketing ploy had worked in any way.

The moment he walked inside he almost turned right back around.

"Well, if it isn't Quinton Cantrell," said Louisa Kirk, with her tight-fitting floral sundress and floppy summer hat to match, giving him a huge smile.

She sat at a table—a regular-height table—with her partner in crime, as Quinn and the twins used to call them, Marabelle Stanley. He remembered the two were just about inseparable. Gramma used to say she wondered how either of them had broken apart long enough to meet and marry a man of her own. And even after their marriages you never saw them with said men, just together as usual.

Well, as much as he'd like to, Quinn knew he couldn't avoid them. And should probably thank Louisa for saying his name so loudly that everyone sitting inside the coffee shop, including the two clerks working behind the counter, had looked up to meet his arrival. To them he nodded with a small smile as he moved to the table near the front window where the ladies sat.

"Hello, Mrs. Kirk, Mrs. Stanley, it's wonderful to see you both again," he said in his famous doctor-talking-to-possible-investors voice and completed it with his leave-the-females-wanting-more smile.

Reaction: Marabelle with her butter-yellow complexion blushed right to the roots of her coal-black hair, which Quinn knew instinctively had been dyed—probably because her eyebrows and the few tendrils of hair at her chin were a much lighter shade. As for Louisa, the sterner, much more astute member of this twosome, she smiled as if she knew exactly what Quinn had done.

"Nice to see you out and about, Quinton. Sweetland's missed one of its younger citizens. It's too bad such a horrible event had to bring you back," Louisa told him.

"I wouldn't say horrible, ma'am. My grandmother lived a very long and very full life. She always said we shouldn't try to live forever, just to live as best we can."

Both ladies shook their heads. They, too, could probably remember Gramma saying that.

"Yes, she did live a full life. And she opened that lovely bed-and-breakfast long before these others decided to try their hands in the hotel business. I swear, we're getting so many copycats down here now. But none of them is like The Silver Spoon," Marabelle remarked. "That's what Nikki and Michelle were saying. It looks like she hit the jackpot with that idea."

"Oh, Mary Janet always aimed high. Marrying Jacob Cantrell was certainly high. His father had just won the mayor's seat from her father since old Jerry had already used up his two terms. Snagging Jacob kept her living high up the way she liked," Louisa said with all the distaste she could muster.

Marabelle didn't look as if she shared Louisa's envy but chewed on a vanilla scone instead of saying anything contrary.

"Those two were a mix-match if ever I'd seen one. But they made it work. Had a good son out of the union, too. And he married . . ." Louisa's voice trailed off.

She was waiting for Quinn's response to her silent jab against his mother. He had no intention of obliging her.

". . . that lovely gal Patricia, and look at all the beautiful children that came from that union," Marabelle picked right up after dabbing a napkin to her mouth.

Quinn had witnessed the two hold these types of conversations before, where one would start a thought and the other would finish it. It was eerie to say the least.

"It was so good seeing all of you back together again," Marabelle said, lifting her cup to her lips for a sip.

Louisa had lifted her napkin, dabbing at lipstick-coated lips as if she were the one who'd just eaten the scone and possibly had crumbs on her face. She wore lots of makeup that made her look more strange than attractive because it was so thick and the colors were clearly outdated. For instance, he'd seen young girls wearing blue eye shadow but doubted this particular shade of turquoise existed anywhere outside of the 1960s.

"A good-looking bunch you all are," Louisa remarked when she'd put her napkin down. "I'm surprised none of you is married yet."

Any line of gossip they could find, Quinn thought.

"No. Not yet," was his only reply.

Louisa, however, had not gained her reputation by letting hot topics like this slip away so easily. "Shame. You're such a fine-looking boy. And making all that money as a big-time doctor. You can certainly afford to buy yourself a couple of houses. I'm sure there has to be a woman running around to scoop you up by now. Women love property."

Quinn couldn't be 100 percent certain because he'd been away for a while, but he was almost positive Ms. Louisa was intimating toward the B&B and its tax obligations.

"I'm doing just fine in the single neighborhood, ma'am," he replied because that was definitely a subject he would not discuss with the old busybody.

It was then that Dixi chose to let out a round of barking that sounded like she was threatening to break out of her travel box at any moment. Quinn silently thanked her for the distraction but held tight to the box.

"Whatcha got there?" Marabelle asked, looking down at the box.

"Why, is that one of Mary Janet's dogs?" Louisa moved over in her seat as if that were going to keep Dixi away from her. "She was as proud of those things as she was of her own human grandchildren."

Louisa's frown prompted Quinn to hold the box up to eye level of both ladies, pushing just a little closer to Louisa so she could get a better look whether she wanted it or not. "This is Sweet Dixi. She's on her way to the vet."

To his muted enjoyment, Louisa backed away using both hands to shoo him and the box out of her face.

"Well, go on with you. I don't like four-legged houseguests. You go see Dr. Bellini, he's right around the corner from here," she instructed him.

"And he's so good with animals," Marabelle added.

"I sure will. It was nice seeing you ladies," Quinn offered with a smile. "I'm just going to get a cup of coffee then I'll be on my way."

"You do that, son," Louisa told him with only the mildest bit of courtesy. The rest was disgust that made Quinn want to laugh out loud.

He went up to the counter and was only partially disappointed to find no caramel macchiato. And since it was a rather warm early evening, even though the sun would surely be setting in about an hour or so, he opted for an iced coffee in the flavor of the day that had been scribbled on the board out front and above the register. It was called Midnight Ice and was the perfect blend of a strong dark coffee and a light hint of vanilla. Sipping it as he walked out of the store, Quinn did smile. Not just at the way Sweet Dixi had been able to shut down Louisa and her probing questions about his personal life, but at how the exchange had felt oddly familiar and more than a bit entertaining.

Kraig Bellini was a transplant to Sweetland. He and his family had arrived, Quinn thought, sometime between his junior and senior year of high school. He only remembered that much because Kraig had an older sister, Alana, who had been in one of Quinn's classes. Alana had been a very attractive girl, which of course had roused all the boys at Easton Senior Academy. Her half-Italian, half-African-American heritage gave her a very exotic look that—coupled with a body that had clearly begun and defeated puberty very early in her teenage life—made her very popular.

So Quinn wasn't shocked when he saw the man in the white coat with tanned olive-toned skin and raven-black close-cropped hair come out to the waiting room carrying a fluffy white cat with startling blue eyes. Quinn wasn't really an animal person, but he sensed this cat might be a purebred just by the way Kraig carried it, placing it gently into the owner's arms. Then the owner placed the cat on a blanket Quinn was sure was silk before easing her body into a travel box vaguely similar to the one he used for Dixi.

Even thinking about the dog made her bark, and the woman along with her precious cat jumped in surprise. Kraig, who was most likely used to unruly pets, smiled.

"I'll be with you in just a second, little one," he said looking at Dixi, who'd pressed her tiny wet nose against the bars.

Quinn tapped the bar hoping to get her attention, but what he received was another high-pitched yelp. Why this dog didn't like him he had no clue, but he figured the sooner he figured out what he needed to do to get her adopted, the better.

"Hi, you must be Quinn Cantrell." A perky female who couldn't have been more than sixteen or seventeen came through the same back door that Kraig had and stood at the front desk.

Quinn stood. "Yes, I am. But I don't have an appointment." He wasn't totally sure how she knew who he was, but news traveled faster in Sweetland than it did on TMZ.

She waved a hand and gave him a brilliant smile—definitely a teenager, probably putting in some hours after school. "It's fine, Michelle called to say you'd probably stop by because you had some questions. Dr. Bellini was at the house for the delivery of Mrs. Cantrell's pups so he knows everything about them."

"Good," Quinn said. Because he knew absolutely nothing.

A bell that he hadn't noticed before chimed above the door as the lady with the precious cat left the office.

"Mr. Cantrell. Good to see you back in Sweetland. So sorry for your loss," Kraig said, extending a hand.

Quinn accepted the handshake. "Please, call me Quinn, Dr. Bellini."

The doctor nodded and smiled. "And you can call me Kraig, considering we did about a year in high school together."

"That's right," Quinn recalled. "You were entering ninth grade when your sister and I were graduating."

"Correct."

"How is Alana?" Quinn asked out of curiosity.

"She's living in Baltimore with her daughter. Lost her husband about a year ago in Afghanistan."

He frowned. "Really? I'm sorry to hear that."

"Yeah, me and my mom are trying to get her and Brittany to move back here but she's determined to stay in the city so Brittany won't have to leave her friends. She's trying to get her own wedding photography business off the ground."

"Wow, a single parent and entrepreneur. Well, if I remember correctly she was always ambitious. If anybody can do it, I'm sure Alana can."

"That's what we're hoping. So which one of those beautiful Labs do you have with you today?"

Quinn pointed to the travel box with a slight frown. "I inherited the one they call Sweet Dixi, but I've got to be totally honest with you. I haven't seen anything sweet about her unless it's cool for Labs to urinate on hundred-dollar shoes and three-hundred-dollar rugs."

Kraig chuckled, his goatee making him look not older but rather more distinguished. He had a decidedly magazine-model look that Quinn figured the ladies of Sweetland probably adored.

"Ah, no, that's not one of their more prominent traits. Let's get her in the back and out of that carrier so I can take a look."

Quinn carried the box back and momentarily thought how ugly the plain white contraption, with holes on its side and a latch lock door on the front, looked in comparison with the lavish gray cloth carrier the woman had used for the precious cat. Maybe they sold better ones here. It would probably go a long way toward finding Dixi a happy home, and maybe it would cheer her up a bit. Not that Quinn's goal was to make the dog happy.

"So you're keeping Dixi?" Kraig asked when they were in a smaller examining room.

It looked strangely just like one of the rooms at his

clinic, with warm beige-colored walls versus stark white that can give off the antiseptic feel people tend to hate about hospitals and doctor's offices. Those walls were decorated with portraits of real animals, not snapshots or posters sent from insurance carriers or pharmaceutical companies. Somebody had a good eye and took excellent pictures because these puppies and full-grown dogs, cats, and kittens looked like something a person—other than Quinn—wouldn't mind having as a pet.

"I inherited Dixi, and my siblings inherited Dixi's siblings," he told Kraig and received a quick questioning glance.

"It seems my grandmother wanted all of us to share in the joy of Ms. Cleo's offspring. She's given all of us a puppy to take care of ourselves or to find a loving home for."

Kraig nodded as he opened the box and took a wiggling, barking Dixi out. "Hey girl, I know you don't like being caged in. Let's get a look at you. My goodness, you're so big now. When she was born"—Kraig spoke to Quinn now—"she was the smallest of the litter and weighed less than a pound. We'll get her weighed in first, but she feels like she's been eating enough."

Quinn watched as he lifted Dixi to his face and let her lick a couple of times. "You're such a friendly girl, aren't you? Yeah, you are," he said.

No, she's not, Quinn thought with mild irritation.

As Kraig placed Dixi on the platform of a scale that looked like a tabletop version of the human ones they used at his clinic, he kept on talking to Quinn.

"One of the first signs of a happy and healthy Lab is their personality. They're one of the friendliest breeds around and usually show their affection with lots of licking and general exuberance."

Kraig continued as he sat Dixi on her feet, lifting both her ears and feeling along her head behind them. He pushed her face back and looked at her teeth, her eyelids, then let her lick him once more. When his hands moved over her belly and her back Dixi panted like she was actually laughing. Quinn caught himself smiling.

"Another thing, you can keep your Lab happy by not keeping her tied up or caged in for long periods of time. They need exercise daily, and they love to run."

"Noted," Quinn said, thinking again that he'd find a better carrier for Dixi but not keep her inside it for too long. "Ah, so where does the urinating all over the place come in?" he asked, trying to remember why he was here. "I can't very well tell a new owner she's not housebroken."

Kraig shook his head. "No, I'm pretty sure she's housebroken. Mrs. Cantrell was a stickler for that training and Maisy, my part-time receptionist out front, went over to the house and worked with the puppies herself. So it's not that."

"Maybe she has a bladder problem, a tumor possibly?"

When Kraig looked at Quinn again it was with another quizzical expression. "You work in the medical field?" he asked.

"How'd you guess?" Quinn asked lightly. "I'm an oncologist."

Kraig nodded. "I see. You're seriously watching this exam like you've made some diagnosis of your own. Only another doctor would do that."

"Sorry about that," Quinn said lightly, making a mental note to dial his own conclusions back a bit. He couldn't help it, though; his mind was usually turning in medical circles. That thought reminded him that Dr. MacNamara hadn't returned his call about William Riley yet. It probably would be a bit later when he heard from him depending on the doctor's rotation schedule at the hospital.

"Come over here and play with her," Kraig was saying. Quinn hurriedly turned his attention back to him and the dog.

He moved closer to the table and reached for Dixi. She

instantly took a step back. She wasn't barking, which Quinn thought was good, but she wasn't jumping in his arms or trying to get a lick of him like she was impatient to do with Kraig.

"Here, let's try this," Kraig said, putting Dixi down on the floor. "Call her," he instructed.

"Here, Dixi, come on girl," Quinn called, kneeling down and reaching an arm out to the dog.

Dixi—he purposely left out the "sweet"—sat back on her butt so hard and so fast you would have thought he'd given her the "sit" command instead and held a handful of doggy treats to reward her.

"Hmmm, she doesn't like you much, huh?"

Quinn laughed. "Guess you could say that."

Kraig shook his head and picked Dixi up. "Nah, she's just not sure you're hers or not. And I get the impression you're walking a tightrope on that decision, too. Labs are very friendly, even with strangers. The fact that she's shying away from you is atypical for this breed."

"I live and work in Seattle. My house is anti-kid, so most likely anti-puppy as well. I work long hours and wouldn't know what to do with a puppy when I got home after twelve hours away. Except if it were Dixi I'm sure I'd be cleaning one puddle after another."

"You are correct there." Kraig chuckled. "Labs don't do well without attention. So if you don't have a couple of hours a day to devote solely to them, I'd say start thinking about another pet. She wants your heart. Once you give it to her she'll give you everything she has, which is loyalty and devotion that compares to nothing a human could offer."

Kraig was talking like a man who'd expected loyalty and devotion from a human but didn't get it. To a certain extent Quinn figured he could relate. Then again, he'd learned that with the love of every human would eventually come the pain. He wasn't looking forward to experiencing that ever again.

"I don't know that I'm up for that type of commitment," he admitted.

Kraig nodded. "Good of you to recognize your limitations and own up to them. Most people are too selfish to do that. So, I'd suggest you start looking for a good home for her because the longer she knows she's not wanted, the harder its going to be to place her."

"Any particular type of owner I should look for?"

"Big house, maybe some kids who like to roll around nonstop. Then again, a good owner could just as easily be a single man with enough space for a Lab to grow and satisfy its inquisitive nature. The key is the attention—it's make or break for this breed. So make sure when you interview prospective owners that they know what they're getting into and that they're ready for the commitment. I'd hate for Dixi to lose another owner so early in life."

It was Quinn's turn to nod as he watched Dixi. Her rich brown color was alluring to say the least. Quinn didn't think he'd ever seen a dog who looked more like milk chocolate in his life. Admittedly, he'd never been obsessed with dogs—or any pet, for that matter—but this one looked absolutely perfect.

"What about those dog shows? Would she be good in them?" he asked offhandedly.

Kraig smiled. "I'm not a professional handler, but from a vet's perspective Dixi's definitely of show quality. I was amazed when Mrs. Cantrell said Mr. Heathrow told her to keep the entire litter. No breeder I know would sell let alone give away a brand-new litter of show-quality puppies. But sure, Dixi would love to show off, and she'd love to please her owner any way she can."

There was a knock on the door then and Maisy poked her head inside.

"Miss McCann is here with her bichon frise but she won't tell me what the problem is. She only wants to speak with you," Maisy told him with an obviously irritated look on her face.

A weary and slightly annoyed look momentarily crossed Kraig's face. Quinn hurriedly looked away. He tried to focus on Dixi, the dog who apparently wasn't getting a good vibe from him.

"I'll be right back," Kraig told Quinn.

As Kraig walked out, Maisy crossed the room and stood next to the table where Dixi was now sitting. Immediately the dog perked up, turning all her attention to Maisy, who opened her arms and played enthusiastically with her. Quinn frowned.

"Miss McCann is so transparent." Maisy began talking almost immediately. "She thinks I don't know why she won't tell me what's wrong with her dog. First of all, there's probably nothing wrong with the pampered pup. She just wants a reason to come in here twice a week and make a play at Dr. Bellini. But he doesn't even like her. She's so easy."

To this mini rant Quinn had no idea what to say. His only other option—and the smarter choice, he surmised—was to keep watching Dixi. The way she rolled over onto her back and panted as Maisy rubbed her belly. The look in her eyes said it was pure bliss.

"And I mean how lame is that to use your dog to try and get a man? Really? Is that the best she can do? Dr. Bellini needs to tell her to get lost. But he won't because she always pays in cash when she comes in. Like lots and lots of cash. I don't know where she gets it because she doesn't work and doesn't have a husband. I kind of wish she did have a husband, then maybe she wouldn't come in here so much. Then again, she might because she's just like that," Maisy finished with a tone that Quinn thought she figured he understood.

"Just like what?" Kraig asked when he came back into the room, no doubt saving Quinn from more of Maisy's mini rant.

Inwardly he sighed with relief by reaching out to mimic the way Maisy had been rubbing Dixi. To his surprise, the normally temperamental pup didn't bark when he touched her, simply lolled her head in the other direction so she could see him.

"Ah, Dixi's just like a princess. She likes to be pampered," Maisy said by way of recovery. Looking at Quinn she silently begged his compliance. He could only nod at the pretty young girl.

"I see what you're saying," he added to the cover-up, but was honestly picking up on what the doctor had said. "If I treat her like she's royalty, she'll stop peeing on my shoes."

Maisy laughed. "Right, that's exactly right."

Kraig nodded. "That would be my assessment as well," he told them. "I can also keep you posted if I hear of anyone looking for a Lab. If you're really desperate to get rid of her, and I hope this isn't the route you'd take, but I at least have to make it known. There's an animal shelter in Easton that you could leave her at. They only give them forty-five days to be adopted, however."

Then they euthanized them—Kraig didn't have to say that part. Quinn already knew and to his further surprise he felt a pang of guilt at the very suggestion.

"No," he said, shaking his head. "Gramma wanted us to find them a loving home. So that's what I'm going to do."

"Good," Kraig told him, nodding his agreement and slipping a hand into his pocket. "So I can give you a call if I hear of anyone looking. How long are you staying in Sweetland?"

"I only planned for the week. Then again, I didn't plan for Dixi."

Could he take her back to Seattle with him? Surely

there were people looking for a puppy there, too? Dixi had come to her feet and was now standing in front of him, looking up expectantly. Going only on instinct, he rubbed behind her ears and didn't pull away as her head turned quickly and her tongue found his wrist and fingers. When his watch fell off from the jostling about, Dixi quickly grabbed it between her teeth and moved to the other side of the table.

"Lab pups are also notorious for taking stuff and walking off with it. The longer you keep her, the more you'll have to focus on training her not to do that."

He nodded. "I'll give you my cell number so you can get in touch with me if you hear from someone. Even once I leave, you can call me to let me know."

"You're going to take her back with you?" Kraig asked.

"Yes. I don't have any other choice."

"My little cousin has always wanted a puppy. My aunt wanted her to wait until she was old enough. She's turning six this Sunday. I could ask her if she wants Dixi?" Maisy offered.

"That'd be great," Quinn said, looking at the way Dixi happily contented herself with his watch.

He wasn't a dog owner, had never even thought of owning a pet. And this was a show quality. She should be shown or trained or at the very least given the attention Kraig said she needed. All Quinn could offer her was a pretty house, plenty of food, and lots of things for her to either steal or pee on.

Chapter 9

It was well after eight when Quinn finally made his way back to The Silver Spoon. After leaving his number with Kraig and taking him up on his offer for drinks on Friday night, he'd walked back down Main Street in search of a pet supply store. He hadn't recalled seeing one on his journey down but figured it was a good tourist lure and sure enough he stumbled upon Sweet Nothings. At first glance the assumption would be that this was a candy store or a store that at least had sweet items to eat. No. It was a store that sold any and everything it could with the Sweetland logo and slogan on it. *Life should be so sweet* was the slogan the town council had come up with five years ago, according to Michelle, when they'd thought to reestablish the town as a tourist destination. And way in the back left-hand corner was a pet section with everything from colored collars with SWEETLAND impressed into the leash to water and food bowls with the same logo.

The first purchase Quinn made was a leash for Dixi, whom he'd taken out of her—what he now considered—ugly box and held in his arms while he made the selection.

"Do you like this one?" he'd asked her, holding up a

black collar with SWEETLAND scrawled in swirling pink letters and a matching leash to go with it.

Dixi's reply was to lick along the collar until he put it back and offered her a hot pink one with white writing. This one she actually tried to grab out of his hand.

"So that's the one, huh? Okay, I take it you like pink," he said, moving on to the bowls then finally stopping to search for a new box.

The options were four different designs in an array of colors. Kneeling on the floor with his bowls under one arm, he let Dixi get down. She ran straight to a pale pink carrier that looked much more comfortable than the one he'd been using. He was just about to try to lift all his items and his dog into his arms and head to the counter when his attention was drawn to pretty painted toenails and strappy high-heeled sandals with sparkly clips at the ankles.

"Need some help?" a feminine voice inquired.

Dixi moved to the female immediately, looking upward as if she expected to be picked up. Quinn scooped her up with one arm and stood after he'd stuffed the bowls, collar, and leash into the carrier and held that in his other hand.

"Thanks, but I think I've got it now."

She was a tall woman, the top of her head almost passing his shoulders—and Quinn was six foot one. Her eyes were a subtle green color, like ocean water he'd dare not venture into, her skin flawless with makeup that looked so delicate it could have been natural. However, when she smiled, Quinn felt a slight sense of dread.

"Quinton Cantrell in the flesh," she said. "I was wondering if I'd run into you while you were here."

It took him another second before the eyes, the sultry sound of her voice, and the long painted nails he'd spotted when she lifted a hand to rub across her chin jogged his memory.

"Diana McCann." He said her name slowly. "It's been a long time."

"Yes, it has. Like almost twenty years," Diana said, still smiling at him. "I was so sorry to hear about your grandmother."

"Thank you." Dixi was becoming fidgety in his arms and Quinn looked down at her, making a shushing sound in the hope of keeping her quiet. She'd been like a different dog once they left the vet; he was almost getting used to her not barking so loudy or moving around in the case like she was destined to break out.

"So you've got a dog. I have one, too, but she's a little under the weather. I just left her with Dr. Bellini to figure out what's wrong with her."

And you were the one who upset pretty little Maisy. Quinn looked at Diana a little differently now that he'd connected the dots so to speak.

"We just had a visit with the doctor as well. Dixi here is just fine. Now that we've gotten her everything she needs to be comfortable, she should be even better."

Diana nodded, the long ponytail that waved ridiculously from the top of her head to what he suspected was near the middle of her back bobbing slightly. If Quinn's memory served correctly, Diana had been in school with the twins so she was about three years younger than him. Her parents owned a bunch of real estate all over the world and thus made a tremendous amount of money. That, of course, meant they didn't have much time to raise their only child, whom they sent to live with her great-uncle George Bellmont on his estate beyond Yates Passage. It looked as if Diana hadn't changed much over the years.

"So all of you are back, huh? How long are you planning to stay? Surely you can't all live in that bed-and-breakfast place; it would never make any money. Even though I'm not sure how much Mrs. Cantrell was able to squeeze out of it anyway."

Nope, she hadn't changed at all. Still thought she was better than everyone in Sweetland, but didn't have enough guts to get herself away from the town she swore was more a hindrance than a benefit. And she was the second person, outside of his family, who had made a remark about the B&B's status.

"The B and B does very well," he told her quickly and with a tinge of attitude. "And no, we're not all planning to stay."

"What about your brothers? Marabelle Stanley was just complaining about a loud vehicle running up and down her block last night. She said it was Parker riding some kind of bike. I believe her since Parker was always the daredevil of the Cantrell men."

Quinn refused to bite. "Parker's here and he's doing just fine."

"You'd think he'd remember how deadly quiet this town is. Riding around on a motorcycle is not the norm."

"Parker's never been known to do the norm," he admitted with a smile because he'd always wished he had just a smidgen of Parker's recklessness.

She'd been standing right at the edge of the aisle so that Quinn couldn't pass her and had no choice but to stand there and keep talking. If there was anything Quinn didn't like, it was feeling as if he was trapped. Finally he skirted around her, saying over his shoulder, "I should get Dixi home so she can play with her new toys."

No luck. Diana followed him, her heels clicking annoyingly on the hardwood floors.

"I would think he'd grown up by now. He was such a little hell raiser. I hear he's a cop now, surely he's matured."

"Parker's a detective," Quinn told her once he was at the register putting his things up on the counter.

The older woman behind the register gave him a warm smile. "Hope you found everything you needed."

"Yes, ma'am, I did. Thanks," was his reply.

As the woman rang up the items Diana kept right on talking. "He should have more respect especially considering he's supposed to be in mourning."

"I'll be sure to tell him that," Quinn replied without looking at her again.

The woman behind the counter rolled her eyes in Diana's direction, causing Quinn to smile.

Once he'd paid for his things, Quinn left the old carrier with the store owner who promised to donate it to the shelter in Easton. He was on his way out the door when Diana yelled out to him.

"I might stop by that little bed-and-breakfast just to see what all the fuss is about. Be sure to tell Parker!"

Quinn only nodded and smiled at her. He'd tell Parker all right. He'd warn his brother that Dirty Diana was once again on the prowl.

That thought had him chuckling all the way down to the corner of Birch and Duncan, where—of all the things he'd never expected to see in Sweetland—he spotted a hot dog cart. The scent was alluring, and Quinn's stomach growled as he grew closer. So he stopped and picked up an all-beef hot dog loaded with mustard, chili, and relish. About fifteen minutes later he was happily walking down Sycamore, loving the scent of the Bay that wafted up through the town and the peaceful sight of evening settling in.

As he stepped onto the front porch of the B&B he noticed Sylvester sitting in a rocker, a table in front of him, chessboard open on top.

Later Quinn would look back on the day and think it was one of the most relaxing and awakening times of his life.

"Got a game going, Mr. Sylvester?" he said, heading for the door.

Sylvester looked up from under the brim of a well-worn Baltimore Orioles hat. "Yep. Join me?"

"No. I don't really play chess."

"I didn't, either, till I came to Sweetland. Come on, sit down, can't be going all your life."

With a shrug Quinn let Dixi out of her carrier, remembering the exercise Kraig said she needed. The front yard was big enough to tire her out.

"See you carrying that dog around like she's a baby," Sylvester said with a chuckle as Quinn pulled another rocker from the opposite end of the porch to sit on the other side of the chess table.

"Didn't know how else to transport her," he told the old man.

"She can walk right well. Look at her running after lightning bugs."

Quinn looked over his shoulder. Sure enough, Dixi was chasing the intermittent flash of light in the air above her.

"I just bought her a leash today so she'll be taking walks soon enough."

"Good. Good. Dogs need exercise. They need to have fun." Sylvester leaned forward with his elbows on his knees, his face down toward the chessboard as if he was really studying his next move.

"So I hear from the vet. Is Savannah still here?" Quinn asked, wanting to change the subject from the dog for some reason.

"Nobody's gone yet. That's a good sign," he told him.

"Guess I'll go see what they're doing for dinner."

Sylvester kept talking, stopping Quinn from leaving.

"Couple of them in the restaurant helping Michelle. That's a good thing, too. She works too hard, that one. Needs to have some time to herself to find a good man."

"She'll find one when she's ready," Quinn stated, not really wanting to talk about his sister's love life.

Sylvester's head shot up quickly, his watery brown eyes looking up at Quinn. "Can't find what she ain't looking for."

Quinn shrugged. "I don't like to mind other people's business, especially when it comes to relationships." He was subtly trying to advise the man of the same courtesy, but Quinn wasn't totally sure it was working.

"She ain't other people. She's your sister," he told Quinn adamantly, as if this were a new fact.

"I know that," Quinn spoke seriously. "But Michelle will know when she's ready to settle down."

"How can she when none of you come around to help her out here? You all got your lives but what about hers? She's been worrying over how to pay those taxes all these weeks. It's a shame to see her like that."

This was a question Quinn had asked himself since he'd returned to Sweetland and watched how integral a part of this place she was. She had her hands in the B&B and the restaurant. It was clear she'd been a tremendous help to their grandmother. Now who was going to help her?

"Michelle should have told us sooner what was going on. As a matter of fact, I'm wondering why Gramma didn't tell Michelle about this before she passed."

Sylvester hadn't responded to that, and Quinn suspected he knew more than he was telling.

"She wouldn't be able to pay it all herself, even if Janet had told her," he grumbled. "You could help her with the money."

Quinn nodded. "Because I'm a doctor, I should have the money to put up for the taxes. Is that what you mean?" Quinn had thought about this last night. He also figured his siblings were thinking along the same lines.

"You know, we could sure use some new doctors here in Sweetland. That one they got is old and grumpy as all get-out. Could use some younger eyes."

Quinn sighed. It was all a ploy. He hadn't wanted to admit this before and he definitely didn't want to let on to this fact to his siblings, but everything that had happened in the last couple of days felt strangely like a setup. He wondered if he could prove it, if it would even be worth mentioning to his siblings. Then decided it didn't matter. He wasn't staying in Sweetland to practice medicine. He wouldn't turn his back on his heritage, but it wasn't his heritage alone. Either they would all agree to save the B&B or they would all agree to let it go. The sooner a decision was made, the better, he figured. He did have a job to get back to.

His cell phone rang and Quinn almost sighed with relief as he reached into his pocket and excused himself from Sylvester's company.

"Always interruptions in life, just depends on how you deal with them," he heard Sylvester mumble as he walked down the porch steps.

"Dr. Cantrell here," he answered the phone.

"Dr. Cantrell, hello. This is Dr. MacNamara returning your call from General Hospital."

"Right, yes. How are you today, Doctor?"

"I'm good as I guess I'll get," he answered with a chuckle. "So you had a run-in with one of my patients? Is Mr. Riley all right?"

"Yes, he was wandering around in the middle of the night. Said he got up to go to the bathroom and couldn't remember where his bedroom was. I saw him while I was out walking my dog. I'm told his house is about five or six blocks from where I am," he told the doctor.

"Mmm," was the doctor's initial response. "Can't say I'm shocked. He's got a frontal lobe tumor that's too damned big to remove and every time I check it there's more growth."

"Did he have chemo even though there was no surgery?"

MacNamara sighed. "Yeah. The wife wanted to try anything. So we tried to see if it would shrink, but it didn't. Last time they were here I told them it didn't look good."

"I was thinking that the chemo had caused his cognitive dysfunction, but if he's that far gone, then this is just the next stage." And it was the saddest stage of all. From this point on William Riley would only get worse. "Is he doing anything for pain?"

"He didn't want it. Wife insisted I write the prescription anyway and she'd have it filled. But I doubt if he'll take them. Says if it's his time, its his time."

Quinn nodded, looking off down the small slope in the backyard. He'd been walking around the house looking for Dixi as he was talking. His steps had slowed as the doctor confirmed Mr. Riley's dismal chances of surviving.

"He's a proud man, doesn't want a whole lot of fussing, especially by his wife. I've known them for a couple of years now."

"So did the tumor just turn up one day?" Part of Quinn's work at the clinic was researching the precursors to all types of cancers, knowing that any attempt to head this disease off before it even started was their best shot at a cure. He'd been working these last five years with massive grants from private companies and philanthropists willing to help. But money was dwindling in this recession, even though more and more patients were dying from cancer.

"We're personal friends, met them through my third wife. I'm a bit hardheaded when it comes to love." Dr. MacNamara chuckled. "He was healthy as far as I could see those first two years. Then one day last winter my wife was talking to Margaret and she told her how Bill had some kind of virus and had been throwing up all weekend. By the end of the week he was still sick. He saw the local doc, who still said it was a virus. But when my wife heard about it she didn't like the sound of it, you know she's a surgical nurse and all. So I told them to come up so I could take a look. Found the tumor two days later."

Doesn't life just suck sometimes? was what Quinn was thinking. One day you're rolling along just fine, going to high school during the week, on dates on the weekends. You could be sitting on the bank of the river at Fitzgerald Park, kissing as though your lives depended on every touch, then making plans to go to college and get married and buy a house and have kids and . . .

They weren't talking about Sharane, were they?

"So the question now is, how we can keep him safe?" *Until the end,* Quinn finished in his mind. "It's dangerous for him to be walking out of the house and Mrs. Riley not having any idea he's gone."

"You're right. I'll have my wife give Margaret a call. Talk to her a bit about hiring a live-in nurse who'll keep a better eye on him."

"I guess he wouldn't consider hospice."

"Not in a million years," MacNamara said with another chuckle. "He's a stubborn old goat, I tell you. Besides, there's no hospice in Sweetland, and Bill's definitely not leaving the town where his grandparents were born."

"I understand," Quinn said even though he didn't. It was just a town. There was life outside of this small town and he couldn't figure out why none of the people who lived here could understand that. "Well, I'm thinking about paying him another visit before I leave."

"Yeah, I was gonna ask you when you were going back to your big fancy clinic in Seattle. I looked you up," he told Quinn, laughing again.

Quinn had never met the man in person but he was willing to bet his face was never without a smile.

"Yes, I work at Mark Vincent in Seattle. We've made some terrific strides in early detection but we've still got a way to go," he told him. "I'm scheduled to leave at the end of the week."

"I see. Well I'll let you know if I come up with any solutions while you're here. And I'd appreciate it if you'd give me a call on Bill's condition when you see him again."

"I certainly will. Thanks for calling, Dr. MacNamara."

"Howard," he said, "and you're welcome. Thank you for looking out for my patient."

"No problem, Howard. Call me Quinn."

"All right, Quinn. I'll be talking to you soon."

"Have a good evening."

When Quinn hung up Dixi appeared, running and barking as if she hadn't seen him in ages. His first inclination was to scoop her up and take her inside for some dinner and winding down. But a light breeze blew—not a cool one, but not as stifling as the air had been earlier. It was quiet out here, and if he inhaled really deeply, let the scent of the Bay unleash the true memories inside him, he would close his eyes and see Sharane. He'd hear her voice, her laughter, see her smile, then see her as she lay in that pearl-white casket.

So he didn't do any of that. Instead he called out to Dixi and ran with her when she met up with him. When they were around the front of the house again he fell to his knees, ruffling his hands in her deep brown coat. Lifting her, Quinn let her lick his face and he laughed, laughed as hard as he had in years.

And the memory stayed gone. For the time being.

"Guess who I just saw?" Cordy came into the house grinning madly, hair stiff with holding spray and eyes still a little red from where her eyebrows were arched.

"Who?" Nikki asked. It was around nine thirty and all three kids had been bathed and fed and now lay in their bedrooms faking like they were already asleep when Nikki knew perfectly well they weren't.

"Quinn Cantrell and let me tell you he is one fine-ass doctor! I'd go see him for a headache if I had one." Cordy had put her purse on the sofa table and now plopped onto the couch next to Nikki, who had been watching some crazy reality show.

"Mary Cordelia Brockington, are you looking at another man while still married to my brother-in-law? And a very good brother-in-law I might add," she asked jokingly.

"Girl, please. There's nothing wrong with my eyes. Besides, Barry's probably staring at so many nudie magazines his eyes are about to go crossed," she told Nikki with a wave of her hand. "But really, Quinn is too fine to ignore. He was at Sweet Nothings. I saw him through the window and had to backtrack to see who the handsome stranger was. Once inside I saw him and knew instantly who he was. Tall, broad shoulders, hypnotic brown eyes, skin the color of freshly churned butter, and that five o'clock shadow that on some men just looks dirty. Well, on Quinn it looks downright sinful. Whew, girl, I had to fan myself right there in the store."

Nikki couldn't help it, Cordy was being so dramatic she had no choice but to laugh. "He was all that, huh?"

"Yes he was. You should have seen him," she said then paused. "Oh, wait, you did see him. And you didn't tell me how good he looked."

Nikki shrugged trying not to let all this talk about Quinn move her into that place she used to be with him. That was the past and she was an adult now. Hopeless crushes were for kids.

"He looks like he always looked."

"You lie and you know it. That man looks like he walked off a Hollywood movie screen. Did you see his muscles—and that deep slow drawl of his . . . my, my, my."

"Okay, so would you like your cold shower now or after you've had some dinner? Dad ordered some of Michelle's fried chicken and mashed potatoes. Your kids eat like they're starving but I managed to save you some."

"Oh thanks. You're right, they eat like I never feed them." Cordy laughed. "But back to Quinn. So he's working in Seattle? I think I heard Marabelle, the gossip queen, say that at the funeral."

"Yes. He's chief medical oncologist at Mark Vincent Cancer Center in Seattle." And didn't she sound like an employment recruiter trying to sell him for a position? *Okay, Nikki, calm down. She's just asking about him in general.*

"Well, look at you. What other specifics do you know about him?"

See, she could always count on Cordy to see beyond her words.

"I know he's going back to Seattle at the end of the week just like the rest of the Cantrells. So what did he buy in Sweet Nothings? Some T-shirts to take back home with him? Maybe he needs one for his girlfriend?" Yes, just like that Nikki had done it again. She wanted to bite off her own tongue, especially when she saw Cordy's eyes widen.

"Well," Cordy said, still smiling and nodding just like she did when she'd found their hidden Christmas toys. "Let's see, he had one of the puppies with him so he was getting doggy stuff. Then Diana McCann walked right up to him and I swear that woman is so brazen, she probably should have gone ahead and pinched his butt for as long as she stood there gawking at it."

At her side, the side that Cordy could not see, Nikki's fist clenched. She'd always hated Diana McCann and her snotty attitude.

"Then they were chatting like Diana had been surprised to see him. She'd cornered him like he was a prize deer and she was aiming to shoot and stuff him to go on her wall. Come to think of it, he's not bad to wake up staring at and go to sleep admiring. What do you think?"

"I think Diana McCann's an annoying witch, the same thing I've thought about her for years now," Nikki said, knowing full well that wasn't what her sister was referring to.

"Oh no you don't. You know what I mean."

Nikki sighed. There was no winning with her. "I think Quinn Cantrell is very handsome. And so are Preston and Parker. All the Cantrell men are drop-dead gorgeous. But we already knew that. Every female with eyes and an ounce of sense in Sweetland knows that."

"Okay, I just wanted to make sure I didn't have to rush you over to Doc Stallings to get you checked out."

"Please, Doc Stallings doesn't half know the time of day anymore. It's a good thing Dr. Lorens comes in twice a week to take women's appointments or we'd all be driving over to Easton for checkups."

"You're right about that." Cordy laughed.

"So he's really not staying, huh?"

Nikki shook her head. "No. I don't think so. They all have lives somewhere else. I don't know that it was fair to think they'd come back here just because Mrs. Cantrell died."

"I guess you're right. But we sure can enjoy looking at him now, right?"

Nikki couldn't resist. In fact she was sure she would burst if she didn't agree just this one time. "You've got that right. And Quinn sure is good looking. If I had one wish . . ." She trailed off, knowing she'd gone too far. But before she could backtrack and come up with an ulterior meaning or excuse for her words Cordy had her by the arm, dragging her to the front door. She pulled up, then swung Nikki so she was all but falling outside.

"There's the evening star," she told her.

Nikki folded her arms over her chest. "So what, there goes Mr. Hulligan trying to water his grass with the old hose from his garage because he can't see where the gar-

den hose is. What's your point?" She knew full well what
Cordy's point was.

"Make a wish," Cordy told her with a sugary-sweet
smile.

"We're not kids anymore, Cordy. I'm not wishing on a
star and believing it'll come true."

"Come on, it'll come true. Just do it. Two years ago
Mimi wished on the evening star for a baby sister."

"And four hours ago she was about to sling said baby
sister out the window over a dolly. No, thank you."

"You're just afraid," Cordy taunted.

"I'm not afraid of anything," was Nikki's reply, to
which she had to stomp her foot and growl a fake noise of
despair. Only Cordy could have her standing outside arguing like they were still kids. "I'm not doing it, Cordy.
It's foolish. It'll never happen. Ever."

"The star's so bright tonight. Don't think I've ever seen
an evening star so bright." Cordy stared up to the sky.
"That has to be a good sign, right?"

"He's probably got a girlfriend. I mean, who wouldn't
want to be his girlfriend?" Nikki asked instead.

Cordy ignored her. "And just think, all you have to do
is say the magic words and your dreams could come
true."

"Or a gigantic hole could open up right here on your
lawn and swallow me up."

Cordy took a step toward Nikki, planted her hands on
her hips, and said, "I dare you to make that wish."

Oh dammit, did she have to dare her? Nikki let her
head fall back, her eyes closed, and sighed a heavy sigh.
Some things would never change, not in Sweetland anyway.

Taking a deep breath she looked upon the evening star,
felt a warm breeze tickle her skin, then said the words
under her breath: "I wish Quinn Cantrell would kiss me."

She'd thought about wishing he would become her

man, or at the very least act like he was interested in a serious relationship with her. But she decided that was going too far, putting way more pressure on that tiny old star than was necessary. One kiss would be enough. It would last her another twenty years and she would be content. Really, she would.

Chapter 10

"Hmmm, I can't make up my mind," Quinn said the moment he saw Nikki standing at the front desk, slightly hunched over and reading something in that big book that sat right beside the phone.

It was just after eleven and he'd finished the conference call he'd had with his PA. It was customary on Monday mornings for Quinn and Elena to go through his schedule and the status of all the patients on it. But because his Monday had started out hectic with finding Mr. Riley, then his afternoon had been punctuated by Savannah's meltdown and running behind Dixi to make sure she didn't destroy any other antiques in the house, Quinn hadn't found a moment to call her. Luckily, there was another doctor covering his workload for the week and Elena sounded like everything was under control. "Running smoothly without you," was actually what she'd said. Quinn's reaction to that statement wasn't his normal calm, either; a part of him had wanted to reply, *Maybe you'd like to run smoothly without me for much longer . . . like possibly forever?*

But he'd remained quiet, just as he had for the past few months.

He'd taken Dixi out for her morning walk, which seemed to please her immensely. It hadn't tired her out, however, so he'd just left her in the basement with her siblings. The noise and energy level had been on high as he'd taken the stairs and thankfully closed the door behind him.

With no real plans for the rest of the day, he'd thought about sitting down with Nikki to talk more about the B&B and its daily operating expenses. With his mind always on business, Quinn wanted to check out the financial viability of the B&B before he left. He refused to leave Michelle and quite possibly Raine with a sinking ship.

And he'd wanted to see Nikki again. It seemed he'd gotten his wish.

"Excuse me?" she asked, turning around to see it was him, then turning her attention back to the book.

"At first I thought the curls were a little out of control," he said and was rewarded by a blistering gaze tossed over her shoulder. "But then they were seriously sexy. Now I'm trying to figure out—"

"You're trying to figure out if you really don't like my hairstyle?" she asked with a definite bite to her tone.

Quinn cleared his throat. "Let me start over," he said. "Good morning, Nikki."

Closing the book—with what could probably be called a very attitudinal slam—she turned all the way around to face him. One elegantly arched eyebrow raised, hands coming around to clasp in front of her.

"Good morning, Quinn. Is there something I can do for you?"

Still the chilly tone. He'd botched this up pretty good. But he wasn't out of the running just yet. Quinn could never be called the ladies' man his brothers were reputed to be, but he'd never had any problems getting women, either. The problem had always been that he'd never found a woman he really wanted. Not since Sharane. But he wasn't going there this morning.

This morning was about the very attractive manager of the B&B and the fact that he'd probably, albeit inadvertently, insulted her.

"You look really good this morning," he said, extending his hand to her. "And I apologize if I didn't say that the way I should have in the beginning. Truce?"

She tilted her head. This new style of her hair was straight and bouncy so that when she tilted, it moved with her in a sultry kind of motion that had his blood swirling to his groin. Her lips moved. She tried not to smile. He took a step closer because nothing but nothing was going to keep him away from her now.

He was so wrong.

She lifted her arm abruptly, clasping her hand in his and effectively putting distance between them. At the same time the phone on the front desk rang and Michelle came through the side entrance with trays in hand. Nikki pulled her hand away from his quickly and Quinn turned as if it were all a natural response.

"Good morning, sis. Need some help?" he asked.

If Michelle questioned anything she didn't say, but thrust the trays at him as if they were some type of disease. "Take these into the dining room. Tanya's already in there—she'll know where they go. Then there's a lot more stuff in my car if you could go out and just bring it in. Thanks!"

She was gone the second Quinn took the trays from her. He was just about to turn around when he felt hands on his arms, warm hands that made him want to drop said trays and touch in response.

"Go this way. My mother's here today with the women's auxiliary. They had some meeting down at the library and now they're on their way up here for a luncheon." Nikki was talking as she walked beside him, then crossed in front of him toward the side door to the dining room.

The floor plan of the house was basically a circle

around the living room and what had been converted into the front desk/check-in. All the rooms had previously been connected by French doors. Only the doors leading from the living room to the parlor and from the parlor to the dining room remained. Open entryways had replaced them between the living room and front desk area, as well as the living room and foyer. The entrance to the kitchen was the only one with swinging doors; their dark oak matched the intricately designed original crown molding that mimicked the house's Victorian style. Some of the hardwood floors, dainty wallpapers, rich brocade window coverings, ornate lounges, and antiques had been here when the Cantrells were growing up, but most had been brought in over the years to create a very intriguing and homey feel that Quinn admired.

"Put them here," Tanya directed, her normally jovial tone a little on the stressed side.

"She just called. There are five more added to her final count," Nikki told her.

"Argghh! Really? I hope we have enough food," Tanya said, moving quickly to fit the trays into silver stands with domed covers.

"You know Michelle cooks for an army every time," Nikki added with a chuckle. "And you, sir, need to get outside and get the rest of those things before Michelle goes off. She gets a little crazy when we have catered gatherings."

Quinn took that to mean he was now a part of the staff for this gathering and did as he was told. For the next four and a half hours, to be exact.

It was almost six o'clock that evening when Quinn had a chance to sit down with a glass of lemonade. Of course the momentary solitude was interrupted—but by a prettier face he couldn't have found.

"Look who's ready for some attention," Nikki said

coming out the front door with a very happy Dixi trailing behind her. "Michelle said you left this downstairs with her this morning."

She handed him the leash he'd purchased for Dixi. "It's nice that you bought her some personal things. Does that mean you're thinking about keeping her?"

Throughout the day's business her hair had taken on its usual flyaway look, without the curls. The long strands lay seductively at her shoulders, daring him to touch just once. Quinn refrained only by grasping the coolness of the glass of lemonade in his one hand and using the other to grip the leash she'd just handed him.

"I figure she needs these things no matter who her owner is."

"I guess you're right. Well, I'm going to leave for the evening. Since there are no guests, we don't need anyone on duty."

"When are the next guests due to come in?" he asked, taking a final drink from his glass before standing. Dixi was at his feet the moment he did, going between his legs and coming out the other side as if she were chasing something.

"Not until Friday. Check-in is at three so we'll open the windows to refresh the rooms in the morning. It's a few sorority sisters meeting up after twenty years."

Quinn nodded. "How many?"

"Six. Two to a room."

"So you'll need us to bail out before then?" he asked.

Nikki spun around. She'd been standing at the edge of the porch near one of the wooden railings, looking down the street. The sun was just setting; slashes of its rays fell over her profile, giving her skin a golden glow.

"Oh, I didn't think about that. Hmmm, do you know when Savannah's leaving?"

Quinn shrugged. "She hasn't said anything about it." When he noticed the shocked look on Nikki's face, he smiled. "I know, we can't believe it, either. Parker's strangely content here for the moment so he hasn't mentioned leaving. I think Preston has a trial coming up he needs to get back and prepare for. It doesn't matter. If need be, we'll go to one of the hotels."

"Nonsense, this is your home," she told him.

"It's a business and we all need to respect that. We'll have it worked out by Friday," he told her finally.

For a few moments Quinn couldn't keep his eyes off her and she seemed held in his gaze. Then Dixi's noise permeated their silence.

"I think she needs a walk. Mrs. Cantrell used to take them out in the morning and the evening. She had Sonny Windsor from down the street help her so all of them could go out at the same time."

"Yeah, I took her out yesterday evening and again this morning. So I guess it's time for her next round." He bent down using one hand to try to hold Dixi still while he clamped the leash onto the collar. "Ready to go?" he asked. She wagged her tail so exuberantly it looked like it might fall off. Quinn heard himself laugh as well as Nikki's cute chuckle.

"She's so sweet," Nikki said as he stood up.

"You drive in today?"

She shook her head even though she was still looking at Dixi. "No. I walked. Gas prices are too high to drive all over Sweetland every day when I can just as easily walk. If it's not raining and I'm not running late I usually walk back and forth. Now, if I go out later I might take my car, or if I have somewhere to go after work, but . . . I'm talking too much," she said with a smile. "I'll see you in the morning, Quinn."

"Nonsense, Dixi and I will walk you home."

"I'm not a kid, I can walk home by myself. I've been doing it for years now."

"Believe me, Nikki. I know you're not a kid."

A kid would never elicit this type of heat from Quinn. All he had to do was stand near her, smelling the soft floral scent of her perfume—strangely absent the lemony fragrance he'd begun to associate with her. And no kid had a butt and breasts like hers, that was a definite.

As if she could sense his arousal, or probably because she could see him staring, she folded her arms over her chest and shrugged. "Well, if you say so."

"I say so. Come on, Dixi," he said to the puppy as he and Nikki started down the steps.

Twenty minutes into the walk Nikki couldn't stand it a moment longer: She just had to know.

"So how does your girlfriend feel about you staying away from her for a whole week?" she asked.

Quinn had just come back to stand beside her after Dixi had seen a pretty black-and-gold butterfly and decided she'd chase it as far as her leash would take her. The rest of the way Quinn had run behind her until finally he'd pulled on the leash, calling her name in a stern voice that stopped her cold. She was definitely going to need some formal training; otherwise Quinn was going to strangle her.

When he came back they resumed walking and were now actually crossing onto Elm Road.

"You asked about my girlfriend?" he asked while wrapping the leash around his wrist so that Dixi had a much smaller berth.

"Yes. If I were in a serious relationship I would have wanted to be with my partner in his time of grief. But maybe she couldn't get off work. I guess that's a good enough excuse. Maybe she doesn't like small towns any more than you do. I was just wondering." *And babbling. God can you please get a grip?* Nikki all but screamed the last comment to herself.

Quinn just smiled. "I don't have a girlfriend, Nikki."

"Oh," she said quickly. "Why not? I mean, if you don't mind my asking?"

He shook his head. "No. I don't mind. Especially since you already told me about that hole in your lip."

She decided to laugh off the embarrassing fact that she'd actually told him that, and that he'd actually remembered.

"I don't really have time for a relationship," was his reply.

"Oh, right. You said you work long hours. Are you treating patients all that time?"

"I treat patients most of the morning into early afternoon. Then I do administrative stuff."

"And what do you do at night? When you go home I mean? Do you just sit alone and watch television? Because reality TV really sucks."

Quinn nodded his agreement. "From the tidbits I've seen, I have to agree. But no, I usually do research at night."

"Hmmm, what do you do for fun?"

They stopped at the corner of Pinetree for the red light. "I don't really think I have fun." He gave a wry chuckle but she sensed his response was dead serious.

However, she liked his laugh, even though it sounded a little stilted. Probably because he didn't do it often enough. Another thing Nikki liked was walking with Quinn. He was so much taller than her that he made her feel safe—as if nothing could touch her when he was around. And each time his arm brushed against hers warm spikes trickled up and down, filtering through her body until by now she was practically humming with desire.

What she really liked was that he walked on the curb side of the sidewalk. When they'd come down the steps she'd been on the curb side and he'd immediately walked around her, saying men should walk on the outside. She'd never heard that before and thought it was the most chivalrous thing she'd ever experienced.

"I hear fun is overrated," he was saying.

She shook her head. "That's because you're not having enough of it. And neither is the person who told you that."

"What do you know about fun? You live in Sweetland."

"Out of respect for Mrs. Cantrell I'm not going to take that as an insult," she told him. Then a car passed and she waved at Natalie Hall, the daytime desk clerk at The Silver Spoon and her younger brother Beau as they turned the corner.

"We should go crabbing one day and then to Vito's Pizzeria for dinner. They have the best Hawaiian pizza ever, and they also have pinball machines like they used to have way back when. Now, that'll be fun," she suggested.

They were about two houses down from hers and Dixi was going about her business as they walked. The sky had grown darker but the heat hadn't lifted much. The sound of crickets and other night bugs indicated that summer would definitely start soon.

"Are you asking me out on a date, Nikki?" he said.

She had to look up at him because something told her he was staring at her. It was a feeling she had whenever his gaze was on hers, a molten heat moving like lava over her skin. Now, that sounded really intense, but that's what it felt like to hold Quinn Cantrell's gaze. She wasn't complaining at all.

"I guess I am," she replied boldly. In all her life Nikki had looked ahead. There wasn't a time when she felt like she couldn't do something or shouldn't do something. She'd grown up with two very protective brothers and a loving but often bossy older sister, so at an early age she'd learned to stand her ground. Inside, those butterflies that had reappeared days ago, when she'd watched Quinn walk into the B&B for the first time in years, were scrambling through her like a hoard of bees were chasing them. On the outside, though, she held her head up and looked directly into his eyes. "So are you accepting?"

The smile that spread across his lips was slow, but it was knock-down, drag-out, faint, get up, and faint again gorgeous.

"Sure."

"Great!" she said, unable to hide the relief that washed over her. "How about Saturday morning? We have to get up early to get a good spot on the river because you know everybody'll be out there trying to make a catch. You do remember how to crab, don't you?" When he didn't answer right away she stopped where she stood. "Or were you planning to be back in Seattle by Saturday?"

He turned back to look at her but still didn't reply. He appeared to be contemplating what she'd asked. As if this were really the first time he was considering when he would leave Sweetland.

"I'll be here Saturday morning," he said. "What time shall I pick you up?"

"You don't have a car here," she told him as she resumed her steps.

"Oh, right. Habit. I'm sorry, I usually like to pick up my dates."

"Well, since I asked you on a date—and I do have a car—I'll pick you up around five. Bring Dixi with you, she'll love being out on the water."

"She'll wake everyone else out on the water, including the crabs," he added with a chuckle.

"Here we are," Nikki said, not without a hint of sadness.

"You still live here, huh?" He looked up at the pale blue siding of the house she'd called home. "I remember coming past here to pick up Parker more times than I could count."

"Yeah, he and Cordy were pretty hot there for a minute," she recalled. "I live back here now, over the garage. It's small but it gives me some privacy."

They walked to the back of the house and stopped right at the stairwell that led up to Nikki's front door.

"So thanks for walking me home," she said. Then she bent down to grab Dixi up in her arms. "And thank you, too, Sweet Dixi. You were such a sweet girl to walk with me."

When she stood again it was to be captured in Quinn's gaze once more.

"Why don't you have a boyfriend, Nikki Brockington?" he asked at the same time he lifted a hand to touch her hair.

It was a barely-there touch, one that if done by anybody else on this planet she would have brushed off. But this was Quinn and they were standing in the dark backyard of her house all alone.

"Had one," she said nonchalantly. "He didn't want to stick around."

"Idiot," he quipped, taking another step toward her.

"I guess you could call him that," she replied, the calm in her voice wavering. She hoped Quinn couldn't tell.

"What if I don't stick around?" he asked when his face was only inches from hers.

It was the kiss! The evening-star wish was coming true and he was talking too much. Why had he asked her that? Why, when he should have known it would be like splashing ice-cold water on her very hot body. She took a deep breath, her eyes closing of their own volition.

"I didn't ask you to," was her reply. She hadn't asked. Told herself she wouldn't be fool enough to make that mistake.

"Good," was his barest whisper a second before his lips touched hers.

Nikki was up on her tiptoes, arms wrapping around his neck in a greedy stance that she wasn't taking back no matter how desperate it probably made her look.

The first touch was tentative, just a whisper of his lips over hers. Her breath hitched and she struggled not to pull him down and take more, take faster.

The second touch was like chocolate chip ice cream, sweet and so damned good. His lips brushed over hers once more, more persuasively this time, the tip of his tongue running slowly over her lips.

Then the fireworks came and Nikki struggled to keep all the feelings and sensations inside from bursting free. His kiss matched his personality, seriously intent on making whoever was on the receiving end drown in everything about him.

His arms wrapped around her waist and pulled her closer to him, up off her tiptoes to the point she felt like wrapping her legs around his waist. But she didn't. In fact, Nikki was the one to pull back, to let her lips leave his, her arms loosen around his neck. He still held her close but her feet were at least now back on solid ground. The world was still spinning, though, so she was in no real hurry to let her arms fall completely from him.

"Good night, Nikki," he said.

Still, he did not pull away. Instead he looked down at her as if, again, he were trying to figure something out. She wanted to help him along and say *but you just kissed the hell out of me,* but she refrained.

She removed her arms from him and backed away. "Good night, Quinn."

She'd just been kissed by her childhood crush. Her wish on the evening star had come true. This required some serious thought time.

At their feet Sweet Dixi barked and ran in circles, almost gathering them both up in the extension of her leash.

"Dixi also says good night."

With a smile Nikki backed away toward her steps. When she was at the top of the stairs about to open the door, she looked back to see that Quinn was still standing there watching her. Seeing her inside, she supposed. Retrieving her key from her pocket, she let herself inside, falling back against the door as she closed it wondering what the hell had just happened.

Ever heard of the long walk home? Quinn hadn't, either, until tonight. Just last night he'd walked these streets and his mind had been on things like finding a home for Dixi, making sure the B&B thrived so his grandmother's legacy might live on, what he was going to say to the board of directors at the clinic's next meeting. Nothing that concerned kissing Nikki Brockington.

Because that thought hadn't crossed his mind. Sure, he'd noted how attractive she was. He'd even lain in bed Sunday night thinking about her mouthwatering bottom and breasts. But those were only thoughts. He'd never intended to act on them. At least not until he'd seen her this morning.

He could blame it on the new, more mature-looking hairdo. Or the way her knee-length black skirt had hugged her backside. What would be a little more accurate would be the snug way her tight, compact body had fit against him as he'd moved closer to her at the front desk before Michelle had interrupted. Still, the plan to actually kiss her was never conceived, not consciously anyway. He'd offered to walk her home because it was the right thing to do. Sure, this was Sweetland, small town on Maryland's Eastern Shore. It was still America, and the last time Quinn had looked at the nightly news he'd seen more muggings, sexual assaults, and shootings than he cared to. So, yes, he walked her home. Dixi also needed to be walked.

Kissing was nowhere in the equation.

Until now.

Now it was all he could think about. The B&B crossed his mind only because it was currently within his line of sight as he walked down Sycamore, and Dixi because he could hear her intermittent barking. Other than that Quinn's mind was completely filled with Nikki.

She was feisty and independent and settled in her own life. All things that normally attracted him to a female. On the other hand, she was also kind and loyal and young, he couldn't forget that one. She wasn't tall and leggy as he preferred, and she didn't carry a cell phone in one hand at all times and drive a car as fancy as his Mercedes SL550. She was a hometown girl, complete with the fresh-looking face—no makeup required—and an apartment over her parents' garage. And she wasn't what he'd come back to Sweetland for.

There were certain things that Quinn knew without a doubt—he'd loved his father and missed him every day of his life and he had also loved Sharane and missed her just about every minute of every day. So why had he kissed Nikki? To be truthful he'd kissed other women since Sharane's death; this coming June would mark the twenty-first anniversary of that day. He'd gone on dates, had sex with other women, and moved on with his life as well as he could. But she was always there, in the back of his mind, as the only woman he'd ever loved.

Tonight, when he'd been kissing Nikki, that memory was gone. It was almost like the time he'd spent playing in the front yard with Dixi, when the suffocating pain of losing Sharane had been taken away.

Only this time he felt extremely guilty.

Life was crazy that way, he figured as he walked up the front steps and into the house. Coming back to Sweetland was a definite mistake. That was all there was to it.

Chapter 11

Nikki's cell never rang before eight in the morning, unless it was an emergency. She'd just seen both her parents before she'd set out for work, so she assumed all was well there. Reaching into her purse, she pulled out the phone and grit her teeth. Dr. Epilson would not like that since he'd spent three of her teen years working on her slight overbite and fitting her with the best braces her parents' money could buy.

On about the third ring Nikki decided to just answer it. Obviously the ignore technique wasn't working.

"Hello?" she said in a none-too-chipper voice.

"Hi," was the tentative reply. "I've been trying to call you for days. How are you?"

"I'm fine." *Or at least I was until you started calling me again.*

With a long sigh she reached for a mildly pleasant tone. "What do you want, Randall?"

Because he'd never really wanted her. No matter that she'd given him her heart, a huge chunk of her personal self she could never get back, and about a thousand dollars to get his car fixed that she should have known she'd never see again.

"I wanted to see how you were doing. It's been a while since I've talked to you. I miss you."

And just as soon as she closed her eyes and opened them again she'd see a stampede of cows coming down Elm Road. Nothing Randall ever said could be believed. What she did know, however, was that the man had to be the most creative person on the planet to be able to spout the stories he did in record time.

"I'm doing fine and yes it's been a while."

"Why are you being so cold to me?" he asked, as if he didn't already know.

But Nikki didn't feel like rehashing the past. She'd forgiven him, only because that's what the good Lord said she should do. But no way had she forgotten the longest six months of her life when she'd had to suffer through the pain and disgrace he'd caused.

"Niceties are over, Randall. We did this dance two years ago. I'm on to a new step now."

He sighed. "You'd think you would be mature enough to have a civil conversation. I need your help with something important. You're the only one I can turn to."

He did not just call her immature! She wanted to scream. No, she wanted to hurl the phone across the street and keep on walking. But that would cost her another hundred or so bucks to buy a new one, and Randall Davis was most definitely not worth another dime of her hard-earned money. Nor was he worth another minute of her time.

"You're right, I'm just not mature enough to have a conversation with you. So take that as a hint and don't call me again," she told him with finality and disconnected the call.

With a groan she stuck the phone back into her purse knowing instinctively that would not be the last she heard from him. For whatever reason he wanted back into her life and for a million other reasons she refused to let that happen.

She'd met him during the Bay Day festivities two years ago. He was handsome. No, actually he ripped that word to shreds he looked so good. And he'd smelled good, she still remembered that. His cologne was soft but masculine, and it had rippled through her senses like a fresh summer's breeze. He'd driven right down Main Street in the hottest car Sweetland had ever seen, a silver Jaguar that was shined and in pristine condition. And when he'd parked right across the street from Jana's Java and stepped out of that car even Marabelle and Louisa were speechless.

Sweet Nothings hadn't opened yet but Nikki had volunteered to help with the decorating committee, so she'd been in front of that empty building hanging yellow bows on the doorknob. Sweetland's official colors were yellow, black, and white—representing the black-eyed Susan, the official flower for the state of Maryland. Every door on Main Street wore those bright yellow bows, while tiny white lights that reminded her of Christmas had been strung from one lamppost to another and black and yellow ribbons were intertwined up and down the poles.

Out of the corner of her eye she'd seen the car and heard the whispers as he'd stepped out. She'd glanced at him in his white linen pants and shirt and dock shoes. Then she'd looked away because men weren't her strong point—even back then. There had to have been about thirty people in the immediate area that day. The sun was shining but it wasn't hot, which was a miracle. A cool breeze had been blowing as they'd worked. Mr. Creed had just passed them on the way to the building he'd used for his law firm for more than twenty years, saying it looked like a storm was coming. Sure enough, the next gusts of wind brought the scent of his cologne. The sunlight faded a bit, as if a cloud had covered its brightness, and the next time Nikki had looked up from her task, it had been to stare right into his stormy gray eyes. The fact that Mr. Creed had just predicted a storm and Randall's

eye color correlated should have been warning enough.
But she'd been enamored from that moment on. And by
Sunday, the night of the Sweet Soiree that closed out Bay
Day celebrations, Nikki had arrived at Gentry's Hall on
the arm of Randall Davis, junior stockbroker from New
York City.

Or, as she liked to refer to him now, the con artist from
who-gave-a-crap where.

Everything Randall had ever told her was a lie. He
didn't own his own condo, nor did he work on Wall Street.
And that car wasn't even his. He was a hired driver who
had apparently driven his boss down here for a golfing
weekend. At the time there was only one golf course; it
had just been built on the other side of Yates Passage where
there were still acres and acres of unused land. A large
hotel chain had been first to put up a resort and golf
course in the prime locale.

So the entire week that Randy had been wining and
dining her, he'd also been running back and forth to the
resort to drive his boss wherever he needed to be. But
Nikki hadn't found all this out until months later. After
she'd slept with him and fallen in love with the person
he'd pretended to be.

Her mother had been the first to say there was something about Randall she didn't like. Mrs. Cantrell had
followed up by calling him unsavory. Nikki had foolishly
disregarded both of the well-meant warnings.

The end had come soon enough when Nikki had saved
up her paychecks to make the plane fare to New York and
back. It was a good thing she'd gotten the round-trip ticket.
What she'd found when she arrived at the address Randall had given her was a man who introduced himself as
Aaron Witherspoon and who also told her that the only
Randall Davis he knew was his driver. He'd shown her
the car Randall drove for him, after he'd absently introduced her to the half-naked woman that she would later

learn was not his wife. It had all happened so fast; then
Mr. Witherspoon—who had to be in his early fifties with
a spray of salt-and-pepper hair still thick on top his
head—had driven her to the place where Randall really
lived, a shabby little three-story where he rented a room.
And as if that weren't bad enough, Randall hadn't even
had the foresight to be in his crappy little apartment
alone. Oh no, it seems both he and his boss had called the
same escort service, as his tramp looked vaguely similar
to the one she'd just left at Mr. Witherspoon's place. Nikki
had quickly changed her return flight and flew home.
Where she knew just about every man her age, where he
lived, what he drove, and whom he was married to, if ap-
plicable. She took refuge in the place she knew and loved,
vowing to never become a fool for love again. Ever!

So no, she was not taking Randall's calls, because
nothing he had to say meant a damned thing to her. Besides, she didn't have time to try to decipher truth from
make believe where he was concerned.

As she walked into the back door of The Silver Spoon
she was greeted by Michelle, already in the kitchen with
her apron on and her long black hair pulled back into a bun.

"Mornin'." Michelle barely looked up from the three
long pans lined up on the table in front of her.

"Good morning," Nikki said, hanging up her purse.
"Ah, Wednesday is southern seaside fried chicken and
buttermilk biscuits day."

"You know it. And we already have four reservations
for lunch."

"What's that I smell cooking?" Nikki moved to the
refrigerator to pull out a bottle of water. It was already
humid outside, which was never a good sign. If at eight in
the morning the sun was already sitting high in the sky,
its rays beaming down onto the sidewalk and humidity
threading its fingers around the base of your neck, it was
going to be a hell of a scorcher!

"Marcus Godfrey stopped by this morning on his way back from Easton where he'd been to the butcher. He had some slab ribs that looked too good to pass up. I put the invoice over there." Michelle nodded toward the countertop where the sink was.

"I'll make barbecued ribs the lunch special and leave the fried chicken, biscuits, and baked beans as the regular daily deal."

"Good idea. Plenty of iced tea today. It's hot already."

Michelle was dipping chicken legs that looked big enough to be human into the buttermilk that filled one long pan. Then she dipped the leg into her special seasonsings, of which Nikki only knew some of the ingredients, one being a healthy dousing of Old Bay. Afterward, she'd go back to double-dip in the buttermilk, then on to the bleached flour breading before they landed on a cookie sheet that had been pre-sprayed with olive oil. Once those pieces hit that piping-hot canola oil the kitchen would fill with the savory scent that drew customers from as far as the pier to have some of Michelle's Famous Seaside Fried Chicken—that's the way it was listed on the menu and the way they all asked for it.

Michelle nodded as she worked. "Already have it brewing in the window."

Nikki looked over to the bay window over the sink. Four large barrel-like containers were filled with water and tea bags that by lunchtime would be brewed just right. Once Michelle added the sugar and lemon it would be perfect and ready for the orders that would no doubt come in to quench their customers' throats.

"Is Natalie here?"

"She is. Said she received a call about a group booking for Fourth of July weekend."

"Okay, good."

"You okay?" Michelle asked her.

"Huh?" Nikki said, trying to remember what Michelle

had said. Walking into this kitchen and watching the daily routine left her feeling a bit nostalgic, missing Mrs. Cantrell especially. Maybe because so much was going through her mind at the moment, and usually she'd run right and talk to Mrs. Cantrell about whatever was bothering her. She wasn't as rigid as her mother; nor was she as opinionated as Cordy. There was a delicate balance about Mrs. Cantrell, and Nikki could always count on her to be totally honest and compassionate at the same time.

"I asked if you were okay," Michelle repeated. "You look a little out of it this morning."

"I'm fine," was her quick reply. "Just wondering how we're going to do sales-wise this summer. You know, if we'll make enough over our daily expenses to put a dent in those taxes."

"We're going to do fine, just like every summer. We might even do a little better if I can hire that sous chef who just graduated a few weeks ago. Remember, I told you about her—she lives in Hagerstown but I think I could persuade her to relocate, for the right price I mean."

"I don't know about another salary just yet, Michelle," Nikki said absently, picking up the invoice from the counter.

"Look, Nikki, we've come too far—and by 'we' I mean my grandmother and my family—we've come too far for this to fall apart now. I just have to believe that everything will work out. And maybe I'll just hire the sous chef part-time. I'll talk to her and see what she's looking for. If it's out of our range then I'll pull back."

"Okay," Nikki agreed without much fight because she wasn't really paying that much attention.

Until he came in.

"Good morning," Quinn said the moment he pushed through the swinging door.

"Mornin', Quinn. What has you up so early?" Michelle asked.

"Sweet Dixi does not like to wait for her walk. She actually thinks she's supposed to beat the sun up in the morning," he said with a chuckle.

A very relaxed chuckle that was vastly different from the way he'd sounded last night. And just like that Nikki's melancholy over missing Mrs. Cantrell melted away to be upstaged by the slight uneasiness of last night's kiss.

"Looks like you're frying chicken today," he said, walking over to stand beside Michelle.

"I am."

"And I'll bet there'll be biscuits and baked beans."

"You know me too well." Michelle smiled up at him.

He shook his head. "I know what Gramma used to cook for us all the time. You're just like her, you know."

To that Michelle's grin broadened, pride almost radiating from her. "There are worse people I could be like."

"Can I help?" he asked.

"You know I'm not turning that down. Look over there in those bottom cabinets and grab the navy beans. You can get those rinsed and into the pot and then you can work on the sauce to go on them."

With a nod Quinn headed over to the cabinets—and that's when he saw her.

"Good morning, Nikki," he said, his gaze lingering on hers a moment longer than was probably necessary.

But Nikki didn't look away. To be perfectly honest, she couldn't. Being captured in Quinn's gaze was like a drug, and she was quickly becoming addicted. Besides, it made her feel so warm, so womanly, so wanted. She just couldn't focus on what was bad about it.

"Good morning, Quinn," she finally replied.

From across the room Michelle said, "He can't get to the cans with you standing in front of the cabinets, Nikki."

It was said in a smart way. In fact, Nikki could swear she heard laughter in Michelle's voice. A sound Nikki didn't even want to expound on.

"Sorry," she said, moving out of his way. Then she grabbed her water and her invoice and figured it was time for her to get to work. "I'll just get out of here before Michelle decides to put me to work, too."

Michelle agreed. "You know the deal. If you hang around my kitchen you've got to do some work."

Nikki nodded and smiled. "Uh-huh, that's why I'm leaving your kitchen so I can get to my own work. I'll run some numbers and let you know this afternoon what we might be able to do about your sous chef."

"Thanks, Nikki. You won't regret it," Michelle told her.

"I'm sure *we* won't regret it. See ya later," she said.

"Bye, Nikki," Quinn said with a smile that made her body temperature skyrocket too high, too fast.

"Bye, Quinn," she replied, slipping through the door before she could get caught up in his hypnotic gaze once more.

"Okay, what was all that?" Michelle asked the moment Nikki was out of earshot. "And don't even waste your time telling me nothing. My eyesight is excellent and as you've already stated I'm a lot like Gramma, which means I'm as intuitive as a psychic. So spill it."

She'd been waving hands that were caked with seasonings and flour as she talked concocting what looked like a mini summer snowstorm and Quinn had almost laughed at her. *Almost.* Except he knew not to play with Michelle when she was cooking. As a general rule she was mostly serious when she was in the kitchen.

"Nikki's a very nice woman. She's going to be excellent as a manager here."

"And?" Michelle prodded, once again dipping and coating her chicken.

"And, she's grown up to be quite an attractive female." He figured he'd go ahead and admit that much.

"Uh-huh," Michelle said as she nodded. "One that you've got your sights set on."

"Come on, Michelle. Who even says that anymore? Besides, you know I don't set my sights on females. I just noticed that she's attractive, that's all." At least that's what he'd tried to convince himself for the better part of last night.

"She's looking at you like a woman in love," Michelle continued, not as if she hadn't heard what he'd said, but as if she didn't believe one word of it.

"She's not in love with me and I'm not in love with her. Hell, I've only been here a few days."

"And you're not planning on staying," she said in a quieter voice and was so sure she was right she didn't even wait for his response. "So let me give you a bit of advice. Stay away from her. If there's no future for the two of you then don't start anything in the present. Got it?"

Quinn wasn't surprised to learn that Michelle was still bossy and that, in this case, she was also right. Quinn had begun opening the beans, dumping them in the strainer and running water over them, then pouring the strained beans into a pot that looked big enough to fit a small child inside. Cooking baked beans was a staple in the Cantrell family, and while Quinn didn't know all the seasonings that went into the sweet sauce, he had cleaning the beans down to a science. And as he went about the task, a wave of homesickness so thick and threatening hit him so hard, he almost stopped what he was doing to leave the kitchen altogether.

He couldn't be homesick; he'd never had that feeling before. He'd also never cooked baked beans in Seattle. And did it count as homesickness if you were in the place that was making you feel bad? Hell, he didn't know. More and more each day he stayed in Sweetland, Quinn found he didn't know what to think, do, or say.

"I know how to conduct myself with women," he finally told his sister. "And Nikki's an adult, I think she can make her own decisions."

"She could if she knew what she was dealing with. But since I'm almost positive you haven't told her about Sharane, my stance is the same and it's firm. Stay away from her, Quinn. Because if you don't you're going to break her heart and I don't think Nikki could take that again."

That immediately caught his attention. "Her heart's been broken before?"

Michelle sighed and came to stand beside him at the sink. It was a double stainless-steel sink so she didn't interrupt his bean-cleaning process. She washed the flour and guck off her hands and reached for a paper towel to dry them.

"She's not very experienced with men. Had one a while back and he was a real ass. So I'm telling you that she doesn't need to go through this again. Not now."

"What did he do to her?" Quinn asked, a feeling of immediate anger rising in him. So much so that he ignored his sister's warning just as she'd ignored his earlier words.

Michelle had moved back to the island where she'd been working and pulled out a long box of plastic wrap. She wrapped the tray of seasoned and battered chicken with three sheets of plastic wrap then went to the Sub-Zero double-sided refrigerator and pushed the tray onto a rack. When she closed the door she turned back to face him.

"He was basically a lying, cheating womanizer. He came into town one day and picked himself the ripest little peach he could find and snowed her over with a bunch of lies and misrepresentations. When Nikki found out, she was devastated. End of story."

And it would have been the end of that lying, cheating womanizer's days of lying and cheating women if Quinn had been here. But he hadn't. He'd been in Seattle building his career.

"Don't tell her I told you this," Michelle warned him.

"We're not on that level. Nikki and I are just friends," he said again to convince himself that the kiss and the resulting feelings of desire that had followed were a huge mistake. "And this has nothing to do with Sharane so don't bring her up, either."

He turned his back and concentrated on the beans so he didn't see Michelle shaking her head. Didn't see the look of pure sadness that crossed her face as she spoke again.

"Everything you've done since the day she died has been about her, Quinn. You stayed away because you thought it would be easier—but it's not, is it? You're still grieving for the girl you couldn't save. Then Daddy died and you grieved for him as well because you couldn't do a damned thing about that disease ravaging him. You can't save everybody," she said quietly.

"But I have saved people," he replied without turning around. "I've saved hundreds of people."

"No, the good Lord spared their lives. He wasn't ready for them. Don't for one minute believe you have that type of power no matter how many degrees you've earned."

Quinn slammed the next can down onto the counter. With too much force he slapped the faucet so the water he'd been running to rinse the bean juice down the drain shut off instantly. The motion was so quick it tilted the bowl he'd been draining and some of the beans spilled into the sink.

"You don't know everything, Michelle. Just because you stayed under Gramma's wing doesn't mean you know what you're talking about. You have no idea what I've been through."

"Right," she said softly yet sarcastically. "I didn't lose my father. My mother didn't walk out on me. And my grandmother, my best friend, didn't just die almost a week ago. I have no idea what it feels like to lose someone you love. That's a feeling reserved for The Mighty Quinn himself. You're such a self-centered idiot!"

"And you haven't changed one bit," was his parting retort as he left the kitchen, wishing the door didn't swing. He'd wanted it to slam, to have the noise shock him out of this darkness that threatened to suffocate him.

Every time Quinn thought he had a handle on it, the darkness came back like a raging beast to whack him over the head once more.

Yesterday he'd ordered a new rug for the foyer, he'd played with Sweet Dixi, and he'd kissed a pretty girl. During each of those moments he'd thought he was getting better, moving forward instead of standing still while everything and everyone else moved on around him. Leave it to his sister to swipe away those blinders and slap him in the face with reality.

The real kicker, which Quinn acknowledged when he'd made it outside and around the side of the house, down the small incline to the bench close to the bank that dropped down to the water, was that she wasn't that far off the mark. He was still grieving the loss of Sharane and his father and he was still spitting mad that he hadn't been practicing medicine when both of them had been diagnosed with cancer. Even though they were two different types—stomach and lung—he'd since dealt with both, had made strides in new treatments and increasing longevity and quality of life. He could have helped them, could have saved them.

Unable to hold back any longer he cursed, loud, long, fluently.

"Better out than in, is what I say," Sylvester said.

Quinn startled because he hadn't even noticed the old man sitting on the bench in front of him.

"Go ahead, let it all out. I didn't curse much around Janet, but here's as good a place as any to let all that out of you."

"Sorry. I didn't mean any disrespect," Quinn muttered after taking a deep breath.

"No need for apologies. Not to me anyhow. Why don't you sit down, let some of that stress you're carrying around rest a bit."

Quinn did as the man suggested but had no intention of talking. Instead he looked out to the water, watched as the rays of sun danced along the water like cellophane. Overhead, gulls flew low, screeching loud. In the distance there were boats, three of them, crabbing most likely. Or simply fishing. Sweetland was a huge seafood town, with the majority of menus consisting of some type of seafood. Minutes passed with the two men simply sitting there in silence. A light breeze blew as Quinn concentrated on taking deep breaths and releasing them slowly. It was a relaxation technique he'd overheard one of the therapists using with a patient at the clinic.

He had never sought therapy. Never thought he needed it because grief would pass. Now he was wondering if that little assessment of his was true.

"I miss your grandmother already," Sylvester said. "Thought about going out to the cemetery just to say hello to her."

"I miss her, too," Quinn admitted. If Gramma were alive she would tell him to stop living in the past, to move on with the life he was blessed with. She'd probably warn him away from Nikki as well.

But words were a lot easier to say than to act out, especially for Quinn.

"We could go together, you and me," he offered.

Quinn turned, looked at the older man who sat with his back ramrod-straight. On the side of the bench was his cane. His pants looked worn, a dull blue khaki, and his shirt was plaid, a variety of blue shades. He wore an old baseball cap, this time no Oriole bird in sight, and his glassy eyes stared at the same water Quinn watched.

"Were you in love with her?" he asked out of the blue and was surprised when Sylvester only hesitated a moment.

"I was." He nodded and sighed.

"Did she love you?"

"There wasn't many Janet didn't love. Except maybe those chatty women at the coffee shop. Said she'd been praying for their menacing souls for so long she thought the good Lord might be tired of hearing about them."

He laughed, a low wheezing sound that concerned Quinn—but Quinn let it go. Now was not the time to doctor the man.

"You been in love before?" Sylvester asked him.

Like the man before him, Quinn did not hesitate. "Yes."

"She love you back?"

He nodded. "Yes."

"And now you're alone?"

"She died. Twenty-one years ago." Twenty-one seemingly endless years ago.

"Whew, been a long time."

"Yes, sir, it has."

"Time to let that bird fly away, don't you figure?"

Quinn was quiet, more considering than stalling. Then finally, he admitted, "I don't know how."

There weren't too many things Quinton Cantrell didn't know how to do. If there were, he eventually mastered them because that's the type of man he was. If there was a medication he hadn't heard of, he researched it until he knew all the side effects and benefits by heart. A dish he'd just discovered, he had to know exactly what it was made of and if there were any variations on the recipe. An antique he couldn't place, couldn't price, he looked in every book he owned on the subject, ran through the Internet until his eyes began to cross from staring at the screen. In the end he would have the answer.

Except to this dilemma.

"Ever tried to let it go?" Sylvester asked.

The man seemed to be full of questions today. That was okay because Quinn was looking for answers.

"No. I don't think I really did."

Sylvester nodded. "It's not easy saying good-bye. And sometimes it's said for you and you think, *Well, that's okay, it's done.* But it's really not. If you know what I mean."

Quinn sighed. It sounded strange but he admitted, "I think I do."

"Holding on can keep you holding still. And that's not good. You know what happens to a man who lies in bed all the time, never gets out to walk or see the sun?"

"He develops blood clots in his legs," Quinn said, opting for the medical synopsis. "The clots travel to his heart and he dies."

Sylvester chuckled. "You're right about that. I was gonna say life passes him by. But I guess you got a good point, too." He laughed some more. "Don't let those clots, you call 'em, break your heart to pieces, son. Grief will kill you if you let it."

"I'm healthy and I'm living, helping to save lives," he argued, but not with much heart.

"When the one you need to save is your own. Janet knew this, she knew it about all of you. Your life is missing something and she wanted to bring you all back here so you could figure out what."

"She wanted us all to come back to stay here." But Sweetland wasn't the remedy to Quinn's problem, he was sure of that.

This time Sylvester shook his head. "I don't think so. I think she was more worried you wouldn't get yourselves straightened out if you just kept working and pushing to succeed. She told me one time that all you kids needed was to come back and smell the sweet Bay air."

"You have any idea how polluted the Chesapeake Bay is now? There are dead fish washing up on some shores in Maryland because of the pollutants in the Bay. Being here is not as sweet as Gramma thought."

Sylvester only thought on those words for a few seconds before replying, "Seems to me being away ain't that sweet, either."

When Nikki left The Silver Spoon to head home for the evening she was dead tired. The day had been full of phone calls—to the printer, to possible customers, to vendors, and finally to the accountant in Easton that officially handled the books for The Silver Spoon. She'd wanted a projection about hiring more staff—an assistant for herself and one for Michelle. As the restaurant was also picking up business, Nikki figured Michelle would most likely need more permanent staff instead of just the summer workers they hired. Of course they'd still need the extra summer help, but she felt like a couple of part-time waitresses could help with the influx in catering jobs Michelle was receiving. This extra help could be obtained through the high school to keep costs down.

After the phone calls she'd had a meeting with Walt from The Crab Pot to discuss his forecast for this season's catch and their pricing changes. Michelle also liked to get all her seafood fresh from Walt as well. There were a few other crabbers and fishermen left in the town but they mainly shipped their products out now. Walt had been the only one to keep a good working relationship with The Silver Spoon. Nikki suspected the other locals, like Emory Newsome, were trying to get contracts with that big resort on the other side of Yates Passage and some of the newer places trying to come down here and open up shop. Nikki appreciated Walt's loyalty and showed him that by not looking for outside vendors herself.

When she'd finally hit her street her mind had been so full of work issues that she'd barely registered the two police cars sitting in front of the house. Until she came closer and the officers stepped out of their cars.

"Nicole Brockington?" one of them asked.

He'd gotten out of the passenger side of the first vehicle, along with another one who'd come out from the driver's side, his hand already on his gun. Two others were in the second car, getting out with looks of trepidation and almost sorrow. The day's work fled her mind as Nikki approached and answered, "Yes. Is there something I can do for you, Officers?"

She recognized two of them from the second car, Carl Farraway and Jonah Lincoln; she went to school with both of them. The first two were older, one of them probably closer to Caleb's age and the other one, the one asking the question, was older like her father, his graying hair and paunchy abdomen a dead giveaway. He was the one doing all the talking.

"You know a Randall Davis?"

Dread slithered down her spine and she nodded slowly. "I do."

"When's the last time you talked to him? Saw him?" the older officer asked as he stepped up onto the curb in front of her.

"What's this about?" she asked suddenly feeling like she should be in a small room, sitting in an uncomfortable chair, with dim lights and one angry cop.

"I'm asking the questions, ma'am," he said, his voice a little more irritated.

Carl lifted a hand. "Let's just give her a minute. Maybe we can go inside, Nikki. Let you have a seat. We've just got some questions to ask you."

"Sure. Can I do that?" she asked the mean older officer, who frowned as if he were going to say no. But Carl stepped around him and took Nikki by the arm, leading her to the front porch of her parents' house.

"It's okay. It's just a few questions," Carl said when they were at the front door.

"Am I under arrest?" she asked, the words sounding absolutely crazy to her own ears. The closest she'd ever come to breaking the law was when she was fourteen. She'd wanted to give her mother flowers for Mother's Day but had already spent her allowance—following behind Savannah—on nail polish and lip gloss when they went into Easton on a class trip. She'd snuck into Ms. Vera's backyard and picked most of her prized roses right off the bush. The cuts from all the thorns had given her away when Ms. Vera showed up on her porch to accuse her. But even then she'd only been punished for a weekend, because her father said she'd meant well.

If she were under arrest for something . . . no, Nikki didn't even want to think about that possibility.

Once inside, standing right in her mother's foyer—which smelled like daisies and freesias because Odell Brockington loved flowers and paid a visit to Drew Sidney's Blossoms at least once a week—the older officer finally introduced himself. Nikki figured it clicked that they were standing in the house of the fire chief, who was just coming down the stairs with his astute and socialite wife behind him.

"What's going on here?" Ralph Brockington asked in his gruff voice. "Carl, Jonah, is something wrong?"

They were at the bottom of the steps when the old cop started, "Good evening, Chief Brockington, I'm Officer Dorchester from the Easton Police Department."

And that's why his uniform was different, Nikki noted. And so different she wondered why she hadn't noticed it immediately. The two officers from the first car wore dark gray uniforms, while Carl and Jonah wore black. Their cars might have been a little different, too, but all she'd needed to notice about them were the flashing lights on top.

"Officer," Ralph said, shaking the hand that was extended.

Odell had come to stand right beside her daughter, placing her right hand on Nikki's shoulder. "Is there a problem, Officers?"

"We're here to ask your daughter a few questions, sir," Carl said, a tinge of nervousness in his voice.

"Nikki? Questions about what?" Ralph asked.

"About the murder of Randall Davis."

Chapter 12

"Randall's been murdered?" Nikki heard herself asking as she backed up, using the wall to catch her and stop her from falling to the floor.

"Here, let's go into the living room and have a seat," Odell Brockington said. She was a woman of small build, a genteel manner, and the fury of a fire-breathing dragon if crossed.

"That's a good idea. Officers, this way." Ralph, who was used to going out of his way to make sure his wife wasn't crossed or irritated too often, extended an arm to show the officers into the living room.

"Why don't you start by telling us what the hell is going on?" Ralph said when they were all seated.

Nikki clasped her hands together as she sat on the couch she'd seen a million times. Her mother loved to decorate and redecorate, as her father always said. So this was the new contemporary look she'd adopted, with soft-fabric furniture reupholstered because while Ralph tried his best to accommodate his wife, he wasn't about to bankrupt them so their house could look like some type of museum. Anyway, right about now Nikki was enjoying the comfort of the couch and the arm of her mother's that had circled her shoulders.

"When? Where? What happened to him?" she finally managed.

"His body was found in Easton, about two hours ago," Officer Dorchester said, looking straight at Nikki. "And before you say another word, you should know that your cell phone number was the last number he called before he was killed."

Nikki gasped.

"Looks like cause of death will be a gunshot wound to the head. Kind of looks like a professional hit," Jonah put in, only to get a warning glare from Dorchester.

"Since you were probably the last person to talk to him before he was killed, that makes you the first person we want to talk to," Dorchester finished.

Nikki was already shaking her head. "Not without my attorney." She knew how this must look, the angry ex-girlfriend kills the low-life, lying scum of an ex-boyfriend. He calls her to reconcile and she's had enough so she shoots him in the head. Yes, she had an active imagination. That and the shows that were on TV these days had her mind whirling. "I want my attorney right now," she said louder.

"Your attorney," Odell whispered in her ear. "You don't have an attorney, honey."

"Yes, I do. Call Preston Cantrell. He's staying at The Silver Spoon."

For a few seconds nobody in the room moved. Then Carl stood, reaching into his pocket for his cell phone. "I'll make that call."

Quinn was perfectly silent in the car as they drove the short distance to the Brockington house. He'd been sitting in the parlor with Preston and Parker, the three of them having drinks and sharing memories of their pasts when

Natalie had come in telling Preston there was a call for him. The fact that Natalie was still there after seven in the evening had been shock number one, but only a mild one. The moment Preston disconnected the call he'd taken right there in the parlor shock number two had taken hold.

Both Quinn and Parker had said they were going with him the moment Preston told them about Nikki. They hadn't told any of their sisters, for one reason because they didn't know where they were. Raine had announced earlier that afternoon that they were going out for dinner just as soon as Michelle could break away. And Quinn had been ducking Michelle since their morning conversation. So it was just the Cantrell men piling into Preston's SUV and heading over to see what they could do to keep Nikki out of jail.

Quinn still couldn't fathom why the words *jail* and *Nikki* would even be mentioned in the same sentence. Anybody could look at her and see she had innocence practically stamped across her forehead. Well, not anybody. If Quinn had seen that last night maybe he would have kept his hands . . . and his lips off her. At any rate, he wasn't happy about the fact that there were policemen attempting to question her about a crime as heinous as murder.

"I'm the attorney here so I'll do all the talking," Preston said when they'd gotten out of the car.

They traveled up the walkway single-file with Preston in front, turning to look over his shoulder as he spoke to them. Quinn, who was in the middle, added, "I don't know when you became her attorney, but I guess I'll go along with it."

Parker picked up the rear in his usual fashion. "Well, I'm a cop, so I can ask questions just like they are."

Preston was already shaking his head as he made it to the front door and lifted his hand to knock. He wore slacks and a button-up shirt, which he'd quickly changed into before they left. Appearance, to Preston, was everything. Quinn wore the jeans and T-shirt he'd put on earlier this morning, while Parker followed his lead in worn jeans, boots—because he'd been riding his bike earlier—and a black T-shirt. They were a formidable threesome at any rate. And the moment Odell Brockington opened the door for them, Quinn could see in her eyes that she'd acknowledged that fact.

"Well. Well. Well. All of the Cantrell boys on my doorstep. I would have never imagined." She gave each of them a smile and warm hug as they passed the threshold.

Quinn looked around more because he wanted to see Nikki than he wanted to pay attention the decor of the house. They moved through the foyer, which was longer and narrower than the one at The Silver Spoon and completely carpeted. Odell took a left at the first doorway and they were in the living room, where it appeared everyone had assembled. Nikki sat on the couch, her slight build giving her a vulnerable, almost childlike appearance. Only the moment she looked up to meet his gaze, heat soared through Quinn. Heat and an undeniable urge to protect. He went to her instantly, taking a seat to her left. She turned to him, giving him a look that asked what he was doing there. Instead of answering Quinn took her hand in his—which seemed a little weird even to him. Still, he looked up and gave Preston a nod. Both his brothers had stopped in the doorway, while Odell Brockington had gone to the right to stand with her husband. The officers stood to Quinn's left looking stern and unyielding. One in particular was giving Quinn a not-too-happy look.

"I'm Preston Cantrell, Ms. Brockington's attorney. I understand you have some questions for her in reference to a murder that occurred," he began.

"Officer Dorchester," the older officer introduced himself and took a step to stand in front of Preston. "My partner and I are down here from Easton. Our guys found a body in a motel off I-33 a couple of hours ago. Her number was the last dialed from his cell phone."

Preston nodded. "Okay. What else?"

"What else?" Dorchester asked. "What else do we need?"

"That depends," Preston told him. "If you're accusing her of murder you need a hell of a lot more evidence than her number in his cell phone."

"She's got motive seeing as she used to date the guy," Dorchester's counterpart put in.

"It's not a crime to date someone," Preston added with finality.

"I want to know where she was and what their last conversation was about. That's all for now," Dorchester told him.

Preston looked to Nikki then back to Dorchester. "What's the time of death?"

Dorchester's lips thinned as he frowned. "I want to know where she was all day. From the time he made that call up to now."

Preston shook his head. "No. Give us a time of death and she'll provide an alibi for that time. Either that or go back up to Easton and come back with a warrant to arrest her."

"You really should be more cooperative," Dorchester's sidekick said to Preston, placing his hands on his belt, the right hand landing closer to his gun than Quinn liked.

That's when Parker stepped up. "Allow me to introduce myself, Officers. I'm Detective Parker Cantrell from the Baltimore City Police Department."

Dorchester barely looked Parker's way. "No jurisdiction here," he claimed.

Parker chuckled. "You may be right. But harassment by a police officer is the same all over the state. Now, I figure you're not the investigating officers on this case. They would still be in Easton doing a canvass of the neighborhood where the body was found and notifying the next of kin. That means you're either here on your own pulling a rogue interrogation that you hope'll make you look good when you ride back to Easton, or you're not the brightest two officers on the force." Parker shrugged. "I'm wavering back and forth on which one."

"Look, I don't have time for this circus," Dorchester snapped, looking from Parker to Preston. "Look-alikes showing up when I'm trying to question a suspect is not what I'm used to. Now, if you please, Ms. Brockington, where were you from seven thirty this morning until we just saw you walking up the street?"

Preston was about to object, but Nikki held up a hand to stop him. "I'll answer him. I left my house to walk to work at seven fifteen. I arrived at The Silver Spoon around seven forty and didn't leave again until six thirty. I walked back home and that's when you saw me."

Her hand shook slightly as she spoke, so Quinn gripped it a little tighter, to let her know it was okay. She took a deep breath and let it out slowly.

"What did you talk about when he called you?"

She kept her back straight, her eyes focused on the cop. "We didn't talk. He said hello, called me immature, and I hung up. That's it."

"The call lasted about forty-two seconds," Carl added.

Dorchester gave him a scathing look. "Let me handle this, Deputy," he told Carl, who frowned right back at him.

"Okay, she's given you an alibi. That's all you get," Preston told him. He reached into his back pocket for his wallet and pulled out a card. "Call me if you have any more questions. Do not contact my client directly," he added with a tone of warning while passing Dorchester the card.

With a snatch the officer took the card and looked back at Nikki. "Witnesses who saw you at work?"

This time Quinn answered. "I'm staying at The Silver Spoon. Came down into the kitchen a little after eight this morning and she was already there."

Dorchester gave Quinn a skeptical look. "And who are you? The new boyfriend?"

Nikki immediately pulled her hand from Quinn's and shook her head. If he was going to say yes she'd certainly blown a hole in that comment with her quick reaction. But Quinn wasn't going to say yes. "My name's Quinn Cantrell. I'm one of the owners of The Silver Spoon. Ms. Brockington works for me."

Again, the look Dorchester was giving them said he didn't buy it. But Quinn knew he didn't have any other choice.

"Who saw her leave and who knows if she stayed there all day? Easton's only about an hour and a half away. She could have left, done the murder, and come back before being noticed."

"I made a lot of calls today, from my office. Check the phone records, you'll see I was right there all day. And I worked in the restaurant during lunchtime so I'm sure some of the patrons there will remember seeing me. Marabelle Stanley and Louisa Kirk were there and so was Inez King, meeting with some man I didn't recognize. They'll all say I was there," Nikki told him.

"Now I'll show you gentleman to the door," Preston told them.

"We're not finished," Dorchester's sidekick protested.

"Oh yes you are," Parker told him, touching an arm to his elbow and extending his arm as if to tell him to take this way out.

The guy didn't like Parker touching him, and when he pulled away again his hand went to his side and his gun.

"You've got an itchy trigger finger there, Officer," Parker grinned, but it wasn't a funny look. It was lethal and laced with a silent threat that had the officer's hand moving just slightly in the opposite direction. "Better get that checked out. Once you get back to Easton, that is."

"This way, gentlemen," Ralph Brockington said, moving past them and into the foyer.

Quinn could hear him saying something about calling commanding officers to report the disrespect to his home and his daughter.

"Why are you here?" Nikki asked Quinn the moment the police were gone.

"Preston told me what was going on. I wasn't going to let you go through that alone," he replied.

"I wasn't alone," she argued, standing. "My parents are here."

Quinn nodded and stood with her. "And now so am I." She was shaken up so he wasn't going to let her jabs get to him. He'd come here to support her and he was going to do that whether or not she liked it.

"You've certainly grown up, Quinton," Odell interrupted. "What are you doing with yourself now?"

"I'm an oncologist in Seattle," he told her.

Her lips formed a perfect O. "Really? Hmmm, I guess that was your calling."

"I enjoy it," he said for lack of anything better to say.

Nikki's mother was a little taller than Nikki, her complexion much darker. It was obvious Nikki was a mixture of her mother's African-American heritage and her father's Caucasian. Odell's hair was neatly pinned up in fat curls that would probably fall to her shoulders when loose, and her eyes were assessing, knowledgeable. Quinn felt mildly uncomfortable.

"We were very sorry to hear about Janet's passing," Odell continued, her smile never wavering, her eyes never slipping past him.

"Thank you."

With a nod Odell continued, "How are you and the family getting along?"

"We're getting along just fine, ma'am," he answered,

but he really wanted a moment alone with Nikki. Despite how serious this situation was, his desire to touch her was stronger than ever.

By that time Preston and Parker had come back into the living room with Nikki's father right behind them.

Ralph Brockington was a broad man, tall and almost fierce looking with his bushy black-and-gray beard and his slightly receding hairline. His eyes were dark and at this very moment angry as he set them firmly on Quinn and Nikki.

"I want somebody to tell me what's going on here," he said, hooking and running his thumbs up and down the plaid suspenders he wore.

Mr. Brockington still had a good build, Quinn suspected because he remained pretty active even as the chief of firemen. Sweetland wasn't that big so they wouldn't have as many firemen as a department in a major city would have. Which meant that, even as chief, he was probably fighting right alongside his men.

"I don't know what's going on, Dad," Nikki spoke up. "I went to work this morning and came home to police at my door."

"But this guy, he called you this morning?" Ralph asked.

With a sigh Nikki folded her arms over her chest and moved toward the window. She touched the sheer curtains with a hand that Quinn saw still shook and looked outside, as if to assure herself the cops had gone.

"It happened just like I said. He called, I told him not to call me anymore, and he accused me of being immature. End of conversation," she said quietly.

"How frequently did you receive these types of calls from this man?" Preston asked.

"We dated for about six months, two years ago. It was over the first week in December and he didn't start calling again until this year, around Valentine's Day I think. It was just off and on leaving messages that I never returned. In the last week he's called a lot more."

While she talked Quinn thought back to his conversation with Michelle this morning. He figured Nikki was talking about the guy who'd lied and betrayed her. In that moment Quinn experienced an emotion he never had before—jealousy. The way Nikki was looking at that window, the breathy soft whisper of her voice as she spoke gave the distinct impression that she'd still been in love with this man.

"Randall Davis was a liar and a con," Odell stated without a stitch of remorse. "He waltzed into this town looking for an innocent to have his way with. And he told all kinds of lies to get what he wanted."

"Thanks, Mom, you make me sound like the innocent idiot that fell into his trap," Nikki scoffed.

Odell shook her head. "That's not what I meant. He was a smooth one," she continued. "With his fancy clothes and fancy car. He was always throwing money around like he had it to spare. A real pro, like he was used to doing this same thing to women all the time."

"I didn't kill him," Nikki said, raising her voice a notch. "It doesn't matter what kind of man he was or what lies he told me, the thought of killing him never crossed my mind. He wasn't even worth my thoughts after I found out the truth about him. So that's that." She took a deep breath, blowing it out again as if she'd held it for ages.

"Thanks, Preston, for coming. You can let me know what your fee is and I'll gladly pay it," she said.

Preston was already shaking his head before she could finish her sentence. "Don't worry about it. I'll let you know if they have any more questions. You don't have to talk to the Easton police or the locals about this. They should all contact me."

She nodded.

"I'm going to make a few calls, have this guy's name

run to see what I can come up with. Was he from Easton?"
Parker asked.

Nikki shook her head. "No. Well, he told me he was
from New York and that's where I went to see him. He
had an apartment there but I don't remember the address.
I have the name of the guy he was working for on a card
somewhere. He gave it to me when I was in New York
and I kept it because he was in advertising and I figured I
might be able to use his company someday for help with
the B and B."

"Okay, why don't you bring that card to work with you
in the morning and I'll see what I can find out. Jonah said
he was shot at point-blank range three times to the back
of his head."

"Execution-style," Preston said.

"What are you boys thinking?" Ralph asked.

"They're thinking that a con artist getting killed hundreds of miles away from his home execution-style isn't
the kind of murder an ex-girlfriend would commit," Quinn
said.

He wasn't a cop or a criminal lawyer, but he wasn't
totally out of the loop, either. In the snatches of spare
time he had, when the medical world became too much
for him to dedicate another moment to—which had become more and more of an issue lately—he liked to watch
some of the crime drama television shows. Of course, he
had the ones he liked on DVD, because catching them at
their scheduled time was not an option. Listening to what
Nikki said about their relationship—which was slight—
combining that with Odell and Michelle's rendition of
what happened had Quinn following what he thought was
the same thought process his brothers were.

"The question is—what was he doing in Easton?" Preston asked. "Did he say anything about coming to see you?"

"No. Nothing. I didn't really give him a chance," Nikki
answered.

"When was the last time you heard from him before this morning?" Quinn asked even though she'd already been over how long he'd been calling her.

Her head shot up, her gaze turning in his direction. She didn't look like she wanted to talk about this anymore, especially not to him. He got the distinct impression that he was making her nervous—not so much because of the current situation, but more about the kiss they'd shared last night.

"Like I said, he's been calling me every day since last week. Today was the first time I answered because I was tired of all the calls. Now, if this is over for the night, Parker, I'll bring you the card tomorrow. Preston, thanks again. Mom and Dad, good night."

She'd already headed to the door when Odell made a move like she was going to follow her.

"I'll go," Quinn said placing a hand on Odell's shoulder. "I'll walk her around to her apartment, make sure she gets inside safely."

Ralph gave him a questioning look, but Odell smiled knowingly. "Thank you, Quinn."

He wasn't sure he wanted to assume what Odell thought she knew but he wasn't about to let Nikki be alone for another second, so he simply nodded and headed toward the door. "You go on back to the house, I'll walk over later," he said to Preston and Parker, who nodded even though they weren't entirely sure what he was up to.

For that matter, Quinn wasn't entirely sure. All he knew as he walked out the door was that he wanted—no, he needed—to talk to Nikki alone, to maybe hold her. As much as she gave the appearance that she was in control, Quinn didn't believe her. It was in her eyes, in the slight slump of her shoulders, the way her fingers shook as she talked. And try as he might, he couldn't let her go through this alone. He *wouldn't* let her go through this alone.

Chapter 13

Nikki had just stepped onto the first step that would carry her safely to her apartment when she felt a hand to the small of her back. She knew it was Quinn even without turning around. And she knew she couldn't turn around because if she did the tears filling her eyes might fall.

Instead she just walked up the steps. Quinn wouldn't leave even if she told him to. Stubbornness was a trait all the Cantrells had. It was most likely the largest and most dominant string in their DNA, she thought and almost laughed, except she felt like her world was just beginning to collapse around her. When she got to the door she slipped her hand into the bag she always carried and pulled out her key.

"Dammit!" she cursed when the key slipped right through her fingers to the wooden plank of the top step.

"I got it," Quinn said, stooping.

She held out her hand but he pushed it aside, moving her out of the way so he could slip the key into the lock and push the door open. When he stepped aside, she walked past him and hit the switch to her right to turn on the lights. Behind her she heard the door close, but still Nikki refused to turn around. Instead she went straight to the small kitchenette that was to the right of what she used as the living room.

Her place was small but then she was only one person so it suited her needs. To the left was a sofa bed she'd bought from Mike and Liza Fitzgerald when they'd had that huge yard sale because Mike's aunt Bethany had passed away and they were moving into her wing of the Fitzgerald estate. Now that Liza was the mayor Nikki liked to amuse herself by saying she had the furniture of royalty—at least Sweetland royalty anyway. There was a small desk pushed up against the wall right beneath the only window in this part of the apartment. When she sat down to write—which she did often, as she liked to practice her verbiage for the B&B a lot—she enjoyed looking outside, to the streets of the town she knew so well. She also kept a journal, had since she was thirteen years old, but that was nobody's business but her own.

In the kitchenette there was a wooden table that her brother Caleb had built when he was convinced he would be a furniture maker instead of a fireman, the sides dropped down so that when it was just her she had enough space, and if she had company—which she rarely ever did— there'd be space as well. The sink had a counter beside it that was about two feet long. At the end of that short wall was a mini refrigerator with a microwave on top. She bent over and retrieved a bottled water from the refrigerator. Twisting off the top, she drank and drank until the dryness of her throat seemed to subside, the tears in her eyes temporarily held at bay.

"You want to talk about it?" Quinn asked from behind her.

Nikki shook her head.

"How about I talk and you answer questions," he suggested.

Taking one last swallow, Nikki licked her lips before finally turning to face him. "Didn't I just do that dance?"

"Humor me," he said, extending a hand to her. "Let's sit down."

There was no place for her to run, if that were a thought. Her bedroom was about twenty steps away but once in there she would truly be trapped. And Quinn would follow her; her temples throbbed with another set of issues she didn't want to deal with.

"Fine," she said, giving up and putting her hand once again in his, while setting the half-empty water bottle on the counter.

They were close on the couch, even though there was more room on both sides of them. And Quinn kept her hand in his, linking their fingers together.

"So you met this guy, he lied to you, you dumped him, and now he's dead."

Nikki nodded. "That about sums it up."

"And you still love him?"

"No!" she replied immediately then clapped her lips shut. "No," this time in a calmer tone. "I do not still love him. Actually, I doubt what I felt for him was love in the first place. All I know for sure is that I trusted him, completely. And to find out that was all a lie, that I'd fallen for every word he said, every gift he bought me, every look he'd given me, well, that was embarrassing."

"And painful," he continued. He was using his other hand, those long, strong doctor's fingers, to rub along the back of her hand. It was a soft distraction, one she barely noticed, one that sent tiny spikes of heat through her body.

"I should have been smarter but he was worldlier. He'd performed this act before. Me, it was my first romantic episode so it took me completely by surprise." She shrugged. "You live and you learn, I guess."

"You don't have to pretend with me, Nikki. I can see that he hurt you."

She nodded but wouldn't look at him. She couldn't. Inside her chest felt heavy, like one of those puppies might be sitting right above her rib cage, staring down into her face. He was right: It had been painful. More painful than anything she'd ever experienced. The worst part was you'd think she'd be over it by now. Still, the sting of embarrassment was swift and irritating as hell. The tears she wanted to shed were tears of agitation, of anger and disappointment, in herself.

"He hurt me, yes," she said and drew a deep breath. Then she did look at him because she wanted him to see that she was serious. "But he didn't break me. I made a mistake. I shouldn't have trusted him. But there's a point in all mistakes, there's a lesson to be learned. I learned it. I worked hard to achieve my goals and I kept my chin up, just like everybody told me to do. And still he came back to haunt me. That pisses me off!"

Quinn smiled. Of all things she expected, this was not it.

"I can see that you're a little pissed off."

"More than a little," she said, letting out a whoosh of breath. "I just . . . I felt so helpless when it all happened."

"And you hate to feel helpless," he commented.

Using her free hand, she ran her fingers through hair that was still straight from the salon styling but threatening to curl at any moment. Nikki wanted to tell him he was absolutely right. Instead she remained quiet, wishing this entire exchange would be over.

"Why don't you tell me about it," Quinn prompted, pulling her back with him.

He extended an arm across, let his hand drop along her shoulder, and tugged until she had no choice but to move closer. Right where he wanted her. From the moment Quinn heard about her situation he'd wanted to do this, to fold her in his arms and assure her that everything would be fine. Of course, he had no idea how that was going to happen at the time, but he wanted to offer it to her anyway.

Knowing what he did now, he was positive she'd be okay—and if those cops didn't leave her the hell alone they'd have him to deal with. Him, Preston, and Parker, he thought. His brothers were going to run with this case like Dixi had taken off with the remote control to his television just this morning. They'd probably find Randall Davis's killer before that oaf of an officer from Easton did.

"I'm the youngest, you know." Nikki had begun talking.

The soft pitch of her voice lulled about in the silence of her apartment. Quinn looked around as he listened. Her furnishings were sparse, right down to only the items she needed. She wasn't a frivolous type, he thought.

"My brothers were always very overprotective of Cordy because she was pretty and bubbly and all the boys wanted her. You know she had a thing with Parker for a while."

"I recall that," Quinn said letting his fingers rub along her shoulder, down a little on her arm. She wore a short-sleeved shirt, so it wasn't long before his skin was touching hers.

There was a desk that might have been an antique except the engraved design at the helm was American and the table legs weren't original. The wood was different, almost a perfect match in color, no doubt because the legs had been stained. Nothing in here was of any particular value except that everything in here was hers. He suspected she took great pride in that fact, and that pride alone made each piece priceless. Nikki was a woman who worked hard for what she wanted and cherished every one of her milestones. Quinn was impressed by that fact because even though he'd had many milestones, he couldn't remember them all and didn't really care to. All he could think about was getting a step farther, reaching just a little farther no matter how high he stood.

"So they treated me like the 'other' sister. I mean, they loved me, no doubt, but they never had to worry about me getting mixed up with the wrong guy. Cordy gave me tons of advice, tons and tons. And when Randall first came to town she, too, was in awe. Then when he went back to New York and our relationship became mostly long distance she started to tell me I should move on, look for someone who could focus on making me happy and wasn't so impressed by the material things. I'm not impressed by material things, you know," she said.

The last part had been spoken even more quietly, like she thought if she said it too loud it would be something he really didn't want to hear.

"That's not a bad thing," he replied. "You can't take those material things with you. It's what's in your heart that lasts." Even as Quinn said those words he was wondering why he hadn't told himself that for years past.

"I like how that sounds," she said and actually snuggled closer to him.

Quinn turned his head, let his chin rest on top of hers and inhaled deeply. Her hair smelled fresh with the faintest hint of citrus. That wasn't a normal scent to be associated with a female, not what some would call a sexy scent. But men were obsessed with food scents—not that many women knew that—so instead of a heady floral fragrance, he preferred the smells that made him think more of nature, of . . . home.

"I like how you sound," he said out of nowhere. "Your voice is soft but confident. Your stature is slight but there's a fierceness about you that rests right on your shoulders when you stand. At first glance I thought, young, fresh, don't touch. Then there's this other part of you, like a parallel world, a very seductive and enticing you that I'm having a really hard time resisting."

For a second she stiffened in his grasp, and he wondered if he'd scared her away. But no, Nicole Brockington was not a skittish female, she wasn't one of the independent medical professionals he'd dated in Seattle, who had worked too long and too hard to let him do things like open doors for them or walk them home. They'd actually preferred to pick him up for dates, drop him off at his door, schedule their next date months in advance on the iPhones that were glued to the palms of their hands.

"I'm trying to resist, too," she reluctantly admitted, shifting a little so that she could now look up at him.

"I know better. I've been taught better. Don't take what's not yours. Don't touch what you can't hope to hold on to," he whispered, his head lowering even as he spoke.

"I wished for you," she told him. "On the evening star, I wished that you would kiss me."

Her lips parted slightly, her bottom lip just a pinch fuller than the top. Her eyelids lowered, like they were as heady with the intensity of this moment as he was.

"For you, Nicole, wishes can come true," Quinn told her, his voice a whisper just above her lips.

Then he was lost in the sweet taste of her. It was like sinking in quicksand, he figured, if he'd ever had that experience for real. The slowest of descents, with the pulling and tugging against every part of his body as his mouth covered hers. There was no prelude this time; their tongues immediately collided, as if waiting for the chance at this reunion. Like a slow duel they clashed and rubbed, touched and glided along until his heartbeat slammed against his chest. He reached another arm around, pulling her so that she now straddled his lap. His hands went directly to her buttocks then, fingers grasping those enticing globes as if his very next breath depended on that touch.

She pressed into him, arching her back only slightly, taking his bottom lip into her mouth for a long, tortuous suckle. His mind clouded, seeing only her in the distance.

This pert and lively female with the great body and the small-town values that he could no longer deny he wanted.

Her hands cupped his face as she pulled back only slightly.

"I want you to take me to bed," she said, pinning him with the hottest gaze he'd ever had the pleasure of experiencing.

If saying no had even the slightest fraction of possibility in his mind, her words sliced that thought to pieces like a master swordsman.

He stood without a word, his teeth nibbling along the line of her jaw as he wrapped her legs around his waist and took a step toward the far end of the room he figured was her bedroom. They kissed as he walked. No, that wasn't really the correct term: Two hungry mouths made every human attempt to devour each other. He kicked something, heard something else hit the floor.

"Forget it," she mumbled and pressed her breasts closer to his chest.

"Forgotten," he growled, his fingers grasping her buttocks then slipping farther between her legs to rub along her center. She arched at his touch, her head falling back as she moaned and his tongue traced a heated trail down the line of her neck.

They hit her bedroom. Through his one open eye he found the full-sized bed, dropping her down without another word. In seconds he was on top of her, pulling at her pants until the snap popped. Later, much later, he might consider buying her another pair if these were destroyed by his eagerness.

Looking down at her, legs partially spread, top pushed up so that the bottom half of her torso was bared to him right along with her panty-clad juncture, he inhaled deeply before reaching for her again. His breath came in a quick whoosh as his fingers immediately found the band of her panties, pulling them down her thighs, his fingers grazing her soft skin on the way. Need raged through him like a summer storm and Quinn thought he heard the thunder of waves crashing in his head. He grasped her thighs then, spreading them wide so he could have a better view.

All thoughts of age and sisters and the cloak of the small town they were in faded. His focus was solely on her dampened folds. With one finger that he wasn't willing to admit shook just slightly, he touched her there, heard her intake of breath and licked his lips longingly. She felt like velvet, hot, soft, pliant. He touched along both sides, dragging his finger slowly upward to press against the hood of her vagina. He found the tightened pearl and rubbed it adoringly. Below him her head thrashed. She called his name, and Quinn closed his eyes to the pleasure.

"Sweet Nikki," he whispered, letting his thumb massage her bud, his fingers slipping through her wetness to plunge into her waiting center.

"Oh God, Quinn!" she yelled, and the sound simply speared him on.

He thrust his finger deeper, rubbed with his thumb with more persistence. She rotated her hips, meeting his thrusts.

"Yes, just like that, baby," he told her, his hips jerking with the motion.

"Quinn, I need . . ." Her words trailed off and he used his other hand to reach up under her shirt.

Pushing aside the lace front of her bra he found her waiting nipple and pinched slightly before cupping her entire breast. She grabbed his wrist, holding his hand firmly against her breast. He thrust his finger in and out of her with more urgency, the pain of his erection pressing against the zipper of his pants. He wanted . . . no, he desperately needed relief.

"I need, too, Nikki. Oh God, do I need." The words were wrenched from him as he struggled to hold on just a second longer. That's all Nikki needed.

She tightened her thighs and grabbed the sheets tightly in her fists.

"Is that what you need, baby? Is that it?" he asked, staring down into her pretty face, cheeks flushed with arousal, eyes clouded with the rush of release.

She didn't answer verbally; Quinn wasn't sure she could. But her head thrashed as her body stopped the mild quaking motion. He slipped his hand slowly from her, loving the feel of her essence along his fingers. Gently, because her breath was still coming in quick pants, he pulled her shirt up and over her head. With a quick motion he unhooked her bra and pushed it from her arms. Without a doubt he was going to lower his head, his tongue immediately licking still-puckered nipples. He felt her hands at the back of his head, holding him there, pushing him closer.

She was so desirable, so willing and seemingly uninhibited that Quinn could do nothing more than groan. This was the woman he'd thought was an innocent—or at least innocent as far as he was concerned. He'd tried to look at her as a little sister, but that had been futile. And now that he'd seen her in a different light, he'd never be able to go back. Gripping her other breast in his hand as he continued to suckle its twin, his mind sighed once more: *Never.*

And now, that's what his next thought was: *Now!*

Reluctantly he pulled away from her. "One sec, baby. Just give me one second."

His fingers fumbled over his buckle. Yes, he was thirty-six years old and way past his first sexual experience, but his fingers were shaking as he tried to undo the belt.

"Let me," she said, coming to sit on the edge of the bed and reaching for his belt.

She smiled up at him while pushing his hands away.

"Mighty Quinn Cantrell, it's okay if you're not in control all the time," she told him.

But really Quinn could hardly decipher what she was saying to him. All he knew was that he needed to be inside her sooner much rather than later. If that could be achieved by her undressing him, so be it.

Her fingers were surprisingly steady considering the orgasm she'd just had. But she undid his belt, pushed down the zipper of his pants, then reached inside and wrapped her fingers around him.

"Did you think you were the only one who liked to touch?" she asked.

His answer was to grab the hem of his T-shirt and pull it quickly over his head.

"You can touch all you want," he told her. "Just hurry up!"

She smiled and pushed his pants and boxers down his legs. "You still have your shoes on."

Quinn cursed and bent over to get them off. He finished the deed with his pants and pushed her back onto the bed in a swift motion. They both laughed as his hands wrapped around her, squeezing her butt cheeks in his palms.

"I can't believe we're going to do this," she said, her smile faltering only slightly.

He lowered his head to hers, kissed her lips, then licked over them twice, until she was breathless.

"We're definitely doing this," he told her. Then he cursed and let her go as fast as he'd pushed her down.

She made a sound of surprise as he took to the floor to find his pants, then riffled through his pockets to find the gold packet that would forever be his lifesaver. He sheathed himself with her eyes fixated on his erection, his hands moving over his length. Then she licked her lips, while she watched, and Quinn thought he was going to blow right then and there.

*   *   *

Wow.

No, wait a minute, that didn't seem to actually describe how good he looked naked.

Wow!

Yes, that was much better.

Quinn Cantrell was standing in her bedroom. He was a little over six feet tall, honey-toned skin, dark eyes, great smile, tight muscled ass, and the rest . . . well, let's just say her mouth never watered . . . ever. Until now. Until Quinn.

A part of her wondered if she should be nervous, but Nikki ignored that. Instead she reached for him, extended her arms and welcomed the feel of his strong shoulders beneath her hands. He spread her legs and her heart beat a little faster. She felt the tip of him touch her center and she wanted to scream, or writhe, which is what she ended up doing.

He moaned and inside she smiled. He wanted her. Quinn Cantrell really wanted her.

She lifted her hips a bit because for a man with wants he was moving kind of slow. Or maybe it was just too slow for her at the moment. When he entered her it was quick and complete. She gasped and he moaned and they both remained perfectly still for endless moments.

He set the pace; she immediately followed, loving the feel of him so thick and sensuous inside her. She wrapped her legs around his waist and he plunged deeper, her nails scraping along his back as delicious ripples of pleasure soared through her. It was a repeat of the feeling she'd had minutes ago when he was touching and suckling her. She hadn't thought she would recover from that, but damn if she wasn't gearing up for another ride.

"Quinn," she whispered in a shaky voice as her body lifted to his, then shattered in a million pieces because of his.

Her release must have triggered his because it was only seconds later that he murmured, "Sweet, sweet Nikki," into the crook of her neck. But it sounded anything but sweet. Instead it sounded like regret.

Chapter 14

The very first thing Nikki realized when she rolled over after sleeping like the dead for who knew how long was that this was not how sex was two years ago.

Of course, there had been more fundamental differences in this experience. The man. The moment. The location. *The man.*

The man who was lying on his back, one arm tucked beneath his head, while she—the woman—had half her body sprawled over his. Her palm resting on his chest, which had minimal hair—something she silently thanked the heavens for. Her thigh was thrown over his; her toes, when they wiggled, rubbed along muscled calves that did have a light spray of hair that felt kind of sexy when she actually thought about it.

Her bedroom was dark. There was only one window besides the one in the living room and luckily it was in her bedroom. She'd hung a plain cotton turquoise curtain there because it seemed to match the geometric bedspread's rainbow of colors. His chest moved up and down, a slow rhythm that she thought her heartbeat now matched. He was a big man, which was a surprise since he didn't look all that big when completely dressed. Tall, yes, and fit, she'd known that just by the way his suit had looked on him as he made his way into the church. But these muscles, the tight abs, bulging biceps, even his hands had strength, she thought with a sigh as memories of him gripping her bottom sent pangs of lust right to her center.

She'd had sex with Quinn Cantrell. A smile tickled her lips and she shifted ever so slightly closer to him, daring this to be a dream.

"You're asking for trouble, young lady," the deep voice echoed above her.

"And if I ask, will I receive?" It was a brave question, a bold and almost uncharacteristically ambitious one on her part. But Nikki figured he was here and so was she; their clothes were somewhere else, and it was still night. What the hell, they might as well make the best of their time together. Because who knew what would happen come morning. Regrets, recriminations, apologies— anything was possible.

"You shall definitely receive," he said, wrapping his arms around her and pulling her until she was on top of him. "Just let me know when you've had enough."

He'd taken her face in his hands, pulling her down so that his lips were just inches from hers. "I'll keep that in mind," was her reply before she nipped his bottom lip.

He gave a light slap to her behind and Nikki yelped. Yes, it was probably the most unsexy sound she'd ever heard, but she did it and he chuckled. "Like that, huh?"

When he did it again she moaned, spread her legs, and settled over him, feeling the persistent nudge of his arousal at her center.

"I like that."

And she liked being on top of him, guiding his thick erection into her waiting core, setting the pace for this next round of lovemaking. Because for Nikki, that's ex- actly what this was. It was the dream that she'd never thought would come true, the experience she'd figured she'd never know.

He held her hips tightly, thrusting upward to meet the pump and sway of her hips. Her hands rested first on his chest then, when she sat straight up, gripped her breasts, tweaking her own nipples in the same way he'd done before.

"You're beautiful," he whispered and a blush spread throughout her body.

Her breath came in quick pants as he seemed to press deeper inside her, filling her until she thought they might have been born connected. The air around her was thick with their scents, filled with the sound of his moans of pleasure, her gasps of surprise to be followed by his name on her lips like lyrics to some intense love song.

For the duration of the night, Nikki had asked and received. Quinn gave and he accepted. His whispers of her beauty, his pleasure, her acquiescence, his undying need, all filtered through her like the finest of wines, the best of miracles.

It was everything good and everything equally terrifying—as she would discover all too soon.

"I thought you were dying to get out of town," Preston asked on a bright sunny morning in the kitchen of The Silver Spoon.

"That was then, this is now," was Savannah's flippant reply.

"Something happen to change your mind?" Parker asked this time.

"Is this a tag team?" Savannah shot back. Then she looked up, saw Quinn coming through the back door, and frowned. "Oh, no, it's a triple team."

Preston and Parker turned to see Quinn. It was just after nine in the morning. He'd been back at the B&B since around four thirty when he'd left Nikki's very warm and equally welcoming bed to come home and walk his puppy so she wouldn't pee on yet another rug, or perhaps his bed since he wasn't there to put her out of it. And Dixi had been waiting, tail wagging while her paws pushed his hairbrush around on the floor. How she'd gotten that out of his suitcase, Quinn still wasn't sure. But today was going to be her first lesson in boundaries.

"Good morning," he said with a smile nobody returned. Well, Parker had a smirk, but Quinn figured it was best to ignore that, at least for now. "What seems to be the problem now?"

"No problem. None of anybody's business. I'm staying in Sweetland for a couple more days, maybe a week . . . or two," Savannah said, speaking more into her cup of coffee than to the three men standing there staring at her.

Parker looked at Preston, who deferred to Quinn, who decided only to shrug. He knew there was something going on with Savannah, didn't know what, but knew better than to push.

"That's a good idea. You could get some rest, maybe help Michelle out a bit," Quinn said, then almost bit off his own tongue.

"Help Michelle do what? She's perfect, you know? She doesn't need any help," Savannah raved.

"Whatever the case, if you're staying a while and I'm not leaving until this mess with Nikki is cleared up, then we'd better all talk about making other accommodations. Guests are checking in on Friday," Quinn told them.

"How do you know that?" Savannah asked with a frown. She'd been wearing that expression quite a bit lately.

"Nikki told me a sorority reunion is booked for the weekend. Which means we can't all be here taking up rooms."

"I have a case I need to prepare for," Preston began. "But I wanted to unload the puppy before I went back."

"I took two weeks off, was thinking of heading down south after this," Parker added.

"Move into the caretaker's suite," Michelle said, pushing her way backward through the swinging door to the kitchen.

Savannah made a tsking sound. "Were you listening at the door?"

Michelle put down the two bags full of groceries she'd been carrying, glaring at Savannah over the tops. "No, as usual you're too loud.

"If you guys are staying for a while," she continued, her voice obviously lighter since this was no doubt what she'd wanted all along, "Quinn, you and the twins can take the caretaker's suite. It has a private bathroom, the master bedroom, and a sitting room that has a sofa bed."

"Three guys and two beds," Preston began. "Not a good match."

"Two beds and a couch. You want to draw straws?" she asked with a smile.

"No need," Preston added. "I'll take the couch since I need to get back to Baltimore this weekend anyway."

"What about Nikki?" Quinn asked.

"I can handle that from there and if it comes down to it I'm only an hour and a half away. But I think that's going to go away fairly soon," Preston answered.

"What's going to go away? What happened to Nikki?" Savannah asked, concern edging out the bitterness in her voice.

Quinn obviously wasn't the only one to hear it because everyone in the kitchen stopped to stare at her.

"What? She's my best friend. I mean, she was my best friend. And now she works for us, practically lives here like family, and . . . whatever. What happened to her?"

It was going to be common knowledge by noon anyway, if it wasn't already. If Quinn walked into the restaurant right now he'd more than likely overhear someone talking about it over their morning coffee.

"Randall Davis was found dead yesterday. Police were

at Nikki's door to question her when she got home," Quinn stated simply.

But it wasn't a simple matter. In his mind it was ludicrous, but for Nikki's sake he wanted it over and done with, sooner rather than later.

"Oh my God," Michelle sighed. "That poor girl. Didn't that bastard put her through enough? Is she here yet?"

"No, she's not in yet," Quinn answered quickly.

Too quickly by the looks he received.

"They only came looking her way because she was easy. Her number was in his cell phone because he'd called her yesterday morning. She has an airtight alibi and he was killed in Easton. They know they have to look someplace else," Parker said, opening the refrigerator for Michelle, who had been holding two gallons of milk and standing completely still.

"They think Nikki killed some guy?" Savannah asked.

"Not some guy, her ex," Preston stated.

"Her ex that was an ass," Quinn added. He'd moved to the coffeepot and grabbed himself a mug. Just as he was pouring he heard the silence, which was never good where his siblings were concerned.

"And why did you say she wasn't in yet?" Michelle asked, her voice suspicious.

There was a pot of creamer right beside the coffeepot, its dainty white handle just like the one Gramma used to use. It sat inside a bowl of ice and Quinn momentarily wondered how Michelle knew to take care of every detail, every damned time. Maybe she was perfect, as Savannah said.

"I don't know why because I'm not Nikki," he answered when he'd fixed his coffee to his liking and turned to face what looked like a sad rendition of the firing squad.

Preston and Savannah were both sitting at the table staring at him. Parker was closing the refrigerator, and Michelle was standing near the island with her arms folded.

"But you know she's not here. Strange," Michelle noted quietly.

"Any of you would know she's not here if you checked her office." Or if you'd spent the night having sex with her and told her to sleep in when you'd left her tired and completely sated about four and a half hours ago.

Quinn's cell phone was his saving grace as its loud ring echoed throughout the kitchen. Pulling it from his hip, he looked down and weighed the options. Stand here and continue to be scrutinized by his siblings—which could not possibly end well—or take the call from Elena and get more grief about the clinic. He opted for what he thought was the lesser of two evils.

"Excuse me," he said, leaving the kitchen.

"The funding didn't come through," Elena told him the moment he answered.

Quinn cursed.

"What about The Transor Group, did they answer?"

"We've heard from everywhere we applied. Donations were low, other diseases are taking precedence, there's a wide range of excuses but no checks is our bottom line."

He sighed, dropping down into the chair by the window in the dining room. Research and development was his department at the clinic. He managed treatment plans and four doctors working below him, but R&D had been his sole purpose in working for a private clinic, versus a hospital. At a hospital he would have never had the time to look for a cure or at least a part of the cure. He would no doubt be on a surgical rotation and have triple the number of patients he did in private practice. That wasn't what he'd wanted.

For the last three or four months Quinn had known his department was in trouble; he'd sensed the shift in the tide at the clinic. The board wasn't pleased with his slow results, nor were they keen on the idea of a younger, more experienced doctor telling them to shut up and give him room to breathe. Yes, he'd said that at their last meeting when they'd been on his back about results.

"Do you think the cure is just under the next hat? Am I supposed to take unhealthy risks and shortcuts just to meet your bottom line?" he'd yelled at them.

"You're supposed to contribute to the financial stability of this clinic," Albert Lomax had replied in his old, starchy tone.

"Then give me time to do that and stop nitpicking at every invoice that crosses your desk."

"It's not the invoices we're concerned about. It's more like the lack of checks we see coming in," Lomax countered.

"Then get your cheap friends to unclench their fists and give us some money!" he'd yelled in response.

That meeting had ended badly, and from that point on the place he'd loved to work had become a source of tension and discord. His relationship with his patients was fine—he gave them 100 percent regardless of what was going on. But everything else had been twisting in the wind like debris from a tornado, waiting to be swept away, he figured, as he looked out the window to see Sylvester once again sitting on Gramma's bench.

"They've called an emergency board meeting first thing tomorrow morning. I think you should be here," Elena said in that no-nonsense way she had.

"I can't," Quinn replied quicker than he intended.

"You've already buried your grandmother. What's left to do in that country town?" she asked.

Quinn had told Elena where he was from and most of how he'd come to be in Seattle. After two dates and one unsuccessful attempt at sex they'd both decided being co-workers was a lot better than trying to be lovers. So she knew things the board of directors didn't. He wondered how many times he'd called Sweetland a "country" town. Probably a lot if she'd adopted the term for her own use.

"I inherited a bed-and-breakfast and I have to stay until I know things are running smoothly." That was only half the truth, but Quinn didn't really care. He didn't owe Elena any explanation, and the only reason he was partially willing to give the board of directors one was because he still received a paycheck from them.

"Let John continue to see my patients. I'll call you next week to let you know when I'll be back."

"Quinn," she said, then paused.

"What is it, Elena?"

When she didn't respond, Quinn grew impatient. He needed to call Nikki to make sure she was okay and on her way to work before his siblings converged on him once more. He also needed to go check on Dixi to make sure she wasn't up to mischief, and he needed to move his things from his current room to the caretaker's suite. He did not have any more time to talk to Elena.

"If you have something to say, just say it," he told her.

"I think they're leaning toward letting you go," she said quickly and quietly.

For the first time since he'd come in here Quinn tore his gaze from the window. He stared down at the floor instead. Fired. He'd never been fired before, didn't really know how that felt. Then again, the only real feeling Quinn could lay claim to experiencing so far in his life had been grief. He rubbed a hand over his face and took a deep breath.

"I'll call you back by the end of the day to let you know my plans," he said slowly, deliberately.

"What do you mean your plans? Your travel plans? Quinn, if you want to save your job I think you should hit the road now. They're serious about this. And—" She paused. "I think they've already interviewed a replacement for you. Some guy from UCLA who married into this billionaire philanthropy family."

So they could control him and his money, Quinn

thought with a smirk. That was the game at Mark Vincent: You either did what the board of directors said or they found someone who would. In the five years that Quinn had been there he'd tried to walk their line because to him, the end justified the means. Sitting here in his grandmother's parlor, with his siblings in the other room, the beauty of a sunny Eastern Shore day just outside and the distant sound of playing puppies in the backyard, he thought maybe he'd been wrong.

"They're going to do what they want when they want, Elena. I'm not worried about it. I'll call you by five this afternoon."

Quinn disconnected the call because he didn't want to hear any more of Elena's questions. She was a good woman with a caring heart that was unfortunately at war with her ambitions. She didn't think Quinn knew that she'd been sleeping with Lomax. That was no doubt how she'd known about them interviewing the UCLA guy. He was twenty-five years her senior, but obviously that didn't matter to her. Quinn wished them the best; it wasn't his concern. Neither was the medical center, he thought with a sigh.

He stood looking out the window once more. Sylvester had stood from the bench and was watching as the puppies ran around. Michelle probably let them all out of the basement for a while. She liked to do that in the morning, said they needed to stretch their legs and socialize. Quinn thought that was good, brothers and sisters playing as nicely as they could. Sylvester rotated throwing a red and a yellow ball, watching as the puppies pushed them around with their noses, fell over their big feet trying to bite them. Then he'd take his time walking over and picking up the ball just to see them jumping around him for it before tossing it again. The puppies looked as if they enjoyed themselves and so did Sylvester. It was a simple task for a simple day, to a person who led a simple life.

Quinn wondered how that would feel. Could he live in Sweetland again? Could he wake up in the mornings and do nothing more than play with the dogs? Could he walk around this B&B all day taking care of guest issues, or sit in the restaurant listening to Marabelle and Louisa talk about anybody and everybody they knew, and some they didn't? The answer to most of those questions would be no if he didn't figure out the tax issue on the house. With that in mind, Quinn put thoughts of Seattle and the flux his job was in to the side, and stepped outside—his destination, city hall.

Quinn had kissed her before leaving. He'd gone to walk Sweet Dixi. He hadn't left her. Not like Randall had.

The morning after with Randall had been eye opening in a couple of ways. One, Nikki accepted that she was no longer a virgin. Two, she acknowledged that she didn't feel much different at that moment than she had the day before. If this was what all the fuss was about, she might be able to pass on sex for a while longer. And finally, the man she'd slept with had left her in a hotel room just off I-33 all alone.

It was one month after she'd met him, numerous marathon phone calls and emails later. He'd come into town and picked her up on a Friday night for dinner. They hadn't eaten in town but had traveled on the outskirts to a little Italian restaurant nestled close to the river. The food and atmosphere had been excellent, the company mind blowing to her naive mind. When he'd told her how much he missed her, how he'd been wanting to break away sooner so he could see her, Nikki was flattered, and she was excited because she'd known how this night would end. Or at least she thought she had.

Fast-forward two years. There'd been no dinner, only one lovely walk home and that first enticing kiss. Then like three superheroes to the rescue he and his two brothers had appeared at her time of need, assuring her that all would be well. He'd stayed, not because he wanted to sleep with her, but because he'd wanted to ensure she was all right. Nikki knew that instinctively. Quinn Cantrell was not a man with ulterior motives. With him, what you saw was what you got and she was thankful, because what Nikki saw, she liked . . . a lot.

With Quinn it would be different; she knew that without him even touching her. The moment she rested her head on his shoulders and admitted to things she'd never confessed to another soul, she'd known it would be good with him. And it had been. Actually, it had been more than good, it had been sort of liberating. On each occasion after the first with Randall she'd always left feeling like something was missing, like somehow the episode had missed its mark.

Well, Quinn had hit the mark a couple of times, and as she stood in her small shower this morning the soreness between her legs was a welcome reminder of her true induction into womanhood.

An hour later when she walked into The Silver Spoon to two sets of imploring eyes she realized she was now inducted into something else . . . the Cantrell family.

The kitchen was bright as by now, a little after ten in the morning, the sun was high up in the sky, shining as brightly as it possibly could. Intense rays poured in through the open curtains of the kitchen because Michelle loved working by sunlight. The natural light bounced off the cheery yellow walls so that it was more than a little intense walking inside.

At the table, with her feet propped in the chair across from her, a magazine in her hands, Savannah sat. Said magazine had been lowered the moment she heard the door open and now lay flat on the table as she watched Nikki intently. Michelle had been at the stove, transferring peeled potatoes into a huge pot. Today was crab soup day. After she'd finished she set the strainer in the sink and wiped her hands on her apron as her eyes found Nikki's.

"Good morning," she said, her voice sounding saucy and southern all at the same time. Her smile was wide, bright, knowing.

"Good morning," Nikki replied, taking her usual steps to the other side of the kitchen to hang up her purse.

"Late night?" Savannah asked, tapping her nails on the table.

"Okay," Nikki said with a huff, turning to face them both. "You've probably heard by now that the Easton police were at my house when I got home yesterday. They wanted to know if I'd killed Randall Davis."

"I heard that. Fools, why would they think a thing like that? Of course because they weren't from Sweetland they don't know any better. You won't even tell your slightly overbearing mother to back off, let alone kill a man," Michelle replied with a bite to her tone.

Nikki could only nod, because Michelle's comparison was on the mark. Odell Brockington could be overbearing and not just with her children. Nikki had a feeling every woman in town probably had the same take on her mother.

"So you were dating this guy and he got himself killed?" Savannah asked.

Nikki shook her head and went to the refrigerator. If she was going to be giving out explanations—which it appeared she was—she needed a beverage. As usual there were two big crystal jugs on the top shelf, one with lemonade and one with iced tea, both with fresh lemon slices floating on top. There were two additional containers filled with the drinks on the lower shelf of the right-hand side. The left-hand side of the refrigerator contained all the pre-prepped dishes for the day. Below, there were more packaged items such as sausage and other breakfast meats.

Seafood and most of the meats Michelle purchased from the local butcher were cooked fresh. Nikki took out the jug of iced tea and put it on the counter. When she found a glass she poured some in and took a sip.

"We dated two years ago. He was a jerk. I found that out about ten minutes too late." She shrugged, already tired of rehashing this story. "He's been calling me a lot in the last week or so. The last time and the first time I actually answered was yesterday morning while I was walking to work. I told him to get lost and I guess he took that to mean get killed." As she took another sip she figured her flippant words might have come off as more than a little morbid. But really, she couldn't find much sympathy for the guy. Except that getting shot in the back of the head three times was a pretty crappy way to die, if offered the choice.

"So what did he want when he called? I mean, he had to want something to keep calling you even though you weren't answering," Savannah said.

"I don't know and I don't care." She really didn't want to know whatever Randall's reasoning was for calling her.

Savannah's perfectly arched eyebrow raised. "What if it was to get back together?"

"Then he was a bigger fool than I thought he was," Michelle said. "You don't get a second chance when you mess up so royally the first time around."

"Right," Nikki agreed with a nod and finished off her tea. She was just about to leave when she heard Michelle clear her throat.

"So you haven't told us why you're so late this morning," she said.

Nikki paused, her hand already on the door. "Decided to sleep in."

"Alone or with company?" Savannah prompted.

It didn't show. Did it? They could not know because Nikki was positive Quinn was not the kiss-and-tell type.

"I slept in alone," she said because that was true, for the most part.

"But did you fall asleep alone?" Savannah persisted.

Michelle knew, Nikki could tell. It was in her eyes, that assessing and knowledgeable look she gave. Nikki sighed. She hadn't told anyone, had considered calling Cordy on her walk over but decided against it knowing she didn't have enough time to answer all her sister's inevitable questions. So how would she deal with Quinn's sisters? And did he even want her to deal with them?

"No, I didn't," she said with finality. "I slept with a man and woke up alone. End of story." She pushed through the door and left the kitchen praying with everything that was in her that this was the end of that conversation.

Why she never used the brain God gave her Nikki had no clue.

Savannah was right on her heels, Michelle right on hers. Nikki kept moving to her office even though she heard them both behind her.

"So who was the man?" Savannah asked with a smile as she leaned against one side of the doorjamb.

Michelle took residence on the other side, one hand on her hip. "I'll bet I know."

Nikki dropped down into her chair, slamming her palms on her desk. "You do not."

Michelle never faltered. "Want me to guess?"

"I want both of you to go find something else to do. The lunch crowd will be flowing in in about an hour. They'll expect crab soup and corn bread. And you, I'm certain there are more magazines in the living room."

"Uh-huh, I'm staying right here until I get the full scoop. This is the most fun I've had here all week," Savannah quipped. And she smiled.

Nikki hadn't seen Savannah smile since she'd arrived. It warmed her heart because it was so familiar, right down to the deep dimple she had in her left cheek. Michelle was the only sister with matching dimples in each cheek. Raine had been left out of the dimple market altogether.

"There is no scoop to get. And no, Michelle, you are not guessing," Nikki told them sternly.

"Oh yes I am. I say his name starts with a . . .." She hesitated and Nikki all but bounced on the edge of her seat.

Papers on her desk were crumbled beneath her fingers. "Stop it," she begged.

"Q," Michelle finished.

"Q?" Savannah looked quizzical. "What kind of name starts with a Q? Who would name their child something with a Q? Q like . . ." Then Savannah paused and looked at Michelle, who was smiling broadly, those dimples all but twinkling at her sister as she nodded in agreement.

"Oh. My. God! You did not sleep with my brother! Did you?" Savannah implored while Michelle's laughter exploded.

Nikki let her head fall into her palms and groaned.

Savannah had come all the way into the room by this point, resting her very narrow hip on the side of Nikki's already-scuffed desk. "You did! How could you, Nikki? He's like old as forever and he's my brother and . . . and . . . was it good?"

"Yes! That's what I want to know. Was it good?" Michelle echoed.

Nikki made a gurgling sound and lay her head back against her chair. "He's your brother, you shouldn't want to know these things," she finally replied.

Savannah waved a hand. "He's a man first, and besides I don't want to know details like how big or how long he lasted. I just want to know if you enjoyed it. Are you going to do it again?"

"Oh, yeah, when are you going to do it again?" Michelle chimed in.

"Stop. Stop. Please." She used the base of her hand to rub her eyes.

"Okay, seriously," Michelle said even though she was still laughing. "Now what?"

Nikki looked at her and replied as honestly as she knew how, because she'd sort of been asking herself the same thing all morning. "I don't know."

"He lives in Seattle," Savannah said like a splash of cold water.

"I know."

"He could move back here, start his own practice," Michelle said hopefully. "What better reason to stay then that he's in love with you?"

"Oh no," Nikki said shaking her head. "I did not mention love. Not at all."

"That doesn't mean you're not thinking it. And judging from the way you two were looking at each other yesterday . . ."

"It's not love," she adamantly confessed and meant it. Because the last thing Nikki could afford to do was give her heart and have it slammed back in her face another time. She wouldn't survive it again, she just knew it.

Chapter 15

Quinn had waited as long as he possibly could.

Hell, he'd even left the house for a couple of hours, visiting city hall and its newest mayor, whom it just so happened he'd met at a conference in Washington, DC, a little more than five years ago. Of course he'd been introduced to her as Liza Palamari, PhD, and she'd been giving a lecture on why it was important to have new legislation on stem cell research. On his first trip to city hall he'd recognized her in the mayoral portraits and made a note to visit with her personally. Today had seemed like as good a time as any.

Liza was married to Michael Fitzgerald, who instead of following in the family business had shown a talent for painting over any political ambitions. She was an attractive woman, tall and lean, with aristocratic features and a warm smile.

"So you want me to talk to the town council about back taxes owed on the inn?" she'd asked Quinn point-blank as he sat in her office explaining all he knew of the situation.

"Here's the thing, Liza, I don't think my grandmother would have not paid her taxes. From what my sister tells me, the bills are all paid up at the B and B, so why leave

the taxes unpaid? Besides that, fifty thousand seems like
a pretty steep amount for two years' worth of property
tax. The interest rate must be astronomical. I also understand that the Kings are looking to sell as much property
in town as they possibly can." He hadn't come right out
and said he thought something fishy was going on but he
could tell by the way Liza had nodded that she was following his line of thought.

"It does sound unlikely. I knew Mrs. Cantrell fairly
well and she didn't strike me as the type of person who
wouldn't pay her debts. Besides, like you said, the inn is
doing great business. I can look into it for you, find out if
there's any discrepancy."

"Apparently they've received a few notices," he added.

"And she didn't pay any of them or call to try to make
arrangements? Huh, that doesn't sound like Mrs. Cantrell,"
she'd said.

No, it didn't, and after leaving the mayor's office Quinn
was even more convinced that something wasn't quite
right about the way his grandmother had died or the status of the inn.

That had held his attention for about two hours, but the
desire to see Nikki, to touch her, was still as potent as ever.

If he closed his eyes and inhaled deep enough he could
still smell the lemon scent of her hair, taste the softness of
her skin, feel the heat of her embrace. She'd taken him to
a place Quinn didn't ever remember traveling before and
with a startling revelation he accepted that he wanted to
venture there again, and again.

She was working, he'd tried to tell himself. And yet his
feet were still trekking along the carpeted floors, going
through one doorway to another until he was right at her
office door. She was just hanging up the phone when he
stepped inside, closing the door behind him.

"Hi," she said, a tentative smile playing at her lips.

Quinn wasn't really in the mood for formalities so he

skirted the desk. Grasping her shoulders, he pulled her to a standing position and planted his lips firmly on hers. Her lips parted, their tongues reuniting, heat flashing immediately between them. His hands moved quickly down her back to cup his favorite part of her anatomy in his palms. She pressed into him, moaning softly. The kiss deepened, his body hardened, and he felt dizzy with desire. He was about to put her on the desk and have his way with her when the sound of voices reminded him they were in her office. The office that faced the side of the house where the entrance to The Silver Spoon was located—and it was pretty close to lunchtime.

Reluctantly and with more control than he'd ever realized he had, he pulled away. "Hi," he whispered, resting his forehead against hers.

"Hi again," she replied, clearing her throat. "You okay?"

He took a deep steadying breath. "I've been thinking about that all day," he told her.

"Good." Nikki laughed a bit as she spoke. "I didn't want to be the only one of us thinking that way."

Quinn did finally remove his hands and took a step back from her. She sat back in her chair, spinning around so that he had space to lean back on the desk.

It was his turn to clear his throat. "That's not all I was thinking about. I wanted to talk about business as well."

"Oh, really? Are there more questions I need to answer?" she asked him playfully.

"Actually, there are a couple of things," he said, folding his arms over his chest so he wouldn't be as tempted to touch her again. It probably wasn't going to work, but he needed the pretense.

"I went to see Mayor Fitzgerald today and we talked about the back taxes on the house," he began.

"You just went to see the mayor about this? Why not the town council; they're the ones who generate the bills?" she asked.

"I met the mayor before she was a mayor. Actually, before she was even married to Mike Fitzgerald. So I figured I'd just go and see what she knew."

"Oh," she said but still looked a little leery. Quinn couldn't figure that out and decided it was best just to keep going. "She agrees that it doesn't sound like Gramma not to pay the taxes. And Mr. Creed had no idea about them, either. I called him yesterday and he said all he knew about was in the will. The new deed to the house is ready for us to sign and there aren't any liens on it. So where is this tax debt coming from and why is it so high?"

She bit on her bottom lip, which was kind of cute since he could tell she was thinking about what he'd said. It was also a little bit sexy and had an erection brewing slowly. He swallowed deeply, trying to focus.

"All I know is the bill came two months before Mrs. Cantrell passed away. I showed it to Michelle first because Mrs. Cantrell had seemed a little preoccupied and we'd both agreed to take over as much responsibility around here as possible to give her some rest time."

"Do you still have the bill?" he asked her.

She nodded. "I do. I filed it over here." She stood and moved to a file cabinet right beside the door.

Of course Quinn watched her walk. He loved the sway of her hips, the sweet curve of her buttocks, and the way her feet tilted slightly outward as she moved. She reached into the cabinet and pulled out a folder. When she was standing close enough to him she handed Quinn the file.

The bill looked official, he thought as he surveyed the piece of paper. But the figures still seemed off to him. He'd paid property taxes in Seattle for the last few years, and even if he'd gone two years his debt would still be a fraction of what this was.

"You said you and Michelle had decided to take on most of the work around here. Just how much is Michelle actually doing? I mean, I know she runs the kitchen for the restaurant and the guests, but I was wondering about her catering assignments. Do you know anything about those?"

Nikki nodded. "I sure do," she told him, returning to the other side of her desk.

Quinn kept looking at the tax bill even though there was nothing new there for him to see. When he heard her shuffling things around on her desk he looked up.

She was sliding things from the center of her desk and pulled out a black appointment book that looked much like the one she'd just closed.

"I keep her schedule, too," she said. "Right now she has three off-site catering appointments for the month of June. That might pick up as we get farther into wedding season."

"She caters weddings as well?"

Nikki nodded. "Last year we had the Phillips and Crandon wedding. The bridal party stayed here. They married at Sweetland Presbyterian then came back here for the reception."

Sweetland had two churches, one Baptist and one Presbyterian. Which meant that unfortunately if someone was any other denomination, they had to travel up to Easton for fellowship experience. There were some aspects of this town that felt small and confining to Quinn. And then there were others, like the golf course and resort and the new restaurant he spied down by the pier that was about to open, that made him feel like they were steadily trying to come into the twenty-first century.

"Does she hire additional staff for that or does she use the staff from the restaurant?"

"Well, the interns usually help out because she actually pays them out of pocket for off-site catering events. Then we all just sort of pitch in. My sister Cordy gets a babysitter and she and I become servers. We work it out."

"Hmmm," Quinn said, rubbing a hand over his chin. That was working for now but he had a feeling that might be changing soon.

"You do this on your job, don't you?" she asked. "Supervise, I mean. I can see it comes really natural to you."

That was a part of his job at the clinic, supervising the doctors and other staff that worked under him, as well as organizing fund-raisers and soliciting research funds. The latter he apparently wasn't doing well enough.

"Yes, I do."

"Do you like supervising more than you like practicing medicine?"

"Why do you ask that?" Quinn didn't want to discuss his job but he couldn't tell if what she was asking was out of curiosity or if there was some other motive.

She shrugged. "You don't talk about your work much. I keep hearing everyone say that you're a doctor, but you don't talk about your patients or anything."

"For one, there's patient confidentiality," Quinn told her. "And for two, I don't like to bring work home with me." Which wasn't a total untruth. When he was back in Seattle he'd always have some reading to do pertaining to work, and on some occasions conference calls that couldn't be handled during his regular workweek, or meetings with potential donors. But when he'd packed up to come back to Sweetland, Quinn hadn't brought anything that pertained to work with him, not in his luggage and not in his mind. Until Elena's call this morning. He'd checked in with her out of habit, not necessarily out of any great concern for what was going on back there. Which should have been his first sign that the situation at the clinic had changed.

"Do you miss not being at work? Your grandmother said how devoted you were to your patients. Is it hard being here in Sweetland?"

She'd looked back down at the appointment book as she asked the last question, and Quinn wondered once again what information Nikki was really fishing for. Which was crazy. He had no reason not to trust her, no reason not to believe she was simply interested in his life.

That's why in the end he decided to answer her honestly. "It's not what it used to be. And that's all we're going to say about that. Come," he said, taking her hand and standing so he could pull her up out of her chair. "Have lunch with me, and then we can take Dixi out for a while."

"I still have some calls to make," she said even though she stood and fell naturally into his embrace, looking up at him with that smile he was becoming very familiar with.

"Take a break. I promise I won't keep you long. I want to go over and see Mr. Riley later this afternoon." Quinn was rubbing his hands up and down her back as he talked, loving the feel of her soft body against his, even if they were fully clothed. "We can get us a bowl of soup in the restaurant and then go down by the water with Dixi. I know how much you like it down there," he teased. The memory of her half naked and dripping wet rising from the river was one of his favorites.

"Well," she said, still hesitating and now blushing slightly. "I haven't seen Sweet Dixi today."

Quinn shook his head. "I don't know why you insist on calling that dog sweet. She's moody and demanding and—"

"All things men say about women," she cut in with a quick laugh.

"If you say so." He shrugged, not willing to take that comment any farther.

"Okay, let's go. But we have to make it quick."

There was definitely something else Quinn wanted to make quick with Nikki, but lunch was the smarter option.

Requesting a quick meal was pointless. It was almost three thirty by the time Nikki had finished having lunch with Quinn, since just as they'd finished Louisa and Marabelle had joined them.

"They're coming over," Nikki had whispered. Tanya had just taken away their empty bowls and refilled their glasses of lemonade.

"Then we'll just be polite," he'd said with a smile already in place.

"Aren't you a good-looking couple," Marabelle said with a jovial look on her face.

In Nikki's mind she was the nicer of the two ladies. Always quick to laugh and quicker to compliment than Louisa ever was. Most times she seemed to fall behind Louisa's shadow and followed the other woman without a qualm.

"Hello, Mrs. Stanley, Mrs. Kirk." Nikki was always polite to them, never wanting to give either woman cause to talk about her even though she knew most people didn't give them cause, but that still hadn't stopped them.

"You taking a break from work?" was Louisa's stiff question, which seemed more like an accusation.

"We decided to enjoy the soup with the rest of the customers today," Quinn said.

They'd taken a seat on the outside deck, which faced the water. An overhead canopy protected them from the sun, but it still was a warm afternoon. Marabelle wore a yellow dress with capped sleeves and the biggest, brightest turquoise flowers Nikki had ever seen on printed material. Coupled with her light complexion, she looked like she, too, could be a ray of sunshine. Louisa's dress was a little more understated, a pale green color with much smaller multicolored flowers all over. Both ladies wore large-brimmed hats and carried their white gloves in one hand while pillbox purses hung on the opposite wrist. Like most of Sweetland, they were stuck in their own little time warp, resisting change as much as they possibly could.

"The soup was fabulous as usual. Your sister is a master in the kitchen," Marabelle said.

"I'll be sure to tell her that, Mrs. Kirk. She works really hard at doing a good job," Quinn offered.

"Hmph, more restaurants opening up here than we need," Louisa chirped. "Heard you had a run-in with the law yesterday. They think you killed somebody," Louisa finished with what was supposed to be a whisper.

Nikki's smile faltered. She couldn't help it. Of course she'd known word would get around town sooner rather than later, but she hadn't been prepared to face the gossip head-on. After a momentary lapse she squared her shoulders and said, "My lawyer is straightening all that out."

Louisa nodded, her multicolored stud earrings catching rays of sunlight. "Your lawyer? Oh yeah, saw your brother heading into the police station when we were on our way over here," she said, nodding at Quinn. "Guess he's trying to clear her name while you wine and dine her. Cantrell boys are certainly at it again."

"Nikki's innocent and Preston's just making sure the police know that," Quinn told them, keeping his smile in place.

"But I'm fine, Mrs. Kirk, thanks for asking. I wasn't worried about being carted off to jail or anything," Nikki heard herself saying. She kept her gaze focused on the great Louisa Kirk with her beady and assessing brown eyes and overly made-up face. The woman was a witch, dressed like a 1960s matron. She thrived on cutting down anyone she chose for no other reason than that she could, and Nikki was sick of her. Even her own husband didn't like the woman. The husband who rarely ever left their little house down by the river.

"Don't get snippy with me," was Louisa's retort. "I thought Odell had raised you better. Then again, you've always had your head buried in the sand except when Savannah was around. That one you followed around like a lost puppy." She again gestured toward Quinn. "Guess she's following a different Cantrell around these days."

"Good afternoon, Mrs. Stanley, Mrs. Kirk, I know you ladies aren't leaving without trying my apple turnovers," Michelle said as she walked up to the table, touching a hand to Nikki's shoulders.

For a second Nikki felt embarrassed. Here she was the manager of this establishment and she was getting into a petty argument with the town gossips whom most people simply chose to ignore. What happened to Miss Personality? She'd taken a lunch break, Nikki thought dismally. But she wouldn't apologize for her comment; Louisa deserved it and then some. Unfortunately, her mother would probably have a headache by the time Nikki arrived home this evening: She knew without a shadow of a doubt that at the very soonest opportunity Louisa could find, she'd be telling Odell how rude her youngest daughter was.

"Oh, I love apple turnovers. Godfrey's sells them in these cute little wrappers. Don't tell Sam, but I have a couple stashed in the bread box for special occasions," Marabelle said with a quick laugh that shook her entire body and every one of those bright turquoise flowers on her dress.

Sam was her husband of about fifty or so years now. Like Louisa's husband, Granger, he barely left their house anymore. Nikki wondered if either man was still alive.

"But mine are fresh, just baked this morning." Michelle teased the woman with a brilliant smile. "The kitchen smells absolutely heavenly with the scent of cooked apples. I can have Tanya bring you out a couple with a glass of iced tea." The last was said in a sweet voice but was the equivalent of wagging a bone in front of a dog.

Marabelle's eyes bulged, her lips smacking as she probably imagined the taste. "Oh, that sounds lovely. We'll just head back to our table," she told Michelle. Then she touched Louisa's arm. "Come on, Louisa, let's have dessert."

"You don't need any more dessert, Marabelle," Louisa said, her glare still on Nikki. "But I guess other people do have to get back to work. Wonder how the customers will feel staying in a place run by an accused murderer," she said as her parting shot.

Before Nikki could say another word Quinn had reached across the table to take her hand, the one she hadn't even realized had been shaking.

"That's right, have a seat and I'll send Tanya right over," Michelle told the two old biddies and watched them walk away.

"Count to ten," she said out of the corner of her mouth to Nikki. Michelle kept looking in the direction of the town gossips, a smile plastered on her face just in case any customers were enjoying this exchange.

Nikki tried to scrounge up her own smile but when she couldn't she picked up her glass to take a drink. Unfortunately she'd drank all the lemonade and the cubes of ice just fell against her lips. With a heavy sigh she put the glass down.

"She's just doing what she always does," Quinn was saying.

"Yeah, but today she was vicious," Michelle said. "I overheard her comment as I was coming over to see you guys. That's why I stepped in. I didn't want Nikki to get up and slap her." Michelle chuckled.

"I wouldn't have struck her," Nikki said even though she wasn't 100 percent sure of that claim. "She just caught me off guard. I knew everybody would be talking about it today, but I didn't expect her to come right up to me and say something."

Quinn shook his head. "They don't have anything better to do."

"You're right," she agreed with another sigh, sitting back in the chair. "But what if she's right about the customers? Maybe I should take some time off. The last thing we need right now is bad publicity. We're already at a loss with Mrs. Cantrell and her natural hospitality gone."

Michelle shook her head. "We'll be fine. People know rumors when they hear them. As long as you're here every day smiling and giving them the same service we're known for, there won't be a problem."

"I agree. We should continue on as if none of this happened. Don't give them any reason to think you're guilty, especially since you're not," Quinn added.

"I guess you're right," Nikki said again. But she didn't feel better. Not by a long shot.

"Hey, I hear someone calling for you," Quinn said, still holding her hand.

"What? Who?"

"Sweet Dixi." He gave her a huge grin that she knew was sarcastic since Dixi was still making his stay here difficult.

A part of Nikki wished she could take the puppy and keep it as her own, but a small apartment over a garage was no home for a Lab. Of course she had all the love an owner could give a dog of that nature, but right now she just didn't have the space.

"Yeah, I think I hear her, too," she said, figuring if anything could cheer her up after that confrontation it would be Sweet Dixi.

Sweet Dixi was more than happy to see Nikki, Quinn noted. The dog had taken to her, he suspected, since the day it was born. Watching the two of them together in the backyard of the house was more than amusing. She held the dog in her lap, rubbed her stomach, and scratched behind her ears, all things Dixi absolutely loved. Then when she put her down Nikki laughed along with Dixi as she ran and stopped, ran and stopped, any and everything grabbing her attention.

For a moment the scene seemed like déjà vu to Quinn. A big beautiful yard, lush green grass, beaming sunlight and blue waters, the female and the puppy, the family. Slipping his hands into his pockets, he blinked to clear his mind, but the scene stayed the same. Only the female changed.

Short curly hair was replaced by long straight black hair with blunt-cut bangs in front. The cute little mouth had changed to full lush lips, a brilliant smile, and deep-toned laughter. Instead of capris and a summer blouse, she wore black slacks and a teal tank top, matching teal sandals at her feet, big gold hoop earrings in her ears. When she turned to Quinn and said his name, it was in a husky timbre he remembered whispering in his ear while he kissed her neck, laughing as he tickled her feet and they rolled together in the grass one summer's evening.

It was so intense, the stark clarity of this moment. She was right there; all he had to do was reach out and he would touch her. His fingers would skate lightly over her jawline, touching the smoothness of her mocha-colored skin. Hazel eyes would stare at him adoringly. She'd reach up a hand and tuck the long strands of hair behind her ear, then she'd reach out and touch him, pull his face down to hers.

His lips would touch hers, sweetly at first, then longingly, and the kiss would go on forever and ever, just like their love.

"You keep treating me to afternoons like this and I'll never get any work done," Nikki whispered when he'd finally pulled his mouth away from hers.

Quinn struggled to open his eyes, and when he did he felt like crap. No, he felt worse than crap, if that were possible. Nikki's brown eyes stared back up at him, twinkling with satisfaction. Her small lips were red from the kiss. Her skin was like heavily creamed coffee. It wasn't dark. And her hair . . . absently he lifted a hand to touch the springy curls that caught rays of the sun and looked more golden brown than black.

"Hey, you okay?" she asked, lifting a hand to touch his cheek.

No. I'm an ass, he wanted to say but didn't. "I'm good. Just got a little sidetracked."

"Oh, did I sidetrack you, Dr. Cantrell?" she asked playfully.

He mustered a smile because she was pretty and attractive, and smart and honest, and everything good there was in the world was found in her. And yet she was different. Too different from the woman he'd loved with all his heart, too different from Sharane.

"No, actually I was thinking about Mr. Riley again."

"Oh, right. You said you wanted to go see him. Why don't you go ahead and call me later with an update."

Because she would want to know how he was doing. Bill Riley lived in this town with her, she knew his wife and most likely his children, and as he'd seen her do with people in the restaurant or people she saw on the streets, she simply took an interest in everyone. Her heart was too big not to. Another thing for Quinn to admire about Nikki.

"I'll stop by your place when I'm finished and we can go out to dinner," he said when he knew he shouldn't have. He should come back home alone, go to his room, and think about what the hell he was doing in this town and with this woman. This was not the life he wanted for himself, not the dream he'd dreamed because Sharane was dead.

"Are you asking me out on a date?" she asked playfully, the rays of the sun dancing merrily off her hair.

Quinn shook his head, dropping his hands from her because everything he was doing felt like a betrayal. "Or if you'd rather just eat in, I can bring something over," he said, because try as he might he just couldn't walk away.

"Too late, you said we could go out. Amore has great manicotti. I can make us a reservation."

And she would, Quinn thought. She'd go right back into the hotel and make all the arrangements for a lovely date, one that would be full of romance and promise. "It's okay, I'll take care of everything," he told her.

When he'd walked away it was with a heaviness on his

shoulders that seemed magnified. She was excited about their date—and why shouldn't she be? Women loved dates, they loved romance, they loved . . . period. With that in mind Quinn knew with absolute certainty that when Nikki loved she'd love with her whole heart, her entire being. That thought frightened him. As mighty as she often accused him of being, Quinn would be first to admit—to himself, that is—that this seemingly innocent nymph of a female had him scared. He was afraid of what might be developing between them and how she'd react when she found out he couldn't be what she wanted.

Chapter 16

This was it, their first official date. For the first few moments after Quinn had walked her into Amore, Nikki had felt like she was walking into her senior prom, with the captain of the football team on her arm. Except she'd gone to her prom with her cousin, stayed an hour and a half, and left immediately after Savannah and her date—the actual captain of the football team—headed out to that motel they'd often frequented just outside of Sweetland.

And just like at prom, the minute they walked into Salvatore Gionelli's restaurant, every person who'd been seated at one of the small booths had turned to look at them. Her heart hammered in her chest as she caught Carl Farraway's gaze. He was with a female whom Nikki didn't recognize, which meant she probably wasn't from Sweetland. Seeing him immediately recalled the questioning in her parents' house last night and Louisa's rude remarks about the same earlier today. Carl waved, and she found herself lifting a shaky hand and giving him a stilted smile in return.

"Would you all like a booth?" the hostess standing behind a shiny black podium asked.

Nikki welcomed the interruption and moved with Quinn as he stood in front of the woman to reply.

"Sure," he said, which totaled three sentences from him since she'd returned to the inn for their date.

She'd gone home around four thirty to get ready and texted him that she'd be back at six. To her surprise, he hadn't allowed her to drive them down to the dock to the restaurant. Instead, he'd borrowed Preston's car. So it was a real date, she thought. A real, honest-to-goodness date with the Mighty Quinn Cantrell. Sure, the realization was dulled slightly by the fact that she'd already slept with the Mighty Quinn, but only slightly.

Nikki had been to Amore a handful of times since it opened about two years ago. All of those times had been with Cordy and the kids or her entire family for some celebratory event or another. So she was already acclimated to the dim lighting and the little ivory votive candles on a table covered with a red-and-white-checked picnic cloth. White napkins were carefully folded, silverware shined until it almost sparkled were both on the table as well. In the far left corner, past the door and the little alcove where the bathrooms were cleverly hidden, was a huge black piano that was being played by a young gentleman who might also be new to town.

"This is a nice establishment," Quinn said, picking up the menu in front of him and opening it.

And that was sentence number four. There was something definitely wrong with him tonight. She wondered if it had to do with his job, the one he never talked about. For some reason Nikki got the impression that wasn't a happy situation. She'd thought about asking him what was going on, but had refrained. If Quinn wanted to open up and share his life with her, he would. She hoped.

She didn't even want to think it may be something else bothering him, something or someone else.

Shaking her head, she opened her menu and said, "Mr. Sal's been here for about two years now. My dad says he moved here after a pretty messy divorce. She got the house and the cats, he got the restaurant name because that's all he cared about, and he came down here for some peace and quiet."

"So Sweetland's a refuge now," he murmured. "I can see that."

"I guess for some it could be. For me, it's just home."

"And you'd never leave home, would you?"

She looked up at him because the question was a shock. From the look on his face, it was to him as well. Did Quinn want her to go back to Seattle with him? Would she if he did? Mentally she shook those questions off, swearing she was getting ahead of herself. Instead she put her menu down and folded her hands on the table.

"I was born here. I love it here. So far there's been no reason to leave." *But you could give me one, please give me one,* she almost finished.

"I think Michelle feels the same way," was his follow-up, and Nikki had to really focus on not letting her disappointment show.

It was totally ridiculous, she knew. How many times had she warned herself about this very thing? And hadn't she just told Michelle and Savannah that this thing between her and Quinn wasn't about love? Well, she'd lied. Big time.

That's right, steer the conversation away from anything having to do with the two of them. Why? Because it was the only defense Quinn had left. Denial had always worked for him. Or had it?

Nikki looked great tonight. That's the first thing he'd noticed when she walked into the living room where he'd just finished with his call to Seattle. If he hadn't been

tempted to cancel the date a dozen times throughout the
rest of the afternoon, after that call he'd definitely been
ready to spend the evening alone with his thoughts. But
she'd walked in wearing a soft yellow sundress that hugged
her breasts like a glove, offering a very alluring peek at
the bounty beneath the material. The material wrapped
around her torso and waist to swing outward in a flirty
motion as she moved from the hips down. Her hair was
curly again—the way he liked it, Quinn decided right
there on the spot—a pretty yellow flower tucked in its
rich depths just above her left ear. Whimsical star and
moon earrings dangled from her ears to touch her neck,
and bracelets jingled on her wrists as she'd crossed the
room to stand in front of him.

She'd looked up at him expectantly and he'd obliged,
leaning forward to kiss her waiting lips. He didn't have
any other choice.

Now they were in this restaurant that was about five
seconds short of serenading them with a bounty of romance to start their evening off. He'd tried to focus on the
fact that he was truly hungry and he could just think of
this as a shared meal. But each time he'd looked into
Nikki's eyes, he knew that was a lie. Just like everything
he was doing.

The waiter arrived to Quinn's relief and took their orders quickly and efficiently because almost twenty minutes later their food, and the bottle of wine he'd ordered
to go along with it, had arrived.

They ate in silence but for a few comments about the
taste of the food. Nikki really loved their manicotti while
Quinn was having a hard time enjoying his penne vodka
even though it was very tasty.

"Fancy meeting you here," Hoover King said, stepping
up to stand right in front of their booth.

Quinn hadn't seen him since the night he'd pulled the

man off Nikki in the kitchen. He looked remarkably better this time around. The tall woman wearing a lovely scowl right beside him might be the cause of that.

"I'd heard you two were an item, but I didn't believe it," the woman said snidely.

"Hello, Hoover, Inez, it's nice to see you here," Nikki said.

Her smile was brilliant, the calm soothing tone of her voice professional, practiced, and perfected.

"Hello, I'm Quinn Cantrell," Quinn said, extending his hand to Inez because while Hoover had been just getting started on his town drunk reputation when Quinn had left, Inez had not been on his radar at all.

Michelle had told him that Inez was actually a third cousin to the Fitzgeralds, which would explain the air of superiority that circled her even though her husband could barely stay sober for a twenty-four-hour stint.

She accepted his hand, albeit reluctantly.

"Inez King. It's convenient that we're meeting with you here. I spoke to Mr. Creed earlier today and he informed me that you and your siblings now own The Silver Spoon and the property it's located on."

Quinn nodded, keeping eye contact with Inez, but very aware of the way Hoover was glancing at Nikki.

"We do," he answered, feeling really skeptical about where this conversation was going.

"For now," Hoover attempted to whisper, but Quinn heard him clearly.

"The inn is doing wonderfully," Nikki put in. "Michelle's garnering rave reviews with the restaurant and we're booking steadily."

Quinn got the impression that Nikki knew something he didn't.

"And yet you still owe on the taxes," Inez stated, touching her bright red-painted nails to the edge of the table. "We've been very lenient in that department. But now that ownership is changing hands we'll have to request immediate payment."

"That's not the information I received from my meeting with the mayor," Quinn said. He wasn't comfortable having this discussion in this setting where anyone could overhear. Obviously the town council of Sweetland didn't have those same reservations.

"Payment is due immediately," Hoover added emphatically, then coughed a wheezing sound that most likely indicated his liquor consumption tank was on empty.

On a better day, under different circumstances, Quinn might have offered to buy him a drink—probably non-alcoholic—or to offer his assistance in some way. Not tonight.

"Or we'll foreclose and sell that property faster than your brother rides that bike of his," Hoover finished, his eyes now watering after the coughing exertion.

Nikki looked alarmed. "You cannot sell The Silver Spoon. Mrs. Cantrell was a member of one of the founding families. She was a matriarch in this town. How can you even stand there and threaten something like that?"

"Because we're the town council. We do what's in the best interest of Sweetland. If Mrs. Cantrell, the good matriarch, didn't have the foresight to pay her bills before she croaked—"

"That's enough," Quinn interjected sternly.

"I'm not finished," Inez started again.

"Oh yes you are," Quinn told her with a tone that he knew would get no argument.

Inez's lips snapped shut and Hoover stood mutely beside her.

"The tax bill will be paid," he stated firmly. "Now, if you'll excuse us, we were having dinner."

"Wanted her all to yourself, huh?" Hoover said eyeing Quinn.

"Don't," Quinn warned him with a glare and a shake

of his head. The way he was feeling at this moment he couldn't promise he wouldn't punch the man in his sweat-riddled face.

"Is there a problem?" A tall man wearing a black suit arrived to ask. Over his shoulder Quinn could see their waiter peeking as if he wanted to help but was afraid to.

"Mr. Sal," Nikki said with what sounded like a sigh of relief. "Everything is fine."

"Everything is not fine," Quinn stated. "These two are interrupting our dinner."

"We are the town council," Inez repeated, as if that meant something to Quinn.

It did not. And he was beyond pissed off that these two walked around like they alone were the law in this town. If this was how things were going in Sweetland . . . no, he didn't dare finish that thought.

"You are interrupting," Quinn insisted.

"Let's just go," Nikki said, dropping her napkin onto her plate.

"No, you are not finished with your meal," Sal insisted.

But Nikki was already standing, which said she was ready to go. Quinn's head throbbed as he once again felt like he should have canceled this date this afternoon. Reaching into his pocket, he pulled out his wallet and gave the waiter his credit card.

"This is not finished," Inez said with a scowl.

"For me it is," Quinn told her as he stood face-to-face with what he thought might be one of the meanest women he'd ever known.

For all that Marabelle and Louisa could be totally vicious in their gossiping, they were generally harmless. This woman, Quinn decided in the seconds he stared back at her, was not. For that he felt supremely sorry for Hoover, who had just plopped his big body down in the seat Quinn had vacated and was presently drinking the remainder of the wine he'd left in his glass.

There was silence, once again, as they walked along the pier. Not complete silence thanks to the soft rustle of the water just a few feet below and the click of her heels on the wooden planks as they moved closer to where he'd parked the car.

"They want to sell the land. It's all about money to them," she said more to herself than to Quinn actually. She hadn't expected him to reply, didn't really know that she wanted him to.

The scene with the Kings had rocked her just a little harder than the one she'd had earlier today with Louisa. What was going on with the people in Sweetland? They all seemed to be losing their minds.

"My grandmother's work will not be in vain," he said solemnly then suddenly stopped walking and reached for her hand. "I want to thank you for your loyalty and your dedication to the inn. I assure you that we'll take care of the taxes. Your job will remain intact."

She wanted to pull her hand away from his because she didn't like his tone, or the stilted look in his eyes when he stared down at her. There was a light breeze, so her dress danced around her legs, and the scent of his cologne was lifted wafting in her face in quiet enticement.

"This isn't about a job for me. Mrs. Cantrell was like my family. That inn means as much to me as it does to you and your siblings. Possibly more," she couldn't resist adding.

"What's that supposed to mean?" he questioned immediately.

Nikki hadn't wanted to say this. Actually, she'd hoped to keep her professional and personal feelings separate in this matter. But she should have known that wasn't going to work.

"All of you walked away. You left her here and moved on with your lives. Now, I'm not saying you weren't entitled to your own lives, because I think everyone should make their own decisions, walk their own paths. But none of you ever looked back. All she wanted was for you to love the inn, the legacy as much as she did, but you couldn't." She shrugged because now that she'd said all that she didn't know what she wanted him to do with the information.

"I guess what I'm saying is that it's time for all of you to step up and do what's right."

"And what's right, Nikki? Should all of us pack up and move back here? Should we all walk away from the lives we've built to come back to a town that never gave us anything but grief?"

"Grief isn't in one place, Quinn. It follows you wherever you take it," she told him honestly. She'd thought about this earlier and had hurriedly pushed the subject out of her mind. Denial, she figured. Or maybe it was just hope.

"What if we don't belong here?"

"What if you do?" was her counteroffer.

What did she know, Nikki questioned herself. She'd never been anywhere, never branched out from Sweetland or her family. Well, when she'd done so it hadn't been successful. What if this place had been her safety net all along? Could she really stand here and tell Quinn she thought he and his siblings should come back?

"Look, Quinn, I don't have all the answers. I wasn't the smartest or the prettiest girl in high school, and it took me a little longer than others to find my way. But I did that once I decided to follow my heart. Your grandmother taught me that."

He kept walking, kept looking out toward the water. He was distant and he was confusing. Hot and desirable one minute, brooding and borderline angry the next, and she should walk away right now. She should turn around and go back to her apartment, back to the safest place she knew, the place where she loved and that love was reciprocated without question.

But she didn't.

Instead, Nikki reached for his hand. She twined her fingers in his and let the bare skin of her arm rub along his.

"Follow your heart," she said again, quietly letting the words hang in the air a few seconds before they continued to walk.

Chapter 17

Two days later Nikki found herself following her tired feet and growling stomach into her apartment after a long day at the inn. A Fortune 500 company headquartered in Virginia had decided it would be nice to host their company picnic in Sweetland. They'd booked a year ago through a travel agent who had completely sold them on a new upscale resort that would cater to their request for a small-town picnic for two hundred guests. Only that upscale resort had fallen into financial difficulties and as yet still had not been completed. It would have been nice for the travel agent to tell her client this well before today. Better yet, it would have been even lovelier if said travel agent had called The Silver Spoon before yesterday morning.

They weren't prepared for something this big, weren't sure they could pull it all together in time. But after a powwow with Michelle and Raine, who had walked in on the meeting, the three of them had decided that with the tax bill looming they couldn't say no. So Nikki had called the agent back, assured her that they would have a lovely picnic awaiting her clients the next day at eleven thirty, and set out to do exactly that.

"We've got a situation so I called you all here to tell

you that it's all hands on deck," Michelle had said as they sat in the kitchen.

For some reason this seemed to be the gathering place in the house for the family. And as of late, Nikki found herself right there with the six of them.

"What's going on?" Preston asked.

Michelle explained about the event while Savannah hissed and rolled her eyes.

"You can't possibly get all that done in one day," Savannah quipped. "No matter how perfect you think you are."

"You're right," Quinn put in to everyone's chagrin.

Nikki had looked at him with shock. Their date had been the night before last and since then he'd been nice to her, cordial and even mildly affectionate, but there had been distance. She'd tried not to think too much on it because it wasn't wise to dwell on things she couldn't change. But she had to admit she was itching to say some choice words to him at this moment.

Then he held up a hand to stop what was most likely going to be Michelle's heated response. "Michelle can't get all this together in one day. But *we* can."

"He's right," Parker added.

"We're planning a party," Raine said with a squee.

And as the plans had begun to take shape, Michelle at the helm passing out orders, Raine taking notes, Quinn had caught Nikki's gaze. As it was with him, Nikki couldn't look away. When he smiled, she smiled back. Then she'd pulled out her own address book and started making calls.

The picnic had gone as smoothly as if they'd planned it for an entire year. If you didn't count the tent collapsing twice as Parker, Quinn, and Preston tried to set it up; the puppies running wildly throughout the house since they couldn't go out in the yard; Savannah dropping two trays of finger sandwiches on the floor, subsequently feeding the already-hyper puppies; and Michelle spending the day flip-flopping between evil dictator and cordial host.

Of the last twelve hours Nikki would have to admit the highlight for her was when Quinn had found her sitting on the rocks by the water, about twenty minutes after they'd finally finished the cleanup.

"Hey," he'd said stepping lightly over the rocks before sitting on one right beside her.

"Hey," she'd replied without even opening her eyes. She'd been resting her head on her arms, which were folded over her knees. There was no breeze today, just the stiff humidity of mid-May in Maryland. But it was quiet and it was still, so she'd sat here and almost drifted off to sleep.

"I owe you an apology."

Now, that had her eyes opening. "You do?"

He smiled. His black polo shirt was sprinkled with all types of things from the day's work, his khaki shorts wrinkled. He'd sweat so much and wiped his face so much there were red marks on his forehead from the towel he kept stuffed in his back pocket. And yet he was still gorgeous.

She swallowed that thought and waited for this apology he thought he owed her.

"I was a little rude the other night. I had some things going on and I took it out on you. That was wrong of me and I apologize."

Clean-cut and to the point; she could live with that.

"Apology accepted."

"Just like that?" he asked, one brow raised in confusion.

It was a cute look, Quinn Cantrell confused. She couldn't resist reaching out to tap his cheek with her palm. "I'm too tired to come up with anything else," she told him with a weak chuckle.

He laughed and the tension that had lay between them the past two days dissolved.

"Come on, I'll drive you home," he said, standing and reaching for her hands to help her up.

She was shaking her head as she stood. "I drove in this

morning because I had a ton of flowers from Drew's shop to bring over."

"Then I tell you what, you go on home, get a hot bath and relax. I'll grab a shower and Dixi and we'll bring you dinner. How does pizza sound?"

He'd been rubbing her shoulders as he talked and Nikki had rested her head against his chest because she was almost too tired to hold herself upright a moment longer.

"With extra cheese, pepperoni and ham, and a glass of wine? That sounds heavenly." She sighed.

"You got it," Quinn said before kissing the top of her head. If she weren't in an almost-debilitated state she would have thought that was a chaste action. Instead she allowed him to walk her to her car and even snap her into the seat belt.

It was then that he'd leaned in, touched his lips lightly to hers. "I'm really sorry. You said some really smart things, some things I needed to hear. So thanks for that."

"You're very welcome," she said, suddenly feeling a little less tired.

He stared at her a moment, and heat spread quickly throughout her body. Then he kissed her. She'd expected and welcomed it. The soft touch of his lips on hers, the gentle brush of their tongues in reunion, then the deep hunger that punched like a prizefighter deep in her gut were graciously welcomed. His hand gripped the back of her neck, pulling her upward as he continued to take, to devour, to mesmerize her completely.

She was still dazed when he pulled away. "I'll be there in a couple of hours," he whispered.

"I'll be there, too," was her bewildered reply, which garnered another one of his smiles.

When Nikki arrived home it was to a FedEx box sitting in her doorway. She picked it up and let herself inside. Placing the box on the table, she headed straight to the shower.

After taking much longer than usual to select an outfit and arguing with herself about the necessity for makeup—especially since she rarely wore the stuff—Nikki slipped into comfortable white shorts and a peach tank top. She hummed as she walked through her place, picking up this and straightening that. It wasn't until about an hour after she'd come in and placed the box on her table that she noticed it was still there.

Checking the time, she figured Quinn would be arriving soon but reached into the drawer where she tended to throw everything that didn't have a definite space in her tiny house. Grabbing the scissors, she cut the taped portions of the box and opened it. The gasp came quick, one hand flying to her mouth to stifle a full-on scream.

It was filled with money, stacks and stacks of money. Only because her brain swore her eyes were playing a cruel trick on her did she reach into the box and pick up one thick stack of bills. Rubbing her finger over the crisp one-hundred-dollar bill, she could do nothing but sigh. A few startled moments later she saw the envelope that had been on top of the bills, the one with her name written in blue ink. Her heart hammered in her chest as she placed the stack of bills back into its slot in the box and picked up the envelope. She used her finger to slip through the seal and open it, all the while thinking, praying this wasn't from who she thought it was. The moment she unfolded the letter and began to read, dread filled her like water seeping into a bucket.

Nikki,
You would not listen when I called. I will be in Sweetland soon to pick up this box and to see you. I hope things will work out for both of us.
Yours,
Randall

Why? Why couldn't this man leave her alone? Wasn't it enough that he'd made a fool out of her? Obviously not; now he had to taunt her, even in death. That's right, Randall was dead. And the police thought she had something to do with his death. And now she'd received this.

She hurriedly closed the box. The flaps, having already been opened, immediately flipped open again. She pressed her hand down on top of the box to keep it closed, then figured how idiotic that seemed. Acting purely on instinct, she turned and was immediately facing her small refrigerator. Reaching inside she pulled out the first thing she saw, a pack of defrosted chicken wings she'd originally planned for her dinner tonight. She put the chicken on the top of the box and sighed when it stayed closed. But she didn't know what to do with the letter. The thought of burning it crossed her mind briefly, but then there came a knock at her door. Nikki jumped, dropping the letter on the floor. Her scream wasn't loud, but it was loud enough that the knock came even quicker on the door and only a second later he was calling out to her.

"Nikki? You in there? Open the door," Quinn yelled.

Bending quickly, she scooped up the letter and envelope and headed for the door. She'd tucked one hand behind her back—the hand with the letter—and used the other hand to open the door.

"Hey," she said trying desperately to sound normal.

His frown was instant. "Hey," he replied. Stepping into her apartment, he immediately reached for her hand. "You okay? I thought I heard you scream."

"Um, I'm fine," she told him and felt her lips shake with a smile. She was so not fine it was unbelievable.

"Ed Toriana's gonna send his son Vinny over with the pizza in about twenty minutes. I'm thinking I might need to go up to Easton this weekend and rent a car. I'm not really used to walking all around Sweetland anymore," he told her after he'd closed the door and began walking them both toward the couch.

Nikki kept her hand behind her back, walking along with him, swallowing deeply so that the next time she spoke her voice hopefully wouldn't crack. She didn't know if she should tell him about this or just keep it to herself. Nobody knew about the delivery but her and the FedEx guy who dropped it off. But FedEx kept a paper trail, she thought dismally. That box could be traced if somebody wanted to trace it. But why would they? Nobody knew about this money, right? Her temples throbbed with questions, her heart almost jackhammering right out of her chest as she sat on the couch next to Quinn.

"I'm going to give you one more minute to sit there like nothing's going on. Then I want you to tell me what the problem is," Quinn said, sitting with his elbows on his knees, his face turned to her.

"What?" she asked, only vaguely aware that he was still here and talking to her, or rather expecting her to say something to him.

"What's going on, Nikki?" he implored, his voice softer, his hand reaching out to touch hers.

She couldn't help it, didn't know what else to do. So Nikki pulled the envelope from behind her back and thrust it at him. "It was here when I got home," she said.

Quinn took the letter, opened it, read it quietly. With a serious expression he looked back at her. "Where?"

She nodded. "On the table."

Nikki didn't move, but watched him as he went into the kitchen, picked up the pack of chicken, staring at it quizzically for a minute before putting it on the table and pushing back the flaps of the box. He didn't say a word, just reached into his pocket for his cell phone.

"Yeah, it's me. I need you to get over to Nikki's place and bring Preston with you."

When he disconnected, Quinn came back into the

living room and sat down. This time he pulled her onto his lap, holding her as if she were a child. Nikki couldn't help it, she let her head rest on his shoulder.

"This is not your fault. He was a nutcase and you couldn't have predicted that."

"But it doesn't look good. It looks like I was involved with whatever he was doing that got him killed."

"Circumstantial," Quinn told her. "Try not to worry. We're going to fix this."

"How?" she asked in a voice that sounded so small, so vulnerable, so weak. Nikki hated it. She absolutely hated that Randall still had this power over her even from the grave.

"You are innocent," Quinn stated firmly. "That's the bottom line."

"Right," she whispered with a slight nod of her head. "I'm innocent." The words didn't necessarily convince her.

But there was a box of money sitting on her kitchen table that came from a dead man, a pack of chicken that would probably go bad before she got a chance to cook it, and the pizza delivery guy at her door.

Nikki wasn't sure what she felt right at this moment, but innocent wasn't at the top of the list.

Deputy Jonah Lincoln pulled up in front of the Brockington house for the second time this week. Carl, the only other deputy in the town and the son of Sheriff Kyle Farraway, was out on a date. And Jonah was about to turn puke green with envy.

Okay, maybe it wasn't that bad. So Jonah hadn't been on a date in about four months; there weren't that many available females in Sweetland. Most of the women were over thirty-five and either married or shacked up with longtime boyfriends. As a native of the town Jonah knew that if he hadn't snagged one by his thirtieth birthday, the prospects began to go downhill. But he already had a prospect and as he walked up the walkway and around to the back of the house his heartbeat sped up just a bit. He was about to see her again. Maybe this time he'd have the nerve to ask her out. Maybe not since he was kind of here in an official capacity, investigating that murder in Easton and making sure Nikki—his prospect—wasn't really a suspect.

As he took the steps he wondered what he was going to find out. The call had come from Preston Cantrell, Nikki's attorney, who seemed like a nice enough guy. When he'd pulled up he'd seen the motorcycle he'd heard Parker Cantrell driving through town in the last few days. It was likely the other one, Quinn, was in there, too. Even though Jonah was the cop and the one with the gun, these three guys intimidated him a little. He'd worked for years on defeating his shyness; going to the police academy in Easton had helped with that a lot. Still, standing up next to these three was almost as bad as trying to arrest Hoover King for drinking too much and being a public nuisance by urinating in Vera Moog's rosebushes.

The door swung open before Jonah could lift his hand to knock.

"Good evening, Deputy," Preston—or at least he thought this one was Preston since he was dressed kind of business-like in slacks and a dress shirt—said with a grim look on his face.

"Evening," Jonah replied before entering the apartment.

He saw Nikki first. He could always find her; even in a crowd, she stood out to him. Her pretty brown eyes were red-rimmed, which made him feel like crap. Then she stood from the couch she'd been sitting on and Quinn Cantrell stood with her, dropping a protective arm over her shoulders. That action officially made Jonah feel like whatever was lower than crap.

"Hi, Jonah," Nikki said, her voice a little shaky.

The other twin, Parker, who was wearing jeans and a

KISS T-shirt, was standing near the kitchen table, his arms folded over his chest. This was the cop, a big-city cop he would add for clarification. Everything about him said confrontation, in your face, loud and with authority, even without a gun holstered to his side. Still, Jonah was willing to bet his biweekly salary the guy had a gun on him somewhere.

"Thanks for coming so soon," Preston began from behind him.

Quinn had only given him a polite nod, to which Jonah had replied in kind. No need to be rude to the man with his arm around the only woman Jonah thought he could ever love.

To keep his mind on the business at hand, Jonah turned back to Preston and watched as he moved to stand near the table with his brother.

"No problem. What's going on?"

Parker nodded toward the table, where there was an open box.

"This was here when Nikki came home, about two hours ago. Her prints are on it because she opened the box, opened the letter," Parker said, giving him the rundown.

Jonah took a step closer to the table and heard Nikki add, "I touched some of the money, too. Just because, I don't know, just because, I guess."

Looking over his shoulder, he saw her shrug. He smiled and told her, "It's okay, just let me have a look."

Pulling back the flap Jonah almost gasped himself; luckily he kept his cool. The box was maybe a foot wide, close to two feet deep. Hundred-dollar-bills were lined neatly inside. He'd never been real good with math but figured there might be about fifty thousand in there.

"Where'd the box come from?" he asked.

"FedEx tracked it as being received in one of their satellite locations in Easton at nine twenty-seven yesterday morning. Truck number two-eight-one-nine picked it up at five forty-seven on yesterday afternoon. Shipper is listed as R. Davis. Sent overnight directly to Nikki," Parker told him.

Jonah gave him a look.

"Yeah, I checked," he said like he was daring Jonah to question him further.

"Appreciate your efforts, but I'd rather you let us do the investigating," Jonah replied, because the sheriff would have his ass if something went wrong with a case because of him.

"I'd rather this freak show stop harassing her, even from the grave," was Parker's quick retort.

"Here's the letter that came with it," Preston told him. "We've all touched it."

"Great, more fingerprints." Johah sighed. "Look guys, next time if you could just leave everything as is and wait until the local police show up that would be better."

"That's not how we work," Quinn told him from the other side of the room. "If something affects one of us, all of us are involved."

Jonah did not like his tone. "Nikki's not one of you," was his quick reply.

Parker was first to interrupt that line of thinking. "As long as she works for us she is. Now, what do you plan to do about this? I'm sure you know how it looks."

Sighing again, Jonah put one hand on his utility belt out of habit. His other hand went to the radio that rested over his shoulder. "Yeah, this is nine-oh-two-one, tell Roxy to get her gear and get over to the Brockington place. I'm around back in Nikki's apartment."

"Am I going to be arrested?" Nikki asked tentatively.

He'd almost forgotten she was in the room, his mind was so focused on the meddling Cantrell men.

"No," Jonah replied immediately. "I'm just going to have Roxy come over and take this box. She can dust for fingerprints since there's no need to do any trace work.

We'll see what comes back, then we'll send it on to Easton."

She nodded and actually looked a little relieved, which made him feel pretty crappy about what he was going to say next.

"Do you know why he would send you this money, Nik?" he asked and didn't miss the frown that marred Quinn's face.

Nikki shook her head, wrapping her arms around herself as if she were cold. "He never said anything to me about money. I mean, not that kind of money. I've been sitting here thinking and thinking, trying to figure out if he ever let on to having money like this. The answer to that would be yes. Randall wanted me to believe he was rich and important, that he could get whatever he wanted whenever he wanted."

"He was making about thirty thousand a year as a personal driver. That's including tips and bonuses. Not a bad salary, but it's not putting him in the rich bracket," Preston added. "My assistant did some research on him. And before you say it"—he looked straight at Jonah—"it is my job to find out everything I can that will help vindicate my client."

Jonah wasn't going to keep arguing about the Cantrell family meddling in police business; he figured he had better things to do. Besides, all three of those guys were giving him stubborn-as-a-bull looks that he'd rather not be getting at the moment. Instead, he took out his notepad and started jotting down some of the things Preston and Nikki said. Even though he was feeling really uncomfortable around these guys, he had to respect how much time and effort they were putting into this. They seemed pretty dedicated to Nikki even though they were just back in town for their grandmother's funeral.

"I don't know what this money means," Nikki said. "I don't have any idea where he would have gotten it or why he sent it to me."

"You sure he never mentioned it in all the times he called you?" Jonah asked. He hadn't been happy about the ex-boyfriend calling her at all, and it sure would have made this case a lot easier if he didn't have to do this, but there was no way around it. Those buttheads in Easton would certainly ask if Preston would give them the chance to talk to her. But so far, Jonah was the only cop afforded that privilege. He had to feel good about that at least.

"Not that I know of," she said shaking her head.

"Good," he couldn't help but say.

Ten minutes later Roxy showed up with her flaming red hair and multiple piercings that tended to throw some people off. Roxy had just turned twenty-one and would be heading into her senior year at Salisbury University, where she was studying forensic science, this fall. She worked sort of by contract with the sheriff's department since they really couldn't afford a full-time forensic person and rarely had a need for one in Sweetland. Most people pre-judged Roxy because of her piercings and her Gothic style of dressing, but the Cantrells didn't seem bothered and Parker actually played along as Roxy flirted with him. Quinn seemed so serious, not really all that concerned with Roxy or what she was doing there. He was much more in tune to Nikki. Everywhere she went, every word she said, the guy's eyes were on her like he was in some kind of trance. Jonah knew how that felt. And sadly, after being there for an hour and a half, he left Nikki with the Cantrell men just as he'd found her. He walked away with the knowledge that his prospects were now looking a lot dimmer.

Chapter 18

Quinn thought they'd never leave. Nikki was nervous and second-guessing herself left and right. She'd gnawed on her bottom lip so much there might actually be a scar come morning. To say that he didn't like seeing her this way was a huge understatement.

He hated it, and if Randall Davis were still living and breathing he'd break the guy's jaw for the mere fact that he'd upset her. Quinn was not the one prone to physical altercations in his family. That was all Parker. Still, he would do bodily harm to anyone who upset or hurt Nikki. That was a serious revelation.

"Relax," he said, touching his hands to her shoulders and massaging. "I can heat up a slice of pizza, pour you a glass of wine."

"I can't eat when I'm upset," she said, letting her head fall back against his chest.

She'd been standing by the door after she'd walked Parker and Preston out, thanking them both profusely once more. They were both putting a lot of effort into this for her and she really appreciated it.

"Then I'll pour you some wine."

"I don't have wine," she told him with a bewildered look.

"You requested it earlier with your extra cheese, pepperoni, and ham pizza," he told her with a small smile he hoped would soothe her.

Vinny had stopped by while Jonah, Parker, and Preston were here so Quinn had taken the delivery and paid him as quickly as possible.

"You go lie on the bed and I'll bring it to you."

He was still massaging her shoulders, and she moaned with what to Quinn sounded like pure pleasure. Hanging on the wall near her refrigerator was the base holding her cordless phone, which began ringing the minute she stepped away from him.

"It's my sister. I'll call her in the morning," Nikki told him.

"How do you know?"

"Vinny Toriana delivered the pizza. Jonah's police cruiser was parked out front when he pulled up and Jonah was in here with Parker, Preston, and you when he came in. The moment Vinny was back at the pizza parlor he told his father and anybody else who'd been working tonight—namely, Marin Sager, who sometimes babysits for Cordy. The moment Marin heard my name she would have taken out the cell phone that is rarely away from her ear and called to tell Cordy what happened. That"—she pointed to the still-ringing phone—"is Cordy wanting every detail and to find out if I need her to come over or if I want to come spend the night with her."

Quinn could only smile after all that. "Family," he stated simply. "You've got to love them."

She nodded as she walked away. And after Quinn answered the phone and assured Cordy that Nikki was all right, he'd begun thinking about his own sisters. He thought about Michelle, who was extremely busy and possibly gaining more business with the catering orders coming in, and Raine, who was still kind of quiet, even for her, but hadn't made any announcements about when she was leaving Sweetland. He always worried about Savannah, like most of his siblings did. She was awfully quiet now, not squawking about getting out of town, even though today was the day she'd supposedly rescheduled her flight. With those three alone, Quinn's head would throb. The fact that Dr. Stallings had just gotten back to him today about when he could stop by and talk about his grandmother was another issue weighing on him. One that would have to wait until next week, it now appeared.

In the midst of all the family drama going on, there was Nikki. The silver lining to that gray cloud, his grandmother would say. He'd tried to push her away the other night, felt like it was the best thing to do. But here he was once again, in her apartment, craving her closeness.

He'd poured two glasses of white wine, walking them back to her bedroom. She'd turned out the other light in the living room and Quinn had turned off the one in the kitchenette. There was a lamp on the table beside her bed. A Tiffany lamp with a jewel-toned design that he didn't figure out was dragonflies until he was setting the glasses down on the table. It suited her, the whimsical part of her personality that he caught glimpses of usually when she was with Dixi.

She lay on her stomach, her eyes closed. Her shirt had hiked up because she'd probably flopped down on the bed—that's just something he could see her doing after the evening she'd had. A good amount of skin around her midriff was visible. The undeniable curve of her buttocks in shorts that fit her sinfully well was alluring. But she was still tense and while there was no doubt Quinn wanted her, he wanted her relaxed, her mind clear of the other man and all the issues he was creating.

"Thanks," she said, rolling over and taking one glass from his hand.

She sipped instantly. Quinn put his own glass to his lips, watching as she took her first drink, then her second.

Her pert lips touched the glass lightly, leaving a slight imprint from the gloss she was wearing. A quick peek of her tongue had his pulse tripping, an erection clearly on the horizon.

"We always end up here," she told him, and Quinn almost choked on his wine.

"By here you mean in your bed?" he asked after clearing his throat. He couldn't tell if she meant that as a good or bad thing.

She tilted her head, a small smile playing on her lips. "'Here' meaning you coming to my rescue."

"Oh," he replied with relief. He put his glass on the end table, then took hers in an attempt to do the same.

Nikki shook her head, putting her glass back to her lips and emptying its contents. "I needed that."

"I see," he said, moving so that he was closer to her. She backed up a little. "For the record, I'm not rescuing you. I'm just being here for you. That's what friends do," he said.

He'd touched his hands to her shoulders again, massaging them slowly, watching as her eyes glazed slightly with desire. She licked her lips and he wanted to do the same.

"Is that what we are, friends?" she asked and Quinn knew instinctively he needed to proceed with caution.

When his reply didn't come fast enough she reached a hand up to cup his cheek. "Do you believe in love, Quinn?" she asked him quietly.

"Love can be painful," was his automatic reply. "It's a big commitment, one that requires a lot of work to make it last. It's not easy."

"But it's a necessity," she said with total honesty clear in her eyes. She'd inched forward so that their bodies were just about touching, blinking at him as if to make sure she could really see him. "For me, it's a necessity."

Quinn nodded, hearing her words but admitting to himself how truly finished he was with talking for now.

"You want to know what's a necessity for me right now, Nikki?"

She nodded just as Quinn slipped a hand behind her neck, holding her firmly and pulling her face closer to his.

"What?" It was a breathy whisper, one that was as sexy as any porn flick he'd ever watched as a kid and any female he'd ever dated as an adult.

"Kissing you. I really need to kiss you right now."

Nikki's head was moving again although words were a complete loss. The heat between them had been on a slow boil. From the kiss earlier this evening, to the moment everyone cleared out of her apartment, she'd been hyper-aware of Quinn's presence. No, that wasn't entirely true. She was always aware of his presence because there was a feeling of safety that came with it coupled with a level of desirability she'd never experienced before. Each time he looked at her it was as if he were making two promises— *Nothing will happen to you* and *I'll give you everything you need.* A part of her struggled to figure out if that everything she needed was wrapped in this cocoon of physical attraction they'd been unable to ignore from the start. While another part prayed it was much more. Despite what might seem like a quick development between them, for Nikki this had been a long time coming.

That's why the touch of his lips against hers was like the first strike of a match, the flickering of flames swiftly sparked inside her. So swift that she didn't waste a second but lifted a leg and straddled him before he could take the kiss deeper. He made a sound, a deep moaning that sent shivers down her spine. As if he'd anticipated her reaction, his palms ran up and down her back, down again until they cupped her bottom. God, she loved the feel of his hands on her.

His mouth was hot and hungry on hers and she struggled

to catch her breath while keeping up with the deep engage-
ment. Her arms went around his neck as she pulled him
closer with a feeling she could only describe as power.
She felt like she was more than enough woman for this
man who was so worldly and who she'd at one time thought
was out of her league entirely. Now he wanted her,
couldn't get enough of her if the way his hands moved
impatiently over her body was any indication. When they
slipped under her shirt to touch her bare skin, she could
only sigh. With a small gasp she let her head fall back as
his tongue traced scorching paths up and down her neck.
He cupped her breasts then let his fingers rub over one
tight nipple. She hissed, arching upward to meet his touch.

"I just can't seem to get enough of you," was his gut-
tural reply.

The words were thrilling, coursing through her body
on a heated path that landed right between her legs.
"That's good because I want to give you so much more.
Everything," she gasped as she shivered all over.

"I can't wait," he told her, his teeth scraping along her
skin. "I want to wait. I want to make it good for you,
but—"

"Oh, it's good," she told him. "It's so good."

So good that Nikki wasn't about to wait. She pulled at
her shirt, yanking it over her head quickly. Quinn chuckled then pulled his shirt off in the same passionate effort.
Reluctantly, she moved off his lap, smiling at him as she
did away with her shorts and underwear. He was with her
every step of the way, standing to take off his shoes, pants,
boxers.

She reached for him instantly, letting his length fill her
small hands.

"You drive me nuts," he told her. "Absolutely nuts, waiting for the moment I can touch you."

Nikki licked her lips, stepping closer to him, her head
tilted up toward his. "I'm doing the touching now."

"Oh yeah, you definitely are. And I'm going insane," he murmured, bringing his lips to meet hers in another scorching kiss.

When he pulled away Nikki almost complained. Instead she saw that he was reaching into his wallet for a condom, which she quickly took from him.

"Let me," she whispered.

He simply obliged, standing in front of her in all his naked glory. Rock-hard abs, taut muscle from his arms to his thighs to his calves—he was absolutely beautiful. His shaft was long, hard, hot in her palm as she rolled the latex onto him.

That was it for her savoring the moment. Quinn hadn't lied when he said he couldn't wait. He'd sat back on the bed, pulling her over his hips once more. Before she could sigh in contentment he'd entered her, filling her so completely that the scream she'd been contemplating came rippling free. She shivered over him, moments later reaching another pinnacle and loving every minute of it.

He wrapped her in his arms so gently, transitioning their bodies so that he was now over her. He stared down at her for what seemed like endless moments, his length pulsating inside of her, their hearts beating a matching rapid beat.

"What is it?" she asked, reaching a hand up to cup his cheek. "What's the matter?"

Quinn closed his eyes, shook his head, and took a deep breath. "You're amazing," was his reply.

Nikki's heart leapt, soared for endless seconds before settling into a rhythm she could swear sang, *I love you. I love you. I love you.*

He was in trouble. Quinn knew it, felt a pressure in his chest like a sledgehammer. If it weren't for his medical experience he'd think he was having a heart attack. But he knew differently.

This reaction was purely a result of this woman beneath him. The one who was at this very moment tracing her tongue along the line of his ear, wrapping her legs so tightly around him he didn't think their bodies would ever break apart. As he sank deeper inside her, felt the tight grip of her walls around him, he experienced a sensation of sinking, falling so fast and so unexpectedly that he struggled to catch his breath. At that exact moment his release hit him like a freight train and his entire body convulsed. She hugged him closer, and he rested his face in the crook of her neck.

"Quinn," she whispered.

He thought she wanted to say something else. And then he prayed she didn't. He prayed with everything he had inside him that she didn't because he knew without a doubt what the words would be. Words he didn't have a response to and therefore did not want to hear. Even though as he continued with shallow strokes, in and out of her, as her arms cradled him with such tender ferocity he wanted to bury himself right here in this moment and never leave, Quinn couldn't bring himself to think of what all that might mean.

He couldn't bear to think he might be falling in love.

Chapter 19

Saturday came quicker than Quinn thought, most likely because he'd spent the last two nights in Nikki's bed.

When he wasn't there, he'd started seeing Bill Riley for at least an hour each day. The man wasn't going to get better; there was no cure that Quinn could administer to make him and his wife any happier. But he could sit and play checkers with him, watch *Family Feud* and listen to him laugh like it was the funniest show he'd ever seen. He could give Margaret a much-needed reprieve by staying with Bill while she went to the salon or out to lunch with her friend Carolyn. Yesterday, Michelle had even fixed a basket of food for him to take over to the Riley house so Margaret wouldn't have to cook for a day or two.

While Quinn was at the Rileys' place he noticed that he wasn't the only one making these house calls. From time to time he'd open the door to other townsfolk who just stopped by to see Bill and chat with him for a while. Even Marabelle and Louisa came, bringing a box of vanilla scones from the coffee shop and an earful of gossip for Margaret, who simply sat on the front porch listening to them—with only half an ear, Quinn thought with a chuckle.

Now he sat on his own front porch—the one that belonged to The Silver Spoon and wrapped almost completely around the house. The other half of the house was the part that had been extended for the restaurant. He was on the first step, where he usually preferred sitting instead of in one of the Adirondack or rocking chairs that gave the place an even more homey feel. Dixi sat on the step right beneath him, completely tuckered out from running around the house at least ten times in the half hour they'd been out here. It was now twenty minutes to five and Nikki should be here at any moment to pick him up. Quinn planned to ask her if she wasn't busy tomorrow after church to drive him up to Easton so he could rent a car. Walking was nice, but last night when he'd left the Rileys' house heading to Nikki's he and Dixi had gotten completely soaked in the fifteen-minute thunderstorm that hit unexpectedly—not necessarily unexpectedly as he'd watched the evening news with Bill and saw the prediction. He'd simply thought he could beat the weather. He'd been wrong.

He'd also been laughing while he held a soaked and shivering Dixi in his arms and knocked on Nikki's door. She'd shaken her head and taken Dixi from him. For the next hour Dixi had been cuddled and held on Nikki's lap with a fluffy towel wrapped securely around her while Quinn had been forced to wear Ralph Brockington's robe that was way too big for him. That's when Nikki had suggested he leave some clothes at her house for moments such as these. Quinn had brushed that suggestion off.

And on Friday night after spending time in her arms and bed, Quinn had returned to The Silver Spoon. It was another step back, he knew, but had done it anyway.

He was looking forward to going crabbing, however, because it had been years since he'd sat in a boat and waited patiently for anything. Quinn and Michelle hadn't spoken about Nikki anymore since their argument four days ago. When he'd walked into the kitchen late Friday afternoon he'd been more than a little nervous asking this favor.

"Nikki and I are going crabbing in the morning. I was going to fix us some snacks but I don't want to take supplies you may need from the kitchen." That's how he'd put it.

And she'd seen right through him.

"So you want me to fix you a basket?" she'd asked as she sliced lemons.

"I can fix it myself," he'd immediately replied.

"Yeah, right and I can fly. What do you want, sandwiches or soup?"

The slight quirk of her lips said she was in a good mood. The offer to help said she'd forgiven him for his purely male attitude the other day. The way she'd paused and stared at him for just a second before making the offer said she was still questioning his involvement with Nikki.

"Both," was his response. "If you don't mind?"

She'd shaken her head again. "You know I don't mind fixing food. But you haven't been crabbing in a while. You sure you know what you're doing?"

"It's like riding a bike," he'd told her. While she'd been more than happy to give him the food for the Rileys, Quinn had wondered if he could go back and ask his sister for a favor. If this were twenty-five years ago she would surely still not be speaking to him.

As it stood now, Quinn looked to his left and saw the basket his sister had packed for him and Nikki. He smiled with love and appreciation for Michelle. No matter what, she'd always been there for them, always forgave, always smiled and helped out. He wanted to do something nice for her; he just had to figure out what.

Nikki pulled up about five minutes later, and Dixi's rounded head immediately perked up. Her little legs carried her down the steps faster than Quinn thought she'd ever moved. He had a pocket full of treats for her as well as a separate thermos of water and a small bowl in case she became thirsty. It could get extremely hot out there on the water.

"Mornin'," he said when he'd walked down to the curb. He leaned into the driver's-side window and kissed her.

"Good morning," she replied cheerfully then waved him back so she could open the door and let Dixi in.

Dixi, the spoiled princess she was quickly becoming, jumped right up in Nikki's lap as if that were her appointed seat. Quinn walked around to the passenger-side door smiling, happy and content for the first time in a very long time.

Half an hour later they were sitting in a boat floating in the river. The sun hadn't come up yet but the sky was doing its usual dance of transformation from night to day. The boat belonged to Ralph Brockington, and Nikki operated it just like an Eastern Shore native. Between the two of them sat a bucket with about an inch of ice at the bottom. Their food basket was on Quinn's left. Without a word they'd both began to bait their lines with chicken necks. Nikki wasn't squeamish at all; then again, Quinn hadn't really expected her to be. She did this with the same systematic grace he'd watched her do many things lately. It wasn't until they had rigged two lines, propping them up against the side so they would catch on their own and then lacing another line to hold on to, that they sat back and relaxed.

"We can steam what we catch for lunch if you'd like," she said.

Quinn resisted looking at her again. He'd already noted how cute she looked in her cutoff shorts and orange tank top. Her normally unruly hair had been pulled back tightly, the ends that resembled a fluffy brown puffball emerging through the back opening of the Orioles cap she wore. Her skin looked smooth, sun-kissed, and delectable. The latter was why he chose to keep his eyes on the water.

"Sounds good," was his reply.

A few minutes later he asked, "Do you have a crabbing license?"

She shook her head. "Today's a free fishing Saturday. They have them a couple times during the season. We'll see plenty of boats out here before long as everybody'll want to take advantage of that."

He nodded. "I see."

"I talked to Savannah last night," she said.

"Really?" Quinn was surprised when he knew he shouldn't be. Savannah and Nikki had once been extremely close. "What'd she have to say?"

"Nothing much, but I know that means she's worried about something. Savannah always has something to talk about, namely herself. But when she called—which was after you left so you know it was late—she said she just wanted to see how I was doing. She asked about us."

Of course she did, he thought dismally. "Sorry about that," he told her.

"Sorry she called me so late or sorry she asked about us?"

Quinn hesitated, trying to figure if that was a trick question. "Both, I guess," was his response, whether it was right or wrong.

"I couldn't really answer her since I don't know much about us."

"You know what's important," he told her. It was vague and purposely so. This conversation wasn't going to go well if they continued. "I put in a leave of absence from my job," he said by way of changing the subject before he sank what might be the very best thing that had ever happened to him.

"Really?" she asked. "Why?"

"It was time to take a break. If you're not too busy tomorrow can you give me a ride to Easton so I can rent a car?"

"You want to rent a car? For how long?" she asked.

Quinn didn't know the answer to that question. He just knew that it was needed. "For a while I guess."

"Wouldn't it be simpler to have your car shipped here?"

No. That would seem permanent.

"I can rent for now," was his only reply.

They sat in silence after that and he knew she wanted to say more, to ask more. Quinn didn't want to answer.

When his line drew tight he sat up in his chair.

"Pull her up quickly," she instructed.

Even though he already knew to do that Quinn acted as if he were doing what she said. Out of the water came a beautiful Chesapeake blue. When his line was safely inside the boat he put the crab down into the bucket and used a ruler to measure it.

"Remember, anything smaller than five inches goes back. And turn it over to see if it's male or female," she continued.

Maryland had imposed tight restrictions on crabbers throughout the state about two years before because of the diminishing numbers of blue crabs. Smaller ones had to be thrown back to allow for more growth; females were off limits so that they could produce as much as possible.

"He's good," Quinn announced, tossing down the ruler.

"Great. Looks like someone else is making a decision, too," she said, using a hand to pat Dixi's head and push her face out of the bucket before the crab snapped her nose off.

Quinn quickly covered the bucket. "She's so silly," he said about Dixi.

"She's curious."

Of course, that was it. The rest of the morning proceeded with their conversation on that same level. Catching and releasing crabs, swatting at Dixi so she'd keep her nose intact, and filling the cooler they'd brought along with the maximum of two dozen crabs for a personal un-licensed crabber.

As they ate the sandwiches and soup that Michelle had packed them Nikki suggested they share the crabs with the Rileys. Quinn figured that was an excellent idea.

They arrived back at The Silver Spoon around six o'clock that evening. Their crabbing excursion had ended around eleven thirty and when they'd come back to dry land they'd gone to the Brockington house to steam the crabs. Once they were finished Nikki drove them over to the Rileys', and that's where they'd been since then.

"I don't know when the last time was we've had this much fun," Margaret had said while she and Nikki cleaned off the picnic table in the backyard.

Quinn and Bill had rolled up the paper they'd piled their empty crab shells on and were taking it to the town Dumpster so the smell wouldn't attract unwelcome ro-dents in the Rileys' trash cans.

"It was nice of you and Quinn to come by this after-noon," Margaret was telling Nikki.

They'd just made a new pitcher of summer punch. Nikki had smiled as they'd made it because just about everyone in Sweetland had a different recipe for summer punch, and most of them were delicious. Margaret's was a mixture of watermelon, white grape juice, and fresh mint. It was refreshing and just lively enough to counter the salt and spicy taste of the steamed crabs. Nikki had enjoyed the pretty day sitting in the Rileys' backyard sipping from a tall glass.

"Quinn likes spending time with Bill," she'd replied.

The Rileys had a bit of land surrounding their house and it was down a small hill before you could even see the windows from their neighbors. They had two children, a boy and a girl, but neither of them had been in Sweetland for what seemed like ages. Whatever visiting was done would be as a result of the senior Rileys heading to the airport to fly out and see them. Nikki thought that was kind of sad.

Margaret let out a long sigh. "Bill likes him, too. Says he's the first doctor he really trusts."

That was another sad thing, the fact that Bill was dying and Margaret seemed to be sitting here dying right along with him. At one time she'd been on one or two of Odell's committees, but Nikki's mother had remarked the other day that she hadn't seen much of Margaret since Bill's diagnosis.

"It's good that he's been able to remember his surroundings," Nikki said, trying to be as optimistic as ever.

"I dead-bolt all the doors at night. Elmer down at the general store came out and installed them. I have this key and I have to use it to lock and open the doors in the morning. I sleep with it around my neck just in case."

It sounded so dire, so serious, and Nikki figured it was. If Quinn hadn't been out that morning to see Bill there was no telling where he would have ended up or if they would've ever found him.

"Does he know they're locked?" she asked out of curiosity. Nikki remembered Bill Riley mostly from being at the church picnic. He always worked the grill with a big happy smile and a bit of conversation. In the winter months after a big snow or ice storm you could hear Bill's truck riding around, the plow he'd hitched to the front scraping along the icy roads. Seeing him sit still and fading in and out of conversations wasn't easy for her, so she was sure it had to be a living hell for him.

"He got up one night and tried to get out. I heard him yelling and woke up. He said he had to go out and cut the grass. He thought the kids were coming in town for a barbecue. It took me two hours and lots of hot tea to get him calm enough to go back to bed. And actually, don't tell the doc," she whispered, "I put one of those pain pills in his tea so he'd go to sleep and stay sleep."

Something about the way she'd said that made Nikki shiver. Quinn and Bill were back by then, and they'd spent another hour talking before Quinn suggested they leave so Bill could get some rest.

Now Nikki was driving and wondering if Quinn was going to stay at her place tonight or not. She wasn't stupid; she knew her suggestion that he bring some of his clothes over had scared him off so that last night he went back to the B&B. She probably would have kicked herself about it all night if Savannah hadn't called her to keep her mind off him.

"I need to walk Dixi," he was saying as Nikki turned onto Main Street.

"Right. I'll drop you off," she said, holding in the disappointment that gripped her chest with his words. Even though he hadn't said he wouldn't come back to her place after the walk, Nikki had a feeling he wouldn't. But she refused to dwell on it.

"Today was a good day," she started saying. "I'll bet my mom's house is still bubbling with chatter as the ladies from the chamber of commerce were discussing plans for Bay Day."

"That still Fourth of July weekend?" he asked, his gaze focused on the many new shops along Main. Even Bud Nesby had finally gotten his permits and put a tentative sign in the window of a newly renovated shop space with the name HOT DIGGITY DOGS! in bright red letters.

"Yep, kicking off on Saturday with the parade and a huge bull roast down at Charlie's. They line tables all along the pier now so everyone can just walk on down and take a seat. Jonah plays the guitar and has a little band he put together. They do songs by request and even let you get up and sing along if that's your preference. It's a grand party and an excellent kickoff to the weekend-long events."

He nodded. "I remember them a little differently."

"You, Parker, and Preston never stuck around for all the festivities. One minute Savannah and I would see you and the next you'd be gone. We wouldn't hear from Parker and Preston again until either the cops were called or my dad was called to get Mrs. Oberlin's cat out of the tree."

Quinn laughed and Nikki settled back in her seat. She loved to hear him laugh, loved his deep voice and that ridge that appeared in his forehead when he was upset—usually with Dixi. He smelled heavenly, even after they'd been on the water all morning and they'd stood over the huge steamers in the Rileys' backyard, he still smelled like man, totally hot man. She wanted him constantly, which she knew was brazen and probably way out of line for a female. But it was a fact. And Nikki wanted more than the physical. She wanted more Saturdays like this, more nights like the ones they'd had before. She wanted to wake up beside him every morning, to sit at dinner with him sharing the details of their day every evening.

And as she pulled up in front of The Silver Spoon she almost told him exactly that. But Parker was standing on the porch when they arrived. She knew it was Parker and not Preston because for one thing, she parked right behind his motorcycle, and for another, his puppy, Rufus, a rowdy male who spent every one of his waking moments running and playing or eating was in the yard doing his thing with what looked like a paper bag he'd found no doubt in the kitchen.

As they stepped out of the car he called to them.

"Got some news from Easton."

Nikki's good mood plummeted. Quinn waited for her

to round the car and took her by the hand before walking up the path.

"What's up?" Quinn asked as they stepped onto the porch.

Parker thrust his hands into his pockets. "Davis was apparently embezzling funds from his employer. Had some woman in the accounting department helping him. The money he sent you was his getaway stash since he knew they were on to him."

Nikki had already begun shaking her head. "So his boss had him killed? I don't believe that. I met Mr. Witherspoon and he seemed like a nice enough guy to me."

"Nobody's nice when you steal their money," Parker told her. "But no, they got another new lead. When they searched deeper into Davis's phone records they found a bunch of calls to a Johnny Tuscaverdi. He's apparently a high-level loan shark who works for a reputable crime family up in New York. Preliminary theory is that Davis was helping Tuscaverdi with some money laundering and stole from him as well. Word on the street is that there's been a bounty on his head for a couple of months now."

"That's why he came down here. He wanted to hide out in Easton," she said disbelievingly. This was definitely the kind of stuff that happened on television. It did not happen to her in real life, and it certainly didn't happen in Sweetland.

"For the record there was two hundred and fifty thousand in that box. Easton was most likely just a stop for him. My bet is he was going to leave the country. Maybe he got scared when he heard Tuscaverdi's men were looking for him and that's why he sent you the money. He probably figured he could give it to you to hold then have you send it to him later. I don't know." Parker shrugged. "But I wanted to tell you that you're no longer a suspect."

"Where's Preston?" she asked. Quinn had been holding her hand but she'd pulled away to fold her arms over her chest. Suddenly she felt vulnerable and exposed. And for whatever reason she wanted her own space.

"He had to go back to Baltimore. He has a big case starting on Monday," Parker said.

She nodded, having remembered that Preston had mentioned that to her the other day.

"Thanks," she finally managed to say. "I'm going to head home now."

She turned to go down the steps, but Quinn's hand on her arm stopped her. "I can come by after I walk Dixi," he told her.

Nikki looked up at him and almost smiled. A few minutes ago she'd wanted him to say just that, but he hadn't. Now, because he thought she needed his shoulder to cry on, he put the offer out there. Well, she'd cried her share when Quinn Cantrell wasn't in town, she figured she could probably get away with doing it again. No way was she going to take his company out of some form of misguided obligation.

"That's okay. I'll be fine. Call me tomorrow if you still want to go to Easton," she said and walked away before he could answer or respond either way.

"I seem to remember you making a comment about Casey O'Hurley being barely legal enough for Preston to mess with. Nikki's a little on the young side, don't you think?" Parker asked when he and Quinn were alone.

"She's almost thirty," Quinn replied through tight lips.

Parker nodded. "And you're almost forty."

"You a math genius all of a sudden?"

Parker laughed. "Nah, just observing. I heard the girls talking about you and Nikki getting closer but I brushed it off, figured you were just hanging around trying to help her out just like me and Preston. I mean, we were thinking of her as one of our sisters, protecting her the same way we'd protect them. I get the impression you're thinking of her in a totally different way."

"I do want to protect her," he said. "But I do not think of her as a sister."

"Because you're sleeping with her?"

Quinn gave his younger brother a look, one that he hoped said mind-your-damned-business. But Parker didn't back down. It was a weird trait found in all the Cantrell men.

"I'm just saying be careful with her. She's not only young, she's also sort of our employee. Think about how things will be around here if you break her heart."

"I'm not going to break her heart. It's not even that serious," Quinn told him.

"Are you blind, man? You really can't see how she's looking at you. Hell, you don't see how you two are always hugged up together with and without the dog, so don't give me that she's-helping-you-with-Dixi crap I heard you tell Raine the other day."

"You know the will says we have to find a good home for the puppies."

Parker rubbed a hand over the stubble of beard growing at his chin. "And you're testing out how good Nikki's home might be for him? That's bull, Quinn, and you know it."

"It's my life, Parker. I've been running it for quite some time now. I know what I'm doing."

"Right. I guess you do. I'm just bringing it to your attention since we all know you have a habit of putting things you don't like to deal with out of your mind."

"Don't go there, man. Just don't," Quinn warned his brother.

"I won't as long as you acknowledge that there is someone you have to deal with before moving forward. Look, I told Michelle I'd talk to you because there's more at stake here now. If you like Nikki, cool, be with her.

She's very attractive and she's a good person. All I'm saying is that if you're not on the same page with her about where this relationship is going, then you should do her a favor and walk away now."

With that Parker was the one to walk away, whistling so that Rufus followed right behind him. Quinn was left on the porch alone, thinking two dismal thoughts: Parker had a good point about Nikki, and Dixi wasn't nearly as obedient as Rufus.

Chapter 20

Grayson W. Stallings, MD, ran the only medical facility in Sweetland. Only that facility wasn't what Quinn was used to seeing. It was an old Victorian-style home, which was the preferred design of most of the original homes in Sweetland. Quinn remembered his grandmother telling him all about the architecture of the homes and the decorations inside them. That was when he was very young and Quinn figured the moment he'd been introduced to antiques and their sentimental and historical value.

With that in mind Quinn could certainly appreciate the folk-style Victorian off-white structure sitting quietly on the corner of Elm Road. Like The Silver Spoon it looked as if it were a corner of this town that progress had forgotten—and that appealed to him. Tulips bordered the wide walkway, ushering him up to original wood steps painted an eerie shade of green. His soft leather-bottomed loafers were mostly quiet as he crossed the threateningly old wood-planked porch to the double wood doors with stained-glass windows on each side. An older woman who'd looked at him like she might recognize him had answered and led him through a short foyer into a parlor that had been converted into a waiting room.

"Doc'll be with you in a few minutes. He's just finishing his lunch," she said, moving around with a shuffle and swishing sound, her round body seemingly agile. Before she left the room she turned again to look at him, peering gray eyes over the rims of tortoiseshell glasses. "You're Mary Janet's grandson, right?"

Quinn nodded. "Yes, ma'am."

"Hmph," was her reply before she left him alone.

He couldn't help feeling engulfed by the homey building. The moldings and windows were most likely original; he suspected the house was built sometime in the 1900s. Unlike his clinic and many other medical facilities he'd been in, this place didn't have that sterile feel. It didn't speak of bad news or dour expressions, distasteful medications or horrifying needles. Instead, cushioned, high-backed chairs lined two of the dark-paneled walls. In the center was a very worn Oriental rug in a faded blue color that vaguely matched the material of the chairs. Around the room were several end tables overflowing with magazines and dim lighting provided by lamps that looked like they'd too seen better days.

He'd spoken to the doctor last week and to his surprise had been given this appointment almost five days later. Even though Quinn doubted how busy the good doctor could possibly be in a town this size, he'd respected the man's schedule and not dropped in the second he felt like finding answers. At any rate, finding out the status of his grandmother's health before she passed had been momentarily forgotten with Nikki being accused of murder. With a sigh Quinn felt relief at replaying Parker's good news in his head once more. He'd told them on Saturday evening and Nikki had taken the news like a champion. The next day they'd driven to Easton and had lunch while Quinn rented a car. When they'd come back, Nikki had gone her way and Quinn had gone his. He wanted to believe she was still dealing with the resolution of her legal problems, but wondered if Parker hadn't been right about what Nikki expected of him and their relationship. As a countermeasure and because he readily admitted to acting cowardly, Quinn had limited their time together to seeing her at The Silver Spoon and walking her home with Dixi in the evenings. He'd spent one night with her since Saturday and while that night had been terrific, his conscience hadn't allowed him to return.

"Quinton Cantrell," a rough, gravelly voice called.

Quinn stood, swallowing hard and wiping thoughts of Nikki out of his mind. He extended a hand to the man who was shorter than him by at least a foot and wider than him by most likely another foot.

"Dr. Stallings," he greeted and acknowledged his strong handshake.

He looked every bit of his seventy-nine years, as Michelle had told Quinn he would. His brown pants were a little above the ankle so that the old black Velcro shoes he wore with bright white socks were clearly visible. Yellow-and-brown suspenders held the pants up and vaguely complemented the beige dress shirt he wore with the sleeves rolled up to his elbows so that the dark hair on his arms attracted more attention. The hair on his head was absent but for a few stubborn strands that were now silvery white. A matching beard was thick and thriving. Dark but alert eyes stared back at Quinn, not smiling, but somber, like this wasn't expected to be a pleasant visit.

Quinn knew that expression all too well.

"Come on back to my office," he told Quinn after their handshake and quiet assessment of each other was complete.

Quinn followed him, noting the old wallpaper that had begun peeling in certain areas and the dining room that was occupied with bookshelves, a desk, and five chairs scattered about. This was his office, Quinn surmised, and took a seat across from the desk. The doctor moved with a slightly slower gait until he was behind the desk, plopping down into his chair.

"You want to know about your grandmother," he said immediately.

"My family and I just have a few questions," Quinn replied.

"And because you're the oldest you had to come and ask me yourself. Or is it because you're a doctor, too?"

Quinn tried to smile. "Probably a little of both."

The doctor surprised him by chuckling himself. "Well, I'm the oldest in my family, too, so I know the responsibility that comes with it." He reached over to a double-shelved tray and pulled a file in front of him. "Mary Janet Cantrell was my patient for years," he started.

"I understand that," Quinn stated with a nod. "We're just wondering if her death was of natural causes or if there were any underlying ailments that we should know about."

"Well," Dr. Stallings said, opening the file with one hand, ruffling his beard with the other. "What you did know and what you should know are two different things."

"And that means?" It meant, it wasn't good. His grandmother had been sick, Quinn knew that now without any doubt. The new question was what had been wrong with her and why she hadn't told anybody.

"I reckon back where you practice this would be a breach of doctor–patient privilege," the doctor said, glancing up at Quinn.

"It would certainly violate HIPAA laws. But from one colleague to another, I'm asking you for a professional courtesy."

The doctor shook his head. "Don't go much by all those fancy rules down here. I just respect my patients' wishes. Don't necessarily agree with 'em, but I respect 'em."

Quinn folded his hands in his lap and nodded. "I understand."

"About two months before she passed Mary Janet

came in for a physical, said she'd been feeling more tired than usual and thought she might have lost some weight even though her appetite hadn't changed much. I ran some tests, blood, urine, all that stuff, and sent everything up to the lab in Easton. Because I could see she didn't look like her usual self I had the people up their put a rush on the results. Three days later I got a call from a doctor up there." The doctor paused and looked straight at Quinn. "He was your kind of doctor."

Quinn's heartbeat slowed and then threatened to burst with anxiousness. He sat forward in the chair. "She had cancer," he said, the last word catching in his throat.

Dr. Stallings nodded. "Stage three lung cancer. A week later we did another round of tests and found out it had already spread to her brain."

Quinn's teeth clenched, his hands fisting and releasing so that he braced the arms of the chair with a death grip. "She was already dying by the time she came to see you."

"Yes, she was. When I told her she just smiled. Mary Janet had one of the prettiest smiles this side of the Mississippi." The doctor himself smiled at that memory. "She told me it was okay, that she'd lived the life the good Lord had for her and if He was ready for her to come home, she'd go without a fuss. I didn't give her anything but something for the pain and that was at the very end."

"And she never told any of us," he whispered more to himself than to the doctor.

"Had her friend come and pick up the prescription for the pain medicine that week or so before."

"Her friend?" Quinn asked, but he knew instinctively who the doctor was talking about.

"Yeah, fellow that was staying over at the inn with her for a while, Sylvester I think his name is. Nice enough man determined to do what Mary Janet wanted."

"No matter what the rest of us wanted."

The doctor shrugged. "Her life. Her call," he said simply.

Quinn didn't even bother asking if there had been something that could have been done for her. He knew there wasn't. Once the cancer metastasized the outcome was grim. Bill Riley could attest to that.

Still, he felt like absolute crap as he walked out of the house and down to the curb where his rental car was parked. Once behind the wheel he pounded both palms on the steering wheel before resting his forehead there and struggling to steady his breathing.

His father had died of lung cancer the year Quinn graduated from college. Now his grandmother had died of the same. *Cancer. Cancer. Cancer.* He hated hearing the word. Closing his eyes, he hated seeing it in his consciousness. Hated every aspect of the disease until he wanted to scream. Instead he started the car and drove to the only place he knew to go.

Sylvester stared down at the grave, dropped to his knees, and ran his fingers over the engraved letters. Tears burned his eyes and clogged his chest, and the next breath was a struggle. He almost didn't care if it came or not. Janet was gone and he wondered if it wouldn't be easier if he were gone, too.

Some people didn't find love until late in life; some never found it at all. Sylvester had thought for sure he was one of the latter group, going through his days without ever really knowing true love. Then he'd come to Sweetland and met Janet, and his whole life had changed. She was not like any other woman he'd ever met. All the others he'd only liked marginally; he could only talk to them about common things like jobs or the lack of, weather, food when they wanted him to buy dinner, stuff like that. Nothing too deep. He could sleep with them and move on; most of them didn't care. The ones who did only cared once they found out they were pregnant. And while he wasn't proud of the legacy he would leave behind—five children out of wedlock by five different females—Sylvester had made peace with his past. He'd made peace with the man he'd been one Sunday morning as he'd sat on a pew at the Redeemer's Baptist Church with Janet wearing that peach-colored suit and matching hat he loved to see her in. Pastor Ben Ellersby had preached a mighty sermon that morning, touching on scriptures that seemed to speak directly to Sylvester and to mending his ways. It was a teary and emotional moment—one Michelle would later describe as his come-to-Jesus moment. But afterward he'd felt like a new man, and Janet had looked at him like he was one.

They'd had dinner that night at the restaurant, just the two of them. She'd smiled across the table at him and he'd taken her hands in his.

"You're a real fine woman, Mary Janet Cantrell," he told her, searching deep within himself for the courage to continue.

"And you've turned out to be a fine man, Sylvester. I would have never guessed what type of man you really were five months ago when you appeared on my doorstep."

It had been raining that day and he was cold and his feet hurt. She'd let him come inside and get dry before asking him what he wanted. Anyone other than Janet might have handled that situation differently.

"I am what I am because of you."

"Nonsense. You've always been a good man. You just needed to be reminded. I suspect the Reverend Ellersby's sermon did all the reminding you needed."

"It was eye opening," he admitted. "But there's something that I didn't need my eyes opened about. I just needed the courage to tell you."

"To tell me what?"

He took a deep steadying breath, letting the feel of her soft hands in his calm him. "I love you, Janet. I think I fell in love with you on that rainy day when you let me come inside and sit by your fireplace to get warm. I know I've loved you every Sunday morning when you come knocking on my door reminding me to get ready for church. Then as we sit on that pew clapping and singing and rejoicing each Sunday I feel like I love you even more. Especially today, Janet. Especially today when I've done had my eyes opened about so much stuff, I just feel so full of love for you because if it weren't for you I wouldn't be at this place in my life."

She'd been quiet for a few seconds, blinking and then lowering her head so he couldn't see what she was doing. He would have thought she was praying but hoped she wasn't choosing this moment to have her own come-to-Jesus moment. A few seconds later she looked up at him with tears in her eyes.

"Nobody's talked to me like that since my Jacob passed on," she said, then had to clear her throat. "I don't know how to respond."

Sylvester had rubbed the backs of her hands, giving her an assuring smile. "You don't have to say or do anything. I'm happy just being here with you. That's just fine with me," he'd told her. Then Michelle had brought out her beef stew and they'd shared a meal.

Janet didn't tell him she loved him until more than two years later, the day she'd come from seeing Dr. Stallings. He remembered that morning like it was yesterday. He'd been sitting on the porch playing cards when he noticed that old cab pulling up in front of the house. When Janet stepped out of the backseat, Sylvester had stood. Janet walked everywhere in Sweetland, prided herself on being healthy enough to still use her feet to get her around. Why was Mr. King driving her home?

About an hour later as they still sat on the porch where Janet had come up and taken a seat beside him, she'd said simply, "I've got the cancer, Sylvester. Doc Stallings said I won't be here much longer."

Sylvester's heart had ached and cracked right in half at

her words. "Then we'll take you to see somebody else," he told her hopefully. "Didn't you say your grandson was a doctor and he took care of people with cancer? We can call him up right now, tell him to get down here and fix you up."

Janet was already shaking her head. "Ain't no fixing Quinton can do. It's already done and once the good Lord has His final word, won't be nothing for nobody else to say."

Sylvester had wanted to say more, had plenty of words stored up in his mind, but he knew from the tone of her voice Janet wouldn't listen to any of them. Her mind was made up. Later that night she'd asked him if he would help her take care of things. "I'll do anything you ask, Janet, honey. I love you too much not to."

She'd nodded and held his hands tightly. "I love you, too, Sylvester."

Sylvester could still hear her saying those words right here today. His shoulders shook as tears spilled from his eyes. She'd lived exactly six months from the day Doc Stallings had told her she had cancer. And then she'd died and Sylvester thought a part of him had died right along with her. He would have packed up and left had one of her last requests not been to look out for her grandchildren.

"Mr. Sylvester." He heard the male voice from behind him and thought to himself how this moment must be what some called fate.

Pulling a handkerchief from his back pocket, Sylvester mopped the tears from his face before placing his hands on the headstone to help him stand. When he was upright he turned to face Quinn Cantrell. The good doctor had found out what Janet had vowed to tell no one other than Sylvester. He could see it in his eyes.

"How long did you know my grandmother was sick? And why didn't you tell anyone?" Quinn asked, his hands slipping in the pockets of his pants, the early-evening breeze blowing his loose-fitting shirt.

A storm was coming, Sylvester thought as he looked at

the young man. A storm that would hopefully wash away old hurts and bring joy in the morning.

"She told me when she came back from Doc Stallings's office. Said he told her she was dying," Sylvester reported to him evenly. He hadn't agreed with Janet keeping the secret from her family but had vowed not to betray her wishes.

"Why didn't you tell Michelle? Or call one of us? Why didn't you call me?"

This one of Janet's grandchildren had looked tortured from the first moment he had stepped into that house. There was much on his mind, even more weighing down heavily on his shoulders. And it wasn't all about his grandmother, Sylvester suspected.

"Janet asked me not to. She was happy with the life she'd led, son. You should know that. And she was proud of all of you grandchildren."

"I don't give a damn about her being happy or proud! She's not here anymore and I could have prevented that. I could have saved her!" Quinn yelled.

"No," Sylvester said, shaking his head. "Only the good Lord could work that miracle."

"I'm a doctor. An accomplished oncologist. I heal cancer patients for a living."

"You use the tools God gave you to take care of those patients. If it's in His will that they live they do, if it's not, they don't. Believing you are more powerful than Him is a slap in the face of all your grandmother tried to teach you."

"There are medications and new studies that could have helped her. I could have tried," he said stubbornly.

"No." Sylvester sighed. "That's not what she wanted."

"What about what I wanted?" he yelled once more, finally lifting his hands to cover his face.

Sylvester took the couple of steps to close the gap between them. He reached out, touched Quinn's arm.

"Let it go, son. You'll feel so much better when you understand that you're not in control of everything. Don't hold on to guilt that isn't yours. You got to let that stuff go."

Quinn didn't want to hear a word this man was saying. He'd known Quinn's grandmother was dying and he hadn't said a word. Every day he'd watched her die and Quinn wanted to punch him for that, yell, curse him out, scream to the top of his lungs how unfair and cruel that was. But he didn't.

Tears burned the backs of his eyes, his hands clenching at his sides. He didn't do any of those things because deep down he knew Sylvester was right. His grandmother had asked this man to keep her secret and he'd loved her enough to do as she'd asked. Quinn remembered so many occasions when his grandmother had asked him to come back to Sweetland, if even just for a visit. And he hadn't loved her enough to do either.

"Mr. Creed said she changed her will two months prior to her death," he said because the memory had just come over him. "She changed it after she found out, leaving us those puppies because she knew she wouldn't be here to take care of them."

Sylvester scratched his head. "She loved those dogs and she loved you children. I guess she just wanted all of you to be together."

"She wanted us to have a reason to stay here in Sweetland. Is that why she didn't pay those taxes?"

"Janet wanted you all back here, that's the truth. She wanted that more than she wanted to live. I don't know much about the taxes. Just that she said she would pay only what she owed. Don't know why she didn't do that in the end," Sylvester told him.

Quinn had a suspicion why she hadn't paid and vowed to visit the town council very soon.

"But we can take the dogs back to where we live. We can let the house go. We don't have to stay here," he told Sylvester.

He shook his head. "You can do what you wanna do. You always have. But at least now you know."

Yeah, now he knew. He knew that his grandmother loved them fiercely, knew that she'd given everything she had to them and when she realized she would no longer be here to give, she left them what she cherished the most. How could he not keep Dixi now? How could he not do whatever was necessary to keep the inn open and thriving? How could he go against her wishes now after she'd given him so much and asked so little?

As Quinn left the cemetery he wondered how he would wake up the next morning. Would the pain that squeezed his entire being so tightly he thought he would crumble to pieces at any moment ever cease?

And through all those dark thoughts there was one shining light. He went to her without hesitation, went to her and prayed she could save him.

Chapter 21

Nikki hadn't heard from Quinn all afternoon and she was more than a little worried. Not so much that he hadn't been around the inn or that he hadn't called her personally, but because things between them had been a little off the last couple of days.

"He's a guy, Nik," Cordy had told her earlier on the phone when she'd been complaining to her about it. "And besides that, it hasn't really been that long since you two got involved. It's way too soon to think it'll be smooth sailing."

"No. I think it's way too early for it not to be smooth sailing," she'd replied, a bit on the hostile side. She let out a deep breath then and stared out her office window to the lovely old-fashioned gazebo draped in ivy. It was one of her favorite places in all of Sweetland.

"Well, tell me what you think the problem is," Cordy said in her best try-to-be-patient-with-my-little-sister-who-doesn't-know-squat voice.

"I think he's backing off, like he thinks he made a mistake," Nikki admitted, the sting of finally saying it aloud vibrating through her body.

"Hmmm," was Cordy's instant reply. "Have you asked him about it?"

"No."

"Then ask him," she said simply.

"Thanks, Cordy," Nikki replied with a roll of her eyes.

"I'm serious," Cordy continued. "Communication is key in any relationship, Nikki. And so is teamwork. Both of you have to work at making a successful go of this. If you feel like he's not doing that, then say something. Why wait until it goes south? By then it's too late to salvage anything."

"That's just my point. I don't even know what his permanent plans are—if he's going to stay here or if one day I'll wake up and he'll be on the other side of the country."

"No, honey, that's just *my* point. Call him up, tell him to get his butt over to your place, and ask him."

Nikki had contemplated that idea for the better part of the afternoon. Around five o'clock, just before she was about to leave the inn for the day and she still hadn't seen him around, she gave in. His cell phone went straight to voice mail.

It was now almost eight o'clock and she still hadn't heard from him. She'd left the inn with an I-don't-give-a-damn attitude knowing full well that it was just a front. The problem was she did care, way too much.

At nine forty-five there was a soft knock at Nikki's door. She almost didn't hear it, but the television had picked that moment to perform one of those national broadcasting tests that made it super-quiet in her room. The knock startled her but she figured the issues with Randall were behind her so she shouldn't be afraid that behind the door would be cops with handcuffs designed to fit her especially.

Her usual night attire was old gym shorts and tank tops, which at this hour of the night anyone coming to her home unannounced deserved to see her in. Her hair was a wild mess, left out to air-dry after her early-evening shower. When she finally made it to the door and pulled it open she wished she'd had the good sense to get herself together first.

"Hey," he said, his voice low, his shoulders almost slumped even lower. Instinctively she knew that something was wrong.

"Hey. Come on in," Nikki told Quinn without hesitation. "Is everything okay?"

He rubbed his hands over his face, taking a deep breath before turning to her. "No. It's not," was his slow reply.

Okay, just brace yourself. You can do this. If he doesn't want you that's fine, you've gone years without him, you can go the rest of your life. You can, she thought, trying desperately to convince herself.

"Tell me," she said simply because a long drawn-out performance wasn't going to work for her.

"I'm tired," he said. "Come sit down."

And just like that he turned and walked toward the couch where he sat first, falling back to let his head rest on the edge.

Nikki followed him, dropping her hands into her lap. He reached for her hand and she was almost hesitant to give it to him. In the end she did and felt warmth spread through her body as his fingers threaded through hers.

"My grandmother had cancer," he said quietly. "She found out she had lung cancer six months before she died. No treatment. No announcement. Nothing. She just came home to die."

Nikki couldn't breathe. She couldn't swallow, couldn't even blink. She'd heard the words but they seemed to be rolling around in her mind in a mix that wasn't coherent. She wanted to ask him to repeat it, to say it all over again just so she could assure herself that what she thought he saw wasn't right. All she ended up doing was remaining quiet.

"Preston is devastated. I called him first since he's the

only one of us not here. He's pretty pissed off at Michelle for not noticing something was wrong. But it wasn't her fault."

The more Quinn talked, the more Nikki's eyes watered. It was like being told of Mrs. Cantrell's death all over again.

"Michelle's holding some guilt, though, even without me letting Preston talk to her. Parker just stormed out of the house. He didn't say where he was going and I hope to God it's not to get drunk. He's been spending way too much time down at Charlie's with a drink in his hand."

Quinn took a deep breath, gripped her fingers a little tighter. "Raine and Savannah are just as upset, as they were at the funeral. Raine says she understands why Gramma didn't tell us. Savannah," he added with an eerie chuckle that didn't reflect an ounce of happiness on his face. "She's accusing Gramma of being selfish and inconsiderate. Can you believe that?"

Tears had been slowly slipping down her face, dropping off her chin to land on the gray shorts she wore, leaving big dark stains. When Quinn's finger touched one, wiped it away, she sighed, breath just coming from her in a whoosh. She'd almost certainly been breathing the entire time, but her mind hadn't registered that function. She wasn't registering anything now but her loss.

"Lung cancer," he said. "Just like my dad."

Nikki nodded, but couldn't look at him. If she did she would break down, she knew it. "How did you find out?"

"I met with Dr. Stallings today. He's got a pretty good setup over there. A little outdated but still functional."

"His parents used to live there. When they died they left him the house," she said, sniffling. Talking about this was better than the other. It didn't stop the tears, but it was better. "Ethel, his assistant, is his girlfriend. They've been together for years but refuse to get married."

"I thought the name Stallings sounded familiar."

Then they were quiet again. Grief filled the room as if it were air. Nikki tried to stop crying, she really did. But it was useless.

"I would have tried to help her," Quinn said quietly. "But she wouldn't have wanted that, huh."

"No," Nikki replied. "She wouldn't have. If she did she would have called you first. And that's what you need to understand about all this." She turned to the side so she could face him. Quinn had only stated that Michelle felt guilty but Nikki knew he did, too.

"By the time Stallings found it, the cancer had spread to her brain. She was already dying."

"And so you couldn't have saved her if you wanted to."

"No. But I could have come home sooner. I would have come home sooner," he said adamantly.

Nikki didn't reply. Quinn was determined to have a battle with himself, to grapple with things he couldn't control and to push away the guilt of not doing the one thing he could have. He could have come home sooner because Mrs. Cantrell had asked him to on numerous occasions. But he'd chosen not to. All of them had. She figured this would be something they'd struggle with for years to come.

"She died thinking we didn't care enough to come back. And she left us those dogs and the inn hoping they would keep us here." He kept talking, reconciling with himself.

Nikki simply held his hand. She listened attentively and every now and then rubbed her fingers along the back of his hand to remind him that she was there.

"I can't bring her back," he said finally. "And I can't change what happened."

"No, you can't," she told him.

"And I can't be what she wanted me to be."

Nikki shook her head. "That's not true. She wanted you to be happy. Whether that happiness was here in

Sweetland or not, that's what she wanted for all of you."
Her chest clenched as she said the words; the thought of
Quinn leaving caused an indescribable pain. But Nikki
wouldn't hold him here, she wouldn't guilt him with her
feelings, adding to what he already felt for what happened
to his grandmother. If leaving was his answer, then she
had to be fine with it. She had to let him go.

The moment she let her mind take hold of that fact
Quinn looked at her saying words that would only con-
fuse her more.

"But now there's you."

She wanted to say *and?* but refrained.

"I never counted on you," he continued. The way he was
looking at her was speaking a lot louder than his words. He
wanted her, there was no mistaking that. Lust was clearly
in his eyes. It was also easy and convenient since they were
here alone.

Nikki looked away, because she'd realized that lust
wasn't enough. Not anymore.

"I thought I'd come back and go to the funeral then go
home. I didn't want to be here, didn't want to stay in this
place because of all the bad memories. The pain."

"That pain travels with you, Quinn. Don't you know
that? Did you really hurt less in Seattle or did you simply
trade that pain for something else? Guilt maybe? Wherever you go your baggage goes right along with you. So at
some point you just have to leave it all behind. You have
to move on."

His lips clenched tightly. He hadn't shaved; his usually
neat and trimmed low-cut beard was thicker, his eyes
darker, giving him a really grim appearance.

"Sometimes things are easier said than done," was his
reply.

"I wish there was something I could say to make it
easier," she told him, lifting a hand to rub along his cheek.

Nikki really did wish she could just speak some words

and he'd magically feel better. She wished she could take all his bad memories away and be there to make new ones with him. But Quinn would have to want the same thing. Something told her he didn't.

"For what it's worth, I'm glad you were here when I came back," he told her. "I don't regret what's happened between us."

The *but* hung ominously in the air.

Only to never come because Quinn had leaned in, touching her lips softly with his own. It was the softest, gentlest kiss he'd ever given her. His tongue stroked hers almost lovingly and despite warning bells all but screeching in her head Nikki melted into that kiss. She leaned in closer, wrapped her arms around his neck. Felt his hands slide down her back, pulling her closer. She straddled him because his hold on her was so tight and this kiss was so sweet. His hands were moving up and down her back, one finally cupping her head to hold her exactly where he wanted her.

When he pulled back they both heaved for breath. He kissed her lips again, just a peck, then rested his forehead against hers.

"Sharane," he whispered, his voice sounding more tortured than she'd ever heard it before.

With an inner start Nikki realized why it was more tortured. Then, as if he was foolish enough to think she hadn't heard him the first time, he whispered it again, this time with his voice cracking, "Sharane."

For one excruciatingly long moment Nikki remained perfectly still. She tried to block out everything but her mind chose this moment to act like a tape recorder, replaying the last second over and over until she flattened her palms on Quinn's chest, pushed against him, and stood up.

"What did you just call me?" she asked. She'd closed her eyes, couldn't stand to look at him as he said it again.

While she waited for his response she shook her head, praying she'd been wrong, knowing she wasn't.

"I . . . I . . . dammit!" he cursed. "Nikki, I'm . . . sorry."

Her head would not stop shaking and now her entire body had joined in. She opened her eyes slowly, taking a couple more backward steps because the distance between them needed to be better than great right now.

"I am not Sharane," she said slowly.

"I know," he said, standing and taking a step toward her.

"No!" Nikki held up both hands to stop him. "No! Don't come near me.

"I am not your dead ex-girlfriend," she continued. "And I never will be."

"I know and I apologize. I don't know why I said that."

"Oh, you know why you said it. If you don't you're in a bigger state of denial than I ever thought possible. You're still in love with her, Quinn. You're in love with a damned ghost!"

"No, Nikki. Listen to me, it was a mistake. A really bad mistake and I'm so sorry but I didn't mean it. It's just been a really long day and I—"

She didn't give a damn how long the day had been. "I want you to go," she told him, her heart breaking with each word.

"Nikki—"

"I want you to go now, Quinn!"

"Not without you understanding. There's been so much going on since I came back. So many memories and feelings and just when I thought I was getting a handle on them. Just when I thought—" He paused, a muscle twitching in his jaw. "I just need you to understand."

"Understand?" she whispered incredulously. "You want me to understand you're so in love with your ex that you've been thinking of her every minute you've been with me. No wonder you can't say how long you're staying and you won't make any plans beyond the next day—because you're still waiting for her, dreaming of her! You're so pathetic! You wouldn't come back to see your dying grandmother because you were too busy mourning a girl who's been dead for twenty years. A girl you can never bring back!"

She wanted to reach out and smack him, or to kick herself for falling for another man who couldn't or wouldn't love her in return. Maybe she was the pathetic one. No, she wasn't. She deserved love and dammit, she was going to have it. If it wasn't with Quinn Cantrell then so be it, but Nikki wasn't about to settle for half a man while the other half was either in love with or still eaten up with guilt about his dead ex-girlfriend!

When he didn't say another word she almost choked on her tears. The pain in her chest was so deep and so profound, she should have fallen to the floor with its intensity. But she didn't. She didn't cry and she didn't break. Not when it was Randall breaking her heart and not for Quinn.

"See, you can't even deny that," she stated in a voice that sounded strong, resilient, and drop-dead-serious.

"Was I your substitute for her while you were here in Sweetland? When you decided it was time to go back to your real life were you just going to leave me here like you hurried to leave Sharane's memory? No," she continued talking while shaking her head. "You won't answer that. You won't open up and share a goddamned thing about your life, your past, your pain. You're too perfect for that, you're the Mighty Quinn, no question about that. But you know what else you are? You're a bastard. A depressing and selfish bastard who doesn't know enough to see good standing right in front of him. Well, I'm through hiding behind corners staring at you, wanting you, needing you. I'm through waiting for you to be the man that I need. I'm just through, Quinn. Now you can just get the hell out of my house!"

There was nothing Quinn could say. There were words rambling around in his head, an explanation or two that he could spurt out and pray the words didn't fall on deaf ears. But he didn't because he'd just done what he'd sworn to her he would never do. He'd hurt her far more than the lying, opportunistic Randall. He could see it in her eyes, hear it in her voice. Not only was Nikki hurt, she was disappointed, and that stabbed at Quinn like a jagged blade.

It would have been better if he'd just left and gone back to Seattle without ever seeing her again. It might have been better if he dropped off the face of the earth altogether. Anything would be an improvement over what he'd just done, leaving had been his only apology, his only attempt at soothing her pain. It was the least he could do.

Getting into the car, he cursed his stupidity and started the engine. He drove in a trance, much as he had earlier, because, dammit, it seemed this day couldn't get any worse.

Then it did.

Quinn's cell phone rang just as he was about to turn onto Sycamore.

"Hello?" he answered, half hoping it was Nikki on the other end, but knowing that this was about as probable as the sky opening up and raining cash all around him.

"Quinn! Parker's been hurt. They're sending a mede-vac to pick him up!" Raine yelled, her voice hitching as she cried.

"What the hell happened?"

"He was on his bike and he crashed somewhere on the highway. The officer that called said he was speeding and lost control. They're taking him to Capital City Hospital since they have a trauma center there."

"Dammit!" Quinn cursed. "I'm about five minutes

from the house. You and Savannah come on out and we'll
get right on the road."

"Okay. Can you call Michelle?" she asked, breaking
down totally.

"It's okay, Raine. He's gonna be fine. I'll stop at Michelle's place on my way to get you. Get Savannah and
wait on the porch."

Ten minutes later the Cantrell siblings were on their
way to Annapolis.

Chapter 22

Preston Cantrell drove like a madman, cutting the forty-five-minute ride from Baltimore to Annapolis short by about twenty minutes. He pulled his car into the parking lot so erratically he ended up taking two parking spaces instead of one. But he didn't care. In what was almost a run he arrived at the double glass doors leading to the emergency room, cursing that they were taking too long to slide open for him.

He was at the front desk giving Parker's name when his cell phone rang.

"Yeah?" he answered after he'd seen Quinn's number on the display screen.

"They're about to take him into surgery."

"Where? I'm at the emergency entrance."

"Third floor, come down to the end of the hall to the left."

The young female at the desk was giving him a look that said speak-now-or-get-the-hell-away. Preston left without a word, running to a bank of elevators he prayed would take him to his destination. When he arrived in his brother's room his racing heart and stalled footsteps held him still.

On a bed seemingly surrounded by tubes and white sheets was his brother. His twin. For all intents and purposes the other part of him. He was five minutes older than Parker and an inch and a half taller. Those were their biggest differences. They were closer to each other than any of their other siblings—hence the reason they'd both ended up in Baltimore instead of in separate locales. They saw each other frequently, either in the courtroom or when they carved out a moment to have dinner and/or drinks. There was nothing Preston would not do for his brother, absolutely nothing, and he knew Parker felt the same.

Seeing him like this was a blow to Preston's already fragile emotional state and his body trembled at the sight.

Raine moved first, coming to stand beside Preston, wrapping her arm around his shoulders.

"He's unconscious. And his leg is broken pretty badly. They have to go in and . . . and remove the shattered pieces of bone," she said, her voice cracking just a bit.

Michelle came to his other side and made a motion to touch him, but Preston chose that moment to move. He wasn't ready for that, not just yet. Coming to a stop beside the bed, he took his brother's swollen hand that was riddled with cuts and blood.

"Hang in there, bro," he whispered, his own voice hitching on the words.

He felt a strong hand clapping on his shoulder and knew that Quinn stood near.

"Let us pray," he heard Michelle say and closed his eyes because that was all he could do at the moment.

The sound of her voice was so familiar, the words of spiritual inspiration rolling like a memorized litany from her lips. His chest tightened, emotion threatening to clog his lungs. His grandmother had prayed just like that, standing right beside the bed when his father died. That had been the only other time—besides at Gramma's funeral—that Preston had shed a tear. Gritting his teeth, he held on as tightly as he could to his emotion. Parker wasn't dying, not today and not anytime soon. They were going to fix him up and he'd be back to normal in no time. They'd go back to the city and work together as they'd done all these years. Everything would be back to normal soon, he convinced himself.

When the nurses came to transport Parker to surgery, Preston moved to the waiting room with his other siblings. He sat in a chair near a wall. Raine sat right next to him, reaching out to take his hand. Quinn sat a short distance away, his elbows propped on his knees, head down. Michelle and Savannah were together, Savannah's head resting on Michelle's shoulder as tears marred her absolutely perfect face.

Nikki and Cordy arrived at the hospital at almost two thirty that morning. Cordy had heard about the accident and called Odell, who told her it might be best to come and tell Nikki in person. Mother and daughter had knocked on Nikki's door until she rolled out of the bed, head pounding, eyes swollen from crying, to answer.

"What? What's wrong?" she'd answered, instantly awake at the sight of both her mother and sister crying.

The moment they'd told her Nikki had slipped on sweatpants and a shirt and they'd driven as fast as Cordy would go without the threat of being pulled over by the police.

"He's still in surgery. The family is in waiting room C," the nurse at the front desk on the third floor told them.

They'd moved quickly to that waiting room, only for Nikki to stop the moment she saw Quinn.

He sat alone, solemn and defiant. He wouldn't want anyone near him right now, wouldn't want the comfort of a friend or of a . . . a . . . what was she to him now?

Instead of spending her time trying to figure that out she went straight to Michelle and Savannah. They were the two Cantrells she was closest to—with the exception of Quinn, that is.

"Hey," Michelle said, looking up to greet her and Cordy. "What are you doing here at this time of night?"

"Jonah heard the call for an ambulance over the police wire and told Caleb, who was working the night shift at the firehouse. Caleb called Cordy and here we are," Nikki said, trying valiantly for a light voice. It wasn't easy since Quinn was so close and her heart ached to go to him. And Savannah was crying quietly, as if her world had just crumbled. Michelle's eyes were puffy and red and Nikki just wanted to hug them both until they felt better.

"Oh, the Sweetland hotline. They're faster and usually more accurate than MSNBC," Michelle said, trying for a bit of humor.

Cordy was the only one to chuckle. "Can I get anyone coffee?" she asked.

Michelle shook her head. "No, thanks. I'm okay."

"I need something," Savannah said, sitting up straighter. "I need to get away from here for a minute."

"Sure. Sure. I'll walk with you," Nikki offered, because suddenly she needed to get away from here, too.

"They say he's going to be okay," Savannah said as they stepped off the elevator to the first floor of the hospital where they were told the canteen and vending machines were located.

"I believe that," Nikki told her unwaveringly. "Parker's too strong and too stubborn not to come out of this okay. Besides, somebody has to curse out the motorcycle that failed to keep him safe."

Savannah almost smiled at that. "Or the road that made him crash into the guardrail. He'll be really pissed about that."

"He will and he'll probably be ready to arrest even the officers that showed up on the scene for one reason or another."

"Yep, that sounds just like Parker," Savannah agreed. "It's been different since we've all been back. Different than before and then again the same," she continued as they walked down a hallway that seemed deserted. "Does that make sense?"

Nikki nodded. "It does. You've all grown up since the last time you were here. You're different people and still you're siblings, connected by blood and tradition."

"And Gramma and that house and those dang dogs." She let out a long sigh.

"Yeah, always connected by something," Nikki agreed.

"He can't die," Savannah whispered, stopping and standing perfectly still.

Nikki stopped with her, looked at the woman who on every magazine, every billboard, every runway, always looked so perfect. Not a hair out of place, makeup that looked as if it were made just for her. There were days Nikki had looked at those pictures of Savannah and felt deep pangs of jealousy, moments when she wished for one second it could have been her, that she'd been bold enough to leave, to reach for something other than what was right in front of her. Then she'd resigned herself to the fact that Savannah's path was her own and that she'd had to make her own way as well.

Now, looking at her as tears poured from swollen and red eyes, slipping down cheeks with absolutely no makeup, slim shoulders racking with the pain she was experiencing, Nikki realized that girl in those pictures and on those runways wasn't her best friend, she wasn't the Savannah she'd grown up with. Here, right at this moment, this woman who had no choice but to feel real feelings and to accept human frailties without the cover of cosmetics or the airbrushing of photographs had been her very best friend. Nikki's heart ached for her.

She pulled Savannah close, holding her in a tight hug. "You're right, he's not going to die. He's going to pull through and we're going to take care of him when he does. You hear me? Remember that time Parker and Preston went on that treasure hunt down at Yates Passage? That was before they'd knocked down all those trees and cleaned up the creek down there. The treasure hunt had led them into what they called the haunted forest and as they'd traipsed along looking for the hidden treasure of Sweetland they'd accidentally knocked down that wasp nest. Parker had been stung three times, but Preston hadn't been stung once since he'd caked on some concoction your grandmother had made him. Parker complained the concoction stank to high heaven and refused to put it on."

Nikki talked as Savannah sobbed, tears streaming down her face now even as she smiled with the memory.

"We were only eight years old then," Savannah whispered.

Nikki nodded. "And we sat right by Parker's bed bringing him lemonade and giving him the Tylenol your grandmother said he needed for the pain."

"His face was all swollen. He looked like a mutant."

Nikki laughed because Savannah had been very concerned with Parker's face. Praying hard every night that the good Lord would fix it so he was cute again, even though at thirteen the last thing Parker wanted to hear his younger sister say to him was that he was cute. Now, if Casey Merriweather had said that to him, it would have been a different story entirely.

"But in a couple of days he was up out of that bed chasing us out of the house and calling us little hellions once more."

Savannah nodded as she pulled away, using her fingers to wipe the tears from beneath her eyes like she thought her eyeliner might have smeared. She wasn't wearing any but Nikki figured old habits were hard to break.

"Yeah, he chased us down to the water that time and we both dirtied our white shorts. My mother yelled for days about that," Savannah said, now smiling with the memory.

"My mother simply shook her head and tossed them in the trash. She said she knew it was a mistake for us to wear white when we could barely keep our denim clothes clean." Nikki took Savannah's hand as they continued to walk.

"Mrs. Brockington was always a different type of mother than my mom."

Nikki didn't know what to say to that. Patricia Cantrell had been a different type of woman than the women of Sweetland. She'd held herself above them and didn't socialize with anyone but her husband. Nikki remembered her mother saying, "That woman's like a bird stuck in a cage. She's trying so hard to break out and when she does she's gonna fly so far and so fast, Clifford Cantrell won't know where to find her."

Well, Clifford Cantrell hadn't needed to worry with how far his wife flew away from Sweetland. She'd stayed until the day after his funeral. Only the kids knew how fast she'd gone, leaving them for what Nikki believed was forever.

"We'll take care of Parker, just like Gramma taught us," Savannah said when they came up to the automatic coffee machine.

"We certainly will," Nikki agreed.

"Now, what do you want? Decaf, cappuccino, hot chocolate?"

"Please, I like my caffeine punch hard, fast, and cold as ice." Savannah reached into her pocket and pulled out a couple of dollar bills, slipping them into the machine she retrieved a Coke and opened it instantly. Taking a huge gulp she smacked her lips and smiled at Nikki.

"Dealing with an injured Parker is going to take all the energy I have," she said, laughing.

Nikki laughed along with her, enjoying the memories they shared and the closeness that seemed to be reemerging between them. Parker Cantrell would recover and Nikki would stand by her best friend's side as he did. Nothing else mattered, not even the other Cantrell man who had also brought back memories for her. Quinn hadn't paid her any attention years ago when she'd begun pining after him, and he wasn't paying her any attention now. The difference now was that Nikki had grown up. Pining for Quinn was something she absolutely would not do, not ever again.

One week after Parker's accident, when he was being released and prescribed home physical therapy three times a week, Quinn left Sweetland.

"I can't believe you're just going to leave again!" Michelle protested. "Parker's coming home today, he's going to need a lot of help. I have catering orders and we have guests at the inn. Bay Day celebration is coming up and I have to get ready for that."

"I'll be here for the rest of the summer," Raine announced from her perch near the window. She spent a lot of time simply staring out the window and Quinn wondered if what she found out there was more interesting than what was going on in here. Probably more relaxing, he figured with a frown.

"See, you won't be alone," he told Michelle and knew instinctively he'd messed up with her again.

"That's real grand, Quinn. You said you'd taken a leave of absence from work. So I don't understand your need to run back to Seattle right at this moment."

She might understand if he explained, but Quinn wasn't 100 percent sure himself. He just knew that this was what he had to do. He was already packed and had arranged to turn in his rental car at the airport. This was the right decision, he was sure of it.

"We haven't even figured out what to do about the taxes. The money Raine and I have put up isn't enough.

And I'm pouring every extra dime I have into my catering business. Quinn, this needs to be taken care of sooner rather than later. Inez called me the other day to ask when we'd be making payment."

"You tell Inez King she can deal directly with me," he said, more than a little annoyed.

"Preston went to speak with Inez," Michelle told him with a sigh. "They won't budge on the penalties and interest. It's exactly two years' worth of taxes. If we don't pay in the next thirty days . . ." She trailed off, tears shining in her eyes.

"Don't worry. They won't do a damned thing. Not by the time I get through with that greedy couple. It's all going to work out, Michelle. And I'll call every day to check on Parker's progress. The therapist we hired will be here three times a week so he should be recovering well," he said.

"Parker's a fighter. He'll do just fine," Raine added. She'd looked at Quinn with such sad eyes. But she didn't say anything. Raine never accused or judged, she always waited patiently for explanations and tried her damndest to accept them even when others wouldn't. This time she was at Michelle's side. She wanted him to stay, thought he owed it to all of them, especially Parker, to stay. But he couldn't.

Deciding the conversation with his sisters wasn't going to get any better unless he promised to stay, Quinn walked toward the door. "Tell Savannah I'll call her, too," he told them, knowing the words fell on deaf ears. Neither Michelle nor Raine looked as if they wanted to hear what he'd said.

He was doing the right thing, Quinn told himself as he grabbed his bags from beside the door. Dixi barked in what was probably protest as he picked up her carrier and headed out. She'd want to stay here where she was born because Dixi wasn't like him. She loved her family, loved her home. Now he was making her a deserter as well. As he climbed into the car Quinn promised to make it up to Dixi. He'd make it up to all of them.

"He's gone!" Savannah yelled the moment Nikki opened the door for her that evening.

"Hey, Savannah. Come on in and have a seat," Nikki said with a half smile. She and Savannah had been spending a lot of time together lately.

They'd shopped, had lunch, visited the salon—which Nikki had begun to enjoy—and even gone to a happy hour at Charlie's Bar one night. It had been fun laughing and having drinks—Nikki preferred the fruity type because it masked the taste of the alcohol. At any rate it had been really good to have a friend again.

"Did you hear me?" she asked, flopping down onto the couch. "He's gone. Just like that, he packed his bags, took his yapping dog, and left. I can't believe him sometimes!"

"Who are we talking about?" Nikki asked. She sat cross-legged on the other end of the couch.

"Quinn! He left this morning to go back to Seattle," Savannah said before lying back on the chair. She was a very animated talker; the more her mouth moved, the more her hands, arms, and whatever else she could put in motion on her body to accentuate what she was saying did as well. Right now she'd lifted her arms into the air and let them fall dramatically down at her sides. She was clearly flustered by this event.

Nikki, however, didn't really know how she felt about it. She hadn't spoken to Quinn since the night of the accident, a whole week ago. She'd seen him here and there at the B&B but for the most part he'd stayed at the hospital with Parker. Each day, however, Dixi would come into her office, all feet and wobbly stomach because she was gaining weight. Nikki would take at least an hour to go outside and play with her. After the second day of this happening she figured it wasn't a mistake and that someone must be ushering the puppy to her office—her first guess was that that someone was Quinn. It made her feel like she and Quinn were divorcing parents sharing custody of their child, and for a few moments of each of the hours she spent with Dixi, she allowed herself to feel sad about that correlation.

"So he's gone. Did you say he took Dixi with him?" she asked curiously. From the start Quinn had been resistant to owning a dog, and almost more resistant to Dixi and her needs. It was a fact he'd never hidden or apologized for.

"Yes, he took her. Which makes me feel like crap for not wanting my little bundle of joy," Savannah continued.

"I don't think that was his goal," Nikki heard herself say then clapped her lips shut.

Savannah turned her head to face Nikki. She was still lying back on the chair, trying hard to keep her hands still but not succeeding. "I know you are not defending him. He practically dumped you and ran across the country. Doesn't that piss you off?"

Now that she put it that way . . .

"No," Nikki said shaking her head. "That's not actually what happened. We'd decided to part ways before he left." At least that's what she figured was best. He'd called her another woman's name, a dead woman at that. Hell yeah it was over! No matter how much she still thought about him.

"Right, well that didn't stop him from watching you like some lovesick teenager every chance he could get."

"And when would those chances have been?" she asked, wondering what Savannah was talking about. The woman changed subjects like she changed shoes, frequently and impulsively.

"At the hospital and at the house. It seemed like wherever you were he was lurking around somewhere like a stalker just looking at you. I told him how pitiful it was and he rudely told me to mind my own business."

Nikki almost laughed because that sounded just like how Quinn used to treat them when they were younger. But they weren't young anymore. They were adults and she and Quinn had been lovers. Now it seemed they were back to being nothing. She'd be lying if she said it didn't sting a bit. Like a swarm of angry bees vying for an available spot on her body to take aim.

Her phone rang before she could comment again and Nikki silently thanked the heavens for the reprieve. She wasn't sure what she would have said next or what she didn't actually say would have revealed.

"Hello?" she answered, still wondering about Quinn.

"Hi, Nikki. This is Jonah."

"Hey, Jonah. What's going on?" she asked, instantly on alert. Jonah was a cop and as of late she hadn't had such a good rapport with the police.

"Are you busy? I can call back if you're doing something?"

For as long as she'd known Jonah he'd always been shy. He'd grown into an attractive man with thick, dark blond hair that he kept cut short, and warm brown eyes. After high school he'd even beefed up a bit. Probably due to his training in the police academy, but it had made him one of the best catches in the Sweetland bachelor pool.

"No. Savannah and I are just sitting here talking. Did you need something?"

"Yes, ah, I wanted to ask you something." He cleared his throat.

"Okay."

"Bud Nesby's having a grand opening party for his new hot dog joint tomorrow night. I was wondering if you'd like to go with me. Nothing fancy, you know, we could just go down and check the place out, have a drink or a bite to eat. If you don't want to go that's fine. I just thought we could go together or something."

Nikki was flattered. Jonah was asking her out on a date. But she should probably say no. That would be the right thing to do. Why? Clearly she wasn't seeing anyone at the moment. Not only was that relationship over, he'd gone back across the country, so that wasn't even a consideration. So she should say yes.

"Nikki?" he asked.

"Ah, yes, I'm sorry. I'm still here," she said with a smile. "Sure, I'd love to go to the opening with you tomorrow."

Hanging up the phone, she heard Savannah laugh.

"Wow, I guess you really don't care that Quinn's gone," Savannah quipped.

Chapter 23

Two weeks later

June was half over. In two weeks, the town would be all decorated and ready to celebrate its annual Bay Day. Even though the all-day events didn't start until Saturday, this year they'd celebrate the entire first week of July, including a huge fireworks display on the Fourth.

With that in mind Odell and Cordy had planned Nikki's congratulatory barbecue for the last Saturday of June. They'd invited just about everyone in Sweetland and rented tents and chairs that now lined Odell's backyard so that it looked like there was a wedding reception going on. Odell probably wished that's what she was celebrating instead of Nikki's promotion to manager of The Silver Spoon.

That wish was totally out of Nikki's control. Marriage wasn't on the horizon for her. In fact, after three dates with Jonah, she'd finally had to tell him that there was only friendship in their future. He just wasn't the one. He'd seemingly accepted that fact without too much response. Nikki got the impression that he'd sensed her hesitance pretty early on. She knew he'd find a really terrific woman to fall in love with someday. As for her, Nikki was almost certain her heart wasn't ready for another trip on the love train.

Savannah had called earlier this morning, telling Nikki she might not make it to the festivities today. She had an emergency Skype meeting set up with her agent. Nikki had heard a lot about Savannah's career and her life in general. For all that it appeared to be glitz and glamour, she sensed it was also stressful and maybe becoming too much for Savannah to handle—hence the reason she was still in Sweetland, a month after Mrs. Cantrell's death.

The only Cantrell whom Nikki actually expected to see today would be Michelle and that was because she was bringing her version of summer punch and four of her almond pound cakes. That's what Odell had told Ralph last night when he'd asked what was on the menu. Nikki's father was a diabetic so he didn't eat much by way of sweets anymore, but Michelle's almond pound cake was one of his favorites so Odell would let him slide today.

As she took the steps from her apartment Nikki was actually in a pretty good mood. The sun was shinning brightly, but the forecast wasn't calling for high humidity, just a nice summer day. The grill was already lit; she could smell the charcoal and saw the billow of smoke over by the trees where Caleb and Brad had set it up early this morning. By now it would be good and hot and ready for all the meat and other goodies they had to go on it.

"Well, hello, and congratulations," Michelle said as she was getting out of her car and heading around to the trunk.

Nikki continued down the walkway until she was standing right beside her. Michelle had a really quiet type of pretty. You tended to forget about it on a daily basis because she was always in the kitchen or in the restaurant or doing something in between the two places. But at times like this, when she just walked up with a smiling face, Nikki was reminded how pretty she was and how awfully lonely she tended to look.

"Hi, let me help you," Nikki offered, reaching into the trunk to pick up one of the cakes wrapped in plastic wrap and aluminum foil.

"You're not supposed to be working today, you're the guest of honor."

Nikki laughed. "Please, you know how it is around here. Everybody pitches in."

"Yeah, I know. It's a good day, though. They were talking about rain earlier in the week but it cleared up pretty nicely."

Both of them had their hands full now and were headed toward the first tent where all the precooked food was being stored.

"It did and I'm so glad. There's even a nice breeze," Nikki noted.

"Sure is. I left Ms. Cleo and Lily in the yard so they could get some air."

"Good idea," Nikki said, nodding. Michelle had purchased an outdoor gate that almost looked like a child's playpen but was much bigger. During the day she let all the dogs go out there to play and get some exercise. This way, nobody had to chase them down when it was time to come in. If it was too humid she'd keep them inside. Most days Savannah's puppy Micah would also join them because Savannah didn't know what to do with the dog besides yell at it or run from it.

While Parker had been in the hospital Michelle had taken care of Rufus for him. And last she'd heard Preston had someone coming to look at Coco for a possible adoption. Raine, who had moved in with Michelle to free up another room at the inn, kept the adorable Loki with her most of the time, almost as if he were her only friend in the world.

"They love being out there," Nikki commented finally when they'd pushed through the open flap that served as a door and crossed to the tables lined in a U shape around the tent.

There were already dishes on the table, some covered with foil and others with glass or plastic tops. It looked as if they were preparing to feed an army. With half the town expected, it would seem like they were doing exactly that. Two tables held Sterno racks lined up neatly. Fires were lit beneath them, and aromas coming from whatever was being kept warm inside the pans filled the tent.

"They do and they're still home where they were born, where they're used to being. I think that's so important," Michelle said when she was satisfied with where she'd set the two glass pitchers full of punch.

Nikki couldn't wait to taste it—Michelle's punch looked more like a really cool, colorful ice cream concoction. She'd already started walking out of the tent, and Nikki followed her.

"The others are thriving, though. They're gaining weight and growing. I think they'll be fine."

"I'm worried about Sweet Dixi," she said when they were once again at the trunk.

Nikki was, too, but she had to let that go. There was nothing she could do about that anymore.

"I'm sure she'll be fine. Quinn's probably found a great home for her by now."

Michelle shook her head as she waited for Nikki to get the last cake and closed the trunk.

"No. He hasn't," she said simply then passed Nikki and headed back inside the tent.

Don't ask. Don't ask. Don't ask.

"So he's keeping her?" So much for listening to her conscience.

"Yes, he is," Michelle replied tightly.

"You don't think that's a good idea?" she pressed when Michelle stood looking at the food, a frown marring her brow.

"Huh? Oh, Quinn. I think he might be getting it together. But who knows, only time will tell."

And that's all she had an opportunity to say because Odell came in at that moment with Daisy and Celia Bellmont, all three of them with more food in hand. For the next forty-five minutes Nikki was either sticking serving spoons into dishes, pulling off foil, rewrapping dishes, or putting out more paper plates and cutlery. Who was the guest of honor again?

Hoover and Inez King lived in a newly built detached Cape Cod house just before the opening to Yates Passage. From what Quinn had learned from Liza, they'd just purchased the land in the last two years and had this house built as a sign that they were the ones responsible for the redevelopment in that area. As Liza put it, "Inez loves to show off, thinks it makes her more of a Fitzgerald if she has money and land. Not that it helps since she's still a third cousin to a family famous for dismissing anyone who isn't first in the bloodline."

Quinn had talked to Liza over the phone several times while he was in Seattle, in an attempt to figure out what exactly had happened with the taxes. His investigation had led him here, back to Sweetland, walking up the steps to the beige-sided house with the pristine white trim.

A young woman dressed in a maid's uniform opened the door with a smile. Quinn almost grimaced because what in the world did the Kings need a maid for? Maybe to pick up after Hoover's drunken habits.

"Good morning, I'm here to see Inez. I'm Quinn Cantrell," he said pleasantly.

"Come on in, sir. I'll get Mrs. King for you right away," she told him with a smile and a lightness to her step that Quinn hoped she wouldn't lose working in this house with two of the craziest people he'd ever met.

He tried not to look around too much, so as not to be

disgusted by all the money they'd spent building and decorating this house. All the money that hadn't been theirs to spend.

"What are you doing here?"

Quinn turned from where he'd been standing admiring the fireplace despite himself. Inez was dressed in white linen pants and a gray top. Her short hair was combed straight down, resting with blunt edges at her chin. On her fingers diamonds sparkled as cool as the glint of her crystalline blue eyes as she glared at him.

"I wanted to take care of this business with my family's inn," he told her, not bothering with any other formalities.

She lifted a hand and waved him away. "Call my office and make an appointment for sometime next week. This is the weekend and I do not do business from my house."

Inez had been all prepared to walk out when Quinn's words stopped her. "Chief Farraway will be pulling up in about ten minutes to take you down to the station for questioning."

She froze, then turned in what was a very poised motion considering what he'd just said to her.

"What are you talking about?" she inquired.

"I'm talking about the money you've been embezzling from the city fund. The exorbitant interest and penalties you've been attaching to everything from local water bills to tax bills and collecting from the fine folks of Sweetland."

"How dare you." She started walking toward him in slow, measured steps. "Do you have any idea who you're messing with?"

Her thin lips had all but disappeared into straight slashes webbed lines forming at the corners.

"It appears I'm dealing with a cheater who likes to abuse her power. What I also found very interesting—and this is courtesy of my brother Preston and a certain PI firm he employs—was the connection you have to A.W. Investments."

She visibly paled then, her eyes growing bigger as she swallowed slowly.

A.W. Investments was owned by Aaron Witherspoon, the same man who had employed Randall Davis. Of course the PI was still following up on leads because Quinn wanted to feed everything he knew about the two cases to the authorities as soon as possible. But it looked as if Nikki hadn't been the only female Randall had met up with two years ago. Inez King's number had also been listed on Davis's cell phone bill. The exact connection, Quinn still wasn't sure of, but together with the bills to Sweetland residents that had been substantially inflated and prepared by Inez, and the deductions from the city accounts that matched deposits into the Kingses' account, Chief Farraway hadn't had any problem securing an arrest warrant from the judge in Easton.

"You have no idea what you're talking about," she said, everything from her bony shoulders to her ring-clad hands shaking. "You don't even belong in this town."

"That's where you're wrong," Quinn stated, taking a step toward her. He wouldn't touch her. No, that was definitely not a possibility no matter how angry he was for the scheme she'd tried to get away with. "My great-grandfather was once mayor of Sweetland. My grandmother was instrumental in Sweetland's revitalization and a pillar of this community. And I was born and raised here. Sweetland is my home," he stated without qualm.

"Since when?" was her reply. "Oh, since you started sleeping with a local. That tramp sleeps with everybody. I've even seen her chasing after Hoover."

Right, Quinn thought and almost laughed. Nikki really wanted Hoover King. "Just so you know, we'll be keeping the inn and the land surrounding it. Just in case you were thinking of offering it to one of your business associates."

"We'll just see about that!" she tossed at him a second before another knock sounded at her front door.

Inez spun around so fast Quinn thought she might lose her balance and hit the floor. Instead a hand went to her neck as she looked back at him, then toward the door once more. She was trying to figure out if she should run or not.

"Don't even think about it," Quinn advised her. If he had to he would hold her down until Chief Farraway could get inside to detain her.

Luckily it didn't come to that. Farraway was walking into the living room just as Inez had taken her first step.

"Let's make this as easy as possible, Inez," he said to her.

Quinn didn't think this was going to end well. So once he knew Inez King would be taken into custody and prosecuted for her crimes, he left without looking back.

The barbecue had started an hour and a half ago. Quinn knew this and had timed himself so he'd arrive late. Making an entrance wasn't his plan; slipping in quietly and unnoticed was. He'd been back in Sweetland since early this morning. His flight had actually come in at six; then he'd taken a shuttle to the garage a couple of miles from the airport where his car had been stored once it arrived from Seattle.

Dixi had sat quietly in her carrier on the backseat, loving the breeze that blew in from the open back windows.

"You're home, Sweet Dixi," he'd told her as he drove down the highway headed back to Sweetland.

The last two weeks had been a flurry of activity for him and his puppy. Sweet Dixi had immediately been enrolled in puppy training classes. He'd been amazed to learn there was even such a thing, but had figured this would be a good idea and was absolutely right. Sweet Dixi had thrived in puppy kindergarten and socialization class. And while they hadn't been able to stay for her progression to puppy middle school—which would cover more of the basics for puppies—he'd received an excellent referral from the school in Seattle to one in Easton. It would only be a forty-five-minute drive to keep Dixi's training current. Quinn definitely planned to keep up with the training as he had quickly fallen in love with his better-behaved puppy, who didn't pee in his shoes but still stole the remote control every couple of days.

Before heading to the inn he'd made a couple of stops, one for Inez King. That confrontation hadn't really been necessary. He could have simply let the police take care of it. But Quinn admitted it was a matter of pride. He needed to show her she hadn't beaten him or his family.

Afterward, feeling almost 100 percent better about his return, he'd headed to the inn. He'd used the restaurant entrance hoping to avoid running into any of his siblings on his way to the caretaker's suite. He should have known better.

"Well, you came back," she'd said when she came out of the kitchen with the spatula that Quinn figured was her weapon of choice in hand.

"I did," he said simply. He'd talked to Michelle over the phone a couple times since he'd been gone. One, to check on how things were going with Parker's rehab—even though he'd talked to Parker himself—and two to find out how Michelle was doing and if she were still upset with him.

"Are you staying?" she'd asked simply.

It was a simple enough question. "I am," he'd replied without hesitation.

"Good," she'd said, the corners of her lips lifting in a smile just before she turned and walked back into the kitchen. Before she was completely out of earshot she'd yelled, "The Brockingtons are having a big celebration for Nikki this afternoon at four, just in case you're interested."

Of course he was interested, Michelle knew that. Quinn smiled, shaking his head as he and Dixi headed back to the caretaker's suite where they would stay with Parker.

Speak of the devil.

"Want to tell me what you're up to?" Parker asked from the recliner where he sat, his leg propped up in the knee-to-ankle brace given to him by his therapist.

"I'm about to take a shower and get dressed to go to the barbecue. You want to go with me?" Quinn asked after digging in his bag for clean clothes since he'd yet to completely unpack.

"You know that's not what I'm talking about," Parker said with a chuckle.

"That's my answer," Quinn replied and headed to the bathroom. There were two full bathrooms upstairs that catered to the four of the guest rooms. The largest room—which they rented out as a suite—had its own bathroom. On the first floor were two full bathrooms, the one in the caretaker's suite and the one that had newly been built with the room Sylvester stayed in, and a powder room just off the foyer.

"Fine. But if you're going to see Nikki I should tell you that she's been going out with that cop, Jonah."

Quinn almost stopped his procession to the bathroom. Almost. But he knew that's exactly the reaction Parker was waiting for. Instead he kept on walking, yelling over his shoulder just as he came to the door.

"Not for long."

It had only taken about twenty minutes for Quinn to see Nikki for the first time since he'd left. She was standing by the swings with her nieces holding a cup as she watched them both go back and forth into the air. The sun shone down directly on her, like a spotlight. Her hair—those soft curls he'd missed rubbing between his fingers—reflected the rays and looked more golden brown than he remembered. The same went for her complexion. She'd tanned, he thought as her smooth skin looked sun-kissed and tempting. Her body hadn't changed and neither had his reaction to it, he figured as he went to take a step and felt himself hardening.

Too many times since he'd been here he'd been stopped by someone to talk about his return, or—in the case of Marabelle and Louisa, who were once again out without their husbands—his departure in the first place. That's why it had taken him so long to get to Nikki.

He moved toward her like a man on a mission, which he was technically. It wasn't until he was about four feet from her that she looked up and caught his gaze. For a moment in time everything went perfectly still. Noise from the other guests faded into the background until he'd swear it was just the two of them standing out here, just as they'd been that first night he kissed her.

She was shocked to see him, he could tell by the way her eyes had momentarily widened. Almost immediately that shock was transformed to cool acceptance. She stood straighter, switched her cup from one hand to another, but did not look away. No, Nikki wouldn't look away. She wouldn't walk away, either. Whatever he had to say and however she decided to deal with it she would not run. That fact made him love her even more.

"Hello, Nicole," he said when he was closer to her.

She tilted her head, raising a brow. "I'm Nicole now?"

Yes, this reception was going to be a cool one. Quinn could only hope that everything he had to say, everything he'd done over the last three weeks, and everything he felt inside for this woman would be enough, because he didn't have a plan B.

"You look really good," he told her instead of responding to her inquiry.

"Thank you," she said with a look that revealed how resigned she was to this meeting no matter what. "When did you come back?"

"This morning."

"How's Dixi?" she asked.

"She's really good. You should see what she's learned."

Again she had a shocked look. "You trained her?"

"I enrolled her in classes and she did really well."

She nodded. "Wow, that's . . . ah, great."

"You didn't think I'd keep her, did you?"

The youngest niece, Zyra was her name, struggled to get down off the swing, calling for Nikki to help. Quinn moved ahead instead, lifting the little girl under her arms and placing her gently on the ground. "There you go, princess," he said with a smile and was rewarded with one right back from Zyra.

"Here you go, sweetie," Nikki said when Zyra walked over to her. She bent down, holding the cup to the little girl's lips, and waited while she took a sip.

"Potty," she said loudly the moment she finished drinking.

Behind Quinn there came an overexaggerated sigh. When he turned it was to see the older sister, Mimi, jumping down from her swing.

"I'll take her, Aunt Nikki. She says she has to go but she doesn't when we get there," Mimi said with frustration.

"She's still learning, right, baby?" Nikki asked Zyra, who nodded her response. "Just be careful walking with her cup and take her all the way upstairs to the bathroom."

"I knoooow," was Mimi's reply.

As Nikki stood she shook her head. "I swear that girl acts like a teenager already."

"They're both really cute. Cordy's doing a wonderful job with them."

"She is. And Barry adores them."

"I'll bet. If I had two beautiful girls like that I'd adore them, too," he replied honestly.

Nikki didn't respond.

"I've been thinking about that a lot lately. Kids, I mean," he said, trying like hell to resist the urge to reach out and touch her.

"Really?"

He nodded. "I'd like kids one day. Guess that means my biological clock is ticking." He chuckled but she didn't join in.

"It's usually the female that goes through that," she quipped.

He shook his head. "You're too young for your clock to be ticking already."

She shrugged but didn't say anything.

"I've also been thinking a lot about you."

"Quinn, don't," she said, shaking her head.

He reached out this time and caught the hand she was just about to raise to ward him off. His fingers gripped her wrist lightly. "No. I have to say this," he told her.

A month ago she wouldn't have believed a word he'd said. He'd done the unspeakable by calling her Sharane, he knew that. And couldn't take it back even if he tried. What he'd wanted to do the moment she stood up and couldn't even look at him was pull her close to him, tell her how much he loved her, how he couldn't possibly be still in love with a ghost because there wasn't enough room in his heart now that she'd taken over.

Then she'd told him to go. He'd thought about insisting he stay, but didn't want to cause a scene for her. He'd done enough. The way Nikki had looked at him at the hospital had said it all. She hated him. And yet he'd felt something else as he'd walked away. There was a little bit of hope—at least he prayed there was.

The thing about Nikki was that she knew how to say

what she meant and mean what she said. If she told you something you believed it because she was honest and candid and as transparent as plastic wrap. She'd given him her heart, even if she hadn't told him she had. And he'd been careless with it. Damn him for being the fool.

Now he was back in Sweetland and this time it was with a purpose. He hadn't been thinking of Sharane when he was with Nikki that night. Okay, yes, he had. But his thoughts were on Sylvester's words from earlier that day. How he should have been able to let Sharane go, how he'd given her as much grieving time as he could and that even Sharane wouldn't have wanted him to waste his life feeling bad about what happened to her. "It just happens, Quinn. I didn't wake up and ask for this but I'm not going to spend the time I have left being angry about it or hating everyone around me for circumstances they had nothing to do with and couldn't prevent even if they'd tried." That's what Sharane had told him the night they'd walked along the riverside and she'd told him she had stomach cancer.

She'd remained optimistic for the next two years and Quinn had devoted every moment that he wasn't in school to making her feel as loved and cherished as a seventeen-year-old could. And she'd still died.

It wasn't his fault and she was right, there was absolutely nothing he could have done to change her course in life. Sure, he now had a good medical education and years of experience under his belt, but at the end of the day the final call just wasn't his. Quinn knew that now, accepted it with each breath he was allowed to take, every sunrise and sunset he was gifted to see. He was not in control.

Still, Quinn had prayed today would go better than the last time he'd seen Nikki. He loved her. There was no doubt in his mind about that fact now. And he planned to not only tell her this today, but to show her.

"First and foremost, I want to tell you something and I want you to know that this is the honest truth."

She tried to pull away. Quinn held her still.

"Nikki, please," he pleaded.

When she stopped resisting Quinn released her arm. "I love you," he said.

She didn't respond.

"That's not something I would make up or lie about," he continued.

Nikki nodded. "And you just came to this realization?"

"No." He shook his head. "I knew that last night we were together. Just like I know how bad I messed up that night."

"You called me another woman's name. I would probably say that was more than messed up."

"It wasn't like that." He took a deep breath and knew how important this moment was, how his next words would either make or break his future. "I'd just found out about my grandmother's disease. I talked to the man she'd loved these last three years at the cemetery where he was still crying for her. Yes, I was thinking about Sharane. I stood in that same cemetery twenty-one years ago crying over a disease I couldn't understand and a girl I thought I'd love forever.

"Should I be over that by now? Yes, I should. Am I? Yes, I'm over the love I had for Sharane. But let me tell you something, Nikki, you never get over losing someone to this disease. Especially not when it feels like it's selecting people you love more and more frequently. Yeah, I know that's not how it works because I've watched plenty of patients die, too. It never gets easy, and each time I feel every single loss I've ever witnessed all over again. So yes, Sharane was on my mind that night. And so was my dad and my grandmother and Mr. Riley and all the other people suffering with some form of cancer who might not make it."

Because he wanted to touch her again, Quinn thrust his hands into his pockets. Just a few feet away the barbecue was still going live and strong. There had to be at least a hundred people crammed into the Brockingtons' backyard and more food than three times that number could eat. Music played from a corner where Quinn had already noticed a fully uniformed Jonah kept staring over at them.

Nikki hadn't moved at all. She stood in front of him, perfectly still, her eyes focused solely on him. Quinn couldn't tell what she was thinking but her silence made it seem like she was waiting for him to either say more or walk away. Well, he wasn't walking away, ever again.

"I went back to Seattle because I realized that I couldn't come to you with empty promises. If I was going to declare my love to you then dammit, I wanted to offer you everything else I had along with it."

He took a step toward her.

"I resigned from the clinic. It's not the place for me anymore. I've known that for a while now, but it took coming back here, seeing you and the people of Sweetland, to realize there was life outside those walls. That I could have a purpose that didn't require me to believe I was some kind of god."

She blinked and looked away.

Quinn reached out, touched a finger to her chin, turning her to face him once more.

"I sold my house, packed up everything including Dixi, and came back to Sweetland to stay."

"Quinn," she started to say.

"Shhh," he whispered, putting a finger to her lip. "Let me finish this. Please."

When she nodded, he continued.

"I came in this morning and met with Netta Harvey—she's Doc's real estate agent. Apparently, he's looking to sell his house and his practice. He and Ethel are finally going to make it official and get married, then they're moving down to Florida."

"What?" she asked.

Quinn gave a quick chuckle. "Guess that hadn't filtered through the Sweetland gossip mill yet. Don't tell Marabelle and Louisa they're slipping."

Nikki began shaking her head. "Quinn, what are you saying to me exactly? What do you want me to do with all this information?"

"First," he said, reaching into his back pocket and pulling out a folded sheet of paper. "I want you to take this receipt and file it in that folder with the tax bill. Then I want to see every bill that comes into the inn from now on. We're never going to get behind again and we're certainly not going to be fooled by crooked town council members."

She took the receipt he'd received from Liza, looked down at it then back up at him, her mouth opening to say something. He touched his fingers to her lips lightly to close them.

"I'll explain the rest later. For now, I want you to just listen and tell me if you hear a lie, or deceit. I know you've been lied to before, Nikki, and I don't want you to feel like that with me. Everything I've said, everything I do by you is honestly from the heart."

There was silence, at least between the two of them, and Quinn began to worry. What if it wasn't enough? What if she'd really moved on with Officer Jonah-goddamned-friendly? What if he was too late?

"Well, you can say something now," he told her with mild impatience.

She blinked and tilted her head a bit.

"Oh, sorry," he said with a slight chuckle when he realized his fingers had been still holding her lips closed.

Nikki cleared her throat and looked down at the receipt once more. "So let me get this straight," she started, then shook her head as if in disbelief.

"You moved from Seattle and plan to open a practice here in Sweetland for me? You gave up what I hear from

Savannah was an excellent salary, a great home, a great car, and everything to come back here and treat things like broken toes and summer colds, just for me? That's what you want me to believe?"

"No, of course not," Quinn said seriously. "I had my car shipped here."

She laughed. Instantly, fully and completely irresistible. The act had probably shocked her as much as it had Quinn, but it was there nonetheless and he took that as a lead. He reached out, cupped her face with both his hands.

"I love you, Nikki. And I would have given up anything and everything to be with you. But there's another woman that pulled me back here. She's been trying for years to get me to come home. I hate that it took her death to knock some sense into my head, but I don't intend to spend another day not living the life I was meant to live. And that's a life with a beautiful wife who agrees to have my children and play with my dog and maybe, just maybe, cook baked beans like my gramma once in a while."

"Michelle's the cook in the family," Nikki said, biting her bottom lip as tearful eyes stared back at him.

Quinn had just bent his head to kiss her, had waited so long he thought he'd die of desire if his lips didn't touch hers, when the sirens blared.

Ralph, Caleb, and Brad Brockington went tearing out of the barbecue, each headed for Ralph's big pickup truck. Jonah was next to jump into his cruiser, tires screeching as he pulled out into the street.

Nikki and Quinn had just gotten to the front of the yard in time to see them leave.

"What's going on?" Quinn asked Michelle, who was standing there with a worried look on her face.

"The Riley place is on fire," she stated with disbelief.

Quinn looked at Nikki and she knew. "I'm going with you," she told him.

He didn't even argue but ran to his car, reaching in his pockets as he went and retrieving the keys so the doors would be opened when he got there. Nikki slid into the passenger seat and they, too, sped off.

It took about two minutes before the smoke was visible in the air. Huge black funnels reaching up toward the sky. Nikki rolled down her window, the smoky smell of burning wood sifting through her nostrils. Inside her heart hammered against her chest as she thought the unthinkable.

Another three minutes and Quinn was turning down their street, stopping behind the two fire engines and three police cars. Jumping out, they tried to get past all the people who'd gathered on the sidewalk. The house where they'd had steamed crabs and summer punch was engulfed in flames. The frame of the house was almost unrecognizable, the smoke was so thick.

"Cover your nose and mouth," Quinn yelled to her.

She did as he told her, tears stinging her eyes. "Where are they?" she asked even though she knew her words were muffled.

"I don't know," Quinn replied, shaking his head. He'd lifted his arm to cover the lower half of his face as well.

The police had used yellow tape to mark a perimeter around the house, a boundary for all the spectators.

"Stay here, I'm going to try and get closer," Quinn told her.

When she took a step to follow him he turned back and grabbed her by the shoulders. He shook his head adamantly. "Stay here. Do not move."

She didn't, but tears rolled down her cheeks as she watched. The fire was devouring everything in its path. Glass exploded out of windows; siding or wood or she had no idea what fell from the house in burning embers onto the ground. Around her people were everywhere, some crying, some yelling. It was total chaos and yet there was a kind of serenity hovering around.

Nikki coughed as she tried to wipe her tears and keep her nose and mouth protected from the smoke. Through blurry eyes she saw Quinn coming back toward her. "Where are they? Did they get out? Are they with Doc Stallings?"

He didn't answer right away and Nikki felt a clutching in her chest.

"They think they're still in there," he said. But his face said they knew.

She was already shaking her head, but in her peripheral vision she could see the old Buick that Bill Riley used to drive but lately Margaret had used. "No," she whispered, going to her knees with overwhelming grief.

Quinn wrapped his arms around her, holding her tightly. "Shhh, baby. Shhhh."

But there was to be no silence, not in Sweetland, not tonight.

Chapter 24

Two days later Ralph Brockington ruled the fire an arson. The bodies of William and Margaret Riley had been found lying in their bed fully dressed, two empty cans of kerosene on the back porch where the blaze had begun. The back and front doors dead-bolted.

Quinn figured it had been a suicide. Bill Riley was finished living with the pain that grew more intense with each day. Margaret was finished watching her husband die. They both decided it was easier this way. As sad as it all seemed, Quinn recognized their anguish because he'd seen it so many times before with other patients.

The memorial for William and Margaret Riley took place three days after the fire completely destroyed their property. Both William and Margaret had left instructions to be cremated so there would be no burial to follow as there was with Gramma.

Still, Quinn sat in the fifth row of pews inside Redeemer's Baptist Church, once more listening to Brother Thurgood Hemsley playing a somber hymnal on the organ. Behind him were the twelve women and three men that Michelle had told him made up the entire mass choir for the church, each of them looking as old as the building itself.

In the pulpit the Reverend Ben Ellersby spoke in a quiet tone, asking blessings upon Bill Jr. and Katie Riley as they sat in the first row, both bent over in grief. Quinn watched them as the ushers hovered close with boxes of tissues in one hand, quiet consolations on their lips. He wondered if it was guilt instead of solely grief that kept them both bent forward. They hadn't looked at anyone at all today, their faces always cast down or buried in tissue. Quinn knew for a fact that Margaret had called both her children after Bill's walking incident; he'd heard her make the calls himself. And he was certain that the children already knew of their father's ailment. The day after they'd had the crabs with Bill and Margaret, Quinn had done something he'd never done in his entire career as a doctor. He went against a patient's wishes and called Bill Jr. and Katie himself. Despite their father's stance that they had their own busy lives to lead and he didn't want to bother them, Quinn had thought they should be there with their father in his last days. He knew Bill wouldn't live long and he'd told both his children that. And yet they hadn't arrived until the morning after the fire. They'd come too late, just as he had with Gramma.

Quinn recognized the next hymn Mr. Hemsley played as the Reverend Ellersby closed out the program. He hummed and looked down as Nikki took his hand in hers. She'd been sitting right beside him, with Michelle and Raine on the other side of her. As they processed out of the church he thought that they hadn't had a moment alone since the fire. As it was with the people of Sweetland, and just as they'd done with Gramma, all the women pitched in and cooked, taking dishes and beverages over to the family who'd suffered the loss. Unfortunately, the Riley home wasn't available. So Michelle had invited Bill Jr. and Katie to stay at the inn. Each day Quinn had been up early helping Michelle in the kitchen, or helping Nikki see to the people filing in and out of the place. Pulling double duty they also walked all the dogs, fed them, and made sure they all had exercise time as Parker still wasn't 100 percent on his feet. Raine and Michelle were supervising all the food coming in and cooking their own for the restaurant, so they could barely make it out of the kitchen to take bathroom breaks.

When they arrived back at the house Quinn watched Bill Jr. and Katie go straight to their rooms.

"Ungrateful little brats," Savannah, who had stayed at the inn to take care of the guests who had just checked in that morning, said with a frown. "They haven't thanked any of us since they've been here."

"They're grieving, Savannah," Raine commented with a sigh.

"They're spoiled and inconsiderate, that's what they are," she said in a huff and walked away.

"She doesn't look in the mirror often, does she?" Michelle asked with a chuckle.

Raine shook her head. "I think she looks in the mirror too much and that's her problem."

"I'll help you two put all that leftover food into containers," Nikki offered, moving away from Quinn's side.

"No, that's okay. It's not that much. Raine and I can manage," Michelle told her. "You and Quinn go take a rest; you've been running for the last few days."

"So have you," Quinn stated. "Let us help in the kitchen. That way we'll finish sooner and all of us can take a rest."

Michelle was shaking her head. "No. We'll do it. You two go."

Quinn was too tired and knew Michelle's stubborn streak too well to argue. Taking Nikki's hand, he led her out the door they'd just come in and down the porch steps. He didn't stop walking until they were at the gazebo. He turned and sat on the step, pulling her down onto his lap and hugging her tightly.

"I should have come back sooner. Those kids should have come back sooner," he whispered.

"We can't undo the past," she told him, rubbing her hands up and down his back. "All we can do is work toward a better future."

Quinn nodded and then pulled away so he could look into her eyes. "Tomorrow is not promised to any of us. So I don't want to waste any more time. I want you to be my future, Nikki. I want to marry you and raise children with you. I want it all, with you."

For a few seconds she simply stared at him. Her mind had gone completely blank. Well, not completely. Scenes played in her head like a movie trailer.

Quinn standing in a white tuxedo looking as handsome as any man she'd ever seen in her life. Beside him Parker and Preston were dressed in white as well. They were standing under the gazebo. She walked down a white runner filled with red, pink, and white rose petals from Ms. Vera's garden, toward Quinn. Cordy, Savannah, Michelle, and Raine stood opposite Quinn and his brothers, dressed in dresses a shade of pink so pale it almost looked white. The Reverend Ellersby stood between them, a Bible in his hand, waiting patiently for her.

Her arm was tucked tightly in her father's; Caleb and Brad had previously escorted her mother to a seat in the first row of white chairs that had been rented for this event. It was her dream wedding, in her dream location, with her dream man. And it was perfect.

"Hey, you still with me?" Quinn asked, dropping a kiss on the tip of her nose.

"Yes, I'm still with you," she said, lifting a finger to trace along his cheek. "I'll always be with you, Quinn. And I'll love you and marry you and raise children with you."

Quinn smiled, his gaze holding hers until she was

smiling right along with him. "Could you do something else first?" he asked her.

"What?"

"Kiss me?"

She laughed. "Of course."

And this time when their lips touched it was more than magical, more than anything either of them had ever experienced. It was a real, true homecoming.

The Silver Spoon Recipes

Almost Heaven Almond Pound Cake

3	cups all-purpose flour
1	teaspoon baking powder
1¼	teaspoons salt
2¾	cups granulated sugar
1¼	cups butter, softened
2½	teaspoons almond extract
5	eggs
1	cup evaporated milk
½	cup powdered sugar*

Directions

1. Heat the oven to 350°F. Generously spray a 10-inch angel food tube, 12-cup fluted tube cake pan, or Bundt pan with butter-flavored cooking spray.
2. Mix the flour, baking powder, and salt; set aside.
3. Beat the sugar, butter, almond extract, and eggs in a large bowl with an electric mixer on low speed for 40

seconds, scraping the bowl constantly. Beat in the flour mixture alternately with the milk on low speed. Pour into the pan.

4. Bake 1 hour, 15 minutes or until a toothpick inserted in the center comes away clean. Cool. Remove from the pan to cool completely on a wire rack 45 minutes.

*Sprinkle with powdered sugar.
*Optional.

Southern Seaside Fried Chicken

2   cups buttermilk
1   tablespoon Dijon mustard
1   teaspoon salt
1   teaspoon ground black pepper
1   teaspoon cayenne pepper
1   whole chicken, cut into pieces
2   cups all-purpose flour
1   tablespoon baking powder
3   tablespoons Old Bay seasoning
5   cups vegetable or peanut oil, for frying

Directions

1. Whisk together the buttermilk, mustard, salt, pepper, and cayenne in a bowl. Add the chicken pieces, making sure each piece is generously coated with the marinade. Tightly cover the bowl with two layers of plastic wrap and refrigerate 3 to 6 hours.

2. Combine the flour, baking powder, and Old Bay Seasoning in a resealable plastic bag. Transfer a few pieces

of marinated chicken at a time (breasts should go in one at a time) into the plastic bag of dry ingredients and shake well to ensure complete coverage.

3. Repeat the process by submerging the coated chicken pieces into the buttermilk marinade again, then into the dry ingredients, shaking well to ensure complete coverage once more.

4. Heat the oil in a large frying pan over medium-high heat until a dab of flour in the oil begins to bubble. Fry the chicken in the hot oil until the juices run clear and the chicken is golden brown, turning periodically to allow even browning.

Read on for an excerpt from Lacey Baker's next book

Just Like Heaven

Coming soon from St. Martin's Paperbacks

The backyard wasn't exactly what Heaven expected. It was huge, which she should have assumed since the inn with the restaurant neatly tucked into its side would easily take up half the block of the street she lived on in Boston.

What surprised her was all the lush green grass. It went on for what seemed like miles and miles only to drop suddenly into big gray rocks that formed a slope right down to water she assumed, from her minimal knowledge of Maryland, was the Chesapeake Bay.

"The Bay is really pretty from here," she said quietly but didn't mean for him to hear or to actually respond.

"That's the Miles River. It's a tributary to the Bay so I guess it'll accept the compliment," was his bland reply.

A response that almost had the effect of cold water splashing onto the minute rise in her body temperature at his proximity. It was ridiculous, she knew, to feel any type of reaction to a man she'd just met, especially since their meeting was the furthest thing from a hook-up. Admittedly, men and interacting with them were not Heaven's forte. She accepted that just as she accepted all the other ups and downs of her life, and normally it didn't bother her. But today, with this man . . .

She shook her head, closing her eyes momentarily and reminding herself again that she didn't like this man. The decision came quickly and decisively and all other thoughts of Preston Cantrell sifted slowly away as she opened her eyes and looked to her left where there was a large gated area containing six puppies and one adult Labrador Retriever. Just beyond their outdoor playpen was a lovely white gazebo that was the exact image she'd seen in the pamphlet she'd flipped through on her ride into town. From the airport Heaven had had to hire a car service to bring her the hour-and-ten-minute drive to Sweetland. The service was apparently familiar with the town because it had a lot of literature about it in the pouch behind the passenger-side seat.

"Which one is Coco?" she asked, stepping down from the two steps and planting her feet solidly in the plush grass.

Today, for a change, she'd forgone the pant suit or skirt and jacket she normally wore. This time, because this appointment was purely about her and her personal contentment, and since she was desperately trying to separate the Heaven who used to work twelve- to eighteen-hour days from the Heaven who someday wanted a real life, and because the airline had lost her luggage so she could not change, she wore a more casual outfit. As of right now, her wardrobe didn't really consist of a lot of casual pieces but she'd found this pair of jeans and a shirt and figured that was sufficient. On her feet she'd decided on flats, leather, sensible. Now, she wished she'd had something more feminine, more summer-like and open-toed so she could feel what she assumed was coolness from the soft-looking blades.

"How long are you staying in Sweetland?" he asked as they walked towards the playpen.

Heaven had forgotten he was there. Or at least she'd tried to. He wasn't making much effort to conceal the fact that he didn't really want her to take his dog. But if that was the case, why put the ad online? *Stop it! It's not your job to analyze him or anybody else for that matter.*

It had only taken two months of intense psychotherapy three times a week to get her to accept that point. And her trip to this small Eastern Shore town was part of her recovery. She had to keep reminding herself of that fact.

"Long enough to take care of all the remaining legalities of adopting Coco," she told him. She'd already filled out an adoption application, submitted it, and had a telephone interview and a house visit by one of the Loving-Labs liaisons. This was the next to final step, meeting the Lab she'd fallen in love with. After this, there was just the signing of the adoption contract and receiving temporary licensing and tags. Then she and Coco could be on their way. She hoped all that could be handled today, but was prepared to find a hotel and stay overnight if need be.

"We both have to sign the contract," he told her matter-of-factly.

"You're the one who listed her on the website as available. That was a foolish idea if you really don't want to give her up," she replied with a tinge of annoyance.

They'd stopped right at the gate and reluctantly she looked up at him. He was too handsome, she told herself. That was another reason she didn't like him. Handsome men were trouble and, for the most part, ignored Heaven like the plague. And he looked dangerous, not like he was going to turn around and choke her. That would be insane and later she would admonish herself for being overly dramatic. But right now, she couldn't help but look at him, at his dreamy dark brown eyes and thick neat eyebrows. He had an easy smile—or he had when he'd answered the door and when his sister had first entered the room. His complexion was almost golden, as if he spent a lot of time in the sun, and his hair was raven-black, cut short, waving a bit on the top.

She was in the process of gritting her teeth and trying to look away from him when he spoke again.

"I knew what I was doing when I listed her."

He didn't sound so much annoyed now as he did thoughtful. But Heaven didn't want to think too hard on the emotional state of Preston Cantrell. His physical state was already wreaking havoc with her senses. "That's good to know," she finally replied.

They were standing at the gate, side by side, when Preston leaned forward and flipped the latch. The minute the gate was open, every one of the puppies bounded for the exit, big feet and floppy ears whizzing past Heaven so fast she couldn't help but let out a full-bodied laugh. Something she hadn't done in a very long time.

It took about two minutes for her to figure out what had been an explosion of too-cute and adorably furry little feet running through the grass was not as hilarious as she'd first thought. Or at least, Preston didn't think so.

He ran after one puppy, stooping to scoop it up in his arms, then immediately bounding in the opposite direction for another. She figured she should help or meeting Coco might take even longer. A couple of steps, she'd barely broken into a run and her hand was easily slipping beneath the collar of the adult Lab. Its pug nose and milk-chocolate brown eyes stared up at Heaven, inciting another smile and a warmth that started a small swarm in the pit of her stomach.

Ushering her back to the pen, Heaven secured the gate, then took off to find another one of the runaway pups. In the midst of the hide 'n seek she played with the one pup that had found shelter behind a fat and cheerful azalea bush, she allowed herself to once again forget about her handsome host. Until she heard him curse loudly as he took off after another puppy. The curse didn't sound friendly or as remotely cheerful as she'd begun to feel during her merry little chase. Her smile had only faltered slightly as she decided to give Preston a hand.

He'd run all the way across the yard, down to where the border of rocks started the incline. It didn't take her long to catch up as she'd run track and field in high school, one of the few times she'd had a rebellious moment against her parents and won. By the time she hit the rocks, Preston had already begun his trek down, taking slow steps, one in front of the other. The puppy, with its large feet and flopping ears, seemed to smile up at Preston; with each step the human took forward, the pup took one back.

"Come here, you little nightmare!" Preston yelled.

The puppy's ears flopped and one of his back feet slipped on a rock. Heaven gasped.

"Maybe you should talk nicely to him, coax him to come back up," she suggested.

"I know how to handle this," he snapped back.

Heaven didn't bother gasping, it was no secret to her that men didn't like to be told what to do, especially by a woman—even though in her experience with them, men rarely knew what to do on their own. Still, that was fine and good for Mr. Rude-Arrogant-And-Totally-Hot. She wouldn't tell him what to do again. She'd simply *show* him.

"Here, cutie pie," she coaxed, taking her first step down onto the rocks. "Come on, girl, come on."

Her voice was soft as she moved slowly. The puppy had stopped its descent, flopping down onto his bottom and staring up at her expectantly.

"That's a good girl. That's a good puppy. You're such a pretty little one." The puppy looked like she was lapping up every word so Heaven continued until she was just an arm's reach from the puppy.

Now she would show Preston Cantrell that she knew what she was talking about, that she could certainly handle a puppy and that he . . . Heaven's words were lost somewhere on the rocks with her balance as she toppled into the chilly river.

Preston saw it coming about three seconds before it happened. He'd already cursed and taken another step to catch her when Coco stood abruptly and, with her always playful and mischievous manner, dived feet first, ears following, into the water. Heaven reached for her and toppled over the last couple of rocks into the water right along with the puppy.

With a curse, Preston made it to the bank, reaching into the water to grab Coco before she could swim away. Beside him, Heaven spluttered, wiping her long hair back out of her face. Her blouse was plastered to her chest and what a delectable chest it was. Hell, he thought with a pang of lust so potent he almost fell back on his own butt gaping at her.

"If you laugh, I'll punch you," she said, her eyes narrowing to mere slivers as she glared at him.

Preston put Coco down on the rocks and pointed directly at her. "Stay," he said firmly, then turned back to Heaven.

"I wouldn't think of laughing," he told her with as straight a face as he could manage. Fifteen years ago, he would have gaped and probably panted like Coco was presently doing. Now, he remained stoic, or at least he hoped that's what he was doing.

"Let me help you," he offered, extending a hand to her.

"I don't need—" she had begun to say, then her narrow gaze shifted and a small smile touched the edge of her mouth. "Thank you, Mr. Cantrell."

She reached for his hand, clasped the palm, and Preston instantly knew how this would end.

The splash of cold water wasn't a total shock; still his body did a little jolt as he too was submerged into the river.

She had some strength to her, this pretty, sexy, wisp of a woman. He hadn't expected that, nor had he really expected she would have the balls to pull him into the water. But she had and Preston was mystified at his reaction to it all.

When she tried to make her way to the bank, standing because the water level at the entry of the river was only about three and a half feet high, he got another glimpse of her extremely fine backside and had an idea of his own. He was just about to reach for her, about to take her by the waist and pull her back into the water with him. It had been a long time since he'd frolicked in the water with a wet and willing female—even though he admitted he might have to work on the willing part with her. But Coco had other plans. The hyperactive dog disobeyed Preston's direct order and bounded back into the river, waddling until she was splashing water all over Preston and giving Heaven the time she needed to get safely onto the rocks.

When he finally made his way out of the river, Coco tucked tightly under his left arm, Preston was no longer in a laughing mood. Heaven had just cleared the rocks when he grabbed her by the arm.

"Heaven Montgomery, meet Coco. Coco, meet Ms. Montgomery," he said, thrusting the puppy into Heaven's arms before stalking off.